"Good fun . . . rewarding surprises . . . like
filled with slow shifts in self-awareness. . . . Fc
ticing amateur analysis, *Spectacular Happines*
do it with a beguiling subject [Chip Samuels]
—*The New York Times* ᴅᴏᴏᴋ ...

"You could say that *Spectacular Happiness* makes for explosive beach reading.
It's about an eco-terrorist who blows up shorefront mansions on Cape Cod.
The effect is something like reading *Jaws* from the shark's point of view. . . .
It's wacky and wicked and brilliant—the sort of novel you want to argue with
and about. (Attention, book clubs.) By the end, Kramer has set off explosives
throughout the structure of our consumer culture and everything feels danger-
ously unstable."

—*The Christian Science Monitor*

"Starting with the fact that it is fiction, *Spectacular Happiness* defies our
expectations of Kramer. It breathes life into a certain kind of radical politics
in a way that makes you wish Kramer had tried fiction sooner. None of our
more practiced leftist novelists—including Thomas Pynchon, Don DeLillo,
and E. L. Doctorow—has generated as tantalizing a vision of contemporary
radicalism minus dogma. . . . This elegantly crafted novel restores faith in
politics."

—*The American Prospect*

"A serious novel of ideas . . . the intellectual conflicts lend the book all the tension anybody should need."

—*Newsweek*

"Kramer's chief claim to fame to date is his passionate anti-Prozac treatise
(*Listening to Prozac*), but this debut novel . . . should help earn him a serious
literary audience as well. . . . The depth, quality, and ambition of Kramer's
prose will surprise those expecting a superficial crossover effort."

—*Publishers Weekly* (starred review)

". . . a mordantly funny novel bursting with profound observations about
faded idealism, parental love, and the evanescent nature of fame . . . achingly
beautiful . . . eloquent passages suffused with a parent's boundless devotion
and patience. This complex weaving of social satire and family drama is what
makes *Spectacular Happiness* so compelling."

—*Time Out New York*

"The voice—measured, pensive, soft-spoken, self-deprecating, lightly ironic,
quizzically humane—recalls the early Walker Percy."

—*Kirkus Reviews*

"The author of *Listening to Prozac* and *Should You Leave?* brings his consid-
erable literary skills and insight into human nature to this stunning first novel."

—*Booklist*

"*Spectacular Happiness* is an explosion of ideals and a blasting comment on our era of conspicuous consumption."

—*Bookpage*

"Kramer's new prescription is a blast: Kramer writes a beautiful, brooding tale of failed radical views, alienation, and social responsibility. At the same time, he creates a deft social satire of class, wealth, and celebrity in America. . . . Kramer's media parody is hilarious and withering, a passionate call for radical social change."

—*Boston Phoenix*

"In an era increasingly scarred by terrorism of all kinds, *Spectacular Happiness* is more than just a witty, compelling work of fiction: It is an important commentary on the twin spectacles of greed and rage that have overtaken our age."

—Gerald Shapiro, *Forward*

"Intriguing . . . Kramer is once again challenging our beliefs about the fixedness of both moral principles and human personality . . . a stop on the journey of a renaissance intellect."

—*Chronicle of Higher Education*

"A brilliant and completely original novel that dazzles, shocks, entertains, and ultimately transforms. Kramer's writing is razor sharp and cuts to expose the soft center of modern society. What makes *Spectacular Happiness* so memorable is a narrator whose intimate, intelligent, and humane voice lingers with us long after we put the book down."

—Abraham Verghese, author of *The Tennis Partner* and *My Own Country*

"[An] aching novel of fractured families and class alienation . . . an over-the-top satire . . . Kramer uses the bombing campaign to create a kind of forensic analysis of society and the individual."

—*City Pages* (Minneapolis–St. Paul)

"This rich and wonderful book defies distillation. Somehow, Kramer successfully weaves together a poignant family saga with anarchist theory, suspenseful intrigue with social criticism, dark cynicism with hope for humanity. . . . The provocative aspects of this book are in some ways prescient and, perhaps, especially relevant to a nation engaged in a war against terrorism. . . . Kramer's indictment of modern society is indeed penetrating, but ultimately he writes of people saving one another. He has written a subversive and triumphant work that asks us to do all we can for one another. The attacks of September 11 may complicate the feelings aroused by this book, but by all means read it and enjoy Peter Kramer's deeply thoughtful fiction."

—*The American Journal of Psychiatry*

Spectacular Happiness

✳ A NOVEL ✳

Peter D. Kramer

SCRIBNER PAPERBACK FICTION
PUBLISHED BY SIMON & SCHUSTER
NEW YORK   LONDON   TORONTO   SYDNEY   SINGAPORE

SCRIBNER PAPERBACK FICTION
Simon & Schuster, Inc.
Rockefeller Center
1230 Avenue of the Americas
New York, NY 10020

First Scribner Paperback Fiction edition 2002
SCRIBNER PAPERBACK FICTION and design are trademarks of Macmillan Library Reference USA, Inc., used under license by Simon & Schuster, the publisher of this work.
For information regarding special discounts for bulk purchases, please contact Simon & Schuster Special Sales at 1-800-456-6798 or *business@simonandschuster.com*

Designed by Kyoko Watanabe

Manufactured in the United States of America

1 3 5 7 9 10 8 6 4 2

The Library of Congress has cataloged the original Scribner edition as follows:
Kramer, Peter D.
Spectacular happiness : a novel / Peter D. Kramer.
p. cm.
I. Title.

PS3611 R36 S64 2001
813'.54—dc21   2001020790

ISBN 0-684-86430-4
0-7432-2324-1

for Rachel

Who can gauge the striking-power of an impassioned daydream, of pleasure taken in love, of a nascent desire, of a rush of sympathy?

—Raoul Vaneigem,
The Revolution of Everyday Life

PART ONE

Obscurity

1

*

Calling

I saw you today on the midday news: a teenage boy, skinny body draped in an oversized Chicago Bulls shirt, eyes shaded by a Swoosh cap, matching red, with brim curved just so. I knew you instantly, before the label was added to the picture, before you spoke. I was struck by an emotion that had more force than direction. It could as easily have been despair as elation. A phrase ran through my mind: *already grown*. Words that toward the end of his life my father repeated when he caught sight of me. In the midst of disorientation, what abides is wonder at a child's taking adult form.

You looked thinner than I had imagined. The effect of Ritalin, I suppose. You were taller than the reporter, so it seems not to have stunted your growth. Like a daytime talk-show hostess, the reporter prompted, If you could speak to your dad, what would you say? She held the microphone to your mouth. For a moment you stared at her tongue-tied. Hi, Dad, you said, perhaps because that is the first thing one says into microphones.

The television people were telling a story with your image. It said ordinary, normal, the youngster next door. Not a bad appearance to have in these times when too many try to stand out.

The microphone rested by your mouth, urging further speech. You thought and then asked, Dad, did you do it? After another silence, you giggled, which struck me as appropriate for a young man asked to betray private feelings in public. Appropriate, and wonderful for being so. The reporter pulled the microphone away, so that it did not quite catch your afterthought: Why?

That is the picture the video editor ended with, the lips of the "son of accused bomber" pursing and parting in silent query.

As soon as I could collect myself, I phoned Sukey Kuykendahl. You will remember Sukey. We saw a good deal of her the spring and summer your mother was gone. Sukey was down on her luck then—booze and man trouble—but she perked up around you. She had a way of getting you to do things, by saying out loud what was on your mind: Those kids look too big for you. You don't want to play with them. You want to sit on the sidelines and eat cookies.

Once she named your fear, it seemed foolish, and you would head back to the game. The reporters like her frankness of manner and that forceful, high-pitched New Englander's voice, at once throaty and twittery. They have her pegged as a Cape Cod type, the lady realtor, the Yankee straight-shooter. She's the stoutish "long-time neighbor" you see saying, Good Lord, of course I know Chip Samuels. Known him for years. He grew up on my mother's estate. Salt of the earth, honest as the day is long. That man never did a violent thing in his life.

On tape, she sounds something like Julia Child.

Sukey is a strategist. If you have been following the news, you know that I have not yet been charged with any crime. When the FBI cannot make a case, they leak the name of a suspect in the hopes that citizens will come forward with evidence. Sukey thinks the FBI's approach has backfired. She tells me that people remember times the FBI stumbled. They remember how the FBI had the press convinced that Richard Jewell set the bomb at the Olympics in Atlanta. In the end the feds exonerated the fellow and apologized, which is what Wendy Moro, my lawyer, is calling on them to do now.

For the meanwhile, I am more or less on home confinement. The media are too intrusive for me so much as to walk down Bridge Way. And there have been threats, some vicious and anonymous, some open and milder, couched in language meant to evade this or that criminal statute. The open threats come from families whose houses have lost value or been destroyed. Wendy says I am safest in the cottage, watched over by the agents investigating me.

I have little need to venture out. The community college has placed me on leave, and there is no question of my continuing with the handyman jobs I used to do. For all that certain neighbors express belief in my innocence, I doubt there's a sober citizen on the Cape who would let me bring a toolbox into his home.

When I phoned, Sukey picked up on the first ring. Is that you? she said. I just saw your boy on television.

Me, too, I said. How did he seem?

You at sixteen.

Did he look thin?

Not a bit of it. Your spitting image. Wouldn't have surprised me if he'd jumped off the screen and tried to shanghai me up to the attic.

Sukey was speaking my mind. I have always considered your resemblance to me uncanny. I once heard on the radio—I caught only the end of the story but I believe I have it right—that a child who looks decidedly like a given family member may resemble that relative in talents or temperament, that external appearance provides a fair sampling of the ways the genes express themselves. *Overidentification* was a word the court psychologist used in the custody evaluation; she said I exaggerate what you and I have in common.

That remark caused me much soul-searching. But on seeing you again, I find my opinion is unchanged. You do have my manner.

The shyness, the hesitancy, those are me. Sukey is right, I was wiry as a youngster.

I never shanghaied anyone. That was a little joke. It was Sukey who dragged me to the attic. I will write about that incident in time. I will set down everything if there is time.

Shanghaiing is a concern, I said, believing Sukey would know what I meant. Now that you have been located, you may be in danger. You are in Milwaukee, the reporter indicated. Living in a neighborhood of substantial houses, judging from the background you were shot against. Even in this era of ubiquitous trophy homes, how many such neighborhoods can there be in Milwaukee? I suppose you will be safe while the press keeps an eye on you. But when their attention flags?

Sukey and I talked on about how it was to see you, how a thirty-second video clip enriches and impoverishes the imagination. I wanted the conversation to flow naturally, without rapid changes in topic. After a couple of minutes, I declared myself. I said: Sukey, I need to ask a favor. I'm hemmed in here, by cops and reporters and rubberneckers. I wonder if you could bring by a few bags of groceries.

That is the code we had arranged. If I wanted to sign on to Sukey's next plan, the plan for me to appear in public, I was to ask for groceries.

Sukey suspects the phone is tapped and the cottage is bugged. For important communication, we use key words. *Repair* means to install explosives. *Astonish* indicates a project has come to fruition. When a house has been blown, I may phone Sukey and mention that I find this or that news item astonishing. *Groceries* means a new phase of the Movement.

Sukey said, I imagined you might need groceries. Is that all? Do you want company? I can bring round some friends.

No need to involve others, I told Sukey.

She had in mind a media event, I suspected, a parade of well-wishers to give visual confirmation to the claim that I am a regular guy. I have resisted the temptation to engage in conventional publicity. I believe our success to date is due to our invisibility. To what the old anarchists called *propagande par le fait*. Letting the explosions speak for themselves. Sukey has said that in the end human faces are always needed, faces and words. She tends to be right. I hope she is right now, that if I break my silence, there is a chance of keeping you safe, even bringing you home. Safe home, most desired of endings.

By home, I mean the cottage where you spent your early years. I believe you found it cozy. I did, and do still. But a person can feel exposed on the bayfront.

Your mother never adjusted. She complained of the freight-train sounds of the north wind on winter mornings and the stink of rotting shellfish at ebb tide on summer afternoons. Sometimes I think she left the marriage because she could not bear to live on this sandbank, and she could not bear to ask me to live anywhere else. I would have moved, of course, would have done anything for her and you.

But I am at home here. In the Vietnam days, boys I grew up with went AWOL from basic training because they missed the sea. I always felt a bit like them, lost away from this bay. If the cottage has its shortcomings, I overlook them as we should overlook the failings of those who sustain us. I do not know how I would endure prison; I fear that I would find myself unable even to do what I am doing now, put my thoughts in writing. But I am comfortable for the moment, with my view of the small boats at anchor.

There is a spot at the crest of the bank where reporters like to be videotaped. From that angle, the cottage looks ramshackle. In truth it is sturdy. Whatever his shortcomings, my father knew the ways of buildings. This one will last until the land beneath it is worn away. The television image is political, meant to make a visual comparison to Theodore Kaczynski's cabin or Randy Weaver's— though I believe I am no more like those men than Sesuit, Massachusetts, is like Lincoln, Montana, or Ruby Ridge, Idaho.

You can see from the same shot how much the bay has encroached. They say we lose a foot a year, but the losses are so irregular that they have the power to surprise and dishearten. Some seasons beach builds at the foot of the bank. This past March a no-name storm—the same storm we took advantage of toward the start of our campaign, when we breached the seawalls on Quivet Cove—took a bite ten feet deep and fifteen wide, to the far side of the path. A chance event, perhaps, though nowadays people connect bad weather with the cataclysms we humans have brought upon ourselves, the rash of tornadoes and floods and mudslides that plague the planet as it warms.

On the sandbank, I did the tasks you used to help with. Replaced storm fencing, planted plugs of American beach grass, strewed seeds of weeping love grass. I fear the trampling of the press corps—human erosion—has undone my work. And to think that your mother used to scold you for running down the bank with your kite! I have never been one to feel outrage. All work is Sisyphean. We make our fruitless contribution, playing at shaping chaos. At the shoreline, planting grass, like planting explosives, is mostly symbolic. Wind and waves do what they will.

Despite the isolation, my life has assumed the breathless pace the media imposes on its chosen subject. Revelations intrude hourly. I learn on the news that hairs believed to be mine (and so few are in evidence on my scalp!) have turned up in the Altschuler house. I learn that in my college years I worked on the fringe of a radical clique. That I have reason to be bitter over the circumstances of my divorce. That I am a local boy with community ties and no history of mental illness. That I fit no profile. Half of what is said is false, and the rest is not quite right. Having seen your face, I feel a need for time. Time to write the story as I know it—so different from the public version, moralized by television.

Last week, Wendy Moro presented me with the leather-bound blank book in which I am writing. She wanted me to use it as a place to gather memories that might help in my defense. Fill it with thoughts, she said. The form of the recollections did not matter, so long as I set them down while they were fresh. If I was reluctant to share the memoir with her now, I might want to do so later. (By later, I suspect she meant in the "sentencing phase," after I am convicted.) All would be confidential, protected by attorney-client privilege.

I wanted to oblige but found I could not. Any account of my activities would reveal past crimes and—surely these Wendy would not want to read about—preparations for future ones. I understood that certain details might prove useful. Evidence that I was here when a witness claims I was there. Sukey says that the right wing has made the public so mistrustful of the government that the state cannot win any prominent case where there is room for doubt. I could, perhaps, generate doubt. But the work should do that on its own. Crafting installations, Sukey and I took care to introduce red herrings, to cast suspicion away from me.

I do want to please Wendy. In person, she is the way she looks on television, patient and reasonable. I believe her presence conveys humility, a modest hope that in time the rest of the world will arrive at her viewpoint.

News analysts have asked why I do not hire seasoned defense attorneys. Many, seeking publicity, have offered their services. My policy is not to explain myself to the press. But I can tell you that I think we all might benefit from less brash assertion of our individual rights. I like that Wendy has nothing in common with the slick men we are used to seeing—Johnnie Cochran, Alan Dershowitz, Stephen Jones, Barry Shenk, Gerry Spence, F. Lee Bailey. I like how slight and fine-boned Wendy is, as if she were intent on not taking up space in the world.

Sometimes I think it is an odd thing for a man of my age to place his faith in women with girls' names, Sukey and Wendy. But that is what I have done, and without regret. When Sukey was recovering from drink, I found myself speaking with her psychologist, Emmanuel Abelman, a quirky and unhappy old gentleman whose opinion I came to respect. Manny said that I have a talent for faith and that I should rely on my talent. I have tried to do so, though it would take someone of greater capacity than mine to sit sequestered with the FBI at the door and not worry at all.

Much of this I said to Wendy. Not the bit about girls' names—I am sure Wendy finds it equally odd that her fortunes should be tied to those of a community-college teacher named Chip—but about my mixture of faith and doubt. She asked only how she could make it easy for me to set down my recollections. I had no answer. Manny often said I was dogged in my efforts for others but resourceless when it came to helping myself. He worked to change that in me, but the transformation went only so far.

Then I saw you on the screen. Wendy's notebook came to hand, and I felt moved to write, justify, explain. To the son I have followed in imagination all these years.

I have come to respect these drives, to respect the absurd—a posture that has served well this past year, the year of installations. It is absurd to write you. I do not imagine this journal in your hands. The stories I need to tell would only disturb a boy of (almost) sixteen. Too many explosions. Too many delicate family matters. Even if you were here—fond wish—I would hold back. The understanding I have with Sukey is that we will keep the secrets of the Movement to ourselves. As for the separation, mine from you, I would want my version to emerge gradually, gently, alongside your mother's, in the course of our efforts to create a new life together: wife, husband, child.

Only from this standpoint does the compulsion make sense: I write you anyway, compose letters in my mind, incessantly. The way Herzog writes his former wives, I write my absent son. About events of the day, stray ideas, foolish jokes. The latest on Leno: Good news and bad—you just inherited a waterfront home . . . in Sesuit.

If I am to respond to Wendy's request, why not in this form, the form of my thought? It occurs to me that Herzog often writes on paper, too, unsent letters, a precedent that though it is fictional makes my compulsion seem less strange to me. For as long as I can remember, I have found literature a reliable companion, surely the best guide to how we live when we are by ourselves.

In his essay on walking, Thoreau makes a quiet pun. He writes of returning to his senses, when he means his sight and hearing and smell, as if it were only when we take in the world with intensity that our judgment is trustworthy. The week you were born—in this cottage, with the help of a midwife—your mother was hospitalized, and you and I were left alone together. I was fiercely alive, suffused with love of you and worry over her. Without error, I heard in your breathing whether you wanted rocking or swaddling or burping or being let alone. Once I had an inkling that my own father was near. I smelled the sourness of liquor, as if he were leaning over the bed toward me. I prayed to my dead father as a religious man prays to a saint, for your good fortune.

I needed no sleep. I lay in bed with you resting on my chest. I hummed you a hum that seemed to come from beyond me and that said, All will be okay. My job for that brief while, beyond the diapering and feeding and bathing, was to will health for you and your mother. I tried to be an antenna for the good luck in the cosmos, to direct that luck into you and let you broadcast it to her. Your mother did return to us, and I slept for twelve hours. When she let me, I slept for another twelve, and then I no longer heard the harmonies of the world or the messages in babies' breath. But neither did I fully revert to my former state. I felt alive in a new way.

How does one come to one's senses? In high school, I read a play where Helen of Troy explains herself. She says that she sees the world in black and white except when men are at war. Then she sees color. I don't suppose you will have encountered that play, though in my imaginings you are a voracious reader. I was, from an early age. I was a child saved by reading.

When I came across the play about Helen, I was searching in literature, as certain teenage boys will, for clues to the nature of women. I thought Helen's lines were meant to lay bare her cruelty. I was ready to believe women could be exotically uncaring. Now I see the matter differently. Helen had found her calling. Her calling was to inspire war. I believe fatherhood might be a calling for me. Not that I claim to be expert at fathering, but I was alive when I was engaged in it.

After your mother took you away, the world turned gray. Later—a year ago—when Sukey led me to the Giampiccolo house, I began to return to my senses. I mention that house now, up front, because I remember you as a child who, when you were very young, could not tolerate suspense—could not bear waiting to discover whether the bunny found his way safe home, whether the elephant came to love himself as he was. As the tension built, you seemed almost unable to stay within your body. Daddy, you would demand, tell me how it ends. I would, and then you could stand to listen to what we had skipped, the heart of the story. (How can you call it an attention deficit? I would ask the teachers. He has always been possessed by what he hears.)

In case you are still impatient, I will start by answering the question you posed on television. Yes, I did it. I am responsible for the explosions that captured the public's imagination, though Sukey deserves the lion's share of credit. Sukey was the producer. I favored quiet, limited destruction. Sukey planned extravaganzas. She was the one with the energy, the matériel, and the methods of accessing the media. Sukey supplied the vision. I did the work.

I did the work and returned to my senses, which is what makes me imagine that terrorism, the fastidious version I have practiced, might also be a calling for me. The two tasks, parenting and sabotage, are not so distant as one might imagine. Both express love and devotion. Both demand the exercise of every talent a man might possess.

In college, your mother poked fun at me: The revolutionary who reads directions, she would tease. I yearned to be loose and laid-back—and ever more so as, in time, her joshing turned to open annoyance. Not until years later, in my talks with Manny, did I achieve a level of comfort with my discomfort. Use what you have, Manny taught. What I have is the standard my father passed on, perfectionism. Hank, if you are built that way, I hope you will find, as I have, that meticulousness has its merit.

Care in planning, care in execution, these are what have allowed our deeds, Sukey's and mine, to shape a new story. The old story of anarchism is the death of children. Even in Zola—Zola with his anarchist sympathies, Zola unique among the greats in his appetite for change—when a bomb goes off, a child dies. A lowly errand girl, pretty, slim, fair-haired, her stomach ripped open, her delicate face intact. Hers is the tale the culture must retell continually. Be the terrorist young or old, man or woman, idealist or cynic, the result is identical. And so in Joseph Conrad, there is poor Stevie, a mentally defective boy, *delicate*, like Zola's errand girl, as if a child's delicacy were the inevitable target of a bomb's brutality. More recently, in Doris Lessing—*The Good Terrorist*—a timer is misset; of the dying innocents, only one is identified, a girl of fifteen.

Putting obsessionality to use, I checked and rechecked in order not to tell that story. I practiced an anarchism of overcaution. I believe that uptightness can lead to explosions with their full measure of wit. Terror may be the wrong word for what I have practiced—many people seem less frightened than amused.

Our story, the comedy produced by Sukey, is a satire on the fruits of capitalism, satire epitomized in the collapse of the Giampiccolo house. By now everyone has seen the video: the monstrous mock-Victorian, a seaside abomination, imploding on itself and slumping ignominiously to earth, like a condemned Atlantic City hotel. The sequence has become a visual word in our national vernacular.

The inherent humor and rightness of that word, the incarnation of haughtiness going before a fall, the self-evidently overweening brought to its knees—all that is the fruit of Sukey's talent for what your mother used to call *détournement,* diverting an object from its conventional purpose, allowing it to be seen afresh. That was what we talked about in the sixties, your mother and her friends and I, gestures that might use the products of capitalism to strip capitalism bare, though we never made those gestures. To cause the Giampiccolo house to quake and totter and capitulate is to ask what it was doing on the sand in the first place. By what right had it desecrated the water's edge?

Sukey knows that I have always felt inadequacy in the face of my father's work. Heinrich "Sam" Samuels, the man after whom you arc named, was a fine finish carpenter. Sam could replace a scallop on a Goddard highboy with such precision that an expert might not know the chest had been damaged. When the Kuykendahl collection went to auction, more than one piece he had restored was cataloged by Sotheby's as Excellent condition, no repair or replacement. He could dovetail joints that met at odd angles, measuring by eye and using hand tools to make the cuts.

My father never taught me his trade. He meant to. Beyond starting me off as a real American, his naming me Chip was a joke that contained a father's hopes. But my clumsiness frustrated him.

I learned nonetheless, in the way that a child whose parents speak another language to each other will pick up the accent, even if the words remain foreign. What I got from my father was familiarity with clamps and jigs and bench vises. My particular knowledge comes from public television, *The New Yankee Workshop* and *This Old House* and *The Woodwright's Shop.*

Seeing my father at work made me aware of the importance of skill, persistence, and exactitude. But I am not certain that carpentry was Sam's calling. Perhaps drink was, or romance—he was a gruff man who was capable of devotion to women. The sign of a calling is the life it brings. I think of those lines from Henry James: We work in the dark—we do what we can—we give what we have. Our doubt is our passion and our passion is our task.

Comforting, to know that our most masterly writer understands doubt rather than abundant talent to define calling. My recent work has taught me the importance of passion and of tolerance for uncertainty. I say this to you as one whose skills, when you were a young child, were often called into question.

When Sukey signaled that we had found our time and place, I thought she meant merely that Johnny "Little John" Giampiccolo was a storybook villain: bully, polluter, manipulator, Mafia front man. Ruthless, with a facade of charm. In the 1980s, Giampiccolo headed a company suspected of dumping hospital needles in the waters off Long Island beaches. He was someone the press could revile even when he was wronged. In telling a story, it helps to have a bad guy. But Sukey's wisdom went deeper. She knew the bind Giampiccolo was in. And she knew how the Giampiccolo house would affect me.

I had been there in the construction phase. Anyone on the Cape who could swing a hammer had been there. Part of the fun of building, for Giampiccolo, was fighting with contractors and firing them, unpaid. Then he would flog the next hapless fellow to speed the schedule, to the point where all sorts of incompetents were hired including, for a brief stint, your father. No one person was on the job for long. I had not seen the inside of the finished house until Sukey took me there.

She brought me on a blustery September afternoon, unseasonably cold, the kind of day your mother could not abide. The tide was low, and we could see the perches and groynes scarring the flats. Those were the names my father used for them—sunken posts and boards crisscrossing the beach below the high-tide mark, holding sand and slowing erosion. You may remember the truck tires people on Harm's Way set in front of the dunes—marsh grass grew in them. You and I used to gather the mussels that attached themselves to the tires, and the occasional oyster in the grass. After you left, the Audubon group sued to have the tires removed, on the grounds that they trapped sand that should have swept northward toward the piping-plover nesting grounds. Same thing—perches and groynes. Ways for a man to hold sand in front of his home while starving the downcurrent beach.

Nationally, Giampiccolo became known because his house went down in spectacular fashion and because he was nowhere to be found. But the local story, like every story on Cape Cod, concerned real estate. Here, Giampiccolo was famous for getting permission to build perches and groynes at a time when neighbors were fighting losing battles to erect a seawall. There's the real measure of power in America, winning the right to mess with nature.

In the early nineties, Giampiccolo bought a plot of unbuildable land on the Sesuit beachfront, a long, wide strip of dune. Then he hired engineers and lawyers to say the dune was not a dune but a sandbank and therefore buildable, and more engineers and lawyers to say the septic systems would not affect the bay, and then architects and lawyers to say that height restrictions should not apply since he was reproducing a structure of historic importance, a Victorian building that had once graced the King's Highway at the Sesuit crossroads. What was rumored must surely have been true, that Giampiccolo's finagling was enhanced by bribes and corrupt promises and, when necessary, strong-arm tactics. In the end, Giampiccolo had permission to build a seafront monstrosity and a seawall to protect it—an ecological and aesthetic nightmare, complete with perches and groynes the lawyers claimed as an ancient right attaching to the property.

I don't suppose Sukey felt moral outrage at Giampiccolo's having skirted communal rules. She was a realtor, she had seen it all. As for me, I had been too well schooled in political skepticism to worry over planning boards. I assume laws will favor the rich or be broken by them. But it is true that I did not like to see the beach scarred, did not like seeing a selfish man's imprint on what should belong to all of us in common.

Unfair, I protested. I was referring not to the perches and groynes but to Sukey's marching me past them, knowing how they would disturb me. She answered by wrapping her arms around mine and sliding her hands into my coat pockets. Funny, how a woman can slip a hand into yours and mean almost anything by it. Your mother would press up against me when we walked on cold days. With Anais—that was how your mother used to spell her name—the gesture asked why I had brought her to a home where the elements are harsh. Sukey's hands say only, we share. Warmth, adventures. Like musketeers, all for one and one for all. My pockets are her pockets; she takes without asking.

Come along, Chip, she said. Can't a body take you for a stroll?

Two hummocks of dune met at the beach side of the Giampiccolo house. Stairs ran between them. The beach juts eastward at that point. As you walk up the strand from the cottage, you round the bend and disappear from view. That was one of many promising aspects to the Giampiccolo site. From any distance, there was no way to see me enter or leave. What characterizes successful gambles is favorable odds. Sukey is a master gambler.

Turning in to the house, we headed up the beach stairs and then passed beside fat pilings, sunk deep through the dune, anchoring the deck and great room above. Sukey punched in the code to the outside alarm and admitted us to a ground-level mudroom—more exactly, a sandroom—that would later be for me what a space station air lock is for an astronaut in the movies, a place to brush off and don work clothes. She disarmed the second system, from a keypad in the mudroom closet, and we climbed the steps to the main floor.

I felt no fear. I do not want you to imagine that your father is a brave man. You have nothing to live up to on that score. But for a long while after you left, my capacity for fear was muted. What more had I to lose?

Though the exterior looked Victorian, indoors all was modern—cavernousness meant to denote wealth. The great room was vaulted in limed red oak, the walls held apart by enormous rough oak beams, salvaged timbers from old ships. Hanging from them incongruously were chandeliers made of Chihuly glass—translucent purple cones melting over one another, like a braid of radioactive jalapeños. The effect of the whole was bombast. Bombast and shoddy workmanship. The framing did not sit tight on the windows, the floor had already settled to the north side. The floorboards were face-nailed, but they had not been properly spaced and the sealant had been applied too thick, so that the boards were panelized and had begun to cup. The baseboard molding had not been scribed to the floor. Sand was finding its way under a door, and two skylights leaked. I thought, It wants to come down. There was Sukey's genius, knowing that I was sensitive to place. The Giampiccolo house spoke to me. It asked to be destroyed.

I remember when you were five bringing you to the home of a classmate who was new to your kindergarten. The house was a sterile, barnlike affair in a development at the far northern tip of Sesuit, a cluster perched atop a hostile bluff no one had thought to build on until the Cape became so popular that every inch turned valuable. I walked you up the path and into the entry. Your friend was there, armed with a Nerf gun and ready to play. But you looked around the house and out the sliders to the bay in the distance, and you began to cry. It was the vastness, I think, in contrast to the snugness of our cottage. Your friend's house did not feel to you like a place where people should live. Take me home, you insisted. I could not calm you. You left and would not return. So I suspect houses have spoken to you as well.

Perhaps they should not. When I was in college, the essays of the French novelist Alain Robbe-Grillet were required reading for young radicals. Your mother lent me her copy, to bring me along ideologically. Robbe-Grillet's theme was the danger of investing objects with metaphorical meaning. Man must face the unresponsiveness of his surround. The world is not significant. It is simply other.

Robbe-Grillet's own method was to fill a novel with objects and then render those objects unreliable. Obsessively, repetitiously, he would describe a set of window blinds, or an eraser such as a child might carry in a pencil box. These incidentals were at the center of his work, but the depictions of them were inconsistent—neither the eraser nor the novel's plotline could be grasped. That was Robbe-Grillet's principle, *construire en détruisant,* creation of meaning through destruction of expectations.

Robbe-Grillet was especially dismissive of old novels—Zola's or Balzac's—in which house and owner suffer identical fates. No matter how progressive the novelist's ideology, the old false realism sustains overly reassuring beliefs about man's place in the material world. For the new novelist, a house is only a house, incomprehensible, external, opaque.

I was poisoned young by the old novel. Sukey's mom's house had a library whose walls were lined with leather-bound sets: Dickens and Trollope, Eliot and Hardy, and, yes, Zola and Balzac. It would be understatement to say that those books were more real to me than daily life. They were what made daily life real. Daily life made no sense to me until I saw it through the lens of those books.

For years I thought I was living in *Great Expectations.* (*Lady Chatterley's Lover* might have been more to the point, but I had not yet read that book, and it was some time before I understood the relationship between my dad and Sukey's mom.) I expected to be scorned by the pretty girl in the big house. I expected the houses of the corrupt to fall to the ground.

For me, houses have always been noble or degraded, humble or overbearing. Or think of the ocean. It is freedom and comfort and danger and return and tedium and cleansing and renewal and power and endlessness and indifference and home. What would it be to see the ocean and not find meaning? Hardly human. That is why the Free the Beaches movement has succeeded, because the ocean signifies. The ocean is what is beyond man. We may be on the ocean or in it or beside it, but it is never ours. Someone blows up a beachfront house, and no matter what the pundits say, the public thinks, By golly it *is* strange to believe a strip of ocean belongs to a person. The idea is precisely absurd. And if this nugget of capitalism is absurd, perhaps we should reconsider the whole.

Which is not to say that in struggling to devise a narrative style for the Movement I dismissed Robbe-Grillet. No modern story-teller can ignore what he has to say about the importance of incon-sistency. Neat patterns, even within a program of explosions, are too reassuring, their message too easily debunked or co-opted. We chose certain houses at random, so as to cede control of meaning.

And though I know I do not use it as Robbe-Grillet intends, I admire that phrase, *to create through destruction*. Its influence is evident in our well-wrought dramas, the ones that contradict Robbe-Grillet. A house sits presumptuously on a fragile dune, overlooking a bay. The house is a character, reflecting aspects of its builder, its owner, and the society that sanctions its use. The dune and bay are characters, too. When the explosives go off, we are satisfied because we know, all of us, that this story evolves from the characters' nature. Destruction brings forth a tale that has wanted to be told.

In Giampiccolo's great room, I had an inkling of that tale. I did not yet know how perfect the setup was. Sukey had not shown me the woodshop. She had not told me of Giampiccolo's circumstances nor how she had influenced them. But as I stood beside her, I expe-rienced a change in my apprehension of my surroundings. The room was gray, but now the gray had nuance. It was dove gray, or rather pigeon gray, brightened by iridescent pinks and purples. I was like one of those people whose sight or hearing has been restored, the type you read about in popular medical essays. I enjoyed a pleasant incomprehension of the familiar. What were these goods arrayed before me?

Perhaps it was only that the light was dim. The broad panes of glass had been shuttered against the autumn wind. Clouds showed through skylights, and fog through transom windows above the French doors. In the sitting area at the bayside end, track lights flooded the occasional sculpture. A timing mechanism had gone awry. From a second sitting area, behind the dining table—bowling-alley length, to entertain who knows what obscene crowd—a television added its glow. Another precaution against burglars, or a mistake by whoever was here last. On-screen, a businessman described how he had made a fortune in telemarketing. The interviewer looked bored. She wore a mauve jacket with pointed lapels. Her lips, also mauve, were like pillows. The man planned to bring telemarketing into inner-city tenements, so welfare mothers could enter the job market from their own apartments. Close-up on the mauve lips. It could have been a student video project, The Way We Live Now.

Sukey and I stood near the kitchen amidst a welter of displayed possessions: cookware and crystal, porcelain and paintings, CD racks and speakers. No doubt models that bespoke power, though not in a language I understand. I did recognize a pair of John Dowds. No reason you should know him—a landscape painter who is in his own way a name brand here. Tawdry cottages against vibrant skies, the old Cape. To hang them in this obscene behemoth of a house—perhaps a joke on the part of a decorator.

To my new senses, a single feature was vivid, those oaken beams. Though they were four feet above my head, I could all but feel their texture, wood dry and splintery under my hands. Hewn by what lumberjack, squared by what sawyer? Timbers that had groaned under the pressure of storms, borne honest work, carried men at sea. Objects are not silent.

I put my hand on Sukey's shoulder, to steady myself. Her breath was slow and deep, as if she, too, were entranced. Here is the strange part: In her breathing I heard yours. Yours at age seven, on a night when your mother was away on her private journey. How I loved to kiss you one more time and slip your leg back under the covers. From Sukey's damp parka came your puppy-dog smell, and I felt that you were with me. For weeks, I continued to feel your presence in that house, as if you were a worksite companion, as I was for my father. Which may be why your appearance today on the television—older, and yet yourself—struck me with such force.

In the grayness of the great room, Sukey and I stood side by side, looking, listening. At last I said: I think those beams are structural.

Sukey laid her head on my shoulder, as if she were a teenager saying, You are my man.

You will wonder, I suppose, what I felt for Sukey, what there was between us. Hard for the young to imagine the poignancy of memory. Sukey's thighs and arms have taken on weight, and her bosom has turned from ample to matronly. Years of sun and Scotch and cigarettes have given her face excessive character. The hair that was her glory has faded from spun gold back to straw. I am capable of seeing her as the world does. I am capable of seeing most matters as the world does, though generally I do not. I have always been attracted by the stigma of mortality in a woman's face. The memento mori of European actresses in the art cinema your mother favored. From adolescence, Sukey has had that worldly beauty, has been careening toward the grave. Besides, for me, Sukey as she once was shines through in who she is now.

What she sees in me is less clear. Whatever her recent politics, Sukey's sexual tastes are of the late twentieth-century American variety; they run to power and status and full heads of hair. She returned to me as a friend. She allowed me to help her through her hard time, and I believe she has tried to help me through mine.

You may wonder, too, about the gap between the father you remember and the man I am asking you to imagine, the one who blows up houses. I know you have an image of me, else why say Hi, Dad? Can you call up our mornings in the cottage the summer we worked so hard on reading? I would like to hope I am with you when you turn to a book for consolation. I am sure you experienced me as mild. Too gentle, too stable, those were your mother's complaints. By now you may see me through her eyes.

She may have been right, about stability. To me, it sometimes seems that I have changed the least of any man I know. Sukey likes to say that I am coming into my own, which I hope is true, though I am not certain what that expression means. Lately, it has been hard to avoid self-aggrandizement, in the face of the Movement's success. I have tried to hold steady. Perhaps a man who comes into his own is one who (as Manny advises) lets his character play itself out, in which case you know me still. I would be glad for you to know me. Shakespeare had it backward: It is a wise child, and a lucky one, that knows his own father.

2

*

After Long Silence

Though it is not yet midnight, I can tell already that sleep will not come. I have been prone to two sorts of insomnia. One is the type your mother used to suffer, a wakening in the dead of night to vigilance hedged round with dread and exhaustion. What she called her *nuits blanches,* nights a glaring white in the mind. I first experienced that frightful blankness when she took you, as if she had left it behind in your stead. I did not attempt to drive it away. I clung to sleeplessness, as a link to you, the converse of your nighttime breathing, which soothed me like a lullaby.

The other insomnia is like a second wind, a not unpleasurable upsurge of energy that ends with a refreshing morning nap—the benign sleeplessness I enjoyed the week you were born. In the Giampiccolo basement, in the marvelous woodshop where I prefabricated devices for installations up and down Sesuit, it would come upon me regularly. This wakefulness is full-spectrum, warm and vivid, crowded with memory. I am in that happy state now, as I sit at the kitchen table and write.

The green glass of the student lamp is framed with haze, as it was many happy evenings when you sat in your Sassy Seat, cantilevered off the table end. You would bounce and mouth your crackers and point cheerfully at the lampshade. Your mood would fill the room. Your question fills it now, the Why?

Where should a father begin? Best to start simply, with what you will have seen on television. The installations and the images they have inspired. In the hopes that some of the rest has been implicit in those images, your history and mine.

If the Movement is distinct from prior anarchist efforts, that difference is due to two elements. Minimal program. Obsessive care. Historically, terror has been dogmatic and sloppy. We have gone against the grain.

Most people think explosion is a matter of power, bigger is better. To my mind, the art of explosion is in compactness. Alfred Nobel earned his place in history through stabilizing dynamite, embedding the nitroglycerin in a matrix. *Insensitivity* is the word explosives manuals use. An insensitive installation will not blow if a house burns down or a ground tremor impacts the detonator.

Elegant explosives combine insensitivity with high brisance. Brisance is shattering effect, a measure of the velocity of the explosive front. Detonator cord is high brisance. Wrap detcord around a column, and it cuts through. Low-brisance explosives act through pressure. They are the tool of the heedless terrorist, the high-nitrogen-fertilizer type, the macho braggart. I relied on low-brisance ordnance early in the sequence of home demolitions, to mislead investigators, give them the impression that they need not search for subtler installations. But in my more substantial work, I used low-brisance explosives only selectively and in small amounts, plastique following detcord, say, for the final push, to direct the way a column falls. Cut and push, using small packets in multiple locations. That has been my method when I have had time and access—the method in the Giampiccolo house.

Insensitivity and the clean break, capacities I never aspired to in matters of the heart, these are the characteristics I have favored in explosives. My purpose has been gentle wakening. Inspiring observers to awareness of what they know already. As Thoreau says of the best persuasion, the appeal of them to themselves. I take no pride in brawn. After Giampiccolo, my favorite project might be Warelwast, where there was no detonation at all. Pure insensitivity.

You know the Free the Beaches signature: fireworks. Before a bomb goes off, we send fireworks high into the air. Bright and noisy ones. As a warning in case, despite our precautions, a straggler remains in the house. And as a way of drawing observers to the site. Gather round, there is a tale to be told. That story begins with a metaphor inherent in fireworks. Impossible to see them without thinking of independence—that saying of Thomas Jefferson's: *Light & liberty go together.* My aim has been to find a tool for a job and then allow it to serve multiple functions. Fireworks begin as a safeguard, then serve as a trademark, and later become an instrument of change, sufficient in themselves to bring a structure down.

The Warelwast place seemed beyond us, a house guarded round the clock, all year, even before the Movement had declared itself. Owned by a circumspect banker, a man born to wealth and intent on its preservation. The peculiar name goes back to a pair of twelfth-century English bishops involved in building the cathedral at Exeter. Sukey was drawn by the form of the Warelwast house, stone-fortress modern, one of those incongruous looming presences that have made the bay side of Sesuit look like Hamptons North or Malibu East. As a storyteller, I appreciated the contrast between the ancestors' public architecture and the banker's private. A fine subject for intervention, but how?

In midsummer, after we had already disrupted a dozen houses, Sukey was asked to a dinner reception for the Warelwast son, in honor of his fourth marriage. She was invited because she was still here, at a time when many of the better people had fled the Cape. The party was a gesture of defiance against the Movement. An attempt to shore up property values. A vote of confidence in the FBI's assurance that every beachfront home had been inspected and now all was well.

Like most men at middle age, I suffer a measure of bursitis and sciatica. These ordinary pains are signs of life, almost welcome when seen in that light. Mine accompanied me to the installation. Sukey drove her Lexus. I curled up on the floor behind the front seats, under a blanket. Multiple-listing books sat on the back bench alongside the picnic cooler and black plastic garbage bag that held my matériel. I shifted attention from body to surroundings. In jeopardy, a man hears with acuity. Footfalls, walkie-talkies, mewing of gulls, rattle of surf on the shingle. Tension is close companion to exhilaration.

Most of our installations had been set long in advance. Warelwast was one of only two where I was on-site this past summer. (The other was Woodcock, a project I came to regret.) With me, I had fireworks, a tiny detonator, a programmed cellular modem, and a sandbag to hold the package upright. I had weathered the components—exposed them to sun, wind, rain, and salt air—so that when they were discovered, they would seem to have been in place for months.

An hour into the party, Sukey excused herself to retrieve her purse from the car. She gave me the all clear. I was outdoors only for a minute, to deposit the package in a cellar window well, behind a hydrangea, to the rear of a chimney. The risk was one I would have preferred to do without, but I liked the project. There was randomness in it, pleasure in the play of chance.

So much could have gone wrong. The package might have been discovered the morning after the party, or it might not have been discovered at all. But fortune smiled on us. The weathered fireworks sat in place until the Howell house went and the feds headed back to work, red-faced and intent. They found our deposit at Warelwast and displayed it to great fanfare. A tactical error. Because then they could not locate the explosives.

As terrorists, we had been utterly reliable in our signaling. If fireworks went off, the house blew. No false alarms, no phony bomb threats. The Warelwast house was now unusable and unsalable. It was the one spot on the Cape where a person risked being blown up without warning, the one spot to which the courtesy— the chivalry—of Free the Beaches might not extend.

The search continued, to no avail. The feds' assurances lacked credibility. What could old man Warelwast do? Reinstall the fireworks, in hopes that a saboteur would phone the modem and send up flares before setting off the main explosives? There was no alternative to taking the fortress apart in search of the invisible threat.

The pictures played serially on the nightly news. The decomposition of a structure built over and against the community. Stone by stone, the house diminished. I like to believe that in the images I craft, the pathos extends out from the object to encompass our common vulnerability. No wall is thick enough. Which is not to deny that Warelwast is at heart a droll folktale. The protagonist was the foolish senex who in trying to hold too tight loses the whole sack. The insurance imbroglio added an element of slapstick. When ordinary companies skittered from the Cape, old man Warelwast had turned to Lloyd's. But since the home had sustained no damage, Lloyd's refused to pay unless explosives were found. As the demolition proceeded, the insurers posted agents on the site to make certain that the owner did not import munitions. Now two surveillance forces were on hand, one serving Warelwast and one guarding against him. A fable about the nature of security.

Unlike Giampiccolo, Warelwast was a reasonably sympathetic figure—the congenital skinflint. Only it did seem he might have been happier in a culture that gave less scope to his possessiveness. One wished for a Scrooge- or Marner-like transformation culminating in a donation of beachfront to the public.

In its commentaries, the press insisted that the Warelwast project was an act of violence, just as surely as if dynamite had taken the house down. The assertion was trumpeted as if it were original or paradoxical, counter to the purpose of the work. But it is hard to see how any thoughtful observer could assume the installation is mute on the subject of violence.

Violence does not depend on brisance. When our country embargoes trade, and another country's citizens die of hunger or infection, we have done violence. When the homeless die of exposure or belated medical attention, here in our cities, are those deaths not violent? Six million American families with second homes, six million Americans homeless over the past five years— resonance in those statistics, their symmetry, and the number itself, with its horrific overtones. Violence is built into a system that provides one man two homes and another none. Can we imagine an author of Warelwast who failed to think along these lines?

Over thirteen decades have passed since Karl Marx made his sarcastic observation: The bourgeoisie, which looks complacently upon the wholesale massacre after the battle, is convulsed by horror at the desecration of brick and mortar. And still op-editorialists compete to see who can express the fiercest outrage over the deposit at Warelwast. Fortunately, the images speak for themselves. Fireworks are found in a window well, and a house comes down, until all that can be seen from the roadside is the beauty of bay and sky, marred only by the presence of security guards.

No manifesto, no spokesperson. It is this pattern that Sukey now wants to change, through a campaign of public relations.

Before seeing you on television, I had declined to consider my open entry into what Anais called the world of spectacle. You know about "spectacle." News reporters, basketball stars, seaside mansions. The ubiquitous display that sustains commodities and celebrities and so defines desire and aspiration. *Spectacle* is a word from the sixties, from the French political theory your mother favored. Anais held the belief, though she never acted on it, that the way to resist spectacle is to fashion "situations"—spectacles that contest spectacle. An effective situation allows a moment of freedom, of play, of private desire. What Sukey and I have done is to create a situation.

There is an intensity to life on the Cape this summer, for those (and despite reports of a devastated rental market, there are some) who remain. The sand, the sun, the surf—those clichés—have been renewed for them. The hardy stragglers understand themselves and their passions. They find they would risk everything just to be rocked by the waves. Better than the summer of Hurricane Bob, they say. They share the camaraderie of people in a time of crisis. There are those who claim that the nation has been enlivened.

My concern is that Sukey's next step will end the situation, turn it into standard spectacle. Her intention is to burnish my image. I fear she will succeed halfway, create a persona for me without winning you back. So that you will have less of me than I had of my father. He kept his history private but never hid who he was. That was my father's gift, his legacy—honest presence, a version of how it is to be a man.

3

*

The Fire Last Time

My earliest memory is of him. It is morning, and we are together in a small bathroom. I feel the chill of a tile floor beneath me—tiny black and white squares. What is odd is that the grout is a shiny black. I look up from the floor to my father. He has just shaved, with a brush and straight razor. He is mixing a mouthwash. My attention has been caught by the keenness of mint.

We moved, my father and I, from apartment to apartment in New York. I found each new setting ominous. Mornings soothed me, the constancy of the routine, the brush and the razor and the scent of mouthwash.

In time I lost the particular memory—the cluster of sensations, cold feet, a black shimmer, a sharp smell. Then, sitting in on a college art course with Anais, I saw a slide of a Stuart Davis painting of an Odol bottle, aqua and white like the summer sky, a comedy of juxtaposition, the classically beveled base joined to the awkwardly craned neck. Davis had set the mouthwash bottle before a checkerboard pattern, alternating squares sufficient to signify "bath." On the container's label, the trade name in shadowed letters floats above the motto, It Purifies.

We see, the lecturer said, how the commercial has become the natural and the sacred.

I had a private response, Proustian transport to lost times.

My other early memory is of a woman's face. She is young and pretty. Her hair is black, wavy, bobbed. She has the valentine lips of a silent-movie star, and the languorous, indifferent eyes. When she leans over to be kissed, I taste her face powder. I am uncertain that she cares for me, anxious that she may not.

In childhood, when I tried to conjure my mother, only that moment surfaced. I struggled to hold it in pure form, but soon it merged with the description in *Peter Pan* of Mrs. Darling with her sweet, mocking mouth and the one kiss no one but Peter could get. Later with my school, I saw a local production of the stage play *Peter Pan*, and the memory was further muddled by the face of the actress who played Mrs. Darling. The Pan-Cake makeup linked the two women, as did the moue the actress made when she accepted Michael's hug at bedtime—those details and my belief that my mother was an actress, a rare fact my father once confided when weak with drink.

I was eight. From then on, I imagined that on the evening in the memory my mother was headed off to a performance. I wish now that I could undo the composite and find the original face; though I cannot say for certain whether my mother—your paternal grandmother—is the object of the kiss. That young woman may be someone who cared for me while my father worked. Any young woman at all, looking forward to release from the chore of amusing a toddler, any young woman looking forward to her night on the town.

By the time we moved to Sesuit, the quality of my memories had changed. They assumed the form of stories. Manny Abelman believes the instability of my childhood caused me to retreat, to see my own history from a distance, as if it were a fiction to be wondered at. When will you swing boldly into life? he asked. I have tried of late to answer that challenge. But the early memories, the ones that explain how you came to be born here and how I came to cast my fate with Sukey Kuykendahl, these retain the form of story.

It is an Indian summer night, warm and sweet. I am sleeping in a small room in a vast house, in a strange place, outside the city. I am on a cot, beside my father's twin bed. I waken to a howling noise. It is late, I know, and my father is not in the room.

I go to look for him. I am in a hallway. A foul smell is in the air. Compelled, I move toward it. Already I am crying, Daddy, Daddy.

At the end of the hallway is a kitchen, pitch-dark. The smell has diminished now, replaced for the moment by the mustiness of smoke. I pass into the dining room. I walk beside the long table, steadying myself with a hand on the chair backs. Through the row of windows, I see flames leaping from the building's wall. Beyond the next door a man is bellowing. The light of flame guides me to the door handle.

When I open, I see not my father but an ogre from a fairy tale. He is tall and fat, and he has a blackened hand, which he waves about. His eyes are angry. He shouts bad words. The ogre is dressed in green, shiny pajamas—they are enormous. And the smell has returned, the smell of burnt flesh.

The man is startled to see me. Fetch Sukey, he commands.

Sukey is the name of a girl in a Mother Goose rhyme the kindergarten teacher read us. Sukey is the girl who lived here this summer, the one who was cruel to me at the beach. No one has ever said *fetch* to me before. Wanting to obey, I cross the room to the entry hall. As I turn to climb the stairs, I see that my father is coming down them. He is carrying a beautiful girl in his arms, Sukey. The girl's mother follows, wrapped only in a blanket. She is the woman with the name that means chicken coop, Mrs. Kuykendahl. The ogre is Mr. Kuykendahl, Sukey's father.

We must leave the house, my father says. He is a quiet man. We listen to my father and walk out to the circular drive. Mr. Kuykendahl opens the car, but he realizes he cannot steer. He motions to my father. Smoke is rising from behind the house. They all bundle into the car. The beautiful girl, Sukey, calls: Come, come. Her father wants her in the front seat, but she stays wedged in the back between her mother and me.

We stop, and the men leave the car and then return. They have phoned the firemen, and now we are going to the hospital. And here is my strongest memory of that night of transformation. I am sitting on the smooth, rounded leather of the backseat. I want to cry, but Sukey is excited. She is the loveliest child I have ever seen, a princess with fine blond hair that shows the effects of the hundred brush-strokes at bedtime. She rests her head against me. She squeezes my hand. She was mean to me, but now we are best friends, united in adventure. The car goes over a dip, and she giggles. Her nightgown is made of a fine substance I have never touched before. Gossamer. She is Rapunzel, to my mother's Snow White. Sukey falls asleep beside me. I am awake with wonder. She has my heart forever.

I wish I could provide more of the history that surrounds the night of the fire. I know so little.

My father, your grandfather, was a German Jewish immigrant who had spent the war in an internment camp in Switzerland. He would never talk about his past, not a word. The few facts I have about his family, I learned from papers I came across upon his death. That was in 1968. He died suddenly, of alcoholism. His liver shrank to nothing, a hard little fist of a liver, the doctors said, cirrhosis and hepatitis.

My father's naturalization papers showed that he had been born in Munich in 1916. His father died the same year, his mother in 1941. When I read that date, an image came to mind of my father and his mother walking by foot across the Alps and his losing her on the journey, to cold and hunger. Where I got that impression, I did not remember, even then. It may have been an account that slipped out when my father was drinking. Or I applied to him a story he had told about someone else. My father suffered that misfortune or another. There were misfortunes aplenty in his generation, and his mother's.

My father was raised by a woman who was widowed in one war and who perished in the next. That would explain the sort of father he was, not a bad father, but a father with no sense of what childhood is. I see him as a man who himself was never fathered, a man who began with little and then sustained repeated loss.

He came to New York after the war and found work as a carpenter. I believe he met my mother, the young actress, in a bar. In his nightstand, he kept three identical matchbooks old enough to bear a BUtterfield-8 exchange. I have them still. They show a top hat and straight cane, and they bear the imprint of the Yorkvillager, Lexington Avenue at Seventy-ninth. Why those three matchbooks? He did not smoke. They ask, do they not, to be taken as a clue. I spotted them when I was young, and I would return secretly to visit them, pristine treasures stored in the bedside table alongside the nail clipper, silver pocketknife, and condoms, which were then sold rolled in plastic containers that looked like miniature hatboxes. From the first, I associated the matchbooks with my mother. Perhaps I had asked about them, and my father had responded in a way that made the connection for me.

I believe my mother left shortly after I was born, then returned and left again. Did my father follow her one summer to Sesuit? The Dennis Playhouse, where Gertrude Lawrence reigned, is not far off. I spent hours there once, poring over memorabilia, but it was no use. My mother's maiden name, on my birth certificate, is Jane Jones, so you can imagine. Jane Jones. Protestant. Birthplace, New York. Age, just shy of twenty-two.

Perhaps my father's trip to Sesuit had nothing to do with my mother. He had been working on the Kuykendahls' apartment in Manhattan, and when summer arrived, he was kept on to do repairs on Stone House, their Cape Cod home. The job paid a living wage, and it released him from the city. For the duration of the project, he would have a room in the servants' wing.

*   *   *

I remember arriving at Stone House. Its size intimidated me. I recall anxiety—perhaps a nightmare—about getting lost in endless passageways. What helped was that I had read in a children's book about a boy who had 365 bedrooms and slept each night in a different bed and 365 bathrooms and bathed each day in a different tub. With that story in mind, it became sport for me to go from room to room in Stone House, exploring. It intrigued me that the place had a name and a puzzling one at that. Stone House was clapboarded, in white with dark green shutters, and nary a stone in sight..The place was named after its first owners, I now know, Ezra and Asa Stone, landlubber brothers in a seafaring family. It was the original farmhouse in the neighborhood, expanded half a dozen times, always in Federal style.

No thought was given to my care. I accompanied my father when he worked, until I cut the meat of my left hand on the sharp edge of a chisel. Then Mrs. Kuykendahl enrolled me in the summer program of the local yacht club, a lesser creature there on sufferance. A counselor taught me to swim. Mostly I was paid no mind, except by Sukey, who was horrid. She needed to distance herself from the intruder. But I stood cold water comfortably, could spend all day swimming the length of the jetty or exploring for hermit crabs and starfish. Not knowing how to behave around children, I was content to be let alone. I remember it as a magical summer— little boy in a big house by the endless bay.

Came September, we stayed on. There was work to do—dry-rotted joists to be replaced, window sashes to be repaired, chimneys to be repointed. A man could spend a lifetime restoring that house, and in the end my father did. I was enrolled in the local school you later attended, Sesuit Elementary. There was just the one building, still new, brick with alternating blue and orange fiberglass panels below the classroom windows. My teacher was Mrs. Bloxsom, which made sense to me—the blocks in the classroom, the school that appeared to have been built from blocks, and square-shouldered Mrs. Bloxsom behind her desk. Sukey left for New York with her father. Mrs. Kuykendahl was back and forth, to supervise my father.

Then the Kuykendahls were all here for a fall weekend, and the fire broke out, and my father came down the steps that led from Mrs. Kuykendahl's bedroom, and she was wrapped only in a blanket. Mr. Kuykendahl left for New York and never returned. He took Sukey with him. She showed up on occasional holidays, each time more haughty and more beautiful. I hoped for a sign, acknowledgment of our closeness the night Stone House caught fire. Instead, she played with me grudgingly. I did not know the latest games or songs. I was dense and dull, and she did not scruple to tell me so. She made me cry. When she was gone, I dreamed of her return.

Little you have seen in movies about the 1950s corresponds to the daily reality of my childhood. We did have the usual commodities. We owned a Studebaker and later a Rambler. We graduated from radio to television. (My father liked *The Honeymooners*, and he had an immigrant's—and a beer drinker's—attachment to baseball. He admired Ted Williams's workmanship and his bluntness with the press.) I was vaccinated against polio. Winters, if it snowed, I went sledding with my classmates. After school, I used the electric skillet to grill myself burgers from frozen patties. But we lived, my father and I, like members of the Victorian serving class. Aspects of my father's relationship with Mrs. Kuykendahl were even more antique—feudal. We were serfs on Mrs. Kuykendahl's estate.

For appearance' sake, she had us move out of the main house into a sort of keeper's bungalow on the north end of the property. Using scraps from other projects, my father winterized it and remodeled it into the cottage you know.

He was fanatical about materials. Long before there was an ecology movement, Sam cursed second-growth yellow pine. *Plantation wood*, he called it, proud to have found the words in English.

He preferred wood that was *quarter sawn,* cut radially to the center of the tree, not in tangential or rift cuts that can leave boards unstable or splotched with clusters of knots. For the Stone House library, which he paneled with full-thickness planks, he used Cuban mahogany, a slow-growing subspecies. He insisted on wood from dead-stand trees, since ripening on-site deepens mahogany's burgundy tones.

Only the best would do in my father's work for Mrs. K, and the excess found its way into the cottage. Your bedroom, mine in childhood, is floored with scraps he salvaged from a decayed eighteenth-century farmhouse in Harwich—*king's boards,* pumpkin pine so wide it was meant to be shipped back to England, a law more breached than honored by the rebellious colonists. As for the rest of the cottage, the flooring may be patchwork, but patchwork of the finest woods the world could offer in an era when there was still seasoned, first-growth lumber to be had.

My father taught me to approach materials with a critical eye. That lesson has stood me in good stead in my recent enterprise, where a single discordant detail might negate hours of painstaking labor. My work is a tribute to my father's handcrafting.

Throughout the fifties, in public Mrs. Kuykendahl kept my father at arm's length. When she hosted parties, he was not invited. If she had company, I understood I would be unwelcome at Stone House. I believe she saw my father as a shameful addiction, a perspective that gave the relationship the spice of degradation, for both participants.

Mrs. Kuykendahl had the bluntness you have seen in Sukey, but she was less kind, and when she drank, she could be merciless. She never lost an argument with my father. Perhaps my own mistrust of speech, my preference for deeds, arises from my early observations of my father's social interactions. Storytelling seemed the proper use of language—direct expression never did us Samuels men much good.

I learned to avoid Mrs. K, though she was also the source of much that was sweet in my life, a transistor radio in its own leather case, a wheat-colored, heather-knit pullover that looked just like the other boys'. Emotionally, she withheld everything. I was not to treat her as the mother I longed for, not to indicate to outsiders that I had any relationship to her at all. I was to count on her for nothing, and yet she held possibilities before me. At first it was that she might buy me a bike, and she did, a maroon, antelope-backed Raleigh English racer. Later, I was led to hope that she might subsidize my college studies. You can see how for me Dickens was a window on life.

Dickens was what passed for children's literature in the Germany my father grew up in. He directed me to *David Copperfield* when I was nine. I could see the point of it, the bit about schoolboys tormenting one another.

But it was *Great Expectations* that sealed my attachment to books. I had not known anyone who experienced the world as I did, until I met Pip. From the first page, I knew he was just like me. He used a tombstone to conjure his mother: *From the character and turn of the inscription,* 'Also Georgiana Wife of the Above,' *I drew a childish conclusion that my mother was freckled and sickly.* That was me—from the sweep of italic type on my father's matchbooks, I had elaborated an impression of my mother's grace. And then there was the way that Pip described the countryside, in horizontals and verticals, the flatness of the marsh, the importance of the church steeple. I saw Sesuit that way, as if the landscape had an orderly architecture, one I might understand if I puzzled over it.

The truths of Pip's family life were the truths of mine. Men defer to strong women. Adults find children a nuisance. Children, for their part, develop a sense of injustice, along with an awareness that they can never tell grown-ups the important facts. And here was something that did not happen in the books we read at school: Liquor flowed freely at meals. I was bound to the novel, bonded like a chick to a hen, even before Pip entered Satis House and met Miss Havisham and Estella. When he did—well, you can imagine.

Here was my life on paper: the forbidding, abandoned, wealthy woman on whose charity a boy depends; the lovely and scornful girl whose favor he longs to gain.

I began the book one morning when I was kept in bed by a fever. My father had brought me Mrs. Kuykendahl's copy, an old edition with a nubbly leather cover, comforting to touch, and illustrations by "Phiz," so explorable in their quaint detail. Though I loved school, I faked a second day of illness to learn how Pip fared with Estella. When I found that Dickens had written two endings, I did not feel cheated. The ambiguity struck me as the height of realism, since my own future is what I had stayed home to discover, and that was unknowable.

One event led me to understand that Sukey was, for her part, attached to me. This was years later, in my last weeks of high school, after I had learned I was admitted to Harvard.

Let me tell you about that first—getting into Harvard—since you may worry that you are not the scholar your father was. Here's the truth: I was an indifferent student. I had no talent for math. It disturbed me that what I could write never resembled what I liked to read, so that much of the time I refused to express myself on paper. Worse, I was too shy to speak in class, or too conscious of what other children thought. I would never show up a classmate by giving a better answer. It was the rare teacher who had any take on me.

Mr. Wainwright drew me out, in my junior year of high school. He was another Cape Cod type, the reserved academic who has moved his career here in anticipation of retirement. A man of refinement. Gay, I now suppose, gay and sad, that all too common oxymoron. I don't doubt he spent his summer weekends in Provincetown, stalking the bars, and then felt guilty the year round.

Wainwright taught English. We were starting *Silas Marner*, another novel that contained a piece of my family life, the isolated man who can make no sense of the child with whom fate has saddled him. (When an adult cooed over a child, my father would mutter, *Wo kommen all die alten Esel her?* Where do all the old donkeys come from? Meaning, if kids are as handsome and clever as they are made out to be, why is it that adults are such ugly fools?) Something I said led Wainwright to understand that I was familiar with George Eliot's novels. He held me after class. As I stammered forth my opinions, it emerged that I had read not only *Silas Marner* but *Middlemarch* and *The Mill on the Floss* as well. And half of Trollope. Most of Dickens. And Galsworthy.

I loved Galsworthy, the belabored metaphors. In Mrs. Kuykendahl's collection, the Forsyte novels were bound individually. I remember puzzling over *The Man of Property*. Galsworthy made you turn the phrase in your mind. Which was the owner? Soames Forsyte sometimes seemed a man composed of wealth, controlled by wealth. The plot turns on his impulse to treat his wife as chattel, something I vowed at that young age never to do. Better far to be like my father and hold women in esteem. Wainwright smiled when I mentioned Galsworthy, already out of favor.

Wainwright and I agreed on Thomas Hardy, a favorite of both of ours. He quizzed me on *A Pair of Blue Eyes*, which, being romantic, I knew chapter by chapter. Hardy's perspective—that misfortune is frequent and arbitrary, though also in some way tied up with character—was so close to my own that I did not recognize it as representing a distinct philosophy. I lacked sophistication altogether, had no notion which the important books were. I had been working my way through Mrs. Kuykendahl's bound sets.

I could scarcely explain even to myself why I kept my reading hidden. It was a vice, a compulsion, a lifeline—one that snapped when your mother left with you. I could no longer pick up the old novels, could scarcely make it through the excerpts I now use in class. But throughout my childhood, the Stone House library was my favorite room in the world.

Wainwright believed he had discovered buried treasure. He spent the year buffing me, filling gaps in my reading, directing me to essays that might correct my naive misimpressions. He did not make me discuss books. They spoke to a part of me that did not want to see daylight, and Wainwright respected my reticence. His courtesy allowed me to understand that I was not alone, that others led secret lives. Wainwright gave me one thing more. When I returned for senior year, he arranged for me to travel to Cambridge to meet his old professor at Harvard, Alistair Perkins.

Perkins was of the old school, military bearing, clipped speech. I learned later that he had no graduate degree—he was recruited straight from the College to the English faculty via the old boy network, and he had stayed on forever. For cultural enrichment, he enacted eighteenth-century battle scenes for his classes, with special attention to the advantages of the breech-loading rifle over the muzzle-loader. Of course, he hunted. The proper greeting to him on a Monday morning in autumn was Bag many, sir?

In time, he would introduce me to Swift, Fielding, Burke, Pope, and Johnson, the backbone of a gentleman's education. It was Perkins who got me into Harvard.

He met me at the Faculty Club, examined me through steel-rimmed glasses, with as much dispassion as Miss Havisham ever examined Pip.

Student of Wainwright, are you?

I admitted as much.

Relish horsemeat?

That was his standing joke. He was one of the members who insisted the dish remain on the menu.

I must have looked astonished.

Bring the young gentleman a Salisbury steak and a glass of claret, he admonished the waiter.

Or he may have said plonk—a glass of our plonk. He proceeded to teach me how to conduct myself at table. The main lesson, as I remember it, was after eating salad to chew a slice of bread before returning to the wine, it being sinful to let Bordeaux touch a tongue dulled by the acid of the dressing. Even at the time, it struck me as wrong that a man focused on the trappings of privilege should determine where I went to college—though I liked Perkins, it was impossible not to like him.

He grilled me briefly on *Dombey and Son*. Heavy on the sentiment, wot? He preferred drier prose. Then Perkins proffered advice: Small lives are happiest. He seemed concerned that as a working-class boy, I might be prone to ambition. By the end of the meal, I came to understand that a decision had been made in my favor, Wainwright's recommendation and this luncheon once-over sufficing to win Perkins's backing. Perkins went on to ask about Wainwright, was he tough enough on the lads? Perkins seemed not to know that girls attended public school. All this felt more natural to me than you may imagine. I spent so much time immersed in Dickensian novels that it did not surprise me when a character came to life.

4

*

Shanghaied

Here and now, I am waiting for Sukey and her groceries. I nodded off over this journal and dragged myself to bed in the early hours of the morning. The radio alarm woke me to sunlight filtering through mackerel clouds—so perfect a phrase, bearing the imprint of the fisherman looking skyward.

A story on the all-news station has it that a beachfront owner, Dorothy Arnold, saw my red pickup on the strand the evening before the seawalls blew last March. You had a run-in with Dotty—a white-haired lady with a pair of French bulldogs. She hated for kids to cross her yard en route to the public stretch of Quivet Cove, and she hated if their games spilled over onto her private beach. There's not a chance in a thousand the biddy could tell a Cadillac from a Volkswagen at close range in daylight, but never mind. If the feds are leaking their evidence, it means they are prospecting for more. Sukey hopes her campaign will spur the government to act prematurely. Meanwhile I sit in the quiet of the cottage, with time to write.

I have been postponing the moment when I turn to the episode Sukey joked about in the phone call, the shanghaiing. I doubt I would discuss it if you and I were together. Too much stands between fathers and their teenage sons. Mutual embarrassment. And fear on the father's part that discussion amounts to encouragement, and encouragement to irresponsibility, the dangers of sex today being what they are. So that important aspects of the father's experience are not passed on, and mistakes are repeated.

Lacking stories from our parents, we turn to spectacle for instruction and then feel inadequate when our private pleasures fail to match the glossy fulfillment set before us. We are alienated from the body. Marx wrote of this intimate alienation, and of the alienation of husband from wife, parent from child, in the home. No refuge is free from falseness.

I realize I would withhold these pages—accede to a taboo—if I imagined you were going to read this notebook. But why? I am of the generation that found promise in sexuality. The hope was that your cohort would be free of the awkwardness that distorted ours and our parents' intimate relationships. Your mother and I read in Margaret Mead of South Sea tribes whose teenagers played openly at sex. We imagined our children would share that ease.

For so many reasons, we failed. In the world of spectacle, smarminess rules—as if spectacle could not survive without the audience's repeated surprise at the mildest of variety in appetite. So that now we feel nostalgia for the very era (our own) whose inhibitions we hoped to transcend. Never mind. Even in these parlous times, my wish is for you to grow in confidence. To take pride in the delights of the body. In this as in every realm to fare better than your father did and his father before him.

My relationship with Sukey waxed and waned. It annoyed her to have a child living where she should live, close to her mother, and a graceless boy at that. And yet Sukey found it convenient to have a playmate when she came to visit. She would tell me stories of New York, what children did there and what they owned. Water pistols with a barrel you can twist, so they shoot sideways. Tools for wood-burning and metalcraft. Sukey was good with Erector Sets, had one with motors and pulleys, used it to make a working sandbox steam shovel. She knew what boys liked, what would make me gasp at the plenty about her. Then for weeks she would ignore me in favor of her friends at the club. Later, in my teens, I worked there summers, cleaning private yachts for families and rigging catboats the club kept for the younger kids. Sukey would pass by me without so much as a fare-thee-well.

For a year, Sukey did not appear. Her father had gone to England on business, and she accompanied him, boarding in an exclusive school. When she returned, she had become a young woman. She signaled that we might be friends—like cousins who had squabbled in childhood and now had reconciled as teens. We had much in common. Broken households, shared memories, a love of the Cape, this estate by the bay's edge. And a sense that our childhoods had spilled out of the same odd event, a scandal or a romance from which our parents could not escape.

Sukey was back at boarding school in Connecticut, cutting classes, failing courses. She would be spending an extra year there, unless Mrs. K could get her alma mater, Vassar, to bend a rule or two on behalf of her headstrong daughter. Sukey was a natural at math and science, that was an argument. Meanwhile, I was Harvard bound. Slouch and mumble though I might, I had an aura. Sukey noticed. You're off to Cambridge? she asked when she returned to Stone House on spring break. She gave me a peck on the cheek and then grabbed my hand: Come to the attic. I have something to show you.

She was tall like her father, and full-figured in a way that scared me. What is that fear? That we will be caught looking at a woman the wrong way, that we will act impulsively? She was wearing shorts and a halter top. There was so much of her. I felt shame at the urgency of my desire. As we turned on a landing, a wisp of her Rapunzel hair caught in my mouth. Trying to smooth the strands back in place, I brushed Sukey's shoulder with my hand. Upstairs, she said.

Old furniture had migrated to the attic. Sukey sat on a mattress and motioned me to sit beside. She pushed my hair from my forehead and looked me in the eyes. You are afraid of me, she said.

I thought she was going to make me cry again, that I had come to the attic for an exercise in humiliation. Here, she said. This should help.

From the pocket of her cutoffs she produced a joint and matches. I had smoked before. When you live where rich kids vacation, there will be grass. Or where artists and theater people work. It made me dreamy in company the way I am dreamy without drugs when I am alone. Sukey passed the joint, and she was right, it steadied me. Then she took my face in both her hands and said, I'm going to make up for all the years.

With the freedom the drug gave, I realized I had no wish for change. I was content to be the boy she scorned. I could play that role forever, hold on to her in that way. I did not know if I could do more, and I did not want to lose her.

No need, I said. No need.

She shushed me. She slipped my shirt over my head. She kissed me on the chest and began to suck on my nipples, the way I longed to suck on hers. I was delirious, panicked. If she went on, I would come before I did anything I had fantasized about. I wanted her to stop. I wanted her to go on.

She said, When I was in England, I learned how to give pleasure.

Between kisses, she told me a story. Her art teachers were a handsome young couple of good breeding. Each spring at Easter break they would invite a girl to the Cots. A girl with parents at a distance, a promising girl, a sensuous girl. They would teach her how to give pleasure to men and to women. From among all the lovelies, Sukey had been chosen for this honor.

I felt admiration and wonder. Sukey had been chosen, quite naturally, there was none to match her.

How, I asked, do you give pleasure to a woman?

Look, she said. She parted her Rapunzel mane and, supporting them in her hands, presented her breasts to me. I remember the pattern of veins beneath translucent flesh, like the crackle in the glaze on her mother's China-trade porcelain. Here, Sukey said, running her forefinger around the base of a nipple. She pulled my head to her, and I began to suckle.

Until your birth, that moment was the most intense of my life. Every aspect is emblazoned in memory. Sun filtering through the dust motes of the attic, the coolness of her skin, its sweet taste, the mixed scents of cannabis and Canoe. I moved to kiss her on the mouth. She turned her head so I was nuzzling her below the ear. Then she put her hand between my legs. She said, There's a spot here that will help you to stay big.

She pressed a point below the base of my penis. But it was the wrong spot, or it was too late, or I was too young and too excited.

She sighed in disappointment. She said, You have a lot to learn.

I had missed my chance, I knew. I would never find out how it is that a man gives pleasure to a woman or (which interested me more) how a woman like Sukey can give pleasure to a man. I was certain Sukey would snap at me. I think she was about to—she looked annoyed—but then she smiled as if a clever thought had come to her.

Men enjoy this, she said. She went down and took me in her mouth. My manhood was a peanut, a shrimp, a pinkie. She sucked on it, sucked until a little last drop came out. A sharp suck, a sharp and heavenly twinge. Like what the poets describe, painful pleasure becoming pleasant pain.

Do you like that? she asked. It's called finishing it off.

Then she licked her tongue on my belly and we dozed. When I wakened, she was sitting at the other end of the attic in an old wing chair. She had wrapped herself in an out-of-fashion summer bedcover, white with small white cotton balls sewn on it. But for the long hair, she looked like her mother as she was when she had come down the stairs, blanketed—the aristocratic English face, softened by a hint of Dutchboy roundness.

I understood that what we had just shared referred to that earlier moment, an envoi after a caesura of ten years. Her mother had done something naughty with a servant, and now Sukey had done the same. Like our earlier understanding in her father's car, this one would not be repeated or discussed or even acknowledged. I was beneath her in class and beauty and experience.

I was bitter with myself. In the shuttered shelves behind the wet bar, Mr. K had left a collection of literary pornography, Frank Harris and the rest, that he could not acknowledge or retrieve once he had taken custody of Sukey on moral grounds. I knew that I was unlike the men in the books. Where they sought a series of liaisons, I wanted a woman to love me. But I did not see why my different sort of neediness should disqualify me from the pleasures of the flesh. Here Sukey had offered everything any man might lust for, and despite my reading I had proved unprepared. It was unfair. I needed a second chance. At the same time I was enraptured. To have touched such beauty.

Years later, when I was nursing Sukey back from her entanglement with liquor, I regretted my self-centeredness that day in the attic. Focused on my humiliation, I had overlooked hers. Would it have made a difference, I wondered, for me to have expressed alarm at her adventure in the Cots?

The upper classes often harm their children, and Sukey was harmed repeatedly, through her father's severity, through the substitution of boarding school for family, through the early sexual initiation. I asked Manny, Was she abused at sixteen? By those handsome teachers?

Manny would not answer except to ask, Were you?

Meaning was I overwhelmed by Sukey that day in the attic, overwhelmed indirectly by the couple who inducted Sukey into seduction.

The moment with Sukey was too precious for me to discard. But I could see that much flowed from her rite of passage—my blind attachment, her drinking, our mutual discontentment with society. I said, I suppose it was abuse—not my experience, Sukey's. But she felt privileged to have been chosen by her teachers. And I felt privileged to have been chosen by Sukey even for an afternoon.

You have probably had your first furtive sexual experiences. Did they disappoint? It pains me not to have been close enough to lend you support. My impression is that even a fumbling encounter can have its benefits. My awakening with Sukey laid me open to desire, allowed me, when I met your mother, to express the feelings I had for her.

Your mother was of the world, a realization of the fairy story Sukey represented. Anais was ordinarily lovable, and precious for being so. As I write these words, I find they understate the feelings I have had for your mother. All love is fantastical, all love partakes of the fairy story—that is the pun embedded in the word *romance,* an attachment and a story.

Wrapped in the white summer bedcover, Sukey sat in a blue-gray armchair across the attic from me. On her lap was a small reddish object. Seeing me stir, she placed it in her hand and asked, Can you guess what this is?

A red rock. No, a chunk of old brick.

Sukey said, The night before the fire, I was wakened by a nightmare. I went down the hall to my mother's bedroom. I heard them talking, my mother and your father.

I repeated, My father?

She said, His voice sounded strange to me. The foreign accent, of course. I knew I should not go in. The dream had frightened me, and because your father was with her, I could not turn to my mother. I hated your father, I hated you, I wanted you out of the house.

And so you . . . ?

I had heard my father complaining about the chimney, how it wasn't pointed right. I know he said *pointed,* because it puzzled me—where else could a chimney be pointed but straight up? One more loose bit of mortar, he said, and the whole place will go up in flames.

Your father wanted my father to repoint the chimney? I asked. I was in a haze, from the marijuana and my first experience of sex and the tension of touching the object of my desire. And yet I knew what Sukey was about to tell me. That she had pried this piece of brick from the chimney, in hopes of destroying the house. I said, You pulled out a chunk of brick and hid it.

Here in the attic—there, below the loose boards.

Sukey held the fragment forth for me, and I moved toward her. I wanted to stroke her hair, to hold her and reassure her. Over the years I had heard a dozen explanations for the fire. The chimney was weak throughout. There was no insulation behind the clap-boards, and they were bone-dry. The night was warm; the heat could not dissipate. Creosote lined the stack. Given the state of the bricks and mortar, the house fire hardly needed explaining; the grate should not have been lit that night. But it was not reassurance Sukey wanted. She was proud of the determination she had shown since early childhood.

She said, When I heard noise, I knew it was the fire. I walked to my mother's room. I had punished her. I was happy.

You were kind to me that night.

I don't remember that part. I remember being happy.

Children tell these stories. When parents separate, children invent reasons, make themselves the cause, prefer to be bad themselves than to blame the grown-ups they depend on. You may have a story, how you caused the breakup between your mother and me. I wish I could speak to you, to counter any such misimpression. Though it occurs to me that if you have a private story, you may not want it taken from you. We are our stories. Sukey is the girl who pried loose a piece of masonry and changed the course of her childhood.

The brick was real enough. I have it here before me as I write. I tried years later, when Sukey reentered my life, to get her to fill in the details of our early time together. Her memories had dimmed. Too much drink had come between. Or rather: There are two types of people, those who look back and those who look forward. Sukey plans. I remember. I collect shards—tiles, bricks, matchbooks, the taste of face powder. Rubble from which lost forms can be inferred.

It was May of 1966 when Sukey showed me the chunk of brick. Already she was spinning out of control, with boys, drink, drugs. She was desirable and unprotected. I had lived a childhood—quiet, mundane—that had branched off from hers. For all that I was scorned, to her I had come to represent stability. Whenever she visited, I was there, welcoming, hopeful. I play that role in people's lives. The safe harbor, the mooring. It is not altogether a bad role. If you find you are fated for it, I would not resist too vigorously. People do return.

I see now that my admission to Harvard threatened Sukey. When I left Sesuit, what would remain to her that represented home? A disgraced and tipsy mother, rented apartments in New York, undersized and overheated rooms in a series of boarding schools. So Sukey took care to bind me again, in the usual ways: a glimpse of glamour, sex, shared secrets, dismissal.

She succeeded. I hope there is no shame in my making that admission. We were bound anyway, by our history. We have made good use of that tie, I hope, have not been afraid to extend ourselves in the service of friendship.

5

*

Under the Volcano

I have been warned that there is a bomb in this cottage, a bomb not of my own making. The information is anonymous and second-hand. Years ago, when your mother took her periodic journeys, I vowed not to overreact to what in novels of social manners are called idle reports. From my own work, I know how hard it is to hide emplacements of explosives. I have looked in every room. Nothing seems amiss.

Besides, if there is a bomb here, why has it not gone off already? There is no bomb, or it is not here, or it is not armed, or it is a dud. Or it is set for a particular occasion, and why would that occasion be now? When I have finished this entry, I will undertake a more careful search. Barring the unforeseen, my plan is to stay on until Sukey's new scheme calls me away.

The bomb news came late this morning. There was a knock at the door. I headed over, expecting to help Sukey with the groceries. Instead I saw Wendy Moro. She had an apologetic smile, as if she were sorry to intrude. And that oval face framed by sleek black hair, and the bone structure and skin tone you can't quite place— Modigliani meets Utamaro, a California mix of Italian and Japanese bloodlines. I was pleased to see her.

I invited Wendy in, but she shook her head and stood expectantly at the threshold. Would I mind a walk on the beach?

I found my sandals, and to the racket of snapping shutters we descended the stairs. Police held the photographers at the edge of the property—the press pool pay the Stone House Condo Association for the right to camp out on the lawn but have not succeeded in arranging for access to the beach below. The Association has bravely voted not to give in to the blackmail of terror; so the Stone House beach remains "members only" down to mean low water. I am a member by virtue of rights deeded my father by Mrs. K. I am aware of the irony in my finding this privacy a convenience.

Sesuit has been enjoying one of those brisk fall weeks when the breeze is constantly onshore. Wendy and I took shelter against the eroding sandbank. I spotted a fellow with a telescopic lens out on the jetty. I know the photo that will appear tomorrow: middle-aged suspect and attractive young defense counsel huddled against the elements. It hints at a story that is not there. I am a cause and a challenge, a notorious client in need of a thorough defense. I have been careful not to read anything into Wendy's solicitude.

She was wearing wraparound sunglasses, fashionable, thin, opaque. She glanced at me quickly, then stared at the surf: I need to warn you that you are unsafe in your cottage.

She was embarrassed because recently she had told me that the cottage was the only place on the Cape where I *was* safe.

I wanted to reassure her. I said, I am comfortable with insecurity. Manny Abelman says that is one of my character flaws, lack of paranoia.

Wendy offered a smile. She said, Perhaps I can cure you.

Wendy was readying herself for work this morning when she received a call on her home phone, an unlisted number. The caller said he was a government agent intervening on his own initiative. The FBI had information that a bomb had been planted in Chip Samuels's house.

By whom? Wendy had asked. And would you identify yourself?

The man's voice was distorted, as if run through a machine to disguise his identity. He limited his speech to a brief message: Because of the disturbances on the Cape, the FBI had been following the sales of fertilizer to nonfarmers. An agent had linked a substantial purchase to one Donald Antunes, the local salesman for Northeast Assurance.

I guessed the name of the company before the words came out of Wendy's mouth. Despite the gravity of her message, she responded with an involuntary laugh, the kind you may have seen her give on television, where she nods her head and covers her lips with her thin fingers. Though I could not see through the wraparound glasses, I knew her eyes were squeezed shut. How welcome, for a lawyer to have a helpless, unrehearsed response to the touches of humor in her workday.

Northeast is an insurer whose shares have been "under pressure" in the wake of the bombings. Four of the first five houses that blew were covered by Northeast, and nine of the first dozen. The claims made no dent in the bottom line, but Wall Street, so they say, hates uncertainty.

The uncertainty has been all the greater because of our silence. Will the violence against Northeast spread off-Cape? If it stops, will it resume? So long as the Movement's objectives remain undefined, no one can assess the risk of owning a Northeast policy. It is hard to sell insurance when a contract intended to protect a home instead exposes it to the risk of destruction.

If you have not read Walter Benjamin, you might know his name. A critic of art and society, German, interwar. He was all the rage on campus when his essays were translated into English, in the sixties. Your mother took him to heart as almost French. What appealed to me in Benjamin was his love of books, collecting them. Here is an offbeat epigram for a Marxist: Ownership is the most intimate relationship a man can have with objects. Collections illuminate relations among items selected and, through them, relations among men. Benjamin writes ecstatically of the tension between the chaos of collecting (*chance, whimsy, fate,* and *confusion* are words he loves) and the order of the assemblage that results. Collection renews the world.

I find destruction to be an alternative form of collecting. A way to invite consideration of objects, their origin and function. Destruction preserves a culture at a moment, its artifacts, on videotape and in memory.

When I can pull myself away from current events, I will tell you how Sukey and I select properties. Suffice it to say that we assess prospects on many levels. When we found a cluster of homes covered by one insurer, that coincidence—the combination of arbitrariness and order—appealed to the collector in me. And it satisfied Sukey's thematic requirements. The illusion of security is at the heart of spectacular capitalism. Our collection would draw attention to that fallacy and place it in question.

Collecting through destruction is a praxis that invites responses. Northeast's stock price dipped, and the insurance executives reacted in foreseeable ways. They rewrote contracts to exclude acts of terror—as a homeowner covered by Northeast, I received an overnighted letter that my policy had been changed. That week, explosions brought down two more houses Northeast insured, and of course the owners are suing the company.

Anarchism redistributes anxiety. How different capitalism looks when owners of second homes share a level of exposure felt more usually by the poor. Without insurance, houses become hard to buy—who will provide a mortgage? Who can afford to own real estate if its worth can disappear in an instant?

Public safety is the state's job. Late in the summer, the governor signed interim legislation committing the Commonwealth to cover future losses due to terror bombings, and at property valuations as they were before the Movement began.

Meanwhile, Northeast remains under siege. The company is exposed to what the industry calls "adverse selection" and "moral hazard." People who dislike the anxiety of beachfront ownership and wish to cash out—those who want their homes destroyed or who plan to do the job themselves—will stick with Northeast in hopes of being absorbed into the cascade of Movement bombings, leaving the insurer to argue with the state over what is terror and what self-sabotage. Hardly surprising that Northeast should counterattack, once a target is identified. I feel a paradoxical uplift at Wendy's allegation—a bomb in the cottage. (Speak of "adverse selection" and "moral hazard"!) There is pleasure in seeing a giant corporation engage in terror, and foolishly.

It is oddly reassuring to find an adequate cause for a level of unease I carry anyway. All my life I have lived with risk—of losing mother, father, Anais, you. There is a rightness of fit in my composing my thoughts in a home that may be a powder keg. Besides, it seems fair that I should experience what my fellow Cape Codders have faced these past months, awareness that there is no shelter.

Wendy's caller rang off without indicating whether the FBI had located Antunes or the fertilizer. Regarding the content of the call, Wendy said she had wavered between skepticism and belief. Then, on the way to work, on the car phone she heard from her partner, Bob Willis. Sub rosa, the FBI had applied for a new warrant, to search the cottage a second time. And so she had detoured to pull me out for a strategy session.

How to confer? Wendy's tale contained a request for information. For example: Was I the Sesuibomber? And if so, was I in cahoots with a disgruntled insurance salesman? To give Wendy facts she could work with, I would need to confess to crimes. She would draw further away, as suspicion was replaced by certainty. In a trial, she could never put me on the stand. So I spoke in code, hardly knowing whether to hope Wendy understood or remained in the dark.

I said to Wendy, I have seen Donald Antunes, at town meetings. I wanted to signal her that he was not one of us. I described

Antunes as a shambling, balding, ungainly fellow—like me in appearance. I hoped Wendy would smile at my self-deprecation and was pleased when she did. I mentioned that Antunes had married into the Oakes family, who own the local oil and heating concern. I said: Not a notably competent man, which may be why he is out of the family business and into insurance.

How much . . . ? Wendy began.

I think she was tempted to say, How much competence does it take to build a bomb? But she held back, out of delicacy. Which gave me a window on her beliefs about my innocence.

I said, They've been watching . . .

A week ago, acting on a warrant from a local judge, the feds had searched my home and found nothing. Since then, they have had the place under observation.

Wendy and I sat side by side in the sand and pieced together an unsettling explanation of the morning's phone calls: Northeast considers itself the victim of a conspiracy. The government appears unable to bring the conspirators to justice, so Northeast suggests to Antunes that he do the necessary. He sneaks a bomb into the chief suspect's cottage. There may be government collusion. Or incompetence, a lapse in surveillance. However it enters the home, the bomb promises a convenient ending to the Free the Beaches saga: The cottage explodes with me inside, and it appears that I, like many in the past, have paid the price for playing with fire.

When the bomb does not go off, the feds move to a contingency plan. Search the cottage again, find explosives, bring the indictment. But a member of their team opposes the frame-up. So he phones Wendy.

If I am to be made paranoid, I want to ask: Which constitutes the disorder, to believe or to disbelieve your lawyer's narrative as its elements fall into place? My impression is that paranoia is judged less according to the opinions a man holds than the manner in which he holds them. In our culture, any ideas embraced strongly may come to be judged delusional. That finally was your mother's charge against me, that I was crazy to cling to the values of the sixties. Manny took an opposing view, he faulted not my persistence but my lack of passion.

I have no strong belief about Wendy's tale. I can imagine that the FBI has allowed a bomb to be placed in the cottage. Or that an agent is trying to unnerve me. Or that an odd soul has called Wendy with an odd fable, so that nothing is new between the government and me, the government is trying to get me only in the usual straightforward way.

I always saw you as having this capability, to suspend judgment, to stand poised among possibilities. Your teachers faulted you for obsessing, but they missed your calm in the face of indecision. Letting events take their course can be a virtue and a strategy. As your mother used to say, *Nos défauts sont nos qualités,* our shortcomings and our character strengths are hard to disentangle. I hope Anais has shared that belief with you; it is one from which I have drawn encouragement.

6

*

So This Is Love

Are you sorry you took this case? I asked Wendy.

Rather than answer, she asked, How ever did you choose me to represent you?

I said that Emmanuel Abelman had told me she was a kindred spirit. He thought that compatibility was what I needed in a lawyer.

You are his patient?

I said, I used to drive a patient to his office, an alcoholic woman. Once when she had finished her session, Manny asked whether I wanted to chat, and I said yes, thinking it was for her sake. Then Manny continued inviting me in, as if it were a favor to him, allowing him to exercise his powers, or helping with a problem he was struggling to work out. He never billed me, which allowed me to imagine I was not his patient.

I asked Wendy how she knew Abelman. She said, In much the same way.

She had phoned for a consultation. Manny said he would meet her, but he was not sure he would be able to take her on in treatment. When she arrived, he said he was having a trouble that came upon him periodically, nausea over the therapist-patient relationship. To assume authority put him out of kilter. But he had heard good things about her as a lawyer, and he wondered if she could furnish advice—how to protect his right to practice without keeping formal case notes, whether he needed to opt out of Medicare as a provider. Manny and Wendy began a series of conversations, a barter of legal for psychological expertise.

He mentioned nausea to me as well, I told Wendy.

Four days a week, I used to drive Sukey to see Manny. He lives and works in a 1950s ranch house in a nondescript subdivision in the center of Sesuit, far from the water. His office is in the basement, in what would once have been a "rec room." The building bespeaks failure.

Of the many therapists Sukey worked with in New York, Manny is the one she trusted. She had been sent to him because he had written a book that brought him fame and fortune, *So This Is Love.* Manhattanites who could afford the best went to Emmanuel Abelman. He had a Park Avenue practice.

Near the cash register of the Sesuit Book Barn, I found *So This Is Love,* in one of those small volumes, with hearts and roses bedight, meant to be given (this was Manny's dry characterization when I mentioned the book) by starry-eyed young men to women from whom they unconsciously wish to elicit scorn. With its most sentimental phrases reproduced on the cover, the book is a backlist stalwart, like Erich Fromm's *The Art of Loving,* which it resembles in its emphasis on self-estrangement and greed as the problems of the age. Abelman's book is more cynical than Fromm's, the tone tending toward bitter wit. In its day—the late fifties—it was that odd best-seller that brought its young author both sales and professional respect. Though so far as I can tell, Abelman never wrote another word.

I will tell you why I do not write, he said to me one day. Nausea.

On occasion Manny will rise from apparent lethargy to attempt a moment of grand drama. He has a froglike face—broad mouth, splayed nose, bald dome, bulging eyes emphasized by bottle-glass trifocals. He tends to smile before he speaks, and set in that face, the smile gives an inadvertent comic tone to whatever follows. Unless the comedy is intended. More than once he has said he hopes I take his utterances lightly.

Manny paused significantly before and after the word *nausea*. It was a credo, like *plastics* in that Dustin Hoffman movie. Manny's word to sum up the modern world.

He said that after writing his book he spent a period in the public eye, as a universal expert. Psychologists had that role in those days. *Time* magazine would quote Abelman on any issue from the plight of the family to the national character. I felt a constant queasiness, he said to me, queasiness accompanied by eructation. I began to understand what my patients meant when they said they were off-balance, dizzy, unable to eat, disgusted with those around them, uncomfortable outside the confines of their own room.

Manny said, One day I was passing a bookshop, it was the old Doubleday on the east side of Fifth Avenue at Fifty-third Street, the one with an open spiral staircase at the entrance. There in the window I saw a stack of books wrapped in pink floral paper, a saccharine variant of a William Morris pattern. The jackets caught my eye, mesmerized me, so cloying were they, so unbooklike, so out of place in a store dedicated to consequential products of the human mind. The Pepto-Bismol peonies swam in my visual field, and I found I could not move on. I experienced a gagging in my throat, an urge to vomit on the sidewalk amidst the sweaty summer crowd. And then I realized the books were mine. *So This Is Love* had been reissued as an emetic.

That moment, Manny said, led him to formulate his theory of mental pathology. That there is a certain sort of person, a sensitive or susceptible man or woman, who develops a chronic disgust for contemporary life, its relentless demands and inconsequential rewards, its emotional emptiness, its superficiality, the fifteen hundred advertisements we are exposed to every day. Existential bulimia, Manny called the condition, an interminable sense of something sticking in the craw, a constant impulse to reject what is shoved down the throat.

He later expanded the diagnosis to include those, equally afflicted in his opinion, who should show signs of the illness but do not. Bulimia outside awareness. Manny told me I suffer from a particular variant. Intellectually, I recognize stimuli to nausea. But I lack the affect. Manny said, You must feel it in your gut.

You're a reader, he said, appealing to my reason. You must agree that Sartre had it pegged. The characteristic emotion of modernity is nausea.

After that conversation, I began to notice signs of Abelman's own nausea. The photographs on his waiting-room walls are originals, stark efforts by Joel Meyerowitz, an off-white surface interrupted by the suggestion of a line that on inspection reveals itself as the horizon between bay and sky. The consulting room, too, is decorated with Meyerowitzes, beach scenes from the seventies and eighties. Manny is pale-skinned, as if he had never spent a minute in the sun. As if he had retired to the Cape to sit in a basement far from the water and look at photographs of the beach.

The Lady of Shalott, I said to Wendy.

What?

I have come to think of Dr. Abelman as Tennyson's Lady of Shalott. Under a curse. Pained by the world. Seeing it in a mirror, or in his mind, or through our stories.

Half sick of shadows, Wendy quoted, and then we sat beside each other and listened to the waves. Perhaps that is something we both learned from Manny (I hope you have found your way to the same lesson), not to feel embarrassment over our tendency to speak less than others do, not to be afraid of fading into the woodwork. Sometimes it is hard to distinguish a session with Manny from a nursing home visit to an exhausted old man.

A greenhead fly lit on Wendy's ear, and I shooed it. Wendy began to tell me what had brought her to Manny. I believe her doing so was a tribute to Manny's method. He sometimes places his own problems on the table, as an opportunity for his visitor to display competency. She was doing the same for me. I do not take this gift, of confessional autobiography, as a sign that Wendy has a relationship with me beyond the professional. The newsweeklies say that as a law student she worked with death-row inmates. She externed with the group in South Carolina that opposes capital punishment. I believe Wendy would have offered herself in an intimate way to any isolated client.

Wendy said she had considered herself sad at heart—chronically regretful, but without an object of regret. Manny reframed the problem as queasiness over her own dexterity. Over the successful use of her talents in the service of getting and spending.

Wendy had grown up in San Francisco. Contrary to what the magazine accounts say, her parents' marriage was stormy. Too much to overcome. Not only the disparity between Japanese culture and Italian, but also differences in social standing. Wendy's working-class father continually disappointed her middle-class mother.

Speaking to me—looking out at the water and remembering the past—Wendy gave few details. But the expression on her face said, Not an easy family to grow up in. She tensed when she mentioned her father.

At Cal, as an undergraduate, Wendy struggled, distracted by turmoil at home. For law school, she came as far east as she could, to Boston University. Then she set up shop on the Cape. Domestic law, a way to support herself and live by the beach.

You're too aware of cruelty, Manny had said. It frightens you to see couples argue. Even your victories worry you. I want you back on death row, with the hopeless cases—where the issues are clear, and a sensitive woman can be happy.

Manny had taken that route. After his epiphany on Fifth Avenue he gave his patients a month's notice, shut down his Park Avenue office, and came to Boston to work in the Psychopathic Hospital. When that job felt too cushy, he moved on to the prisons.

Prison must have made an impression on Manny. In his conversations with me, he let drop references to prison life, how even in prison there are callings. *Calling* is a word I take from Manny. He spoke of an inmate who had been a jack-of-all-trades for the mob and now needed help handling his rage and despair. Benny C., Manny called him; Manny said he planned to write a story about the guy, and Benny C. would be the pseudonym.

Benny C. was a bad actor in jail, an impulsive man who would never make parole. I am a guy who works with his hands, he told Manny. Dumb, but handy. Give me what to do.

Manny arranged for Benny to enter an electrical engineering course; there were laws that gave Benny the right. An absurd pursuit for a man who would likely never see the outside. But studying showed him that the work he had done all his life, the technical work of crime, the booby-trapping and the arson, had been the work of a craftsman. That reassessment seemed to help, along with the chance to fiddle.

Manny drew no moral, but what he meant seemed clear. A man needs a calling and an awareness that it is a calling. As a specific against the nausea caused by tasks and goals the society imposes, the grasping and holding and the yearning for recognition.

I suppose therapy calls to Manny, despite his unease with the doctor's role. For years, he had summered in Truro. The problem, he told me once, was that he was lionized there, lionized and demonized, too many jealous colleagues. When his wife died, he sold the Truro home and retired to obscurity in Sesuit. But he could not escape patients. Old med school buddies had moved to the Cape to finish out their careers—an endocrinologist, a rheumatologist. They bullied Manny into taking on this or that poor sufferer. People found Manny, sought him out, a vaguely famous geezer. He could not help helping.

He had encouraged Wendy to take my case.

She said it had been years since she had done criminal law; she would be disbarred for malpractice.

It's a sure loser anyway, Manny answered. How can they disbar you for losing a loser?

Here on the beach, Wendy had been speaking in a sort of trance. When she realized whom she was addressing, she flushed bright red. There is nothing so shameful as being caught in a truth.

No, no, I said to her. Between Sukey's plan and your lawyering, I expect to do fine.

There are grounds for hope. For one thing, the Sesuit police chief and Barnstable County district attorney are school chums of mine. In their investigation, they have done me the courtesy of making haste slowly.

In childhood, the three of us were outsiders in a town whose social life, right through the fifties, revolved around the Congregationalist church. Billy Dineen—now the DA—was Catholic, and the nearest Catholic church was in Harwich. In the main, it served Azores Islands Portuguese families, so it did not figure, though the third boy in our group attended services there—Ildeberto Costas, a fisherman's son linked to me by our common shyness and to Billy by fascination with naughtiness.

I had no religion. My father was an atheist, and I don't suppose my mother had me baptized. But then church was less a matter of religion than of social class—of one's mother serving on the bake-sale committee and cohosting the pre-regatta cocktail party at the Club, of one's father having connections through business or golf with younger Searses or Nickersons. Billy and I were doubly outcast—we each had a single parent, back in the days when single parenthood was rare and socially suspect.

Billy's mother ran the Indian Rock Farm Stand. Billy and I earned pocket money harvesting strawberries and then blueberries and, of course, corn when it came in. If he wasn't needed at the docks, Bert Costas would join us.

When we were older, Billy and Bert and I spent fall days scooping cranberries, not on the farm but in the Shiverick Woods, in bogs too small for machine culling. Billy's mom cut us kneepads from an old muskrat coat. Even today, the sight of cranberry dressing brings back an odd composite smell—dusty leaves, crisp air, and animal fur moistened by damp sand.

Funny that we all ended up in public service, in our different ways. Bert is chief of police. Just installed, in the face of his former boss's failure to stem the attacks on local homes. Race held Bert back, I always thought, prejudice against dark-skinned Azores Islanders. A welcome effect of the Movement, Bert's promotion. His career choice made sense to me from the start. As a boy, he focused on injustice, whether a classroom grade or punishment was fair. But it is funny to think of Billy as the law.

As a kid, Billy was a gap-toothed, freckled, irrepressible imp, constitutionally bent on mischief. I was his sidekick. If Billy borrowed gym equipment during recess, I would take the fall. Fess up, Chip, he'd say, a black mark will be good for your reputation. I stood beside Billy in hopeless schoolyard fights. There was satisfaction in getting pummeled for cockiness, even someone else's. Secretly, my father was pleased to see my bruises. I had too little spunk for his taste.

Writing those words makes me feel what I am missing when I am far from you. The father's role is to mix open disapproval with veiled satisfaction. My intent, when you were here, was to be forgiving, as my father was, but less prone to disappointment—less prone to communicate a wish that you be other than you are.

It is Billy who is presenting evidence to the grand jury. Scrupulous, the media call him; scrupulous or dilatory. Reporters like his deadpan style—dry remarks that cast doubt on the judgment exercised by the police. Not the town cops—Bert's staff is scarcely equipped to investigate a bombing campaign—but the FBI.

Billy's caution has frustrated the Commonwealth attorney general. Caddie Weymouth is a Republican with national aspirations. When I was first named as a suspect, she backed the Barnstable County team, on grounds of local autonomy. But soon she began to lash out, demanding results. We are speaking of crimes against property.

Billy comes off as a sympathetic figure, homegrown prosecutor asking the grand jury to advise on the body of evidence. He represents old-fashioned American justice, neighbors appraising neighbors, weighing character, deliberating.

In exchange for Wendy's snippet of autobiography, and by way of encouragement, I offered up one or two of my childhood escapades with Billy.

She said, There will be pressures on him.

I understand. No one can shield me for long. And I would hate for Billy to look bad. If the time comes for me to confess, I will confess to him. But Billy's presence helped determine our response to the bomb scare. Billy is probing the investigators as well as the suspects, demanding that the feds show their cards. In petitioning to toss the cottage again, they will open the door to the Antunes story, allowing Billy to present the grand jury an alternative theory about the earlier explosions. Disaffected employee. Reasonable doubt. Especially since the main evidence against me, the hair match, is so weak.

I explained to Wendy that I had been in the Altschuler bungalow many times. Not just recently, when I visited as a prospective buyer. I had been a frequent guest of the prior owners, the Sternhells.

Wendy said, It is good to be a good neighbor.

Her voice is soft. As a listener you cannot be certain you detect an edge.

I said I would remain in my cottage. If there were fertilizer and diesel fuel on the loose, they were likely still in the back of Antunes's van, ready to crash into the home of anyone I might stay with. Best not to make a move, not to let the feds know how much we knew. If my house held evidence against another man, best not to let the feds remove it or (if this was their plan) alter it so that it incriminated me. I would live in the cottage, aware that it might be mined. I would follow Sukey's protocol, move ahead with the public relations campaign. Was Wendy on board?

She said she was.

I liked that Wendy could acknowledge what I acknowledge, that we must let those we care about go their own way. I said that time in the cottage is important to me. That I am filling the notebook. That I have found at last that I can write an account of the days we are in and the days that led up to them.

Wendy had been facing away, looking through her wraparound glasses at the bay. Now she turned and said, Be sure to include whatever is difficult for you. How you lost your wife and son.

In its flatness, her voice sounded like the voices of the women (two or three) I dated after your mother left with you. Each time, on perhaps the second date, I would hear a question delivered in just this tight-throated tone. How had I lost my son? How can a man who seems considerate and caring, steady and reliable, devoted in his work to the lives of the young (and who owns waterfront property and shares exclusive rights to the beach down to mean low water), how did such a man lose his wife and child? That was one reason I stopped dating, the wish not to respond to that indictment.

You want to know more about how I lost Hank and Anais?

Goes to motive, Wendy said, apologizing for her intrusiveness. She meant that since there was no apparent reason I should blow up houses, the press has been speculating, as a prosecutor would ask a jury to speculate, about my response to private loss.

Goes to character, I added, filling in a thought that Wendy was too kind to voice. Whether I am a man from whom a wife would have reason to snatch a child.

Wendy said she was sorry to raise the issue. Only she thought that since I was to stay in the cottage to fill the notebook . . .

I knew now why Manny had hooked me up with Wendy. I was her special project, an antidote to the dull pain for which she had sought his help. And she had become my project, another reason for me to work my way out of the hole I have dug—in order to spare Wendy from disappointment in herself. I recognize Manny's formula: When life is desperate, take on an extra obligation.

Wendy ventured, I will visit the judge. To oppose the warrant.

Then, as if to confirm my thoughts about Manny's treatment plan, she looked out at the horizon and said, to no one in particular, I think I would have died if this case had not come along.

7

＊

Groceries

Sukey has phoned to tell me to set aside an hour to look at *Dateline NBC*. I will be the topic.

I am continually the topic nowadays.

She said, I gather this show takes a different approach.

I switched on the TV. After three minutes of Hollywood gossip, the network inserted a teaser containing the first of Sukey's metaphorical groceries. She had delivered Tomas and Deirdre Madeiros to the press. Exclusive interview with Cape Codders who studied anarchism with the accused Sesuibomber. Tune in at nine.

Sukey's goal is to counter the impression that the government and right-wing media will spin, that I am mad. I doubt I am. I hear no voices, suspect no plots save the one my lawyer has brought to my attention. There was a time when I was crazed with grief, but that is a normal and even desirable state—without grief, I would have been desolate. I do worry. What sane man does not question himself when his behavior deviates from the norm?

But then radicalism rests on the assumption that normative behavior can be deranged. Who, taking any distance from his life, would choose to be as inattentive to moral consequence as the average successful American? One assertion in the press strikes me as outright wrong: the claim that the Cape Cod anarchists are in some sense autistic—that they must have no notion of the lives they affect. This indictment mistakes the nature of the work.

I am thinking of the Howell effort, which turned on intimate knowledge of person. Curiosity about the individual and attention to the social surround, those are the great requirements, in this as in any serious endeavor.

We sent Howell up in mid-July. We selected it on our usual grounds, architecture. Shortly after the Second World War, the Howells had put up a center-hall colonial, too grand for the site and for the era, at the bayfront end of Saltworks Circle, near Cole Slough. I have some memory of Charlotte Howell, the matriarch, or of parts of her—strong chin, flaxen chignon, bejeweled bosom. She presided at the summer church socials to which as an outsider I was twice invited in childhood. Her grandson Tyler Howell Jr. I knew well, a superior bully at the yacht club. He showed the same character in his dealings over the beachfront in adult life—he was at the fore of campaigns for owners' rights.

Sukey said the house had always offended her in every aspect, its break with the shoreline tradition of saltboxes and capes, its phony entry portico, its unnecessary height, towering over its neighbors and the beach below. The furnishings were aggressively upper crust: claw-legged settees; velour wing chairs; Martha Washingtons in fussy stripes. Ducks and dogs and dry flies on the walls. A bar full of single-malt Scotches. New England all right, but a bit much for little Sesuit. That was Sukey's focus, the aesthetics. I began the Howell project serving Sukey's vision. I anticipated a major installation, attic and basement, to be rid of the place entirely. But I found I could not get the sequencing right or the placement of charges.

What is said of writing holds for sabotage: apparent failures of technique mask failures of understanding. I go on the assumption that if I reach an impasse, it means I have not used enough of myself, have not dug deep. Stymied, I sat in the Howell kitchen with a drink of water and let my attention wander. I began to thumb through a tattered fifties Junior League cookbook presented to Tyler's mother: To Libby on her twenty-third! Welcome as the newest Howell, dear!

I had gloves on, and I turned the pages clumsily. So many deadly recipes recommended by Libby to herself with exclamation points or emended with notes: More paprika! Biff Jenkins from Kidder loved this one! Too much garlic for Barker, *père*!

The recipes were full of heavy cream and the notes full of anxiety. Mustn't omit baking powder! Utter disaster, check oven temperature! Under a coq au vin, a question was written and then scratched out: How does *she* do it?

Who might *she* have been? The mother-in-law, Charlotte? An arbiter of elegance at the club? A rival? No doubt, a rival. A man like Tyler senior—a Wall Street broker who sent the family off for the summer—would have had a mistress in the City or would have flirted with a pretty young neighbor here on the Cape. Or made comparisons between Libby and her social betters. One way or another he would have used the power of patriarchy to keep his wife insecure and attentive. Bully begetting bully, that pattern seemed likely to me now. Although Tyler senior must have been stressed, too, a man who so needed his wife to make a good impression.

The cookbook fell open to a page featuring a black-and-white photo of a chef beaming at a *bûche de Noël*, cigarette smoke curling from his chubby lips. Opposite was printed a complex recipe for said *bûche*, annotated in Libby Howell's round hand with a self-exhortation that echoed the line from the old English folktale "Mr. Fox": Be bold, be bold!

Bittersweet, the folly of social climbing. All those cocktail parties and church suppers, those deviled eggs and scallops wrapped in bacon, those worries about status and presentation of self. The underscored recipes put me in mind of the tidy Congregationalist church with its spare steeple, and of the struggles, apparent to me even in my teens, for dominance in the church hall—the primping and pushing of children, the petty aspiration and smug satisfaction. Poor Libby. As a child, I had admired her so—wished for Libby Howell as a mother, wondered how such an eager, sensitive woman could produce a monster like little Tyler. Leafing through the cookbook, I felt sympathy over the constraints in the women's lives and the pressures in the men's.

In any work, inspiration arises from empathy—that is the point I am trying to make. I had the stained and dog-eared cookbook in my hand, open to a recipe for Sally Lunn bread, when the solution came to me. One of the affectations of the Howell house was a reproduction beehive oven alongside the fireplace. I had overlooked the oven because in my initial haste I had failed to imagine the house as it was used. Now I envisaged the point in the dinner party, one anxious moment among many, when the Sally Lunn bread was pulled warm from atop the coals.

Once my attention fixed on the oven, I realized there had to be space behind it for a small installation. The brickwork had recently been repaired. I was able to chip that side out, place explosives, and redo the masonry using the same brick—one of those jobs whose pleasure arises from attention to detail, and then routine effort. As luck would have it, the roof antenna wire had been strangely placed; it ran outside the fireboard in the flue serving the fireplace; I could reach it from behind the beehive. I threw timers in as red herrings, but we rarely relied on timers, too much risk of injury to person. Here, we used radio signals to the antenna.

The effect when we set off the charge was modest. Just enough to render the house unlivable—condemned by the town. But Sukey and I had been aiming for narrative thrust, and that we achieved, by pulling the trigger the day (not yet two weeks after Giampiccolo, and shortly before the discovery of fireworks at Warelwast) that the feds declared the homes on the Quivet-to-Saltworks stretch of beach safe for rehabitation. That was it for Sesuit beachfront for the rest of the summer.

After Howell, I noticed a new playfulness in Sukey. She would laugh and throw her arms around me as if she were more than ever grateful for our friendship. She seemed altogether herself—solid, present, commanding. Which made me suspect the Howell project had special meaning for her. I came to wonder whether something had not happened between Sukey and Tyler senior, back when she was a teenage girl who knew how to give pleasure and he was a man who knew how to keep his wife off-balance.

I was not worried that the connection would allow us to be traced—did not imagine that at this late date the old man would disclose his affair with an underaged girl. But if I was right, Sukey had kept an important detail from me. No vendettas, she and I had long since agreed. Free the Beaches was likeliest to succeed if we refrained from acting out of self-interest. I held with Ruskin and with Kierkegaard that purity of heart, or its absence, shows through in the products of a man's labor. Though in truth, I had known all along Sukey would have her exceptions. Giampiccolo was an exception. I could not deny her.

In my own way, I had acted out of private motivation as well. At least, I can say it pleased me to hear, only weeks after the explosion, when rebuilding would have been at issue, that Libby Howell had filed for divorce. In her late seventies. Free at last.

I don't suppose disinterest is ever possible in creative work. For all its absurdity and arbitrariness—those modern virtues—my effort in Sesuit has been a labor of love. For Sukey, to pull her back from the brink. For you and Anais as well, in ways I hope I can explain. But installations often require another sort of love, call it at least affection. I don't know that I could have pulled off Howell had I not hoped, if only in unexamined fashion, to do Libby Howell some good.

As for madness—if a project speaks to ordinary men and women, why not assume that the makers are at worst unexceptional in their strengths and shortcomings? Why not leave personality out of it altogether? The moral emptiness of the spectacle lies in its translating politics into personality.

*   *   *

Speaking of which, I have just seen *Dateline*. I think it is fair to say that the show was as good as Sukey hoped and as bad as I feared.

The program opened with the obligatory video montage, an overview of the crisis. Giampiccolo first—every editor leads with Giampiccolo. The voice-over was by Hugh Crale, the new *Today* show anchor. He said the usual, how the image had been burned into our consciousness. Then he screened a series of lesser clips, in chronological sequence. Not in the order in which I mined the homes, of course. I had worked on the most delicate and detailed interior installations in early winter, on the principle that if I was any good, they would go undetected. The grosser outdoor projects involving bulk explosives or thermite—ordnance that might, if we were unlucky, be exposed by a storm—were left until closer to the target dates.

It was rewarding to see the campaign in overview. Often writers or sculptors say that their early work is beyond them, they have no notion any longer of how those complex objects emerged from their younger self. I am no artist, barely an artisan. But tonight, as I saw how we had structured a *Decameron*-like series of beach stories, disparate tales whose whole is itself a tale, I felt wonder at what I had helped Sukey bring into being.

The report opened with seawall explosions, culminating in that bittersweet shot of the Arlen-Pepper house, newly naked on its diminished peninsula. The bay laps at the base, waiting not a moment to enforce its rightful claim to sand and space.

Then on to the Potter mansion. *Dateline* had gone to the trouble to find a "before" photo, a still from an aborted *Architectural Digest* feature. Hanging far over the sea cliff is a cantilevered room, stiff-necked, insolent, cruising for a bruising. The night we lit the thermite, Sukey used blindly remailed e-messages to alert a local television station. A video crew arrived in time to capture the cantilever melting. The unsupported living room sways and then tumbles into the drink. The camera swings back to find a gargantuan sofa balanced at the edge of the remaining floor. Thousands of dollars of design work and goose-down cushioning and imported fabric. A long moment of indecision, like a basketball hanging interminably on a rim before acceding to the pull of gravity. And then, swoosh. At the edge of the beach cliff, the house gapes openmouthed.

Dateline did quite a run-through: Parlequin, Howell, Abarbanel, Altschuler, McIntyre, Woodcock. And then the Warelwast folly. In the external installations—the mining of seawalls or stanchions early on, and the in-ground interventions (like Abrams)—Sukey and I had ranged up and down the Cape, from Barnstable to Truro. Our intent was to spread the anxiety, and to take advantage of suitable architectural forms. The *Dateline* montage featured only disruptions in Sesuit. That choice may have been calculated to tie the Movement to me, since I live here. But the media has always found our local efforts to be the most evocative. As in drama or fiction, in our compositions there are advantages to observing unity of place and working with what you know best.

For the record, we had nothing to do with Abarbanel. That was faulty wiring and leaking propane, which is why there were no fireworks, beyond the skyrockets the teenage son had hidden in the garage. Abarbanel put the fire department at too much risk for it to be ours—I was grateful when a *Boston Globe* columnist said as much. We were conscientious in that regard, explosions without arson.

Likewise Hopkinton was a copycat crime, an imitation of our work at Parlequin, which was in itself an oddity—a project we did as a favor to the local police. If there is time, I will fill you in on the reasons. Not that they are crucial. Motivation and even authorship matter less than the facts on the ground.

Earlier specials on *Free the Beaches* had stuck with those facts, beginning on the Cape and moving to the national scene. The happenings and teach-ins, the university uprisings, aimed at corporations that degrade workers or the environment. And those contradictory phenomena, the Sesuit Echoes and the Sesuit Silence. The Echoes are the scattered installations that extend ours or comment on them. The Silence is the lack of thunder from either political extreme.

When commentators try to explain the scarcity of Echoes, they focus on the left, where they blame circumstance, the FBI's nationwide roundup of earth liberationists a year back. I indulge myself with a different thought: Comrades have preferred not to divert attention from our narrative.

To me, the conspicuous Silence is on the right. The disparate campaigns to bomb abortion clinics and black churches are in abeyance, operations that dwarfed ours if sheer numbers of explosions are the measure. Months have passed with nary a libertarian kook-group putsch out West. Since the Movement began, the right has held off, for fear of being labeled anarchist. Peace and police is all their cry. So that in aggregate, violence is on the decline. There seems to be a moratorium on invading small countries—we Americans are mercifully focused on our own shortcomings.

Last night, the national story was omitted, in favor of a new emphasis on person. Headlines trumpeting the FBI leak of my name as suspect, yearbook photos from school days, a still of the court order awarding temporary custody to Anais, the standard view of the cottage, from the sandbank. Then the community college, sweatered coeds with arms crossed and books pressed to their bosoms, the American campus in any decade. A dolly shot down the humanities-building corridor to my office door. And finally, before the break to commercial, a live peek at the Madeiroses at home.

I have been friends with Tommy and Dee since I taught them at the college. When the FBI first leaked my name, Tommy phoned and offered to vouch for me in public. I declined. There was a slight chance he thought me innocent. I did not want him to stumble into vouching for a terrorist.

I asked, You're going to say you took my course?

I hadn't thought of that, he said.

He indicated he would make himself available later if I wished.

The course whose name we did not mention was Literature of Anarchism. I taught it in the early seventies, when relevance ruled the curriculum; it earned me a departmental commendation, for getting kids to read old, thick novels. When Tommy phoned, I saw no point in claiming extra expertise in the discipline I was accused of practicing. Besides, I was loath to have anyone polish my image.

But now we had abandoned my strategy in favor of Sukey's media offensive. The Madeiroses' performance was flawless, which is to say fulsome.

Tommy and Dee appeared by remote, from here in Sesuit, accompanied by their plump daughter, Grace, and their plumper granddaughter, Caitlin. The first segment was "human interest." Tommy described how when Dee was pregnant they had come to me asking whether she should get an abortion, and I suggested they marry instead. They have been happy together for going on thirty years. As he gave his testimonial, Tommy patted Dee's hand. His smile mixed public awkwardness and private devotion. Casting an understated glance in the direction of Caitlin, Dee spoke softly of her gratitude to Professor Samuels.

It was effective television. Tommy is muscular, but with enough of a gut to identify him as a beer-drinking laborer. Dee has the peaches-and-cream Irish complexion, and wouldn't her red hair just show up two generations later in baby Kate. The American melting pot was on display in a knickknacked Cape Cod sitting room, the happy consequence of the sage and homely counsel of a beloved teacher.

The interviewer, seated across from the family, was a high-cheekboned correspondent of the new variety that is sliding over from cosmetics commercials. For a moment I thought she was the woman I had seen on Giampiccolo's television, but no, this one's lips were thinner and there was more variety to her facial expressions. Her specialty was the appreciative glance that conveys two double messages. To the subject: I know how you feel, and let's move ahead. And (simultaneously) to the audience: I am here to do a job, but aren't I something to look at this time of night.

She failed to turn me on, this hollow-eyed reporter. I found her haunted and forlorn. I am insufficiently moved by spectacle, or moved in the wrong direction. Sometimes I think it is this idiosyncrasy, rather than any strength of character, that has allowed me to stand fast in my focus on the issues that mattered to Anais.

Tommy smiled the smile of the loyal husband, and the interviewer asked the obvious follow-up: So Professor Samuels is pro-life?

That was a little victory for Sukey right there, the "Professor Samuels." Sukey would have asked Dee to use the phrase as often as possible—positioning me as a wise and harmless academic, rather than an anarchist fanatic. Though, since I had apparently opposed an abortion, the immediate issue was whether I am a right-wing fanatic.

Deirdre was the best student I ever taught. She writes murder mysteries now, set here on the Cape, under her maiden name, Dee O'Connor. She must have experience on television, from the occasional book tour. She looked straight at the camera and emulated the news anchor voice that signifies utter reliability—precise enunciation enhanced by pauses. She said: Professor Samuels supports women's right to choose. But I believe that in any particular case, he would suggest a solution that avoids abortion. I'm grateful that we were able to turn to him. Professor Samuels understood that Tommy and I were meant to have a family together.

If you missed the show, you can believe me that Dee's answer was the high point. Pro-choice but against any particular abortion, as if I were running for office. Sukey had coached Dee to thread the needle. Unless there was no need. We all know how spectacle is fashioned; we know what is required of us.

That moment signaled the end of our situation. I am to enter into spectacle as a conventional figure, the conservative liberal, the ineffectual intellectual, the friend of family values.

On *Dateline,* everything sounded scripted. Tommy said: He's a superb teacher. But I used to work alongside him as a fix-it man. I can tell you he's no wizard with his hands. He can repair a screen door, I'm sure, or stain your deck. As to these invisible installations that fool everyone about where bombs are hidden . . . no offense to the professor, but I highly doubt it.

Dee chimed in: Professor Samuels is not a joiner. . . . If you said Professor Samuels was part of a conspiracy to help found a library, okay.

As she talked, Dee stroked the baby's hair. If I were prone to nausea, I would have felt it then.

After the break, *Dateline* moved on to the real news (the quid pro quo, the reason the producers had let Tom and Dee on the air), the news that I had taught anarchy. The camera panned back from Tommy to reveal a reproduction Early American pie-crust candlestand beside him. On it sat a stack of yellowing paperbacks that looked as if they had never been opened. As he held them toward the camera, Tommy took on the amused look we assume in the face of products of the intellect: Henry James here, *The Princess Casamassima.* Joseph Conrad, *The Secret Agent* and *Under Western Eyes. The Possessed,* by Dostoyevsky. Zola's *Paris.* Tommy's working-class accent added to the humor.

In mint condition, the reporter joked.

The comment had the stale sound of prearrangement. Sure enough, the camera turned to a reproduction Hepplewhite side table next to Dee, where the same novels, in the same editions, appeared tattered. We could see that the Madeiroses are a normal couple, where it is the wife who reads.

I learned enough to tell you this, Tommy offered. These are books *against* anarchism. In this one (he held up the James, which looked no less virginal than the others), they talk revolution for four hundred pages, and in the end the guy who's supposed to act shoots himself—some innocent kid with a flower name. Professor Samuels wasn't pushing terror. He was pushing literature.

And cultural history, Dee chimed in. He talked about Byron's anarchist phase. Shelley's. The great French writers: Mallarmé,

Daudet, Anatole France, Leconte de Lisle. And then the painters: Signac, Seurat, Pissarro. And in America, Thoreau. I think his favorite was Thoreau.

No doubt Sukey had told Deirdre to stop there. Not to mention threatening names on television: Proudhon, Bakunin, Kropotkin. Sacco and Vanzetti. Not to hint at what Thoreau wrote: The only obligation which I have a right to assume is to do at any time what I think is right. Life consists with wildness. In wildness is the preservation of the world.

The interviewer used Deirdre's writing as a segue, to move back to easier territory: Dee O'Connor, you're saying Professor Samuels is not who done it. We have just a minute.

That was all the opening Dee needed to do Sukey's work. She said, Professor Samuels is not a terrorist, he's a teacher. You know your series "Our Master Teachers, Our National Treasures"? He's a national treasure.

The camera lingered on Dee. She said, He doesn't foment anarchy, he explains anarchism's appeal, to the young especially. Its appeal and its failures. In his class, he quoted Clemenceau: I am sorry for anyone who has not been an anarchist at twenty.

The perfect ending, wrapping me in the mantle of fatherly expert and simultaneously arguing that if it emerged that I had held anarchist views in my youth, nothing much should be made of the discovery.

The correspondent gave the camera a long look meant to say she was still in control and still desirable. Although (even as I record it, I know this response was wrong, I am forever getting these things wrong) to me she looked drawn, as if the camera had sucked her lifeblood, as if one more twelve-minute segment of spectacle would about do her in.

In Deirdre, Sukey brought something new to the mass media: that stock character, the Cape Cod granny putting in a good word for anarchism. Byron and Shelley, God bless 'em.

Sukey's defense accepts the premise that acts of terror are reserved for the wild-eyed—never the working man's Mr. Chips, publicly pro-choice and privately pro-life.

Apropos of nothing, except to show how the spectacle gets it wrong: Tommy and Deirdre did turn to me for help, going on thirty years ago. They had just learned that Deirdre was pregnant. I was their teacher, and I seemed young enough to be trusted.

I knew who Deirdre was. She could write a balanced sentence, her hair was the rosy orange of the setting sun, and she let her breasts swing free within the peasant blouses that were the fashion of the day. While I lectured on anarchy, I had thoughts of the color of her skin and the color of her hair and then—I could not avoid these imaginings—the color of parts of her that were hidden: copper, ocher, apricot, peach, strawberry. This is the wise counselor I was. Your mother was always wandering off, and temptation sat before me.

It made me nervous to see Deirdre O'Connor stare attentively at me from her seat in the second row. It made me nervous to have her approach me now, swarthy boyfriend in tow, and more nervous yet when I understood the source of her fullness and her ruddy flush, the fruit of his loins and hers growing inside her. Tommy registered my unease; he offered me a joint. We headed for the privacy of the art-supply closet.

There we crouched on the linoleum floor, below shelves stocked with paper cutters, posterboard, tins of clay, jars of paint powder. Perhaps the dope was laced. After I had taken a few hits, the orange pigment glowed at me in mockery. Deirdre asked if I knew a reliable doctor who performed abortions. This was before *Roe v. Wade*.

I looked at the two of them. Mainly I looked at her. Ripe, luscious. Oh, to taste of that fruit.

She loved Tommy, she said. She wanted to have his baby, only Tommy's father would kill him.

She was a boy-crazy girl who had bounced from college to college, chasing love. When Tommy was dropped from UMass, she followed him here to our third-rate school.

In my hazy way, I took the measure of Tommy. He had not handed in a lick of work. If he passed my course, it would be as a charity case—a tribute to anarchism. He was earning his way through school doing landscaping. He spoke convincingly of repairing and reselling old motorcycles.

I wish I could say I understood that Tommy needed an excuse to drop out of college and work with his back and his hands. Or that I foresaw Deirdre's settling down, once she had secured her man. I did not. I sat in a rosy stupor, thinking that Tommy was the son my father wanted. Thinking that Deirdre was the young woman he would have wanted as a daughter. Impetuous, spirited. My admiration must have shown through, because Tommy and Dee began to make out, in the supply room, on the floor, and there I left them. Months later they asked me to be Maria Gracia's godfather. And may I be struck dead if ever I said a word for or against abortion.

Once I told Manny this very story, out of guilt. Why had I given my students no guidance? I had become a godfather under false pretenses, through lasciviousness.

No, no, Manny had said. Too often we overlook the power of the one who admires. In your gaze, the young people learned who they were, competent and desirable.

That comment consoled me. I gave that gift at least to you and your mother, my admiration.

8

*

How You Learned to Read

I know little about gifts from fathers. From my own, I have what he granted me in death, this solid cottage and the slice of eroding bank it sits upon. That and the legacy of his example, precision in work, devotion in love. He never gave the open gifts that my college friends complained about, gifts that demand displays of gratitude, gifts that distort the self.

In college, your mother introduced me to Sartre. To please her, I tackled the novels, the plays, the autobiography. Sartre writes that he was fortunate not to have a father. Without a father, a son escapes the development of a conscience.

This claim struck me as implausible. Sartre's life task was debating right and wrong. He was all conscience. I took Sartre to mean that without a father, a man does not come to accept convention, does not carry it in his marrow. (Does not get it, when he sees a No Trespassing sign on the beach or a high-cheekboned interviewer on television.) His life becomes a search for moral direction. At least it has struck me that I have had to puzzle matters out for myself, that I continue to puzzle.

My version of the *Aeneid* renders Virgil's famous line as *I fear*

Greeks even (or especially) bearing gifts. I know from my college friends that a son must mistrust a father even (or especially) in his generosity. Now that I am in the spotlight, Free the Beaches risks becoming a paternal gift of the usual variety, burdensome, embarrassing, intrusive, replete with demands for the shaping of your own life.

Sometimes I think every gift I have given you has been a mistake. That may be the proof that I am your father. Sometimes I believe that I lost you when I gave you the summer of reading. I will say this in favor of that gift: It was handcrafted.

I have always favored the handcrafted solution. Part of what the public has enjoyed about our Movement is the fine finish work on the installations, and the tailoring of disruption to site. The imprint of the hand is what I loved about your mother's pottery, before she turned to mass production. Her early pieces are light, dry, fragile, in matte browns, blacks, and ochers, to resemble the urns and amphorae of the ancient Greeks. She favored a slip made of fine-grained red clay—terra sigillata—and an imperfect finish she called weathered engobe wash. On my desk rests a rice bowl meant to fit my left palm. The furrow at the bowl's lip is formed to the width of Anais's pinkie. I wanted the summer of reading to have that quality, fitted to your needs, marked by my love.

It began with a visit to your elementary-school principal, Harriet Bloxsom. A tiny, horse-faced woman. Daughter of the Mrs. Bloxsom who had taught me in first grade. Harriet invited me to meet with her the spring of your first-grade year.

Her office is the size of a classroom. It is decked out with rosewood-veneered filing cabinets and a rosewood-veneered, boat-shaped conference table at whose head Harriet sits, even when meeting with one parent. Despite the profligate use of space, the decor indicates efficiency, prudence, the business mentality. On a rare visit to your elementary school, your mother caught sight of Ms. Bloxsom's office. Give it back to the children, your mother muttered. Principals in the basement, art class in the room over-looking the marsh.

I am uneasy around Harriet. She thinks I avoided her in child-hood because of her appearance. In my attitude, I am always try-ing to say: I was a shy child, and you were bossy. As if it were kinder to have avoided her because of her personality than her looks. As if the personality did not arise in response to the looks. From the earliest age, Harriet was on watch for signs of disre-spect.

The day of our meeting, in the spring of your first-grade year, she sported a dress-for-success suit with padded shoulders, com-manding lapels, and enormous brass buttons. The suit put me in mind of Hermann Broch's *The Sleepwalkers*—1930s. Your mother loved that novel. Once only priestly vestments marked a man off from his fellows as something higher—it begins with words to that effect and goes on to show how modern men have become the property of their uniforms. To wear the right uniform is to guaran-tee security, maintain status. The uniform divides the world into good and evil. A man looks to his uniform for reassurance, guid-ance, self-understanding.

I was not surprised when Harriet began the meeting by boasting of her love of teaching, a habit common to administrators. She prided herself on keeping her hand in, which meant that on rare occasions she took over the classroom when a staff member needed an hour off. Harriet taught Emily Dickinson, whatever the age of the students. Emily Dickinson as a children's poet, sunny Dickin-son.

Once you got used to her appearance, you responded well to Harriet. She read your first grade a riddle poem. You came home and told me you were the one who knew the answer. It made no sense to you that others did not see it. I wish I could remember which poem. Perhaps the woodpecker: His bill an auger is, / His head, a cap and frill. / He laboreth at every tree,— / A worm his utmost goal. You had seen me handle augers.

That incident contains the reasons I thought you would be a

reader: your vocabulary, your comfort with metaphor, your ability to hear straight through to an author's thoughts.

I stared at the brass buttons and said, by way of propitiation: Hank loves it when you take over a class.

Meaning that whatever it was in Harriet's appearance that put children off, it had moderated with the passage of time. Meaning that you—Hank—were a lover of literature, as I had been as a child.

Harriet would not be sidetracked. She said she had doubts that you should be promoted. You had an attention deficit. I had been ignoring the evidence. Your pattern was classic. In groups, you were either withdrawn or impulsive. You had trouble with transitions. You showed problems with large-motor coordination. Your math was spotty—you knew answers but could not show how you got them. You were a bright child, but slow to read.

She wanted you on Ritalin. That was the price of promotion to second grade, a promise that you would visit a child psychiatrist early in the fall, one the school liked to work with, one who would prescribe stimulants.

My concern in that meeting was for you and for Anais. When compelled to visit your school, Anais would return to the cottage, raise a forefinger to the air, and recite: True education worthy of the name will obtain everything by spontaneity alone. That was the credo of the Spanish anarchist Francisco Ferrer, tried and executed in 1909. Ferrer was the inspiration for the sort of education your mother valued before she began taking medication herself, education that draws the child's talents out instead of pouring the teacher's opinions in.

Your mother had been out of town for months. (Her absence would extend through the summer; it was the absence during which she would "find herself" and turn away from me, though I did not know that then.) I believed she would be enraged if I let a doctor put you on Ritalin. Anais would not want you primed to produce.

At first, I mumbled teacherly questions. What was Harriet's

experience with first-graders who work better individually than in groups? I tried in a deferential way to tell her what you were like after school. To allude to your friendships with the twins, Teddy and Janna, and with Todd and, of course, Bert Costas's little one, Fernando. To slip in a reference to your moodiness around your mother's departures. To indicate that you were not attention-deficient, just hungry for love.

Harriet said that every aspect of your behavior fit a pattern, one that demanded medication.

I resorted to speaking about myself. Hank is like me, I said. (That statement is one the child psychologist later fixed on, when she called me "overidentified.") As a child, I, too, was reluctant to give answers. I was slow to learn math. I was shy with girls.

Harriet unbuttoned her jacket and said: Chip, you read books by the gross. Hank can't read.

No, no, I mumbled. He is like me. A secret reader.

You were, in your way. You loved to handle books, make the pictures into stories. You showed every sign of reading readiness. Your learning had been disrupted, by your mother's absences, by the school's emphasis on group process. You needed the steady attention of an adult.

Harriet looked at me with pity. Chip, she said, off medicine Hank will flounder.

I glanced at her shelves. One section was filled with Oz books, the entire series, in hardcover. Her favorites in childhood? I seemed to remember Harriet dragging around a copy of *Ozma of Oz*. I knew what had disappointed her about me in grade school. She had caught wind of my romance with books. She could not stand that I did not embrace her as a comrade in reading.

I had stumbled about for the whole of my meeting with Harriet, but now I spoke the sentence that changed your life. Changed it for the better was my belief for months thereafter, though what I said finally contributed to our family disaster. I made Harriet an offer: At the end of August I will bring Hank here. You can choose at random from the Oz books, and Hank will read to you.

Harriet gave me one of those tolerant grimaces reserved for overzealous parents and the mentally ill. I asked: If he can read to you from the Oz books before school resumes, you will be able to work with him as he is? That would signal a reasonable level of attention for a second-grader?

I tried to address both at once, the woman who had been a child with me and the woman in the suit. In choosing the Oz series I was saying, What if Hank is like us, a socially awkward member of the secret confederacy of readers? At the same time, I hoped that the operational proposal—effectively an achievement test before the next term—might appeal to an executive. I suppose that to Harriet, the offer had the sound of a face-saving compromise. I would work with you, come to see your limitations, and return you to school ready for Ritalin.

She rebuttoned the jacket. Of course, she said. In the meanwhile I will tell Dr. Goetz to expect you at the end of the summer.

I opted out of my summer-school course load. I immersed myself in texts about teaching reading to children. I borrowed structured primers from our education department. I cadged write-to-read materials, exercise books, Orton-Gillingham worksheets. I observed you, I listened to you. I tried to devise a plan that would fit you as you were, an active seven-year-old with an absent mother and trouble learning in groups.

I intended to give you the gift of your own talents. I recognize that any parental gift is suspect. I would love to know your answer to the question the court asked through its psychologist, whether I failed to see you as you were. I know I took advantage of you in one respect: A young child accepts the world as a parent presents it. I told you that we would pass our days in reading and swimming, as if that were a normal way for father and son to spend the summer months.

We read until your attention flagged, and then we swam. We read again. We lunched together. Then we read and swam, read and swam, until Teddy and Janna and Todd and Nando came home from day camp. You played with a friend. We had dinner and read. It was a simple schedule, predictable and focused.

We read, and I observed you, trying to make sense of what made a difference to you in particular. I noticed that when you made a mistake, you would repeat it indefinitely. It was Maggie who found the cat at the beach, but if when you first encountered the name you read it as Molly, Maggie would remain Molly for the whole of the book, however often you were corrected.

Yours was a loyalist brain, true to the first association encoded. So I headed off mistakes. I tried to view the page as you did, effectively to sit beside you, anticipate the next error, step in front of you and pronounce the word. When the verb *saw* approached, I would see it first as our old friend *was*. We would spell it out together, *s-a-w*. You would read *saw*. We would move on.

You liked knowing the rules of reading. Before sounding out a word, we chanted the rules together. When two vowels go walking, the first one does the talking—and it says its own name! I would jump in when an exception loomed, great or chief or pear.

As you became better at reading individual words, scanning problems emerged. I would draw a red line down the left margin of a page and a green line down the right. We read from red to green. From construction paper we cut a window that allowed only one line of text to appear at a time. We worked with the template. We worked without it. I placed my fingers under words and had you read along. Follow the fingers. Now use your finger. Now do it with your eyes alone. You began to read in whole sentences, often sentences that improved on the text. It's what's there, not what you want to be there, I reminded you. We returned to scanning techniques, and I would admonish myself to buy or borrow better books.

You would scrunch up your eyes, shake your shoulders, growl a little animal growl from deep in the throat. You worked hard. Reading was something you wanted. You asked how I knew what words meant. You repeated words and bounced your legs rhythmically and swayed. You read with your whole body. You were my little engine that could.

I remember a particular breakthrough. We had learned the two-vowels-walking rule and the silent *e* rule, and now we came to one of those didactic sentences that pop up in primers: The boy rode down the road.

You said to me, They are not the same.

I asked what you meant.

Rode and *road*.

Not the same?

There is an *a* in road.

I understood. For a real reader it is not quite true that the first vowel does all the talking. The trace of the second remains. We reviewed the O-G categories: Vowel Team, versus Vowel-Consonant-E. We thought about the *oa* sound. About *coal* and *foal*. For a reader they reside in their own part of the mind, separate from the long-*o* words.

I said to you, They are not the same, and you are my darling reader.

Your mind had glitches, on that score the teachers were right. You did reverse letters, scan lines poorly, repeat mistakes. But yours was a reader's mind. And you had many strong qualities—perseverance, an eagerness to please, a storyteller's imagination. Every student has weaknesses. As a teacher I believe it is strengths that count.

The instant you showed signs of flagging, we tumbled down to the bay for a swim. When the tide was out, we drove to the ocean. I would have lunch already packed. We swam on cold days, we swam in the rain. Mostly the weather was hot and dry. A magnificent Cape Cod summer. You had my love of the water and your mother's aptitude for swimming.

We began by aiming for Mooncusser Rock. Then the midway tower on the jetty. Then the tip of the jetty. Then beyond. You were a laughing boy. You loved to swim with your father. You loved to be in the bay beyond the jetty, small boy in the vast ocean.

You could do a creditable six-beat crawl with a full arm pull, that little extra burst in the stroke when the arm follows through from waist to thigh. But you favored the open-ocean crawl your mother had taught you, a high-energy stroke where the pull ends just beyond the shoulder, with no follow-through, a stroke designed to cope with choppy surf. You had the stroke of a boy born by the sea.

Your brown hair took on bronze highlights in the sun. Despite gallons of lotion, your skin tanned and glowed. Your body thinned and lengthened. My laughing seven-year-old.

Our bodies chilled in the water and we warmed on the sand together. Or you leaned against me here on the sofa, fresh from the shower, each of us wrapped in a towel, snuggling and reading. Seductive, the psychologist wrote, in response to your mother's version of your version of that summer of reading. I wonder what else teaching should be but seductive. That is how we learn to read, is it not, from being read to on a parent's lap, feeling the warmth of a body and the coolness of the page. Reveling in the artwork. Reading is sensual, learning is sensual, childhood and parenthood are sensual. The psychologist complained I overworked you in the summer; overworked you and overindulged you. Can it be both? I say it was all indulgence. Learning is an indulgence. Learning is the highest form of play.

In practice, we had little use for the exercise books and worksheets. You wanted to read material that surprised you. I reworked the easy readers, pasting in variant middles or endings. I illustrated with stick figures, colored in with crayons. You would giggle with anticipation as we turned the page to find one of my emendations. You had a keen sense of plot, recognized the unconventional and took pleasure in it. The little tiger who decides to stay a hen. The boy who fails the second of three challenges and then the third as well. The plucky girl who meets no challenges, who is never tested by the fates. You would laugh and laugh and ask to read another.

Your favorite was the plot where transgression is not punished.

The naughty rabbit who stays naughty—as in Marlowe's *Tamburlaine,* where the wheel of fortune takes only half a turn and hubris takes no fall. You wanted to know that you were safe. That you could be a slightly bad little boy and no consequence would ensue. How could you not be drawn to that story line, given your mother's absences, given children's tendency to blame themselves?

I call the plot you favored Happy All the Time, after a book by Laurie Colwin that spoke to me, despite its focus on the moneyed class. I thought of my life with your mother as Happy All the Time, a drawing-room comedy, a cottage comedy, with no arc, where the only suspense comes from the occasional departure of the female love interest. I know Anais came to see matters differently; that very summer she was changing her opinion. But I had found family life blissful. Happy All the Time is the plot I am aiming for now, however long the odds. To make the bold statement and simply have it stand.

By late July, you had got the idea of reading. You were hungry for works that did not insult the intelligence. We tackled harder books. You read what you could, and I jumped in with anything difficult. We were like one reader. You barely noticed which of us spoke the words. In this fashion we ran through the early Beverly Cleary books—*Henry Huggins* and *Ellen Tebbits.* Then all of Mary Poppins. The Mrs. Piggle-Wiggles. The Robert McCloskey stories about Homer Price—those rounded pictures in brown ink, how could the subject not be doughnuts? Your favorites were the Edward Eagers, books built around magic talismans—coins, frogs, turtles—though there I had to help a good deal. You learned that *presently* means "soon." You lived in the ordered world of the 1950s childhood. Though I was always at your side, you had discovered books as a means of private escape.

Escape from the pain of your mother's disappearance, however necessary; and the school system's intolerance of difference; and the inadequacies of my parenting, which I know were plentiful. Anais did not return and did not return, though normally it was only for a part of the winter that she fled. I assumed she was nearby, in Somerville, at her old potters' collective, finding moral sustenance among the aging radicals, reassembling the equanimity to tolerate family life. I thought of her each night, wished her Godspeed and safe return. I was used to her absences.

9

*

Bliss

We met through carpentry and radicalism. I had responded to a notice in the *Crimson* seeking volunteers to rehabilitate houses in a working-class section of Boston. I went looking for a path into social life at college.

A dozen of us gathered at a sagging triple-decker on a quiet street east of Mass. Ave. in what once was and would again be a middle-class neighborhood, between Boston City Hospital and the Symphony. Most of the kids showed up in painter's pants—they were standard on campus, and they seemed the thing to wear to construction work. Painter's pants with Henley T's or chambray workshirts or spaghetti-strap tops in Indian print cotton. The job that first day was hanging plasterboard. I was unfamiliar with the MTA, and the subway stop was blocks from the project. I missed the opening pep talk, about the natural alliance between workers and students, and how rebuilding marginal neighborhoods would help end the war in Vietnam.

I had given no thought to politics. I sought an atmosphere where I would feel at home, and I found one. Naked joists and jerry-rigged wiring were familiar to me. I was no builder, not by my father's standards. But I could swing a hammer, I could measure and trim and run tape. I was comfortable with painter's pants and the tools that hung from them. Amidst dilettantes, my competence got me noticed.

You've done this before.

Those were your mother's first words to me. My mouth was full of nails, and I was craning my neck, judging how a sheet of plasterboard would butt the ceiling. Perhaps that is a lesson I should pass on. When you meet the woman of your dreams, be sure something is plugging your mouth. Ideally, be on a ladder above her.

Try as I may, I can't make the nails behave.

Her voice had baby-talk overtones. I was a lonely young man, unused to attention from women. I wanted the baby talk to continue. If only I could prolong the encounter, postpone the moment when I turned and the girl saw my broad, pedestrian face and my early-balding brow. Mmmm, I hummed, to acknowledge her problem. But the nails resonated like a Jew's harp, and I feared she would think I was mocking her. So I let them drop and they clattered and we laughed, and I stepped down to show her how to hammer.

She was a sweet-faced woman, slender and wavy-haired, with a cupid's-bow mouth like my imagined mother's. Too pretty for me, I would ordinarily have thought, except for this peculiarity: Her skin had an orange cast, like the stain of a cheap sunless-tanning cream. The complexion gave me hope.

Her hammer was too light, so I handed her mine.

A tool should be well-balanced, I said, because that was what I felt competent to say. She rocked the hammer in her hand. She tried tapping a nail, but she swung skew. I adored her intentness. I don't know where my courage came from—perhaps an early memory of my father doing the same with me—but I put my right hand around hers and reached over her left shoulder to secure the nail. I said, A light tap and then a sharp one.

Tap, tap. We reached up two inches, and I was pushed against her. She had a slight vegetable smell, like a glass of wheat-grass juice. Not unpleasant—a homey, unthreatening odor.

We had a beer afterward, at a working-class bar under the T. The room was dark, with oak paneling and an oak counter. I fit in, a young journeyman on break. I had pulled my father out of a similar bar in Hyannis often enough. Your mother signaled for a beer, and I made it two.

She said she was at Radcliffe, at North House, Moors Hall, concentrating in French but focusing on political theory. She was a founding member of the Worker-Student Alliance cell that sponsored the rehab project. Her name was Anais, changed from Annie and pronounced identically. She had chosen the new name as an act of separation from her mother, Ann Holden of Milwaukee, Wisconsin.

I liked it that Anais complained about her mother right away. I felt I was being taken into the family—a troubled family like mine.

Ann Holden was a big fish in a small social pond. Inveterate shopper, fashion plate, a woman who though she did no work had little time for her daughter and less after her husband, Anais's father, passed away. Ann was constantly grooming herself, grooming for remarriage. She was dating a prairie industrialist who had got his start refurbishing huge oil barrels and then branched out into real estate and banking. Buford the Barrel King, he was still called. A man with more money than history, that was how the mother encapsulated his standing.

Anais had contempt for the mother and her beau. Anais's father had been a down-to-earth man, a displaced Yankee content to be led by his wife through the social shoals of the Middle West. He was ill for some years before he died.

Anais had been recognized and nurtured in high school by a French teacher of intense political commitment, a Miss Jean Brodie, only leftist and truly caring, if I got what Anais was trying to say. Anais began to read radical theory in French. The most advanced journal, *Socialisme ou Barbarie,* mocked bureaucratic state communism, decried Stalin's brutality and even Mao's— though it featured Mao's poetry and revolutionary sayings. She went daily to Lamont Library to read the French newspapers. To absorb the European view of the war, to stay up to date on the French student movement.

Your mother studded her speech with French phrases, as a token of her radicalism.

Did I read French?

I said I did, which was not entirely false, and later I managed to, for her sake. French became a bond between us, as young lovers. Even now, to find my sentences peppered with French phrases seems a confirmation of loyalty, to Anais and the values she urged on me.

She adored the *nouvelle vague*. Did I know François Truffaut, Jean-Luc Godard, Alain Resnais? Anais valued intellect. She valued commitment to the welfare of the downtrodden. She loved swimming. She had placed well in a six-mile race in Lake Michigan, one summer when the water was not fouled by alewives. She scorned the immense accumulation of commodities foreseen by Marx. There was a flash of fanaticism in her condemnation of consumer culture. I liked that in her from the start. Admired her outrage, a capacity I lacked.

Anais jabbered away, eager to impress me, the Harvard man at ease with hammers and workingmen's bars. Her skin glowed, and she gave off her comfortable vegetable odor, and I wondered at my good fortune to have found this intense classmate who wanted me to respect her and to care about her, which I did instantly. I recognized her life story as a variant on mine. The death of a parent, the noxious influence of distinctions in social class, the saving power of books and ideas and deep water. Anais was a sort of woman I had not seen before, high-strung and charmingly insecure, in need of a stable man to ballast her life. I thought I could play that role. I was content to be ballast. Ballast, anchor, or harbor.

From the start, she needed time to herself. She moved in with me sophomore year but kept her own room and returned to it for days at a time.

When she was not at political meetings, she spent her evenings at the potters' collective. She had taken up potting as a folk art, a peasant art. To center clay on the wheel made a person centered, that was a metaphor your mother accepted.

At the Worker-Student Alliance, she was shrewd and well-spoken. She would have made a fine politician, but for her absences.

I do not want you to imagine that she was sad or tortured. Despite her anxiety, Anais could be joyful in the manner of a young woman enamored of a cause. She loved art cinema, would go off alone to the Brattle Theater and later the Orson Welles and would return bubbling about the latest Fellini or Antonioni. She quoted Wordsworth's recollection of the French Revolution: *Bliss was it in that dawn to be alive, But to be young was very heaven!* If Anais became overwhelmed at times, still she had the hopefulness of the principled outsider. Conventional happiness, of a person at peace with the world, she rejected as bourgeois self-satisfaction. She disappeared to seek not happiness but centering.

My father was dying in those years.

Mrs. K died first. She was older than my father, though not yet sixty. The illness was unexpected and brief. The diagnosis was not discussed with me, which, given the taboos of the time, meant it was cancer.

I saw Sukey at the funeral. She was treating Vassar as a women's dormitory from which to enjoy society in New York. She brought a date, a publisher in his thirties who sported a razor-cut hairstyle like that of the defense secretary, Robert McNamara. Everyone I knew aimed to appear laid-back; the look of the man served to emphasize Sukey's distance from me. She wore a black silk dress enlivened by pink and purple squiggles that did not betoken mourning, an Emilio Pucci. She seemed a character out of F. Scott Fitzgerald. Other than at church, she had a drink in her hand at all times.

Sukey gave the wake, but she was the one who looked out of

place. The attendees were mostly churchwomen, charitable in the face of death. My father was a figure in the crowd, a local man with rough hands and an ashen complexion. It would soon be jaundiced; he went downhill immediately.

I visited him in the Hyannis hospital or at the cottage. Anais came along. She was impressed by what she called his lack of pretense. She brought sentiment to the visits. She saw a man who was dying in the house he had built by himself, dying of the ultimate working-class ailment, drink. We would pay our respects, and my father would shoo us out.

Anais and I went for long swims, or she would swim alone while I worked on my father's finances, paying his bills, balancing his accounts.

Mrs. K had left Stone House to Sukey, who was soon renting it out and borrowing against it to subsidize her social life in Manhattan. I was not mentioned in the will; Mrs. K's books went to the Sesuit Women's Free Library, whose board she had chaired. It emerged that Mrs. K had subdivided her land and deeded my father a little landlocked portion the house stood upon, along with the cottage and certain rights of access—to the beach via the sandbank and to the cottage via the Stone House drive. There was a catch: The rights attached not to the land but to my father and his heirs, a detail that made the house and land unsalable. The arrangement was in line with Mrs. K's patronage in life, providing for the serfs so long as they stayed on the demesne. We did end up with waterfront when the sandbank in front of us eroded; by the same token, the land was then unprotectable. It is mine and will someday be yours, and then the sea's.

Your grandfather died in the cottage the summer before my junior year. He had about him that puzzled look of the failing, as if life might at last be made sense of. This was when he wondered at my being *already grown*. Often he lapsed into German, *schon wieder erwachsen*, fretting over my presentation in adult form, as if there were plans for my development he had failed to complete.

He had only a few days at home after the final hospital stay. A drinking buddy supplied him with liquor—he took brandy and milk when that was all he could stomach. I cast a blind eye, since it was calories, since it was what he wanted. He was emaciated with a distended belly. The house smelled of his urine.

At the end, his talk was limited to scattered curses, an effect of brain damage, but good to hear again, like a souvenir of the old days. I felt lucky to have known him. Anais was right. He pulled no punches. He gave me a clear sense of my shortcomings. Alcohol aside, he set an example of living without complaint.

To Anais, in sticking with my father in unpleasant circumstances, I showed myself to be the sort of fellow an anxious woman with a disrupted childhood might trust. Now I had come into a small inheritance, a cottage by the bay that we could visit weekends and live in on graduation. We were firmly attached, although we saw no need for church or state to legitimate our union.

I know how I looked to Anais. I fit the image of that romantic figure, the New Man, promised in early Marxist theory, who would parse a sonnet in the morning and shingle a roof in the afternoon. I represented the best of both worlds, a hard-knocks education and a Harvard degree. I personified the worker-student alliance.

I see now that from its beginning our relationship contained the seeds of its own dissolution.

I was no politician. By the lights of the worker-student alliance, what I was good for was teaching. I had taken New York State Board of Regents courses by mail, educational psychology and the like. Public schools were recruiting college students. I intended to teach as a way of averting confrontation with my draft board. Then the teaching deferment was abolished, and the draft lottery came in. I got a high number and was exempt. Your mother and I drank two bottles of champagne the night the numbers were picked; it is the only time I have allowed myself to get drunk.

Take a working-class student and send him home to his community to teach children of the working class and he will look, well, like a worker. I might be a steadfast friend to the proletariat, but I disappointed other of Anais's expectations. Harvard-educated

New Men founded literary magazines, sold screenplays, thought better of radicalism and returned home to run the family business. In the end, Anais was true to a different sixties ideal, her right to self-fulfillment. In the eyes of her therapists, she should have left sooner.

I never fostered the illusion of the New Man, never tried to put one over on your mother. I am not a good Marxist, I would readily confess to her.

I considered Marx to be a nineteenth-century visionary, inferior in his imagination to Zola and Dickens. I found Marx polemical. To my ear, his best passages were found art, excerpts of parliamentary commission hearings that he had stitched together to render portraits of rapacious British industrialists.

When in Marx I read that capital is independent and has individuality, while the living person is dependent and has no individuality, I thought of *Bleak House*. It was not that Marx was wrong but that novelists had expressed the same ideas with more complexity, noticing the gaps in the system, the intersticcs where kindness endured. I faulted Marx as a student of people. In Marx, each acts according to his financial interests or those of his class. I fear it is hard for the world to get far on that principle, the principle on which Marxist and capitalist theory are in accord.

I am no anarchist, I would warn Anais. I had come to anarchism early, through Zola, where the flaw of urban terror is revealed in the death of an errand girl—though Zola respects anarchists, sees them as no more misguided than church or state. I came to anarchism through Conrad and Dostoyevsky. Anarchism as the slaughter of innocents. Anarchism as self-deception.

In response, Anais would speak to me of her French theorists, for whom anarchism was a form of Dada, of surrealism, of existential refusal. That approach had its appeal. But then Weather Underground members began blowing themselves up in basement apartments, and police officers were killed in the name of protest.

More Zola, more Conrad. I had not yet conceived the merger of obsessiveness and absurdity. I saw only the superiority of fiction to political theory.

When I protested that I was no Marxist and no anarchist, Anais would tell me that I was a natural radical. True enough. I found social distinctions unfair, and inheritance, and the consequences of extremes of wealth. The leftist perspective, in which social class is all, was the story of my life. But my passion was not for politics. My dedication was to Anais.

At the same time, I felt unworthy of her. What allowed me hope were her orange complexion and earthy odor, imperfections that led her to underestimate herself.

Soon, those imperfections disappeared. She went to the college health services for a Pap smear, and the gynecologist recognized Anais's condition as carotenemia. Your mother has trouble absorbing certain proteins found in vegetables. The coloring of carrots builds up in her skin. The condition had become more apparent because she had turned vegetarian. Once diagnosed, she cut down on salads. Her color faded, as did the compost smell, and yet she did not leave. She had come to rely on the support I offered.

The smell came back now and again, when Anais was incautious in her diet. I consider it the smell of home. Perhaps you do, too. Here is a secret. Sometimes—rarely—without telling your mother, I grated carrots, or boiled and mashed them, and beat them into a sauce or stew. Ratatouille was one candidate, carrot sweetening the acid of the tomatoes and the bitterness of the eggplant. A couple of helpings, and next morning she would remind me of Henrietta Stackpole, the Henry James character who smelled of America, its prairies and its rivers and the green Pacific. (James says it is the woman's garments that carried the odor, but that is euphemism; he is epitomizing the woman, not her laundress.) I added the carrots to evoke our courtship days. Sabotage by vegetable was my only act of frank dishonesty in the marriage.

Anais came to the Cape and shaped her wondrous pots in the shed with a water view. For a time she had a second wheel and a student or apprentice. I taught at the community college. Comrades from Boston dropped down to visit, though less and less frequently. Anais sold in small shops. She had her women friends. She was anxious and high-strung, and I tried to make the world safe for her.

Fifteen, sixteen years in which little changed. I acquired a master's degree, I assumed and then dropped administrative duties at the college. Radical politics lost its hold on the young. I varied my classroom themes. The Seacoast in Literature had local appeal. Books like *The Sea, the Sea* and *The Waves*. I asked students to read descriptive passages critically. Do we find the ocean the way Iris Murdoch does, radiant and complacent, glowing rather than sparkling? Or as in Virginia Woolf: slightly creased, like a cloth with wrinkles in it, sea indistinguishable from sky? Or as in Chekhov (the story about the young lady with the lapdog): lilac? What does it mean that Chekhov has us imagine a shade of water that we who live at its edge may never have observed in nature? I held the door open for those who like me saw most clearly through books.

I was intent on being a good teacher. I studied developmental psychology and theory of instruction. I took every chance to have my classes critiqued. My model was Maoist: fierce humility, constant improvement. In homage to the teachers who opened up my life, Wainwright and Perkins. Out of respect for my students, the children of working men and women.

My secret love was writing, and for a while I devoted spare time to it. I contributed occasional pieces to the local newspaper, the usual unfocused musings on the seasons: "Autumn in Sesuit," "Walking Thoreau's Sesuit," "Sesuit by Gibbous Moon." Since I lacked training as a naturalist, I was soon outclassed by others. Most of my effort I devoted to fiction. I aspired to craft a book like those I loved, a drama of social class built around a stately home that, for my sins, resembled Stone House.

In time I faced up to the truth that I had neither talent nor the dedication to press on without it. In retrospect, I see that fiction did not allow my personality (I mean my perfectionism) full scope; the modern novel could not bear the attention to architectural detail that has proved, in my recent work, to be a characteristic strength.

Setting writing aside, I supplemented teaching with odd jobs. I liked being a handyman, enjoyed small projects, was willing to go along with homeowners on quick solutions to chronic problems. Nothing lasts forever.

Anais taught the odd course at Castle Hill in Truro. In July she might go off to Horizons, in the Berkshires, to mentor young artists. A shop in Provincetown represented Anais, and another in Northampton, and one in Cambridge. Her pieces sold so long as the prices were modest.

Was Anais depressed? She disdained the word *happiness,* as corrupted by commercial values, but it was not unusual for her to style herself *contente* or *heureuse*—sensible of her good fortune. She disappeared when she wanted, mostly to Boston. I was here on her return. She had her ups and downs, enough downs that she valued the stability of our life together.

The therapists she saw were angry feminists. What they had to say she already knew. That men should share the housework; but then, I kept the cottage neater than Anais required. That she deserved her freedom; but freedom was something she had always assumed. Anais would disappear—disappear from therapy, too. I would get calls from frustrated practitioners: What is holding Anais from treatment? I had no answer. These were women who had told Anais she needed space, women who had told her I was not her keeper.

Anais's swimming habits gave me hints of impending departure. First she would switch from bay to ocean. Then she would head for the Chute.

The Chute is what we called the standing riptide that begins at the Gull Pond outlet by the Farrel mansion on the far side of Sesuit, where the Nantucket Sound roughens up as it meets the open ocean. Depending on the season, the Chute sweeps swimmers maybe forty yards out to sea and then runs parallel to the coast and swings in to a point fifteen yards on a diagonal line from the failing breakwater you see from the soundside town beach. We used to swim the Chute on a dare when I was a boy; every few years a teenager would drown. The shoreline is posted with signs now, Danger and No Trespassing, and the direct route out involves a climb over the Farrel fence or through it.

I made the mistake of introducing your mother to the Chute one summer day when the heat had us down and she was emerging from a stoned state, in need of stimulus. I thought doing the Chute would draw us together. We were young. We felt strong. That first run, Anais was pulled under and I lost sight of her. She emerged far out to sea. In my panic, I tried to yell to her above the rush of surf: Go with it, don't waste energy fighting it. Your mother was a smart swimmer, she had no need of advice. I followed her course, caught up to her near the dock. I had been frightened out of any wish ever to swim the Chute. Your mother was euphoric.

You don't imagine I'm going to die in bed, she said to me when I asked her to promise not to run the Chute again. She said that as a child, when she had swum Lake Michigan, she had understood as in a revelation that she would die in water. Your mother has a sunny laugh, when she is exhilarated.

Over the years, every so often I would find Anais returning flushed and bedraggled from her morning swim and learn that she had done the Chute. To feel something, she said, the way others spoke of slashing their wrists. A few days later she would be gone, which (for all that I missed her) I considered a safer solution to what ailed her.

Sometimes before she disappeared Anais would explain herself. She needed a direct involvement in politics. She was off to Boston to organize hospital workers, secretaries, janitors. More often, she just left. One time she scrawled a note on a kitchen tablet that said everything in a word: *Space!*

This comment will sound odd in society grounded in possessiveness, but granting Anais space was a privilege. As she came and went, I found I believed all the more in the Marxist credo that the free development of each is the basis for the free development of all. I was enlarged by Anais's wandering, learned much about the nature of relationship.

Besides, from early days I had subscribed to Miss Havisham's formulation, that real love is *blind devotion, unquestioning self-humiliation, utter submission, trust and belief against yourself and against the whole world, giving up your whole heart and soul to the smiter.* I know that the line should be read with ironic distance—but isn't it also the case that *Great Expectations* succeeds because the characters' devotion appeals to what is young and vital in us? I felt no less tied to Anais in her absence, though every day I missed her.

Twice, I got calls from women who claimed to have been displaced by Anais. Did I know that my wife was shacked up with the woman's boyfriend? I sympathized with the callers' plight, but when they demanded I act, I replied that Anais and I were not married, she was free to do what she pleased.

We were married, of course, license or no, we had made that sort of commitment. Speaking with the displaced women, I relied on a technicality, in order to be spared idle reports.

For many years Anais did not want a child, thought she was incapable of rearing one. I contented myself with my students and the uses they put me to, tried to satisfy my fatherly urges in that way. Then one month she was pregnant. She was nearing forty; we were too old to assume there would always be another chance. Perhaps one of her therapists had convinced her that motherhood was essential to womanhood or perhaps Anais loved you and wanted you from the start, in the way that people know what they want in these matters.

We had you, and you were wonderful. Anais developed a postpartum infection. She went to the hospital to take antibiotics in her veins, and I was home with you. She was depressed when she returned, nothing terrible, she had her melancholic phases. You were a magnet to her at first. She stayed in Sesuit without a break until you were three. Those were placid years, though (here is a truth I would not divulge, a sign that this odd journal is to you but not for you) Anais was never at ease with motherhood, struggled with it constantly. Too much impingement on her space.

Then there was a time where she went to the Chute regularly. I said I would prefer she did not, that I could not bear the worry every morning. Without a word, she left again. The absence was brief, but more followed.

Her Boston therapists must have changed gears, once you were in the picture. I gathered from stray comments that they thought me overly complaisant. I did too much. The trouble was that the conventional tasks of motherhood disconcerted Anais, and I wanted for her to hang in.

One Saturday she insisted I take the day off; she would have your friends over to play with clay. In retrospect, I imagine a therapist had suggested that Anais use her artisan's skills as a route into parenting. Not an hour had passed before she phoned me at the Sternhells' to say she could not stand the crying and the arguing, the high-pitched voices. She had a blinding headache. What should I have done but return to set things straight? She regrouped—together we managed some lovely pottery mornings, the spring you were four and a half. Your thumb pots and snake-coil baskets stood on the kitchen windowsill for years after.

Not everyone is made for every aspect of family life. My intent was to allow Anais time to grow into the mother's role. Perhaps it was the combination she could not bear, you and me together, two so-similar males.

It seemed hard for her to stay here long. She had business in Boston, her pieces were selling. It was common by then for women to have a career and to travel for it; your day-care counselors and teachers understood. Anais came and went, but all was normal in the fashion of our family until she returned home the fall after the summer of your learning to read.

*　　*　　*

You *had* learned, that was the great thing. It was as I had hoped: once past a certain barrier, you were unstoppable. You leaped from *Little Pear* to *Mr. Popper's Penguins* and then almost anything, including the Oz series.

Actually, there we cheated a bit. We spent four days on *Ozma of Oz.* You would read one page and I would read two. That was the key to your progress, I believe, the closeness of father and son. I was taking advantage of you, admittedly, of your hunger for parental attention. Though I might equally say that I was pouring water on a dry sponge; you absorbed, you grew. I was there, I was consistent, and, of course, I was the only one. You had in effect no grandparents, no aunts or uncles, no cousins. Your mother had been away for months. I adored you. I don't believe you had any wish other than to learn alongside me.

I want to insist: You were comfortable that summer, and secure—as happy as a boy can be when his mother has left without signaling the date of her return. Each morning, you would spring out of bed, primed for action. One moment you lay fast asleep, my guileless boy; the next, you were prancing about the cottage, talking of the past day's adventures, how cool it had been to swim in choppy water, how funny Janna was when she teased Teddy. Asking if we could head to the ocean side even if the tides were wrong. Wondering whether the children caught on the pirate ship would be rescued by the magic turtle. You were utterly at ease with me, running your own tub and then popping out and splashing water everywhere, despite my protestations. Time to eat, time to eat, I'm so hungry I could eat an apatosaurus. Do you remember it as I do?

You might have turned anxious if I had set reading tasks that were beyond you—might have feared displeasing me and losing me as well. But you had talent aplenty. Your sense of plot and humor and language. Your quick intelligence. I think it helped that I tried never to let you read a word wrong.

We homed in on *Ozma of Oz* because of what I knew about Harriet B. I guessed that she would have long since dismissed my challenge—take a kid who can barely make it through *Hop on Pop* and by summer's end bring him in reading Frank Baum. She had insufficient faith in education.

I had my reasons for putting all the chips on *Ozma*. Ms. B would be surprised to see us. She would turn for the bookshelf, and what would she reach for? Her book, the one she had dragged around in fifth grade. Implicitly, she would ask the question that dominates a self-centered person's mind, the question at the heart of capitalism: How does he compare with me?

Toward the end of August, we showed up at school. The day was hot and close. We dripped with sweat as we walked the corridor. There was no secretary. We knocked and let ourselves into Harriet Bloxsom's office. Cold air swept around us. I regretted not having brought a change of shirt for you.

Harriet was wearing a clubwoman's pink shorts and lime green knit blouse. She had done a perfunctory job with makeup. I could see what the years had wrought. Liver spots, jowls, and the face so large. For me, her contemporary, it was like looking into a magnifying mirror. I felt tenderness. I was glad we had dropped in unannounced, found her out of uniform, or in a different one.

What brings you? Harriet asked.

You'll want Hank to read for you.

To read for me.

From *Oz*.

She gave me a perplexed look. Then, with annoyance on her face, she grabbed for *Ozma*. She handed it to me, so that giving it to you would be on my head. My insanity, not hers.

You will be pleased, I told her.

We are all dying together, I wanted to say to her. We can afford to be pleased now and then for one another.

I sat beside you and put my hand on your shoulder. I said, Shall we read this?

Dad, do we have to? was what you asked, and Harriet gave me a kindly look, as if to spare me embarrassment while my delusion was being unmasked. She did not know you, did not know that you had an aversion to rereading, since you had an almost flawless memory for story.

It's one of your principal's favorites, I said.

And so you began: The wind blew hard and joggled the water of the ocean, sending ripples across its surface. Then the wind pushed the edges of the ripples until they became waves, and shoved the waves around until they became billows. The billows rolled dreadfully high: higher even than the tops of houses.

I was happy over *dreadfully*, the three syllables, the short *e*. For *billows* you read *pillows*, which surprised me. In our run-through, I had thought you might mistake *b* for *p*, the less familiar word for the more, so I had given you *billows* the first time round. You were nervous with Ms. Bloxsom present. We had not practiced reading in front of others.

You corrected yourself and smiled sheepishly. You continued to stumble here and there—nervousness, shyness—but the chapter was easy for you. You could visualize a storm at sea, you were a Cape Cod boy. You smiled again when we got to the name Dorothy Gale. We had talked about how the name fit the story—how in order to make *Oz* work, a storm had to blow Dorothy hither and yon.

Now it was Harriet's turn to interrupt. She may have thought it was a prank, that you had memorized chapter one. She flipped to chapter three. No, she said, this chapter is my favorite.

But then it was your favorite, too, where Billinia the hen explains she cannot read, and Dorothy says the letters on the sign are too far apart. You liked it that Baum knew how children think about reading.

Do you know what it means? Harriet asked.

Except for the punita tree, you said. You asked Harriet if she knew what a punita tree was.

She did not, and then you asked her if it really was her favorite book. How could she have a favorite book and not find out what the words mean?

Instead of congratulating you, Harriet looked at me in horror. What did you do to this child? she wanted to know, as if torture were an effective method of teaching reading.

Chip, I heard rumors, I set them aside . . .

Rumors?

That you were sequestering Hank. He wasn't at the day camp, was he? Or swimming lessons at the lake?

Harriet, I said. He can make it from Mooncusser Rock out past the jetty and halfway to the entrance of Barnabash Creek.

Meaning, why would you be at swim lessons? But I saw I had made a claim that would seem incredible to a school principal, an uncoordinated seven-year-old swimming a mile in the bay. Now I was delusional on two counts, reading and swimming, or else torturing my son in two arenas. So I sat quietly. No need to speak. You had read *Oz*.

Okay, Chip, she said, you made a bet and won. But at what cost? In school we can't have a teacher keeping his nose to the grindstone, hour after hour. And what kind of reading did you bully him into? He still mixes letters. He reads without flow or intonation. He sounds like a robot. He jiggles in the chair and sticks his fingers up his nose and shakes his head between paragraphs. This is the same boy who sat through first grade with us. You don't seriously think that because you have made him perform like a talking horse that we will take him into second grade off medication?

She said all this in front of you, and my only hope was that you were not listening. You had pulled *Tik-Tok of Oz* off the shelf and were well into the first chapter, jiggling in the chair and humming to yourself aimlessly.

I was crushed on your behalf and Anais's. And my own as well; I was proud of you. I said, He has been playing with Teddy and Janna and Todd.

This time I did not include Bert's boy, Nando, on the list, since he was so often in trouble. Nando was to you what Billy Dineen had been to me in childhood, or would have been had you stayed here.

I said, Hank is looking forward to spending the school year with his playmates.

Implying that I would fight Harriet all the way. I was an educator. I knew the grounds on which the combat would take place. I could show that I had a boy with "good peer relations" and near-adult athletic skills and reading abilities that would serve a middle schooler. In the face of that sort of evidence, no superintendent on the planet would back a principal for retaining a second-grader over his parents' objections.

It troubled me that I should take this tack. I am not someone who deals in covert threats. In the chill of Ms. Bloxsom's office, I understood that because I had become a husband and a father, because I was intent on protecting your interests and Anais's, I could not escape posturing, could not escape wearing a uniform, in this case the uniform of the litigious parent. My actions were determined, like George Orwell's in "Shooting an Elephant," where because he has donned the uniform of the colonial police, in Burma, he must destroy a poor man's source of livelihood.

Nobody gets to Harriet's level by letting ambiguous cases rise to the superintendent's desk. Harriet had begun to back off already. She was treating me as a colleague now, a fellow educator: Chip, you've seen how much better these kids do on Ritalin.

I buttoned my uniform and said, Some families like drugs and some do not.

Which was unfair. Your mother did like drugs, if they were ones that release a person from the culture. What she did not like—yet—were drugs used to increase productivity. I did not venture this more subtle point as I knew it would detract from the force of my appeal.

The word *drugs* clinched the argument.

Just because it's you, Harriet said to me. But I hope you haven't been browbeating the boy. Kids need to be kids.

I could hear Anais's voice: Oh, sure. Drill kids to cooperate at camp in the summer and drug them to perform at school in the fall. Let kids be kids? Training foot soldiers for the corporate state, is more like it.

Thanks, was all I said. We walked out into the tropical corridor. You asked whether we were going for a swim, a sensible question.

I felt no elation. I had lived too long to imagine that these victories, imposition of one over another, come without a price. The negotiation with Harriet cast its shadow on my later decision, not to try to hold on to you through cunning. I had taken marriage to be a revolutionary act of commitment; even in the absence of an altar, I had pledged to your mother my life, my fortune, my sacred honor. I could not act against her.

She returned mid-September. She had been in treatment in Boston, placed on drugs. Her therapist had insisted Anais needed medication to repair the ravages of a world that undermines women. Anais said that in retrospect she had been depressed for the whole of the time she had known me. She had been distant from her true self.

We had often discussed that passage in the young Marx, in the *Manuscripts of 1844,* where he says that in the truly rich human life, self-realization *(seine eigene Verwirklichung)* exists as an inner necessity. That was the rationale for Anais's absences, *Verwirklichung.* But through political action, not through a pill.

Was she transformed? She laughed only rarely. She seemed less devoted to her potting or her friends. She spoke of a renewed interest in family, but in the cottage she was stiff and distant. She did seem to have worked on her aversion to mothering. This is a subtle matter, but she looked like a mother—like the breezy moms I had seen at the yacht club; even-tempered and encouraging if somewhat inattentive. The yes-dear-how-clever-dear type. Not the worst sort of mother; there were days when I had longed for one like that.

The most obvious change was in Anais's work life. She was on the phone with Boston. She overnighted samples back and forth. Buford was helping her develop, optimize, rationalize her business. She was a manufacturer now, more than a craftsman.

She wore trendier clothes. She had reached out to reconcile with her mother. Anais and Ann had shopped together when the mother and the barrel king visited Boston. Anais's hand-thrown pottery was on display in a shop on Newbury Street. Plates and bowls in hues and patterns based on the paintings of Pierre Bonnard, cheery postimpressionist kitchen items, butter dishes in pink on white. The models for AnnieWare. She had taken back her given name, her mother's name, for the line. AnnieWare was being mass-produced for sale in lesser gift shops, via a subsidiary nestled in one of Buford's holding companies. Your mother was reaching for success.

We were astonished, you and I, although glad to see her, overjoyed.

As I say, she seemed intent on doing better as a mother. Honey, she told you, we will spend more time together. She had taken to calling you *honey*—she was better able to be near you but less liable to remember your name.

She visited your school and came back shaking her head, but not for the old reasons: That principal thinks the boy should be on Ritalin. She says you make him go through hoops rather than accept what is best for him. These medications can help. Mine are helping me.

I had never opposed your mother's wishes. But these wishes did not sound like hers. Like those of a cult convert, rather, given her prior beliefs. For the whole of my time with your mother, I had wished her contentment. But her pill-induced serenity created a discontinuity in her life. The change was in a single direction, toward what until recently she had variously called Disney happiness, Nintendo happiness, Gap happiness—the anodyne and stigma of a dehumanizing culture.

I ventured comments recalling her past formulations. Anais

replied that I was covertly and chronically depressed, that depression had left me stranded self-righteously in the sixties. She said that happiness brings revelations. In happiness one discovers new values, new loves, truer loves and values.

10

*

Space

I don't suppose she goes on anymore about Gap happiness. How Gap happiness is based on the cheapness of a good, without regard to the devil's pact that makes it cheap. The system that outsources jobs to the unfortunates invoked in Anais's favorite song: *les damnés de la terre, les forçats de la faim.* Prisoners of starvation, wretched of the earth.

Before she turned to medication, Anais had a routine about the prisoners of starvation turning out mock turtlenecks. Twenty-seven cents of labor goes into the typical $35 shirt. (This was when branded shirts cost $35.) She had the facts. Eighteen-hour shifts, forced pregnancy tests, dirty drinking water, physical punishments, blacklisting for complainers. While our government trains third-world countries' military personnel, to guarantee internal stability. Even small-time labor organizers disappear without a trace. We might shiver, you and I, at the Dickensian scenes your mother painted, but we loved hearing her care. That was what the doctors overlooked in what they called her chronic depression—the fierce beauty that arose from it.

When she spoke of what she cared about, she was rhapsodic,

inspired. She scorned Gappiness's imagined defenders. Yes, with luck a multinational can be forced into a modest no-sweat compact, promising no child labor and no twenty-hour days. But soon the third-world country's central bank will be exposed as corrupt and overextended. To sustain the infrastructure that sustains the multinationals, a global policing fund will require the country to devalue its currency and raise its interest rates. The worker who in good faith sewed the mock turtleneck will be fired, only to discover that the few pesos she has saved have lost their worth. And now her child will spend twenty-hour days in the town dump scrounging for styrofoam that can be recycled in a plant that pollutes the local river. A child hoping to trade styrofoam for a crust of bread.

I tried to head her off if she got wound up around your bedtime—as tuck-me-ins, you preferred my standard Paddingtons and Ramonas. But you liked being with your mother when she was there, loved her even when she scared you a little.

Of course, it was hard for you to live by her principles, and I saw it would be harder as you grew up. So many objects to desire. Walkmans and Wayfarers, Trek bikes with Indy shocks.

Do you remember the Game Boy with Super Mario cartridge? You brought it home from Todd's house—this was toward the end of our summer of reading. A gift, you said, and for a moment I believed you. But then you handled the object bashfully. A false god, arousing hope and shame. You had pocketed it, your first theft.

We both knew (you with a child's understanding) what your mother would see in the toy. The corrupting content of the games, glorification of competition and aggression. The manufacture of want in the young, chaining yet another generation to the pointless cycle of toil and consumption.

Anais could never understand how others managed to ignore the suffering in the silicon chip. Everyone knows, she would say, everyone knows how Intel pollutes the aquifer in Albuquerque, everyone knows about child and penal labor in Asia. People know and choose not to know. The culture of elective blindness, she called it. I suppose I was open to Manny's theory—that America suffers from nausea outside awareness—because it was also your mother's. She was nauseated and proud of it.

Since for children, for all of us, wishes are close to facts, you half-believed the Game Boy was yours. Still, once we arrived at Todd's, you managed an apology. Todd was at his computer, immersed in virtual aerial warfare, unaware of the loss of his toy and indifferent to its reappearance. His room looked like a set for one of those movies that feature the technologically savvy consumer child, *E.T.* or *Close Encounters,* or the one you loved to watch at the twins' house, *Gremlins,* where the detail that supplies verisimilitude is the child's room stocked with an unremarkable superabundance of electronic paraphernalia. You restored the Game Boy to its place in the riot of its fellows, and you turned to me, palms raised. You said simply, This.

Maybe you said, Look at all this. Or, Why can't I have this? And I heard only the final word. I prefer to believe one word was all you said. *This,* the parfit plea.

You were silent on the ride home and then for hours after. Silent and troubled. Throwing your body around the cottage. Playing the parachute game with your teddy, the one where you tied strings and a washcloth to him and then tossed him to the ceiling and let him crash. You would not eat dinner, could not be distracted or consoled. I hated that evening. It was too much to expect you to reconcile yourself to the family's distance from This.

Your mother's motto was Less. Samuel Gompers said labor wants More, but to Anais it was apparent that More had become a snare. A worker wants more Gap or Guess? for his family, his job is outsourced to the wretched of the earth, and he is reduced to flipping burgers. In the service industry, ministering to unspeakable entrepreneurs and their entitled children in outfits emblazoned with polo ponies. Raj shirts, your mother called them; she looked at a polo pony and saw Orwell shooting the elephant.

You longed for This. You had my sympathy. In my time, I had coveted the heather-knit sweater and antelope-backed English racer. But now This had become More and Excess. I was with your mother, had pledged fealty. Tucking you into bed, I rededicated myself to the project I was already engaged in, trying in my clumsy way to stand in for commodities by being the father you and other children wanted.

I tried to protect your social life, to be a pied piper for your classmates. Setting out materials for collage-making in the kitchen, or helping you and your friends assemble toy boats from wood scraps. Organizing sledding and skating. In hopes of bridging This and Less.

When your mother returned, enamored of More, I found I could not join her. Less had always been Anais's deep truth. She had been worn down, I thought, by others' intolerance of her depression. Therapists' intolerance, and her mother's, and the wide world's. In society's judgment, to be sad amidst Excess is perverse.

I found Anais's transformation painful. She was suffused with the new happiness, which is close kin to dissatisfaction. Thirst for This and More. I saw her as hypnotized, by therapists and pill-pushers. I imagined that if I withheld the drugs for a day or two and then roused her in the middle of the night, she would bless me with one of her old political rants. I never tested my theory.

You are not yourself, I objected. I knew it was a hard case to make, to argue that a woman is lost when she wants what everyone wants, a Palm Pilot, Vuitton luggage, Ritalin for her son. This was early in the legal proceedings. Anais was with me in the cottage. She had come to remove a few belongings. Fine cotton blouses tailored for her by a close friend in a sewing collective—items dating from the days when Anais had bartered with comrades, tableware for clothing, an economy of community among craftspeople.

I urged her to take her books and music: Joan Baez, Malvina Reynolds, the old issues of *Sing Out*. (Were we wrong? I ask, when people scorn the sixties. We loved Bergman and Fellini and Truffaut. We discovered Woody Allen. Rediscovered Tillie Olsen and Norman Mailer. Adored Joyce, Woolf, Salinger, Faulkner. Made room in our artistic pantheon for Cézanne and Man Ray. Listened obsessively to Lennon and Dylan, Stravinsky and Coltrane, Paul Robeson and Bessie Smith. What generation has chosen better? Yes, the revolution was cultural. What more critical level for revolution?) Your mother insisted on leaving it all behind, every vestige of her past. Even *The Golden Notebook,* which she had pushed on friends for years.

What worried me most was her unwillingness to take books for you. I had set aside a bag of your favorites, so you would feel you had two homes. Your E. Nesbit and Edward Eager. She would accept none, as if I had contaminated reading altogether.

Your mother can be stubborn. For weeks, in 1969, she did not believe Richard Nixon was president. She could not be teased about her posture. She suffered dense, angry denial. Not that she respected the Democrats—they had rained war on Asian peasants. But the premise that the country had voted for Nixon was so bizarre that it would take more than mere news reports to make a person accept it as fact.

Anais's obduracy was now directed at me, at the notion that I might be a supportive husband. You are a stone, she said to me, and I am a sapling whose tip you have fixed to the ground.

Whatever can you mean? I asked.

It's an image my psychiatrist gave me. (She meant her pill doctor, Athena Starck.) Dr. Starck said that an adolescent is like a sapling that sways in the breeze. An ice storm may weigh it down in a certain direction. The sapling is resilient. After a thaw, it springs back.

Not a reader of Robert Frost, I thought to myself. No swinger of birches, Dr. Starck.

But you, Chip, have been a boulder, holding me bent. Unnaturally. Through passive aggression and plain passivity. Your "support" inteferred with the normal sequence of adolescence—rebellion and reconciliation. With you removed—and with some extra help, since I am not so young as I once was—I have sprung up straight.

I tried to make sense of the comparison that meant so much to your mother. To consider the sort of weight I might be. A stone that has rolled onto the growth bud of a sapling tacked to the earth in a freak ice storm. I could not see it, resented the clumsiness of the metaphor, the way it stood in contrast to Frost's precise images.

How to understand the infelicitous Dr. Starck? Even if she had learned her poetry in Greece or Austria, the trope would not do. I had let Anais come and go. She had not shown the least impulse to reconcile with her family or with laissez-faire capitalism. And now the doctor styled Anais a victimized woman, one who must be fortified so as to escape her enslaver—the husband who evinces a stultifying constancy and thereby saps her legitimate drive to conform. I stood gravely accused. How can a man be right when his justification implies that everyone around him is in the wrong?

That was the case your mother made in probate court, on your behalf: I stood in the way of your getting the best. With her mother's help Anais could send you to a private school with small class size and an emphasis on individualized programs for the whole child. She would set you up with an after-school tutor and a psychologist. She would manage an education trust fund for you; Buford had established one, contingent on your mother's obtaining custody, that was a big point in the eyes of the judge, Peggy Crow. A schoolteacher's salary no longer suffices for fatherhood. We auction off children now, to the parental high bidder. Though to be clear-eyed about it, the judge would have awarded you to your mother regardless of our relative circumstances. To her credit, Judge Crow was more feminist than capitalist.

It is said that Judge Crow never once handed down a divorce decision that favored a husband. The *Globe* did a series on her. How she removed a daughter from the care of the father who had raised her all her life and granted full custody to an absentee mother days out of drug detox. How Judge Crow took a working stiff with a nonunion job and garnisheed his wages as palimony, so his former live-in girlfriend could attend courses to become a belly dancer. When Judge Crow was overturned on appeal, she would find a new set of reasons to stand by a decision that favored the wife. The ruling your mother won would not make it onto a list of the judge's most egregious. It took the Commonwealth four years to get her off the bench. (I had a grudging respect for Peggy Crow before she sold out—to big tobacco. Virginia Slims signed her on as a personality in cigarette ads, the woman who stands up for women forcefully. She maintains a house in Sesuit, the mansion by the Chute; she is a Farrel by birth.)

We anarchists are with the transcendentalists, Nathaniel Hawthorne in *The Scarlet Letter*. One cannot confess for another. In court, I made no complaint against Anais, for her absences, say, or her high anxiety. She must find her own way to be a mother. I was stung when she let her lawyer say that in ignoring the advice of experts I had done you harm.

Judge Crow granted your mother temporary custody, and you and Anais disappeared, out of the jurisdiction. But not before she said the words that left me paralyzed.

This is a story I have told no one except Manny. A story I doubt I could ever tell you—though how can you understand me or your own past without it?

The judge had suspended my parental rights and set a date for a final disposition. My lawyer tried to calm me. We were walking up the aisle to the leather-padded courtroom doors. Anais approached, let me enter the cloud of pricey perfume, put her lips close to my ear.

Chip, she said, I can't help myself. I need to go forward.

I said, Two parents—

She interrupted: I need space. If you try to get time with him, I won't fight. I will leave him to you.

That was her threat. If I pursued, she would leave you mother-less. The warning took its force from her past behavior. Her response to discomfort was absence.

If you learn of that moment, I hope you will forgive your mother. You know her, understand her need for breathing room. You have to take into account the man I am; for all my solicitude, I may not have been easy to live with—dull and stodgy. No match for the competent navigators of the great world available to a woman of substance.

For my part, I was confused by the word *space*. Anais had always used it to refer to a temporary break from life in the cottage.

Was there nothing I could have done to keep our family intact? I raised this question time and again in my sessions, if they were sessions, with Manny Abelman. That worry is the only one for which he consistently offered absolution. You were blindsided, he would tell me. You never imagined she would go through with it. And then you collapsed in the face of her betrayal.

I did not accept Manny's absolution, nor the premise that Anais was gone forever. I told myself she would waken. (After all, she came to acknowledge that Nixon was president.) Given time, she would return to herself and to radical politics and to me. My task was to keep the home fires burning, to keep the clay and the potter's wheels in readiness.

I did look for you twice, in Madison. I figured, a Wisconsin native on the lam, who makes her living as a potter—where else would Anais flee? So in springtime, less than a year after she had left with you, I showed up for the Madison Self-Management Fair. It was a street celebration—booths on farming, commune life, crafts collectives, minimized consumption as a way to smash capitalism. Held the weekend of May Day, right before the Mifflin Street Block Party, where radicals get drunk alongside frat boys. Anais had often spoken of showing pottery at the fair.

May first was sunny. Light sparkled off the lakes and then off the mica in the sidewalk slabs, as if nature, too, were in a festive and rebellious mood. Unless it was only that I was dazed and agitated at the prospect of being near Anais and you.

I stopped at a table with simple clay bowls on display. I asked a potter if she had heard of Annie Holden. She rolled her eyes as a struggling painter might when Andrew Wyeth is mentioned. The popular fraud. Try Tellus Mater, she said, on State Street. Or a department store out East Towne way.

I turned and saw your mother walking with your grandmother. Anais had let her hair grow to chin length. Rolled and straightened. Fancy dye job, barely any telltale orange sheen. A model breezing down the runway of Mifflin Street. Ann had the identical look, as if her plastic surgeon had used the daughter's face for template. I felt tears well up, as they do when we read a story about a desperate reunion between parent and child. I understood how your mother might take on any persona at all, to reach her own mother.

I had last seen Anais and Ann together in the courtroom. There they were all business. On Mifflin Street, they were relaxed and chatty, two gals out slumming, hairdos swaying in unison. I could understand how Anais might need to be away from me, to create such a moment. My own mother was an actress, a creature of the spectacle. What would I not have done for time with her?

That was what I told myself, but looking at Anais it was hard to avoid thinking she was comfortable in the consumer role. Born to it, which of course she was. I stared—confused, immobilized—and then your mother saw me.

Chip, she said, as if she could scarcely recall the name, assessing whether it made sense for me to be here, a political radical at a celebration of radicalism. She smiled at the potter. Perhaps your mother thought the potter was with me, that I had taken up with another one.

This is Anais herself, I said, making the introduction. The potter glared as if I were crazy. Crazy for having asked whether Annie Holden had a booth, seeing that I knew her and that she was got up like Fifth Avenue, not Mifflin Street.

Your mother looked elegant. Her dress fell just so at her hip. My hand wanted to go there, where it had rested so often as she lay beside me at the cottage. That is what I missed most about her nights, a particular curve of the haunch. I remember a scene in a Jean-Luc Godard movie your mother took me to, *Pierrot le Fou*. A young couple are teasing one another. The woman sings about the short lifeline on her palm—her line of chance, it is in French. The man sings back to her about the sweep of her hip, the line of haunch. A simple dialogue about desire and fortune, love and death. I still adored the sweep of your mother's hip. She was beyond me now, wore the uniform that signaled unapproachability for one of my class.

I searched for you, Hank, and you were there. Three tables back. No longer dressed in baggy clothes from the sewing collective. No, you wore Gap khakis and a Gap pocket T. You were with an identically outfitted friend, playing a sort of tag amidst the exhibits, with much giggling and taunting. You looked immature, as if the trauma of separation had slowed your growth. You bumped into an environmental-action table, scattering leaflets.

It made a darling picture, you pausing to touch your friend's shoulder and whisper in his ear. The coordinated shirt and pants added charm; I recognized their contribution. It is only because of the years with Anais that I saw beside you another child, the one sitting on a rubbish heap, scrounging for anything of the least value.

Your grandmother turned to me. The guards have been warned, she said. And the school. In case you try any funny stuff.

Guards? I asked, but she did not answer. I gathered you were living in a gated community. There couldn't be many in Madison. Not a city of fence-builders. Had the barrel king invested in an upscale development nearby? I seemed to recall a reference to one in a conversation I had had with Anais, posttherapy. Foxhound, Foxhunt, Foxhall—a name your mother would once have deemed unspeakable. I could imagine the barrel king suggesting a gated development as safest for you and your mom.

Hank, I called. You did not hear me.

Your mother said, What I told you in the courtroom still applies.

I said, Separation is the alpha and the omega of the spectacle.

The sentence was from Anais's favorite text, the text she had urged me to learn by heart, one by a French situationist. It referred to a cascade of separations. We are separated from our selves, from our hopes, from any sense of control over our destiny, because we believe that the life of celebrity is truer and more worthwhile than our own shadow life. We are pale, while images are vivid. The Nike swoosh (for example) has more reality than we. We are separated one from another, soul from soul—except as spectators, united by the commercial images we view.

I did feel distant from her. I wanted to ask how AnnieWare compared to the exquisite earthen pots she had once thrown, how a barrel-king trophy home in a new subdivision compared to a cottage built with a father's hands. I felt no acrimony, was genuinely curious, about how it was to cross the line. I wanted to help Anais cross back over. I hoped that the words from the text she had once loved would remind her of her self and of our connection.

I doubt Anais heard me. I mumbled. I was a wreck of a man.

You had been torn from me. I felt like a man operated on for melanoma, with a quarter of the body cut away. I was recovering, as in recovering from surgery, where recovering may mean not likely to recover. Where recovering means continuing to suffer. Under Manny's care, I learned that bearing a loss is like taking a beating; you have to tell yourself it only hurts. But that dispassion came years later. On Mifflin Street, I was a wraith. In that state, I accepted guidance from anyone, from your mother.

She said, Disappear.

Her mother, the barrel queen, said, I will call the police.

As if it were I who had played fast and loose with the law.

Up the street, you were running and jumping with your friend. There amidst the booths, I could smell and taste your skin. The sensation of the good-night kiss. So many missed. I gazed at you and then, to appease your mother, I walked away.

I walked the length of the street, skirting the corner where bigtoothed, blond reporters had themselves photographed with the fair as backdrop, revolution turned local color. I walked past the new public library and the senior center, cubic lumps, the cheapest and grossest of buildings, signs of the degradation of civic life. If Madison, Wisconsin, cannot honor the civil society, is there hope anywhere? At the top of the street I caught a cab.

I told the driver I was looking for a gated community, posh, recently built, I could not remember the name.

Fox Meadows? he asked.

Not so faux-aristocratic as I had remembered. Though it indicated that developers had the same habit in the Midwest as on the Cape, naming a property for what their construction destroyed.

At the gate, the guard was a stocky local kid, studying a text on retail marketing. I knew the type. Mendota Community College? I asked.

He nodded.

Gunderson, I said, taking a guess. Every development in Wisconsin must have a Gunderson.

Mrs. Karen Gunderson?

I'm her nephew. I want to surprise her.

The cabbie turned to look at me.

Number sixteen, behind the lake, the guard motioned.

No, I said, when the cabbie brought me there. I'll recognize it. Let's swing farther round the circle.

I guessed at which incongruous house was yours and settled on one with a midsize bike lying in the circular drive. The entry had tall, white columns, a bit of Georgia plantation lost on the plains. My thought was that your mother had pleaded with Buford to give her "the most house possible." For the greatest psychic contrast with the cottage, which is the least house possible. Here is the peculiar way spectacular symbolism works: a plantation house in the Midwest says Silicon Valley. I imagined your mother in a home office giving onto the swimming pool, her shed and wheel traded for a massive PC dedicated to pottery-by-CAD.

I peered through the sidelights to see if I could spot anything revealing. Family photos, your old quilt, AnnieWare. Nothing. I jumped behind the taxus and ilex to peek through a crack between the curtains. I made out a pile of art books, Bonnard and Miró among them. And then, beside a chintzed wing-back chair of the sort decorators include in model homes to signal elegance and comfort, a jumble of toys—game cartridges and joysticks and electronic board games, and a junior soccer ball.

It made me reel. For a boy to live with his soccer mom in the most substantial house in a tasteless, unexceptional development, in childhood to live the cliché of the moment—it seemed to me what I had wanted in my own childhood, what I had wanted without knowing it. To see the possibility of it (without certainty that the house was yours) made me weak and sentimental and contented with my decision to let go.

I knew how I looked, a vagabond skulking in the shrubbery. I dashed back to the cab. I did not want to frighten a concerned neighbor into phoning the guard so that he and she could be called in to give an affidavit when your mother applied for a restraining order. I had the cabbie take me to the airport. I wanted to be able to return once I had recovered—though that was a conundrum, how to recover without you and Anais.

I did come back four months later. The plantation house was occupied by an elderly couple who owned an Ethan Allen store near the mall. They invited me in to see the coordinated furniture. They had bought the home directly from Foxhall. (I had been right after all about the British imperialist name; it referred to the corporation, not the subdivision.) If you had ever lived in Fox Meadows, you were gone. To Milwaukee, I guessed, hidden in closer holdings of the barrel king.

Beyond those two attempts, I did not pursue you. Out of respect for your mother, and perhaps fear of her. And because faith is difficult.

Other than wanting for you to have a mother, I did not pretend to know what was best for you. Well, the Ritalin—I did have an opinion about that. But what to do now was not clear. I clung to what I knew with confidence. My job was to keep the door open, as a husband might for a wife who has joined a cult. If Anais was Odysseus under Circe's spell, or Starck's, I would be her Penelope, faithful in Sesuit. Living on tofu, teaching workers' children, helping my friends.

There were moments when hope was especially hard to cling to. Two, almost three years back, I was in Filene's at the Hyannis Mall, killing time between dropping Sukey at an AA meeting and picking her up. I turned over a piece of AnnieWare, a soup bowl, and saw a small gold sticker that said Made in China. That was a low point, I can tell you. I had to admit—the next time I saw Manny I did admit—that Anais might not come out of the trance by herself, that to reach her might require drastic measures.

11

*

Hidden Forces

Clouds at daybreak, midtide. Pewter hues—Virginia Woolf sea and sky. Then, a sudden change of spectrum, primary colors, and a horizon line, sharply etched.

With the sun came Sukey at the door. She blew in like a breeze off the bay. Her plan is in motion, and she is her old self, sassy and cocksure.

She brought real groceries: mesclun and sheep's-milk feta, virgin olive oil and balsamic vinegar for salads. Imported pasta and fresh porcini for a first course. Salmon. Snow peas. Sorbet. Trays of tiny blueberries and perfect black raspberries. A bottle of hock and one of claret. Nothing is too good for our National Treasure, she trilled.

There is a message here. That for the next few days at least I am to join the upper-middle class, partake in the familiar bounties of America. Walk in the road pointed to by Alistair Perkins when he instructed me to interpose bread between salad and wine. For years, I have stuck with the brown rice, lentils, and tamari your mother favored. But in a suspected terrorist, peasant food is not a reassuring diet. It signals the quality Sukey wants to deny I possess, fanaticism.

Sometimes I think Sukey doubts my ability to imagine, or my ability to lie. I am to go on the air, and Sukey believes it will give me confidence to know that if I am asked what I had for dinner the previous night, I can tell the host, Pretty much what you had. Or perhaps the delicacies are meant to course through my system and give me the air of respectability.

Can we afford this? I asked.

I thought you believed in spending it all, she said.

She threw the local paper on the table. *DA: Bomb Indictment Near.*

Weymouth was going to force Billy Dineen's hand. Threaten his budget, push him aside with a special prosecutor—whatever it took.

Sukey said, It was time for groceries.

The black raspberries were meant for after dinner, but we picked at them immediately. I wanted to ask Sukey whether she misses the days when the Super Stop & Shop was woodlands, vegetables came from the Dineen farm stand, and we topped our Prince or Ronzoni with mussels picked from the tidal pools at Mooncusser Rock. The Cape was more exclusive—the land was owned by fewer people. But there was *land.* The word has disappeared, given way to *property,* every square inch protected and fought over.

In our childhoods, Sukey and I picked berries the summer long. First the tiny wild strawberries, then high-bush blueberries, and low-bush, too, intense mouthfuls with a flavor I thought of as *blue,* the flavor blue. Every twentieth berry would have a musty and metallic taste that ran up the back of your nose—a thorn-among-roses that elevated berry-picking to a lesson in living.

The seasons marched in fixed succession. Blackberry, raspberry, Concord grape, beach plum. Sukey and I would head out with empty coffee cans tied round our necks with yarn. For these excursions, she was dressed in pedal pushers and a sleeveless blouse, freshly ironed. Everything of hers required ironing. Smooth and crisp. I wore a striped T-shirt, wrinkled, straight from the wash. I was a child, and she was a little lady. I would work hard at a task, she would direct. It was a wonder she did not command me in Dickensian fashion—You are to wait here, you boy.

Certainly I felt common in her presence, though Sukey's charm extended to a different sort of domination. At the least provocation, she would turn tomboy. Crouched over, I would stare a blueberry in its fringed eye. And then I might sneak a shy peek up at Sukey, gawk at the dappling of light on her arms, until she caught me and wrestled me, like as not tearing my shirt in a bramble.

Mrs. K canned each fruit in turn, in Ball jars nested in a wire holder that could be lowered to the bottom of an enameled metal pot—her one distinctive effort at housewifery. All gone now—woods, berry canes, mussel beds, filtered sunlight. Too much fertilizer runoff, too much yacht bilge, the mussels unfit to eat. No woods where trespassing is overlooked. By the time of your childhood, the picking was at the town blueberry patch, disease-resistant cultivars bearing starchy fruit fought over by summer folk who line up at opening time to compete for an insipid taste of country living. And now the tiny wild blueberries are back, in the supermarket, as delicacies.

I did not share these thoughts with Sukey. They have an air of selfishness about them, as if we had committed acts of terror out of nostalgia. I do not want or expect the world to turn back. I do not want or expect much in particular. That has been the source of our success, a combination of boldness and purposelessness. No grand program. No defined ideology. Not collectivist anarchism, not individualist anarchism, not revolutionary anarchism, not pacifist anarchism. Anarchism without adjectives.

I confined myself to straightening up the kitchen. Always wary of secret listeners, Sukey made small talk. When the last dish was dried, Sukey brought forth from her canvas carryall a pair of baggy swim trunks and a baggy overshirt, powder blue, the past summer's color. She said, On sale at Marshalls. I couldn't resist.

I understood her to mean that we were to confer out in the bay, beyond the range of listeners.

Sukey knows I still wear racing trunks at the beach, the way all men did when near-nudity was an emblem of liberalism. Well into the seventies, up and down the Cape you would see potbellied psychoanalysts and fireplug union organizers in tiny nylon Speedos. No jockstraps either. As a toddler, you wore a tank suit like your dad's, only yours was red with a tiny purple dragon. On the wall beside the kitchen table hangs a photo of you in it. We are making a drip sand castle; you hold your hands wide, about to clap with pleasure.

Presidential, I said, holding the new, square-cut trunks at arm's length. Thinking back to Bill and Hillary, how the week before a Paula Jones deposition they had got themselves videotaped in swim gear, the first couple cheek to cheek on the beach, he in his baggies, she with her widening thighs, the middle-aged couple on its way downhill to loyal contentment. The epitome of public relations, it was, the seemingly inadvertent shot that tells a tidy story about gallantry, the aging prodigal returning to his long-suffering dumpling wife (this was before the makeovers) as he will return to the electorate. I mimed a Clinton smile and swagger. Humming "Hail to the Chief," I placed an innocent hand on Sukey's own broad hip. She brushed it aside and retreated to the bathroom to change.

She emerged in a fussy floral one-piece, in consonance with her new image, the spunky dowager. Obediently, I had donned the baggy trunks and overshirt and one distinctive accessory: a Day-Glo orange swim cap, the final item to emerge from the carryall. So that the cameras could pick me up from a distance, I understood. Like good children, we wanted to be seen but not heard.

I have argued against photo ops. Invisible, I remain what I am in the old snapshots, forever the homely small-town teacher and handyman. Once I show my face, I will appear quirky and marginal, the way Richard Jewell continued to look long after the government's declaration of his innocence. Or I will play the game well and seem savvy and corruptible. A small-minded man who wants what we all want, his face on the television. A modest failure who subscribes to the spectacle's definition of success.

In phoning for groceries, I had agreed to follow Sukey's plan. So for the second successive day I shepherded an attractive woman past the chirping cameras and down the wooden stairs to the bay. The networks featured shots of my orange cap bobbing behind Mooncusser Rock. Sukey, who thinks of everything, timed our excursion for two hours after high tide. The water was deep enough for a swim but shallow enough over the sandbar to keep the photo boat at a distance. In the freeze-frame, the one where a white circle is superimposed to point out my head, I resemble Mao Tse-tung in the Yangtze. I am important, but there is doubt as to my reality. I believe that is one measure of celebrity, to have a face that when photographed looks unreal.

The water turned cold suddenly, as it can even on a sunny day. The bay responds to enormous hidden forces—a reality you once found fascinating.

When your second grade did a unit on The Ocean Around Us, you chose to report on rogue waves that rise from a calm sea to crush a strolling beachcomber or snatch a dog to its death. Quiet, and then six tons per square foot of force, arising out of the depths. You were impressed by the number, though you did not know what a ton was. You understood something about the natural world. Force, randomness, cruelty.

Composing your report, you could not wait for summer, could not wait for the chance to swim again and take your risk. I thought, We swim here for that very reason. Like an infant being rocked or bounced or tickled by an enormous parent, we love to be swayed by the sea, love its near-reliable gentleness, its hidden strength.

I did something dangerous with you once. We were at Nauset Beach on a hot August afternoon when a run of bluefish came through, vicious scavengers chomping blindly, roiling the surface of the sea. The lifeguards cleared the water. The crowd turned irritable. No sooner had the school passed and swimming been reopened than the surf rose, eight-foot swells out of nowhere on a still, stifling day. The guards were reluctant to clear the water again. Instead, they all moved to one section, seven guards in front of a ten-yard swath where they allowed swimming to continue. Extraordinary decision. I thought, What an opportunity, to swim in such surf with such protection.

You were five years old. I took you out in my arms, beyond the breakers. We were shot up and tumbled down. There was a regularity to the motion. I could anticipate, I could count on these waves, they were dependable. Although I knew that, minutes earlier, the sea had been six feet lower and full of frenzied predators.

I held you in my arms, giving you a ride no amusement park could equal. You began to squeal and gurgle, making noises I had not heard from you since your infancy, the sound of ideal pleasure. And then a boy with a boogie board was smashed onto the sand, legs broken. An ambulance was called. The lifeguards closed the beach to swimming. We waited for our wave and headed to shore.

Why had I carried you into the surf? Had I thought a second longer, I would have made a different choice. Always I have wanted to offer protection. What bothered me most about the custody proceedings was the allegation that I had endangered you, by not bringing you to a psychiatrist. I answered that I could never harm you. That was why I did not want you medicated—fear of harm. And yet I did take you in the waves that day.

I did not intend to teach you a lesson, but one was there, about the world being powerful in its pleasures and its punishments. It occurs to me that if I say I am at home in the ocean, I might mean that the ocean resembles my home, resembles my life with my father, comforting and indifferent and potentially violent. That day at Nauset I was showing you what my life had been, perhaps that was the impulse. Though I hope at the same time, in holding you close, I promised to provide you what safety I could.

I took your interest in rogue waves, two years later, as an attempt to study and master a puzzling truth you had learned with me. I am sure you are still studying that truth, however far from the ocean your mother has taken you.

You holding up? Sukey asked.

We were treading water in the bay. I related Wendy's news.

You let me come visit when there's a bomb in the cottage? Sukey asked, in mock protest.

I told her how I spent yesterday writing you with the bomb scare as stimulant. And how toward dusk, after dinner but before she phoned about *Dateline,* I put two and two together and walked out the back door, where for a few feet I was screened from the press corps by the pottery shed. Between the shed and the heating-oil standpipe, right where I figured it might be (if an Oakes truck delivered it, that was my line of thought), sat a bag filled with fertilizer and diesel fuel and cotton batting, wired—miswired—to a blasting cap that never had a chance of catching. A couple of sky-rockets had been thrown on top, in halfhearted reference to the Movement's signature.

We do well to rely on our assessment of a neighbor's capacities. Donald Antunes has never done a job right. I was as likely to be caught by a rogue wave and swept to my death chatting with Sukey at midtide in a windless bay.

Oh, Chip, Sukey said, and she reached for my shoulder, to comfort me against the danger past. But immediately she was distracted.

It creates a disposal problem, she said aloud. Sukey began to refine her arrangements and then drilled me on them. Sukey touched me again, to warm me—warm me to the distasteful task of public relations. There is another shot you may have seen. Her fussy floral swim cap behind my Day-Glo orange one, something inexplicable and intriguing in progress on the bay.

12

*

Lucidity

A moment I would love to share with you—something I just heard on the radio. A local author was speaking about his book, *Deer-Proof Your Garden!*—a how-to response to our upsetting the balance of nature, turning graceful creatures into pests. Beyond the usual—select shrubs that don't appeal to deer, caryopteris and buddleia—the fellow favors two concentric fences, spaced a few feet apart, an arrangement that causes deer to imagine they will be trapped. The American solution, walls that shunt the problem to the neighbors. But that's not the point. What got to me was his motivation for writing. When the interviewer thanked him for taking the time to enrich his readers, the guy rejected the compliment. When writing, he had no practical purpose in mind. He was inspired. Driven to write. Art for art's sake, he all but said. It made me smile, to think the Muse flies so low.

Humble creations *can* be inspired. Last winter and spring, I felt compelled to sit in a neighbor's house and discover a fit means of destruction, the performative equivalent of the mot juste. Now, each night when I should be sleeping, I feel your presence, and then well into the day I find myself at work on this journal, the one that is addressed to you and not meant for you. Scribbling under compulsion and without reason.

I am at home now waiting—I assume not for long—for Sukey to arrange our next move with the media, her marketing campaign.

Marketing is Sukey's métier. She worked in public relations when she lived in New York. She continued with freelance jobs here: in-house publicity for BaySky, citizen outreach for the Landmark Commission, community relations for Sesuit Trust, before it was bought out by BankBoston, which was bought out by Fleet. Her first taste of Internet technology, so useful to us, was through a computer strategies course for publicists.

In designing Free the Beaches, Sukey took Uncola as a model: Define a market niche, write clever copy, create an image linked to a personality style—the rebel. She envisioned Unspectacle. Uncommodity. Unconstruction. Politics for those who feel disenfranchised by politics. She was ready to hack into standing sites and post outlaw pages on the Web. Manifestos in the form of advertisements you might see in glossy magazines.

That was Sukey's fantasy, genteel terrorism justified through targeted publicity. I listened, commented, let her find her way.

Sukey's struggles with alcohol continued through the late 1990s. Her license had been suspended after a conviction for driving while intoxicated. Tuesdays and Fridays, I would drop her at the realty office in the morning and then leave the college midafternoon to haul her off to her appointment with Dr. Abelman. She complained that I took her one place to make her crazy and the other to make her sane. I might as well leave her at home.

Home was a run-down golf condo in the Sesuit Shore complex. She'd bought the place cheap and was rehabbing it for resale. Since her sale of Stone House to cover taxes she had neglected to pay, she had been on the move, trading up or down as circumstance dictated.

Without a driver's license Sukey could not sell houses. She structured deals—taking motel cottage-communities condo—and concentrated on publicity. Mostly she fiddled with the computer.

Sukey was maybe six months out of detox when she shared a memory with me, one she had retrieved in a session with Manny.

As a child, she had gone on long walks in the city with her father. He was a querulous, hypochondriacal man whose regimen included the postprandial constitutional, an expedient prescribed by his Park Avenue internist. When Sukey wanted time with him, she would tag along, ignored but secure in her father's presence.

One treat on these outings was a visit to Lascoff's, an ancient-looking pharmacy. Lascoff's sat on the southeast corner of Lexington and Eighty-second, in a German neighborhood, Yorkville. (I am not a superstitious man, but I took it as a further sign of intertwined destinies that Sukey's memory should take place so close to the bar advertised on my father's matchbooks.) The windows of Lascoff's were not filled with merchandise, as they would be today, but with antique ceramic canisters, labeled in Latin, gold leaf on black, decorated with maroon Florentine leaves and filigree. From the ceilings behind the windows hung wrought-iron fixtures holding enormous glass show globes, pointed at the bottom and with ovoid stoppers at the top. The show globes and stoppers were filled with colored liquid, brilliant golds and reds and an especially vibrant medicinal green.

If Sukey ventured inside, when her father picked up his medicine or a packet of Chesterfield regulars, the German-accented pharmacist might call her *Liebchen* and let her climb to the wooden balcony. Up close, the show globes were as big as Sukey was, as big as a child. If she was especially lucky, the pharmacist would walk her along the balcony and let her reach into a ceramic jar and feel leeches, cool and slimy and deliciously frightening, or better, let her feed the leeches a dollop of cornmeal. When a ballplayer got a shiner at Yankee Stadium or the Polo Grounds, the team doctor would send to Lascoff's for leeches to take down the swelling. On the best of nights, her father might buy Sukey a small bag of Lascoff's honey and horehound drops, hard candies that looked like leeches and made her tongue pucker with their sourness. An acquired taste, very adult.

This was an evening in February, dark and frosty. Sukey was maybe eight or nine—home from boarding school for a long weekend. She was bundled in her favorite coat, red with black piping and a black fur collar, but she was wearing shoes, not boots, and her feet were cold. She stomped them on the brownstone steps outside Lascoff's, which, to her disappointment, was closed for the holiday. No leeches, no horehound. She was bored. She pled with her father to flag a cab.

Instead, in a rare display of whimsy, he said that he was going to appoint her Tsarina of New York. The Tsarina had a special job, to rid the city of ugliness. On the walk home, in each block Her Majesty was to select one building for destruction.

Sukey took to her royal obligation with vigor. Should she choose a building with a business she did not like, one where a shopkeeper was curt with children? No, she must stick to her goal, the beauty of her city. What was remarkable once she had taken on the job was how necessary it seemed. A modern apartment that shaded old brownstones, a garish storefront, a standard postwar high-rise built with no effort to accommodate its neighbors—each transgressor was a candidate for demolition. Her father listened to her choices. Sukey found that what she most disliked were facades with undecorated windows, plate glass framed in metal, blank eyes on the city. Windows made only for looking out, the opposite of Lascoff's. These apartments took from the city without giving in return. Down they came.

Until now Sukey had forgotten that evening and her momentary closeness to her father. Was this why she had become a realtor, to exercise a skill he had bestowed? Or did it work the other way round, that she had taken to her father's suggestion because she was the sort of child who cared about her physical surroundings—

who understood what buildings say? As a sales agent, one of her strengths (in addition to her sensuality) was the ability to conjure a house's story for a buyer, what the property meant in the landscape, in the community, in an owner's life. She lent buyers her taste.

I did not know he was so like my father, I said when Sukey told me her story. Both men were harsh and distant, each passed on to his child a feeling for the quality of objects.

Shortly after the memory of the walk home from Lascoff's, Sukey began talking about a Tsarina exercise in Sesuit. She wanted me to help her with it, to plan, to speculate. It seemed a fantasy that might arise in a psychotherapy. Express your anger, hold nothing back, let your mind wander where it will. I played along.

Sukey was grappling with the big issue of midlife, what a person leaves behind. I had known little about her politics, assumed she was a Republican by birth. But she spoke about civil society in utopian terms. She expressed distaste at what she had done with the advantages she had been given. Must her legacy be zoning variances and new subdivisions? She had helped chop Sesuit into little lots on which owners would build the grandest home possible. Satisfying the wishes of unspeakable men. Sometimes it was hard to discern the object of her disgust, the real estate or the men.

She had sold by seduction, that had been her choice, and it had also been a compulsion and what was expected and hoped for from her. If you were a man and you looked at homes with Sukey Kuykendahl, you got to ride beside a stately blonde in a flashy, breezy car—in the seventies a Grand Prix convertible, in the nineties a Lexus with sunroof. You got a whiff of her perfume and of the liquor on her breath and a taste of her energy, her teasing, her frankness, her ability to bring you up short. You got to see her in the property you were considering, could imagine how it would be if you were single, if something happened to your wife, if you left your wife. You saw yourself in a home with one or another feature, water view or water access or wraparound deck, cathedral ceiling, skylights, modern kitchen, gargantuan master bedroom, you in a home with oh so many features and a stately blonde with an air of knowing all the tricks and who understands you, where you belong, which setting corresponds to your character when you are at your most attractive.

If you imagined that after the closing there might be a christening of the purchase, a roll in the hay with the classy realtor who had touched you at just the right moment, grabbed your arm in an access of enthusiasm at the instant you had found your ideal house, or a compromise that came close enough, if you dreamed that there would be a consummation of the contract, you would like as not be right and pleased and satisfied and adult enough to settle for its being just that once. And when a friend asked you how you had found your summer home, he would hear a certain music in your voice or he would have seen this striking figure of a woman around the town and he would say: I see, Sukey Kuykendahl.

He would call and ask her what else there was on the market, what there was to be had, and she would oblige. Or if you had a home to sell, your mind would turn to Sukey whatever you thought of her, and you would remember what you had heard, that she could make things move. Although less so after the drink had gotten to her; she had less glamour as she aged.

Which was why she had reentered Manny's care.

One day—this was not long after the memory of the walk in New York with her father—Sukey grabbed me by the arm, while I was driving, and said: He thinks I have a repetition compulsion.

She enunciated the phrase in her deepest voice, with implicit quotes around it.

He used those words? Already I knew Manny well enough to be surprised that he would use technical language.

He says I am forever my mother the night of the fire. My mother disappointing and enraging my father by betraying him with a man who is beneath her. As if my father were the only man in my life, and I were compelled continually to elicit emotion from him as my mother did, through guilty acts.

Manny said that?

Indirectly. He said, If this were the good old days and I were a Freudian, I might interpret . . .

How did you respond?

I tried yelling at him, she said. He interrupted and said he finds it charming when a life has a theme. I was taken aback. I thought he was mocking me. Then as if thinking aloud, he said, Age is not an absolute impediment, she might be able to carry on for another decade.

So unlike him, I said.

He was talking to himself, considering a possibility.

By now Sukey was whispering. And here she laid her head on my shoulder. She was sobbing, shaken by the understanding that she would have to change, find another way to cope.

Not long after, she began to fantasize about a campaign of destructive beautification. A new life. An undoing of her old life.

I had been through detox enough with Sukey to know how it worked. Six or eight months out, she would enjoy a burst of energy, she would look and feel more solid, she would meet some man who excited her.

This time you are my men, she told me. You and Manny.

Later, I came to think that Manny had assigned me to her—that part of her recovery was to rehabilitate me. His method was to help the paralyzed and the queasy by assigning them one another for rehabilitation.

Regarding the Tsarina project, I found I had opinions. That was a sign of my own recovery. For years after your mother left, I had taught, puttered, listened to the wind on the water. I let others have their head and observed what they did with it. Which wasn't so bad a way to live as you might imagine. Suddenly, the capacity to take a stand returned. Of course, the stances were largely your mother's. She had shaped my politics.

No marketing, I might say, on a typical drive. We are awash in marketing. People's very clothes speak. Declaring their allegiance to what they consume. No hints of Madison Avenue. Remember the anarchists who attacked the world trade meetings, in D.C., in 2000? How their media savvy made them look frivolous? As if for all their complaining about exploitative corporations, they started the day with a sip of Starbucks and ended it with a shot of Absolut.

No manifesto. If you explain a piece of what you intend, you will be accused of committing terror for too trivial a cause. Address the big picture, you'll look nutty. Think of the Unabomber's manifesto, third-rate Thoreau. When he was known only through his fastidious work, the Unabomber was a figure to be reckoned with. Handmade wooden boxes, with electronic elements cobbled together from simple parts—despite the terrible harm they did, those objects were eloquent. Making the case for handcrafting over mass production. Words trivialize. Each act must speak for itself.

With Sukey, I might ask: Why must terrorists propose solutions? If solutions appear distant, that may be the vision appropriate to radicalism in our time. It is a contribution to remind our audience of the supreme theme of art and song: The world is too much with us. Getting and spending we lay waste our powers.

I might say, The summer house has become a form of marketing, boasting on behalf of the owner: Any campaign of anarchism must embody a new ideal, of modesty. It does no good to oppose marketing with marketing.

No change but through marketing, Sukey would insist.

My concern was that revolt is rapidly co-opted. Teens pierce their navels, and immediately a sitcom shows a mock-rebellious daughter discussing belly-button jewels with her mock-scandalized parents. Two days later, a toy company announces it is featuring a line of stick-on TummyGems for children. The spectacle is infinitely absorptive: commerce as ultratampon, with the universal risk of toxic shock.

As Camus says, we are Sisyphus, escaping slavery only in a brief interval, the walk down the hill. How to prolong that hiatus? The more explicit a protest—the closer to advertising in its form—the more quickly it is metabolized. Think of the Seattle riots, over the WTO. No sooner do the protesters declare their goals than the president co-opts them: We, too, want fair labor practices—as if the government and the anarchists shared a concept of fairness. I thought silence stood the best chance of opening an interval of freedom.

Sukey disagreed. The problem with Seattle was not co-optation but symbolism. Men in black shirts shattering windows of small shopkeepers. Look like Nazis, you'll be taken as Nazis. The key to a campaign is control of image. Politics is symbols, Sukey would say. The outstretched fist—black power: transformative.

I would answer: Think of the speed with which defiance is alchemized into spectacle. Now no ad for an amusement park but a tyke shoots up a fist in victory. Yes! The joy of induction into the consumer role. Although I notice that now the fist is as often pulled down toward the body, down and in. Yes!

Hank, do you Yes! when you score a goal? We did manage to express pleasure before the television provided the gestures. I remember a private glow in the body, a modest shake of the head as if to say this time it was my turn and next time it will be yours. A modest shake belied by a small grin despite the effort at self-control. Now there is no small success but it partakes of spectacle, of rebellion co-opted into consumption.

Sukey would respond: The modest pose was gesture in its day, the "aw-shucks" big-screen cowboy on the playing field. Marketing shapes every private gesture, has done so for the whole of our lives.

We had these conversations repeatedly, crossing the pitch-pine forest to mid-Cape, wending our way to Manny's subdivision. So many gray days.

I said, We must have no message.

Sukey said, A high ratio of image to content is the mark of a great publicity campaign. You remember the Harvard strike in '69, Sukey said. Brilliant publicity, about nothing and everything. Strike to seize control of your life. Strike to become more human. Strike because they are trying to squeeze the life out of you. A simple message. Ununiversity. Uncapitalism.

Sukey was tempting me. The Harvard strike came in our glory days, your mother's and mine. Anais's particularly. Riffling through the papers in University Hall. Suffering arrest, but not before having passed incriminating documents on to colleagues on the steps, strategic plans for the university's expansion—evidence that the means of expansion, the method of depressing property values and buying buildings on the cheap, was calculated, not happenstance. I'll tell you who she was back then: Emma Goldman crossed with Greta Garbo, a revolutionary with a need to disappear from view.

Sukey was right. The substance of the strike proved unimportant. The university continued its expansion. A black studies program emerged—conservative, opposed to activism. Banning ROTC from campus had no effect on the military's willingness to send poor inner-city boys to fight poorer farm boys in Indochina.

Critics of the student strike complained it favored style over substance, but the styles had lasting value. A sexual ease and openness that mocked and questioned American conformity and repression. Hippie dress, the Dylan growl, the Ginsberg howl that stood in opposition to the American dream with its fatal flaws of production without meaning, emptiness amidst plenty. If the medium is the message, why is it apt criticism to say a political struggle favors style over substance? Here is where I agreed with Sukey, style matters. But there is something to be said for style that arises from the streets, not Madison Avenue, not marketing campaigns.

We were discussing daydreams, but Sukey demanded we take our choices seriously. Which houses, what sequence.

Was access a problem? For years and without knowing why, Sukey had saved spare keys and alarm codes. I had a similar library of means of entry—in this house, the bulkhead doesn't latch; in that one, the owner hides a key chain in the overturned soap dish in the outdoor shower. My collection seemed a sign that Sukey's fantasy might have come to me independently, had I been open to it.

Access aside, what goes first? That was a game we played often. Sukey favored oceanfront behemoths. In the wake of Giampiccolo's success in skirting the building code, a series of monuments to narcissism had sprung up, landowners using every trick in the book to evade the rules the community had set for itself. Sukey's personal favorite for demolition was a Xanadu still in the framing stage that featured a tower above the roofline that would house a billiards room, the skyline ruined from the beach below so that a Hollywood producer—Harold "Woody" Woodcock—might have a setting in which to smoke cigars twice a year with East Coast sycophants.

The house was an exercise in hubris. Because of the height restrictions, the basement was set fourteen feet below grade, to give space for a screening room and a luxurious gym, its curved walls formed of television screens showing real-time images of sand and surf, broadcast from cameras on the tower above. Instead of a jog along the beach, a guest could enjoy a climb on the StairMaster, in air-conditioned comfort, the arbitrariness of nature averted. A pumping system would work round the clock to keep the sea at bay.

I proposed a gradual approach. Mix small houses in with large. And use an architectural progression. Destroy seawalls first. Then external supports, such as the stilts and pilings holding up overhanging rooms. Then garages, perhaps a small fertilizer bomb in an attached garage, enough to take out the side wall of the home. Then basements. And finally living areas. In the hopes that the police would always be a step behind, searching outside when the next bomb would be in. At each stage, we would increase the level of sophistication of the explosives and igniters.

Not that we had explosives, we were merely outlining our tastes and our standards, as men and women will: I love this movie, I can't stand that song. Discussions that permit us to display ourselves to one another. To strike a balance of sameness and difference. If you have dated a girl, you have had this sort of conversation. The difference is that we chatted about destroying commodities, not consuming them, and that through our conversation, I was trying to keep Sukey alive. Talk of violence seemed to blunt her appetite for liquor and abusive men. Our serialized fantasy gave incentive for her to step into the car and head to the doctor.

She is obsessed, I said to Manny in one of my visits. She rotates among addictions. Booze. Lovers. Now this endless talk of aesthetic anarchism.

He answered, Why is she obsessed and you not?

He seemed to admire her passion. With Manny's permission, I entered more fully into Sukey's fantasy. I discovered that I had my own sense of what an anarchist campaign would look like. I said, We must be in the tradition of the modern, like Monet.

I meant the famous appreciation of the *Water Lilies,* a quotation your mother loved. The one where the critic praises the work for what it is without. Without design or boundary. Without "art." Without the security of form. Without vignette, without anecdote, without fable. Without category. Without body and without face.

Seinfeld, Sukey said, automatically translating into the language of marketing.

Nothing, she said. A campaign about nothing.

Content is everywhere, I said. The spectacle provides all the content anyone could wish for.

We create nothing, she said, and the culture fills the void.

13

✳

Rights

On the crucial point Sukey and I agreed. Our focus would be beachfront homes. For Sukey it was a matter of taste, the ugliness of greedy houses on the dunes. For me, it was a matter of attacking a small exemplar of capitalism. And a matter of memory—memory of you, in our summer of reading.

The press have speculated that the Free the Beaches movement targets the idiosyncratic law allowing the intertidal beach to be private in Massachusetts and its offspring Maine. Though it takes our purpose too narrowly, that reading of our behavior is not wrong.

The law is strange: To develop the Massachusetts seacoast, King Charles I granted colonists land ownership down to mean low water, a right that precedes the U.S. Constitution. The decree was meant to encourage owners to build docks, while the public retained rights to fish, hunt, or navigate, which is most of what anyone did on beaches in the seventeenth century. But under capitalism, private ownership trumps communal use. Now the land's value lies in its exclusivity—the owners' power to ban sunbathers. To ban anyone to mean low water, which on the bay side can be scores of yards out.

When your kite swooped to earth past the boundary at Quivet Cove and Dotty Arnold yelled at you, that is why she had the right. Your kite was on her beach. That moment stuck with me. It is one of the intimate inspirations for Free the Beaches.

We were having a tough day with reading, I remember. The problem was line scanning—you skipped the small words. And so we took what we called a swim break, only you wanted to fly a dragon kite you had been given for your birthday the previous fall. You bounced with excitement as we drove to Quivet Cove.

A breeze at beach level allowed us to get the kite aloft, but the next layer of air was gusty. The kite would rise and tumble, rise again and then crash to earth. The kite was rainbow-colored, intense red blending to intense orange and so on through the spectrum. You loved lucid color. What had appealed to Sukey in a drugstore window appealed to you in your toy.

We headed to the edge of the public beach, to avoid dive-bombing the sunbathers. That was our mistake. The kite shot upward, spiraled, and before we had time to reel the line in, swooped down near Dotty, who sat in splendid isolation on her private stretch of sand.

The kite landed ten feet from her, but she startled as if approached by muggers. This is my beach, don't you know this is my beach, she shrilled.

She was dressed in an Asian peasant's outfit, loose-fitting, pajama-style pants and top, and a wide-brimmed, round hat that attached with a string under the chin, all in lacquer red. She began to flap her arms like a crane about to ascend. You ran toward her to collect your kite, but she kept yelling about her need for privacy and her blood pressure. You froze, in fear of this overwrought grown-up. Rolling string and framing an apology, I headed toward you.

By now Dotty was shooing with her hands, flags of red silk shaking at you. A beefy neighbor chugged in from his own private plot of land to help. Can't people control their kids? he yelled, and he crushed your kite. Just like that. Picked it up by the struts and broke them, snap, snap, snap. It was not enough to disable the kite, he had to mutilate it.

Can't you see that the poor woman is sensitive?

That was his cry. Then he began gathering string from his end, approaching me menacingly, telling me to get off the poor woman's land. I stood my ground. I was beaten up too often as a child to fear a blow or two. And I was made brave by your presence.

I stood beside you while the man blustered. To my surprise he stopped and caught hold of himself. I now think he was imagining what would happen if he, a rich man, struck me, a poor man. Would I sue? Would I sue him even now, for traumatizing a child?

Seeing him collect himself, I imagined he must have a history of violence, this man. Later when I was in his house, I took a good look at the family photos. He is single; there are pictures of grown children from three wives. The correspondence file on his computer has pathetic, begging letters to various of the children. Apologies for past misdeeds, promises of future devotion. I found I wanted to spare the house. The man's life was punishment enough. Besides, revenge is motive; motive leads to capture. Revenge is not absurd.

The man stood nose to nose with me and then—here was perhaps the most telling aspect of the incident—he reached into his swim-trunk pockets and took out a $100 bill and threw it at me.

He said: Here, buy your kid another kite.

And as a parting shot: Don't you think you should teach him to respect other people's property?

I took the money.

You were sobbing now. We would buy another kite, and you would have an ice-cream soda at the Erica's Tuition roadside stand; but the day was ruined. Ruined except for that question, which was a valuable one. What should I teach you about property, about Dotty Arnold and her plot of Quivet beachfront, the plot that allows her to be fussy and self-righteous, buffered (except for the stray kite) from the compromises of communal life?

How does one explain ownership? Via the social contract? Had you made a contract, and when? The moment you emerged from the womb of an anarchist potter? Was it then that you acceded to Dotty Arnold's rights to a stretch of Quivet Cove? Or had you not yet signed on, seeing that you did not understand the basis of Dotty Arnold's right to scream, given that you were, for most purposes, still incompetent to contract?

If you had not joined in an agreement that Dotty Arnold controls the sand the bay washes over, then ownership might need to rest on another basis, not a contract but objective morality. What would that moral basis be, that leaves the earth and its bounties in the hands of the few?

For most of history, men acceded to the divine right of kings. Where is that morality now? There is no contract, no moral equity. There are power and politics, inertia and lack of imagination. Perhaps you were born not to ratify the social contract but to renegotiate it, scrutinize it, mock it, expose its inadequacies by having your kite fall to earth. Those were the fevered thoughts I had that summer day, shaken as I was by the behavior of Dotty Arnold and her irascible neighbor.

As in a Freudian dream, the theme of beach ownership is arbitrary and overdetermined—relating to a particular moment and also to my most profound feelings. The beach was a release for you the summer you learned to read. You taught me how necessary the beach can be.

I know that, objectively seen, beach ownership is a trivial issue. Dotty Arnold notwithstanding, owners' rights are weakly enforced. In many places, strangers may walk on a private beach, so long as they do not sit and sun themselves, so long as they do not go for a swim. Some private beaches are all but unknown to outsiders. (Who had heard of the Sesuit Sachem's Head Association before we completed our attack on the access road to their beach—the explosions that stranded members on their exclusive stretch of coastline, the night of their midsummer cookout?) There is much National Seashore, there are many state and town beaches. Should it matter if a few hundred families have private rights here and there?

Beach ownership is a nonissue. On this field of insubstantiality,

Sukey's dreams and mine might coexist. She could create image in excess of content, I could indulge in anarchism that honors the modern aesthetic. "When Fantasies Overlap" is the title of a chapter in Manny's book. Not that lovers think alike, but that their dreams share common space.

14

*

Where There's a Way

And then in August, Sukey came up with explosives, source unknown.

Take me for a spin, Chip, she said. She produced a pair of keys and swung them tauntingly, like a deb at a dance who has a suite upstairs.

I took out the truck and headed off-Cape with her—a Trip to Nowhere, of the sort that bus companies use to fill their spare weekends. Right at this exit, left at the foot of the ramp. Sukey became garrulous, chattering and joking. I worried that she had resumed drinking or taken up with a flattering lover. What's got into you? I asked, but she answered only with a coquettish look.

That is an aspect of her you do not see on television. For all that she has aged and put on weight, she can still tease suggestively and not seem ridiculous, at least not to me.

Faster, faster, she commanded, impatient with my attention to speed limits. We ended up in an industrial park outside Boston, at one of those rent-a-room storage facilities that advertise with billboards fronting the highway. One key fit a lock on a section of fence at the rear of the property, an unmonitored spot, far from the guard station, free of video cameras. The second key gave entry through a gray metal door opening on a low-ceilinged, ground-floor storeroom.

The room was filled neatly with cardboard cartons, wooden crates, and metal trunks. They were stacked in clusters, with rows between to allow access. Buzzing fluorescent lamps hung from the ceiling. Dust flickered about the boxes, so they appeared through a jaundiced haze. I noticed stenciled exclamation points. Caution! Fireworks! Extreme Care!

Roman candles. Chrysanthemum flares. Sukey looked crestfallen.

You expected . . . ? I asked.

She slid aside a stack of cartons labeled Cherry Bombs. Behind was an unmarked crate. Sukey asked if it could be opened. I went to the truck for a small crowbar. The crate was old. As it splintered, the lid sent a shower of wood chips into the air. The crate contained igniters. Like the cardboard at the center of toilet-paper rolls, only thinner. Half an inch in diameter, two to three inches long. Another row back, we found plastique, like Silly Putty in Saran Wrap. Then boxes of nitrocellulose explosives.

You and me, Sukey said.

The room was filled with matériel. Powders, plastics, tins and canisters, complex equipment. Here and there, Sukey stopped to open a carton. She would call me over to marvel.

In time, I would learn what was what: dynamite, compound A5, compound H6, compound B. Octol, PBXs, cartridged explosives with hole borers and cartridge loaders. Entire systems for excavation and demolition. And old military equipment—launchers and mortars, complete with live shells.

I did not need to know much to appreciate what we had happened upon. Toward the rear was a metal desk flanked by wire baskets interlocked to form bookcases. In the baskets were technical manuals. Some dated back forty years. The most recent were five years old. If the manuals reflected the contents of the boxes, we were in a secret museum of explosives of the late twentieth century.

Sukey had a hilarity about her. Amidst the piles of cartons, she no longer looked stout. Elfin rather, and light on her feet. She picked up the crowbar and danced, tapping it against the crates as she sashayed down an aisle. Half in love with easeful death, I thought, and the quote reminded me of why I had come this far. To save Sukey from self-destruction. Though from the start I must have known also that this project would be mine, that Sukey's wishes were my wishes.

The fireworks, I gathered, were a cover. Whoever had rented the room—an unlicensed contractor? a mob figure? a terrorist group?—had slipped the UStowIt manager some heavy extra cash, insurance against nosiness. We understand each other, pal? If the manager suspected something fishy, he would stick his head in and see Fourth of July paraphernalia, illegal in Massachusetts, a peccadillo.

Hard to believe it's all ours, Sukey said.

From whom? I asked.

A secret admirer, was all Sukey said. I could get nothing more out of her.

In the face of her joy, I felt hurt and betrayal. My guess was that she had seduced or blackmailed a lover into offering this cache. She had opened her fantasy to another man, a fantasy I had believed linked her to me. It struck me as odd that I should feel jealous over Sukey in this way, when I had never been jealous over your mother and her travels. I had changed, unless it was only that my conversations with Sukey, full of illicit imaginings, had seemed more intimate than sex or marriage.

From the start, I suspected that the admirer was Giampiccolo. He was a contractor, he had mob ties, he was a man with whose ways Sukey was familiar. Later I came to believe that Giampiccolo's benefaction was involuntary. There are men who might think it sport to see their house hoist with their own petard, but I doubted he was one.

Had Sukey used her playfulness to draw me into a plot that would now unfold? I asked her how long she had known of the cache.

Yesterday, she said. Out of the blue I got a note with keys enclosed.

Life is not that way. You do not dream up a scheme and then magically happen upon the means to carry it out. I wanted to say: There is something you have done, Sukey, to make this collection appear. But I did not question her further. It was good to see her jubilant.

Even before the visit to the storage shed, we had been playing seriously at Sukey's game. Once more I had dropped my summer courseload, this time to work with Sukey, chauffeuring her with high-end clients. In exchange, BaySky sent fix-up jobs my way and recommended me to other realtors.

Sukey began showing me homes as a prospective buyer. She told her colleagues that I wanted out of the cottage because of its association with your loss. (I do often find the place too poignant to bear. I store my school papers in your room, my own childhood bedroom. Sometimes I sit on your bed and find myself unable to move.) Sukey let on that I wanted another waterfront property, was keen to see the whole range, including ones beyond my means.

The French situationists favored an activity they called *dérive*, drifting—wandering aimlessly through a neighborhood. Appreciating buildings with an artist's eye, disconnected from their usual functions—de-riveted, that was the pun in French. I joined Sukey in her drifting. In retrospect, it served a concrete purpose, creating a record of legitimate visits to beachfront homes that later collapsed with my DNA on-site.

In Sukey's presence, I had begun to peruse houses, ultimately to edit them. Like you, I had my summer of learning to read. And like you, with intimate encouragement, I flourished. At first it was a matter of empathy with Sukey. Standing beside her, I would notice what she noticed, a structure's discourteousness or presumption. I tried to read houses on many levels, how they are used, how they sit on the land, what effect (frightening or humorous) their destruction might bring about, in a sequence of explosions.

But Marx was right: Mankind always sets itself only such tasks as it can solve; since, looking at the matter more closely, we will always find that the task itself arises only when the material conditions necessary for its solution already exist or are at least in formation. Whatever our fantasies, Sukey and I were not terrorists until we opened the storage room door.

Once we had explosives, I came to take in houses operationally—the opportunities they presented for the placement of charges or the wiring of ignition signals. I began to see as an anarchist does. The house de-riveted from its function as trophy or habitation; the house as vulnerable structure. The explosives held a promise of deeper vision yet, vision through praxis, discovering by hand, intimate knowledge.

Not until weeks after we had visited our cache did Sukey walk me to the Giampiccolo house. She was wise to have saved that stroll. Without the explosives, I don't know that I would have seen how the Giampiccolo house wanted to go down.

The house contained another material condition, the tools to craft installations. Sukey showed them to me the evening of that dark September day.

We had toured the remaining sections of the ground floor: ostentatious guest bedrooms, overloaded home office, chinoiserie den with black lacquer walls and a second entertainment system, this one tuned to MTV. We headed upstairs to the master bedroom. Silk sheets, satin bedspread, suggestively placed mirrors. Everywhere photos of the owner with one or another minor celebrity, one or another babe. The playboy suite. In the walk-in cedar closet were rows of clothing, formal and casual, often in trios. Three

Ralph Lauren workshirts. Three pairs of stonewashed Calvin Klein jeans. Armani suits. Bally shoes, Vasque boots, Mephisto sandals. The summerhouse wardrobe.

Anything your size? Sukey asked.

Giampiccolo is my height, roughly six feet, though broader in the shoulders. In photos, he has the exaggerated muscular build that in a well-to-do man of middle age bespeaks a personal trainer. (His bathroom cabinet is stocked with bodybuilding hormones, DHEA and steroids.) My own waist has given way, as waists will. I might not have made it into the suits and bespoke shirts. But I have kept up my swimming, if only as a way of remembering your summer of reading and my honeymoon with Anais. I could see myself in Giampiccolo's less-fitted clothes.

I said, Why do you ask?

A thought, Sukey said. Then she suggested we take a look at the basement, an offer that would prove as seductive as her invitation years before to accompany her to the attic.

The Giampiccolo house contained the means of its own destruction—in the form of an utterly up-to-date woodshop that inhabited a windowless space tucked into the dune. In keeping with the rest of the house, the shop was cavernous and expensively equipped. Band saws, circular saws, routers, drills, lathes, sanders—what did it not contain? The walls were covered with fine hand tools: Japanese handsaws, British planes and files, German miter boxes, and an array of hammers, screwdrivers, and chisels. Clamps hung from ceiling racks. A chest-high caddy displayed a hardware store's worth of nuts and bolts, brads and nails, most in unopened packages. Paints, shellacs, and varnishes had their own case of shelves. Along a wall was stacked an ambitious collection of boards—pine, oak, hickory, fruitwood. Dense-grained, cabinet-quality walnut. Figured woods: bird's-eye maple, spalted maple, curly beech. The concrete floor had already begun to crack, from the weight of the machinery or shoddy construction or the shifting of sands below.

What is it? I asked.

Sukey understood me well enough to answer, A shrine.

To carpentry, she explained. Giampiccolo's father was a union carpenter in Boston until his death ten years ago.

What sort of man? I wondered.

Dismissive, Sukey continued, as if in answer. Dismissive, sarcastic, eternally disappointed.

Like mine, was the implication. Giampiccolo was my doppelgänger, with my height and my history. He had solved the challenges of childhood by different means. Self-aggrandizement. Acquisition. The exercise of arbitrary power. This woodshop was his Rosebud, the sign of the early wishes that made him tick.

Later, Sukey spoke of his childhood. Father a union official in the North End back when unions had clout; "connected"—not "made," but tied in. The Giampiccolos had a cottage in North Eastham, spent summers by Cape Cod Bay. Unhappy ones. Mother chronically ill, father violent, Johnny caught in the middle. The mother was Irish. Apparently a woman who could bring you up short, make you laugh. Her name was Mary Moira. She died when he was a teenager, leaving Little John at the mercy of the tough-guy father. Whom he continued to emulate. Desperately, tastelessly. The basement room contained a single work-in-progress, an Adirondack chair. I recognized the design from *The New Yankee Workshop*.

Giampiccolo had chosen an easy project, begun it sloppily, and given up at an early stage. It exasperated me to think of this wealth of tools in the hands of a man who could not use them. This was the woodshop my father should have had. According to his needs and ability.

The ways of contemporary life. We trust in purchases. First buy the finest golf clubs, then learn to play the game—why begin with a handicap? Even when I was a boy, when I worked cleaning boats in the marina, there were men who bought a yacht first and learned how to sail later.

Then why not equip a woodshop in your summer home to impress the guests? Or to impress yourself, if you are an insecure son who requires a symbolic victory over a dismissive father. Is one form of conspicuous consumption worse than another?

My life would have been easier if, like your mother at midlife, I had come to accept capitalism. My father acquiesced to the distribution of goods. He was an artisan, content to serve a patron. Whereas from the start, I wondered. Why did Mrs. K have walls covered with books when she never opened one? Why did Sukey, who was here rarely, live in Stone House, when I lived year-round in the cottage? What I found hardest to comprehend was my father's condition: How could he be so skilled and have so little? Since childhood, I have lived with confusion about the justification for ownership.

Standing before the pride of machinery in Giampiccolo's basement, I thought of a moment in Zola when a man throws his toolbag into the Seine. Like my father, the man is an artisan, only he is unemployed, unable to feed his family. He has come from planting a bomb at the door of a Parisian mansion, the bomb that will kill the pathetic errand girl. That passing detail moved me. I understood what it is for an artisan to discard his toolbag—despair without mitigation.

My father tended to his tools, sharpened them, oiled them, handled them with affection. Manny asked me once whether I felt my father loved his tools more than he loved me. No, I said. His values were right. The tools were the product of knowledge passed down for centuries. I was an unformed boy, a boy who never learned to dovetail a corner.

About Zola's artisan: He is hunted down like a fox, in the Bois de Boulogne. He has not eaten for three days. The hunt is timed to coincide with a political scandal, in hopes that the capture of an anarchist will divert public attention. There was my introduction to social theory.

Giampiccolo's shop cried out to be put to good use.

Do with it what you will, Sukey said.

She explained that Giampiccolo was not expected back. He had crossed the wrong partners. Among others, a certain Big Eddie. Giampiccolo was in hiding, rumored to be in the South. Not welcome on the Cape.

From scattered stories she told me on our rides home from Manny's, I had a sense of how Sukey knew. She had been involved with Giampiccolo, as an outgrowth of a real-estate transaction. Involved romantically with a cruel and appealing man. Giampiccolo had degraded Sukey. This would have been many months back, toward the end of Sukey's drinking days. She did not tell me the specifics, and I did not ask. Giampiccolo must have gotten her drunk and then humiliated her in a sex act. Videotaped it perhaps and used the tape to mock her, a middle-aged woman who carries on like a femme fatale. Taped her or tricked her into exposing herself in front of others.

I have an impression of what happened, from Sukey's reaction to old movies. One night, we were watching the Robert Altman film *Nashville,* and the stripper scene came on, the scene of sexual degradation. Sukey jumped up and asked to be driven home. Another time she threw Buñuel's *Belle de Jour* into the VCR and then thought better of it.

Humiliating relationships were not new to Sukey. But now she had benefited from therapy with Manny. He encouraged her to sit still long enough to feel what she felt. The nausea that leads to self-degradation and the nausea that arises from it.

I gathered that it was Sukey who got Giampiccolo into trouble, betrayed him to his tough-guy partners. She searched the files in his computer and forwarded relevant ones to interested parties. Or she passed on physical documents relating to real-estate sales whose profits had not been shared. I could imagine her biding her time, playing the dumb blonde, making contacts at cocktail parties in the great room. I could see her cutting a deal with Giampiccolo's associates: I give you the goods, you give me a few months alone in the house. She moved funds out of one of Giampiccolo's accounts, to settle up; such transfers are easily accomplished nowadays.

Giampiccolo had escaped with his life. The pleasure Sukey took in implicating him in our crimes told me as much. That and the way she looked over her shoulder.

Giampiccolo's woodshop came equipped with its own restaurant-size espresso machine, alongside a minifridge that stored the coffee. I fixed us each a cup and we drank to the future, drank Lavazza from Giampiccolo's Empire-style gilt demitasses. Sukey suggested we fling the cups on the floor, to signal life's irreversibility. There was our Rubicon, I suppose, though we were not yet outlaws and (more to the point) I had long since thrown my lot in with Sukey.

Later Sukey would convince me when crafting installations to wear Giampiccolo's boots and work clothes. You look so much alike, Sukey would say.

Giampiccolo had a full-size Ford pickup in the garage, worker chic; we used it to transfer explosives, drove it to job sites.

Sukey added film noir details to our work. For some time, she had gathered Giampiccolo's hair from bathroom brushes. Now she strewed it liberally in spots the FBI would later search. Semen, too, from when he had jerked off watching her; she had scraped it from the sheets or saved the towels. She had read about the technique years ago in a legal mystery, though Ms. Lewinsky has a lot to answer for, too.

Giampiccolo was our silent partner. Where I went, Giampiccolo went. His footprints, his threads, his DNA, his hammers and his nails.

I would love to sit with you someday and discuss the morality of this choice, implicating a man in a cause in which he has no interest. I take it as a given that Giampiccolo is wicked, I trust Sukey's convictions in that regard, and the testimony of the man's house and of the community at large. I am aware, too, that the state may not administer justice against the wealthy or against molesters of women. But my willingness to steal Giampiccolo's identity rested on my belief that, given the trouble he had made for himself, nothing I could do would materially worsen his circumstances. The man had to stay underground or risk death.

Arguments about justice trouble me. In an unjust society there is no privileged spot from which the right can be seen, as regards individuals. It is easy to know that property is theft, harder to know that one person's wealth is more ill-gotten than another's. Beyond Giampiccolo, this agnosticism about justice is an aspect of the Movement that the press got wrong consistently.

If a man has worked, say, importing coffees produced through the burning of rain forests, and if to create a situation I then select that man's beachfront home for destruction, it will not be with the intention of avenging a crime against the planet. I understand the coffee importer's imperative to move enough beans to pay the mortgage on the second home he needs to make himself feel like a winner in a culture that would otherwise brand him a loser. I understand that the coffee importer is, as he would doubtless put it, only a middleman.

Most of us are middlemen. Alongside the coffee importer are arrayed the lawyer who incorporates the business, the accountant who minimizes its tax burden, the politician who creates the loopholes in the tax code, the insurer, the business-software developer, the shipping expediter and the retailer, and their lawyers and accountants, and so on in a long chain. Not forgetting the realtor who sells the importer his second home, a home on the beach that constitutes a sage investment of the coffee profits, nor the handyman who maintains the value of that investment. I am aware that I am a middleman, thoroughly implicated in my neighbor's choices. Even as a junior-college teacher, I am a middleman, when I enhance the consistency of the workforce—supply future wholesalers—by certifying certain youths as slightly less attention-disordered than some other youths. We are all middlemen or abettors of middlemen in an economic system that alchemizes despoiled rain forest into despoiled beachfront and culpability into prerogative.

The middleman is our Everyman. My aim is to let his story tell itself. If in selecting the middleman's house I take his profession into account, it is to enrich a narrative, about how land and houses come to be owned. Whatever delusions I may have, the belief that I can render justice is not among them.

Still, the way Giampiccolo treated women must have eased my conscience. He had photos of women everywhere. His dresser was festooned with them. Commodified women with cantilevered breasts and post-and-beam cheekbones. Icons, relating to womanhood as the computer apple, with the smooth, circular bite, relates to the mottled pippin you hold in your chilled hand as you walk the orchard. Or as the computer apple relates to a Cézanne apple—inadequate even as an ideal. Giampiccolo's women are among the social signals I recognize but do not get.

Except for Patti. Out of public view, in his underwear drawer, Giampiccolo kept a faded snapshot. Himself in his twenties, with shoulder-length hair, floppy mustache, tie-dyed shirt, and striped bell-bottoms. Beside him is a scrawny young woman in a paper dress. They were like hospital johnnies, paper dresses, that material, back before ecology, when disposable was radical because it was cheap. A freckled kid in an aqua paisley paper dress and matching cardboard earrings. A gap-toothed girl, slouching, unathletic, with a silly grin. Just the one snapshot, signed XOXOX Patti. I had seen Patti around Cambridge, years back—a comrade from Anais's affinity group in college, a wild woman who soon dropped out on drugs. I knew from Sukey that Giampiccolo's college job was delivering liquor to undergrads. Liquor and drugs both, I assumed. An easy racket, one that included coeds like Patti on the side.

Here is the best sentence Karl Marx ever wrote: Private property has made us so stupid that an object is *ours* only when we have it. Giampiccolo and I share histories: working-class families, missing mother, tough father, ties to the Cape, careers molded by college life in the sixties, contempt for the System. Where we diverged was at this question of having.

I came to think I understood the disaster with Sukey: Despite the lack of physical resemblance, Sukey momentarily reminded Giampiccolo of XOXOX Patti. Of women before they were in the same category as highflier securities. Sukey moved Giampiccolo with her lack of fitness, her confidence in her body as it is. I tried to picture it: He finds himself investing in the unbankable. Enraging, that Sukey should be unpossessable, and yet of so little objective worth.

Giampiccolo's mistake was desiring Sukey in the first place. A betrayal of the spirit of the age. If Giampiccolo had remained a turn-of-the-millennium consumer, churned women who know they are there to be churned, who are there for the exposure and the trinkets, if he had stuck with the culture of the icon, he would still be weekending in his obscene mansion on the Cape. His humanity did him in, the sentimentality capitalists risk when they have made enough and too much.

A moment of vulnerability to the authentic, and then Giampiccolo awakens from Sukey's spell, horrified at having felt tenderness for sun-damaged skin and sloppy drinking habits. He is gripped by heterosexual panic.

Merely to abandon Sukey will not suffice. He must crush her, deny his unmarketworthy desire, cauterize his mind, burn out the center of compassion. Purge the hard drive of the pathetic mother from childhood and the funky women of the sixties and this new earth-mother sorceress. But what if desire is not in memory only but in the operating system as well? There is the source of panic: the suspicion that the vulnerability cannot be expunged but is his forever. And so he sets out the standard props, maraschino cherries, liquid Godiva chocolate, spray cans of whipped cream . . .

I could not stand to follow these thoughts along. Too painful. But they allowed me to do Giampiccolo wrong, images of Patti and Sukey.

I did ask Sukey if we could make it up to him. To deflect suspicion, create uncertainty, buy ourselves time and room to operate, we would use Giampiccolo as a red herring: communicate from his computers, drive his vehicles, spend his money, use his woodshop to prefabricate elements of installations. But we must leave him something of value. Sukey agreed to give the matter thought, that was her concession to our principle of disinterest.

15

*

Praxis, Praxis

I set about taking measurements in candidate houses, shooting paint colors, checking wiring. Preparing for prefab projects, to be made up in Giampiccolo's shop to minimize time spent on-site. Assessing the possible, stretching my capabilities. Mastering the theory and practice of demolition. Converting the summer of dalliance into a winter of engagement. The key to the campaign turned out to be not carpentry but concept.

We do what we can—we give what we have. From each according to his abilities. What I had was the ability to read and critique. A familiarity with narrative styles. The junior-college English teacher's skills. The campaign is the closest I have come to artistic creation, the closest to crafting a text.

There is a post-and-beam house that was on our list for weeks, the one at the end of Dr. Fisher's Lane. Two well-placed charges in the attic would have done for the whole. It is a smug, disagreeable house, and the owner had profited from a construction deal that led to an S&L collapse, so that the money used to buy the beach was ultimately the public's. To target the home would make a neat fable about how capitalism works in practice.

That perfection was what dissuaded me. The story was too pat, and well-made dramas already crowded our list. Ours is not the era of the straight path. I was aiming for stories that would remain out of focus, set in a picaresque and even whimsical progression, a hypermodern style that reaches far back, to the *Quixote* or Rabelais. As I drove to and from work, I would intone a mantra: structure, form, genre. I passed on the house and never regretted the omission. The feds, expecting conventional narrative, swept the post-and-beam a dozen times.

You were with me, Hank. Drifting down Dr. Fisher's Lane, I thought: That house is an Easy Reader, the type Hank hated. Too predictable.

Just this month, Sukey called my attention to an article in the Hyannis paper: Remember that post-and-beam where you decided against repairs? Says here the daughter devotes herself to services for the homeless.

That's what the conversation is about, if the feds have taped it. Relief that our editorial judgment helped us avoid distractions. We lost the swindling owner, but we were spared the sympathetic daughter and the confusing irony that would have entered the narrative if we had evicted a woman who houses the needy.

While I tended to plotline, Sukey was finding her own calling. She had a heretofore untapped talent for electronics. She was adept with timers and power sources. She rewired security systems so that she could monitor their status from a station in the Giampiccolo study, allowing us to be certain, before we set off bombs, that the mined houses were unoccupied. It was Sukey who thought of using cellular modems—you program them as you would an answering machine, except that the last function of a series of digital commands is to spark an igniter. For more primitive installations, Sukey took radio transmitters from kits for remote-controlled airplanes and tuned the crystals so that they would initiate a cascade of receivers sequenced to set off a blasting cap. Oh, she was extraordinary. There is a sexually attractive trait (or so I find it) that can unfold in later life, the display of mature competencies that contrast, in memory, with early wildness.

Years of boarding school, years of college, and no one had developed Sukey's aptitudes. She is a case study in the miseducation of women. What she cannot do with computers! It was Sukey who sent out the Movement's missives, from Giampiccolo's PCs, via blind remailers in Scandinavia or Eastern Europe to Cape Cod newspapers and television studios. Warning of attacks in progress or attacks to come. A date and time and the quick signature *FtB*. Never the full name, that was part of the mystique. Letting explosions speak for themselves.

It turns out that there is a Free the Beaches organization, right-minded citizens in Marshfield and Duxbury who favor easier beach access for the wheelchair-bound. A *Boston Globe* reporter suggested FtB might mean Free the Beaches, a connection that, once proposed, made such eminent sense that three police organizations descended on the poor South Shore homeowners, to the embarrassment of all concerned.

For a week, TV and radio announcers began stories with the phrase, The putative Free the Beaches movement, not to be confused with the handicapped-rights group Free the Beaches of Massachusetts. You are too young to remember when W. E. B. DuBois Clubs were under investigation and announcers constantly reminded, Not to be confused with the Boys Clubs of America. That was how the new disclaimer sounded: complicit voices retailing the understanding that there is good and there is evil and we all can distinguish the two.

I do not want to leave the impression that Sukey's computer expertise served only for communications with the press. People keep everything on their hard drives. Passwords for office networks. Codes for bank and brokerage accounts. Calendars of upcoming vacations. Where possible, Sukey kept track of each subject's e-mail, arranging for it to be forwarded invisibly to Giampiccolo's account, which she then monitored. The messages were invaluable in keeping us abreast of families' schedule changes.

Of course, Sukey owned Giampiccolo. After locating his electronic Rolodex, she went on-line and requested he be sent replacement bank cards. Sukey had me withdraw cash regularly from the Readyteller at the Stop & Shop, to establish Giampiccolo's presence in Sesuit. Giampiccolo's on-line passwords were in the Rolodex, and they allowed Sukey to buy and sell stocks for him and transfer funds among accounts. She paid his mortgage and utilities via electronic checking.

From catalogs, Sukey had Giampiccolo sent small items that, whatever their role in terrorism, also had a straightforward domestic function: alarm clocks, high-tech batteries, outfits for me to wear on the job, paints to match the decors of targeted homes. From Web sites, using his computers she ordered the portable and wireless equipment she would rely on to monitor installations late in the summer, when the Giampiccolo workspace would be gone. Sukey's aim was to restrict herself to half-complicit purchases an overconfident terrorist might think he could get away with. She had them overnighted, no signature required. However constrained he might be in hiding, the socially critical part of Giampiccolo's identity, his capital, was at liberty here in Sesuit.

Sukey's zest had returned, and not in hectic bursts. She was abstemious and cautious—a conniving nun, joyful in service. She applied the whole of herself, her newfound computer skills and her well-established marketing skills, her playfulness and her rancor.

Following her lead, I saw that I needed to recommit to radicalism, and not halfheartedly, as when I had told your mother that I was not quite Marxist and not quite anarchist. I needed to be both and more. Teacher, reader, parent, lover, son—every role I valued had to find expression in my collaboration with Sukey. There is the lesson Sukey recalled for me, the lesson artists speak of: Save nothing for next time, spend it now.

Like a child entering a new school, I wanted to display traits not heretofore attributed to me: wit, comfort, courage. I do not mean courage in handling explosives. Sukey had the expertise there, and anyway I am a fastidious man, as prudent as any demolition roustabout. I mean courage in the creative sphere. I wanted to do in the world what I lack the talent to accomplish on the page, to create a new narrative with its own quirky thrust and logic. To shape and contribute to a movement that would be quiet and painstaking and limited in its claims, one that would express my love of story and love of ocean. Love for my father, Sukey, Anais, you.

Do you know what a mechanic's gap is? A rectangular cutout in the earth where the plumber and the electrician can stand during construction, before the rat slab is poured, in houses with crawl spaces instead of basements. On the Abrams house, in the old Salt Works section of North Eastham, the mechanic's gap was backfilled sloppily—the error came to light when wind scoured the sand from the foundation. The gap cried out for bulk explosives that require only space and not a special relationship to joist or beams. The project fit only at one point—after the garage bombs, and before the complex installations that signal terrorism's entry into the body of the home—but it fit there well, a rough tale early in a sequence of increasing complexity. Abrams was in other ways unremarkable, like a woman you love for an incidental feature, the curve of her neck when she listens intently. I did love Abrams, for its mechanical aptness—and because it added randomness to what threatened to become an edifying saga.

More often our reading extended to social context. Take Arlen-Pepper, whose seawall led off the explosions. Arlen-Pepper is the one in the famous wire service photo, a lorn dwelling perched at the edge of a carved-out sandbank. All it lacks to serve as a joke greeting card is a caption in the form of a for-sale classified: Waterfront Home, Owners Anxious.

Placement aside, the house is typical, a full Cape added on to twice in the fifties, never modernized, oriented more to road than bay. Before we altered the landscape, Arlen-Pepper sat behind a small peninsula, a phallus jutting onto the beach, its exposed sides protected by a wood-plank seawall. These dull elements masked a domestic farce that I did not appreciate until Sukey invited me inside. The house was in a time warp—avocado kitchen, beanbag chairs, Popsicle-stick lampshades. It had been years since the owners had put a nickel into decor. And every flat surface was covered with notes.

The Arlens tended toward admonition: Sweep under the sofas, check the mousetraps in the basement, and (for when the pump failed) use fresh water, not salt, to refill the toilet tanks. These imperatives were addressed not to unreliable renters but to the Peppers, who had retaliated with ownership labels: Pepper good china, not for general use. Pepper soap supply. Pepper toilet tissue—10 rolls always—replenish if used.

The couples had bought the place together and immediately fallen out. In the real-estate community, the Arlens and the Peppers were infamous. One family would arrange to have the house leased, and the other would countermand the contract. Both needed to be there in August, or both in July. Neither would sell out to the other. They were working couples, New York City public employees, schoolteachers and engineers, who had borrowed against their pensions for a down payment and now owned something valuable they needed to protect and could not bear to share. The families had enjoyed a thirty-year relationship based on contempt, mistrust, and a sense of injustice. Only for one purpose had the families united, to save the house from the sea.

Arlen-Pepper had a makeshift wooden seawall, but the lots on either side had none at all and no right to build any. Here was an undisguised case of beggar-my-neighbor. The sea would slap up against the boards and be diverted full force to the abutting properties, scooping out sand. You can never allow water behind a seawall. The sand becomes impossibly heavy and causes the wall to collapse outward. So the Arlens and the Peppers were perpetually extending the wall back to meet the receding edge of the neighbors' sandbanks, denying the sea entry. Each extension caused further scouring.

By the nineties, in winter the A-P wall was in the water half the day. Even in summer, beachcombers had to head out to sea to walk around it. Now the wall was subject to the force of currents running up or down the beach. Any loose plank, any defect in the filter barrier behind the wood, would allow the sea to saturate the sand inside. Each spring, the wall would be bowed outward, and sinkholes would have formed behind it.

The neighbors had been to court to protect their land. It turns out, in accord with our preference for haves over have-nots, that those with seawalls have near absolute prerogatives and those without (Giampiccolo and the very rich excepted) have none. Not only did the neighbors have no recourse, the Arlens and the Peppers won the right to strengthen their seawall in a fashion in favor on the West Coast. They were planning to pour reinforced-concrete posts deep into the ground at the front of the property near the road. From these indestructible stanchions would run a series of parallel steel cables, first trenched through the earth and then surrounding the seawall, like hoops holding in barrel staves. When a board was damaged, or when the sea took another foot or two from a neighbor's sandbank, another plank would be slipped in behind the cables. House on a barrel. It was the concrete pilings that got to Sukey, the hubris of changing the land forever, to protect one home.

I stood in awe of the barrel plan. Here were two couples who could not manage to share bath supplies, and they were able to come up with a pharaonic scheme for saving their joint investment, their rights, their priority.

The Arlens and the Peppers were folktale characters hobbled by the granting of a wish: Let me own a million-dollar home. From the start, I saw the potential for a comic interlude—a tale heavy on farce, light on moral, I imagined, though in the end I am not sure I got the ratio right.

The execution was simple. Lay explosive in a sinkhole behind the boards, cover with sand, wait for an impending storm. Then walk over, light a fuse, and let the sea reclaim the land. Coming early on, the installation would put the police on the wrong scent, set them to questioning the beggared neighbors. We sent up the A-P seawall in that first series of explosions in March. If the resulting image spoke, it said simply: This land is not theirs or theirs, it is the sea's.

Meanwhile Sukey made sure that her favored Web sites had scans of the renderings for the barrel scheme; in its ultimate extension, it was a wood-planked islet sitting in the bay with a fifties house atop. The networks had it on air in an instant, the man-is-an-island image, a simple visual metaphor for screw-the-consequences individualism.

As you know, we had A & P all summer. The couples were on every talk show. Sitcom rascals is what Sukey called them. The small man with the five-o'clock shadow and threatening gesticulations, the scene-stealing wife with garish hair and smeared-on clown's lipstick. Two couples of this sort, nearly identical, arguing rabidly in Bronx and Brooklyn accents in front of the nation.

What was mesmerizing was their unabashed entitlement. When the sandbank was reclaimed by the bay, the septic field went with it. The families had nowhere to rebuild one, no spot far enough from the house and the well, and meanwhile the property was legally uninhabitable. The Arlens and the Peppers petitioned for what no one before them had been granted, the right to fill in land the sea had swept away. In the meanwhile, they were reduced (or elevated) to talk of a common water district with the very neighbors they had pauperized.

The humor in this metamorphosis, anarchism turning arch-individualists into communitarians, was not lost on media commentators, despite the Arlen-Pepper lawyers' insistent reference to tragedy. One brave op-editorialist jumped on the word: If we term it a tragedy, what is the participants' tragic flaw? Possessiveness?

The human condition is exposed by tragedy: When all is said and done, we need a pot to piss in. Ecology-minded letter-writers extended the argument: We are prideful, building our cities at the ocean's edge, desiccating rivers, erecting barriers that starve beaches of sand. We are a culture of Arlens and Peppers, standing on our rights while bemoaning the erosion of the coastline.

Other responses attacked the essay for making light of misfortune. Editorials celebrated the sanctity of property, demanded that the Arlens and the Peppers be made whole. Made whole, but. Here was Sukey's public relations victory, in the qualifiers at the end of the opinion pieces. The As and the Ps should be made whole, but perhaps we might focus less on self-protection and more on cooperation. The most thoughtful essays evoked the melancholy of the human condition in parlous times. Why should the As and the Ps, who have enjoyed, or managed to fail to enjoy, the beachfront every year for thirty years, why should they be whole when none of the rest of us is? All this early on, before the press knew the form of the narrative.

Arlen-Pepper proved a useful starting point. By beginning with a neatly structured story and then straying from it, we got our readers to seek out patterns where we had planned none. With each succeeding house, members of the press were moved to ask what affront to communal values was under challenge. And they found affronts. The nature of beachfront landownership is such that there are few innocents.

True, Sukey had insisted that we enrich our sample with obvious offenders. We targeted the home of a woman who co-owned an advertising firm that ran a disinformation campaign for energy companies, debunking global warming. The neighboring house, also taken down, belonged to a man who runs two pharmaceutical factories, notorious polluters. We tried to spare artists and artisans, working stiffs and small fry, unless the structural temptations were irresistible.

Most of what reporters saw was a pattern of their own making. They found family involvement with sweatshops, a multinational weapons business, a mass-mailing firm specializing in useless cancer insurance for the elderly. I have said that old man Warelwast was no villain, but it did turn out he had invested in mining schemes that destroyed hectares of Brazilian rain forest. The little Abrams house, where we buried explosives in the mechanic's gap, had been built with gains from mineral-rights scams out West. Then there were the strictly political transgressions. Until I read the accounts in the *Globe,* I had no notion that old Les Altschuler had advised Nixon on the Parrot's Beak incursion into Cambodia or that Walter Jorgen Sr. had named names in the McCarthy era. To Sukey's simultaneous consternation and delight, the media unmasked shady land deals and zoning scams, here and elsewhere, that she had known nothing about. There were private stories regarding spousal abuse and public stories regarding pump-and-dump dot-com stock fraud. These themes overlapped and coincided, more themes than houses. If you attack the rich, you will unmask reaction and corruption. Part of the fun of radicalism is seeing results validate theory.

But for me, the exposure of gross venality had its downside. It distracted from the theme of intimate corruption—capitalism's distortion of relationship, identity, calling. Not the problem with this or that abuse within capitalism, the problem of private ownership altogether, its effect on what we desire, how we conduct our lives. I have never intended to impose political solutions on my neighbors. I have hoped to say at most, We know the dilemma we are in, the human dilemma. A dilemma only exacerbated by our efforts at social organization.

I recognize poignancy in the downfall of seawalls and houses. They are all falling anyway, giving way to the primal elements, time, wind, water. In the best-conserved of seaside homes, the radiators show rust spots, the fascia boards show rot. To stand in such a home in winter is to feel the grandeur and folly of human enterprise. To admire even greed, for the creativity (the barrel islands) it inspires. I would feel a failure if our narrative were simplified into a *Bartholomew Fair,* mocking the venality of this or that landholder. Even greed can be admirably absurd. Deep ambivalence is an underappreciated part of our message, the message we did not put into words.

16

*

Contact

Tonight I am in a hotel suite in New York. Posh, flattering. Outfitted with orchids and leaded crystal that suggest the occupant is a person of importance, sustained by the great forces of the culture, immune and untouchable.

The change in circumstance over the twenty-four hours has been disorienting. This time last night, I was in the cottage on the eroding sandbank. The dishes were dried and put away. Orion was bright in the sky. I sat at the table by the light of the student lamp, not reading, thinking, about Sukey's plan. The phone rang, and it was Anais.

To hear her voice . . . you can't imagine. Despite all I have written about my talent for faith, I was unprepared.

I suppose she introduced herself, made apologies for the long interval, or for the intrusion now. I was immersed in the voice. Firmer than before, less baby and more brass. There was fear in it. That was what absorbed my attention. Anais distraught. Instantly, I was a husband and father intent on making it right for his wife and son. It was true, the unlikely thing I have believed all these years, that we are a family—true in this sense, that when Anais phoned I did not "resume" or "rejoin," felt rather that I was with her still, in married life.

You haven't heard a word I've said.

No, Anais.

I was conscious of the muscular control it took me to say the name, the effort to push air out the throat. That is the other truth, the one that counterbalances the claim of continuity. After the long hiatus, I was unnerved by the novelty of the act, speaking with my wife. I was like a cartoon character whose feet are caught in tar, making progress slowly if at all, while his mind races.

Rumors were circulating that I was about to make an appearance on the *Today* show. I could not help wondering whether it was as Sukey had predicted, that my prominence in the spectacle had attracted Anais.

She said: If it wasn't urgent, I would have left a message with your lawyer, that attractive young woman. Or your old friend . . .

I wanted to explain it all, affirm my loyalty. At the same time, I knew it might strike Anais as odd that I had not been with a woman since she had set off to find herself in Boston, almost nine years ago. Before I had time to resolve the dilemma, she said, But I had to speak with you directly.

Then she brought down the hammer: Hank was accosted today.

I tried to take in the meaning. Accosted. A euphemism for something worse? And why call me? Had you met with no misfortune all these years? I wished it fervently. At the same time, I was frantic. I asked, In what way?

I'm not certain. You know how teenagers are.

I struggled to make sense of phrases whose meaning was obvious to Anais. How teenagers are—something she was confident I knew, and which I do want to know. In the street or at the market, I watch them. I imagine you at each age. I listen to my students when they speak of their high-school years.

How they are.

He didn't tell me until he came home for dinner. He passed it off as if it were nothing.

Like any teenager.

Chip, a man came up to Hank on the street. A man who looked like you. That's why Hank stopped to listen when the man started talking.

Hank was . . .

I don't know why it's hard to make this clear. Hank was walking from school, over to the mall. With his new buddies.

My son has buddies. Ones he did not have before. He walks from school with them. Each sentence needed to be unraveled, as in the grammar exercises I was made to do as a child.

A man sidled up. Hank slowed down because the man looked like you. He's seen you on television. Hank has. Like you, only more haggard.

More haggard.

You know what I mean, Chip. Haggard. But strikingly like you. He put a hand on Hank's arm and said something. Then the man hopped into a car. A woman had been pacing them, driving alongside. The man gave his message, and when something spooked him, he hopped in, and they sped off.

Hank waited until dinnertime—?

He's a self-contained boy anyway, quiet and shy. Like you. And now he's in that private teenager phase . . .

I heard the *like you*. An implicit apology there, I thought, the germ of one. Tell me more about him, please, is what I would have said, if I'd thought she would respond, if she were not so anxious. I found myself asking: But not to tell?

It didn't strike him as important. I mean it wasn't you, was it? Only a man who reminded Hank of you. Physically.

You don't imagine—

I saw you on television, this morning, swimming in the bay. With your friend, in orange caps. Did you always wear a swim cap? And so here in Milwaukee—rationally, I know you couldn't—

I would never, for all these years, you know I have never—

There was that time in Madison—

I was trying to take it in, not only the alarming news, all of it.

That Anais had phoned me and begun conversing as if we were both responsible parents, resolving an issue with consequences for our child's welfare. That she sounded like any apprehensive and frustrated mother, the soccer mom worried over her son and annoyed at the denseness of the soccer dad. I collected my wits enough to say, Why don't you put Hank on and have him tell me the story?

But there I went too far. Anais said, He's been through enough for one day. Besides, he's at a friend's house.

That last was a lie, or would have been had she tried to put it over. I absorbed the blow. I asked, Did you call the police?

I thought it would be wise to phone you first, in case—

I gathered that your mother had been hiding out, more or less, for so long that she was in the habit of not involving the police, as regards you.

The woman, the driver, she looked—?

Middle-aged.

Not a supermodel?

Women my age all look the same to teenage boys.

I said I was all but certain the man had fled.

Is it a private matter? your mother asked, and despite her seriousness, or because of it, I smiled. Back in Cambridge, at Anais's affinity group, if a touchy topic arose in the presence of an unvetted newcomer, one of the regulars would say, That sounds like a *private matter*. Words that compelled silence among the initiated. Decades before Sukey dreamt up *repairs* and *groceries,* Anais had been speaking in code.

Private, yes. I think this incident relates to a private matter.

Chip, I'm sorry this is so hard. But if you've endangered our son . . .

I collected myself enough to ask what the man had said.

Anais said you didn't catch it clearly. Give it to Eddie, that much you remembered. The man who looked like me said, Tell him to give it all to Eddie.

I repeated, Eddie.

Then the man panicked and dove into the car. He rolled down the window and said, Follow through. Tell him to follow through.

They're riddles, I told your mother. You must trust me.

My own language seemed to bear parsing. She could trust me, she had reason to trust, since despite what had been said in court, she understood I was reliable.

I'll try to do what's best for Hank, I assured her. Give him my love. And remember how much I love you. How much I need you.

You seem provided for on that front, she said.

I assume she was referring to Wendy and Sukey.

I phoned Sukey, to bring her up to date. Since the conversation was in code, there was no way to consult in detail. Or perhaps it was that I intentionally omitted the bit about follow-through. Did I sense it referred to an issue on which Sukey and I would disagree? I conveyed the main point: Sukey should get in touch with Big Eddie. I saved for myself the task of figuring out what else Giampiccolo wants.

Not money alone. We had offered money, and he had spurned us. Though, to be fair, the money had strings attached. Sukey had held back assets on Giampiccolo's behalf. In recent weeks, she had put the word out on the street for him, via Big Eddie's minions. The word was Paraguay. Giampiccolo would know what it meant.

Sukey had run through Giampiccolo's cash, to establish his presence on the Cape, to subsidize our remodeling projects. She had used larger portfolios to cancel debts to Big Eddie. That was the deal: for a price, Eddie would keep Giampiccolo on the run. But Sukey had saved Giampiccolo's on-line holdings—had used his Internet access to transfer them to a chain of accounts with new security codes. (*MMoira* was the password Giampiccolo had used. The ultimate tribute.) Those assets Sukey converted into short sales in Northeast Assurance, orders placed before the first Sesuit bomb had gone off. Good news and bad for Giampiccolo. He was a rich man via dealings that further implicated him in terror.

Sukey had arranged for the proceeds to be shipped overseas.

Most to Switzerland, but some to a starter fund in Paraguay. The arrangement was modeled on one Big Eddie makes for associates who need to be convinced that life is better elsewhere. Money goes to a country where Eddie has an ongoing relationship with government officials. A country with currency restrictions and extradition protections. It arrives in stages, contingent on good behavior. The undesirable man emigrates, someone drops a dime on him to the feds, saying he has resurfaced abroad. The man is watched, the airports are watched. Reentry becomes problematic.

Sukey wanted Giampiccolo exiled. Far from us (and you) and far from the feds. Under suspicion and untouchable. A constant source of reasonable doubt as to my guilt. Logically, Giampiccolo should have chosen to deal with us. Our offer came to millions. If I was hanged for the Sesuit crimes and Giampiccolo negotiated directly with Big Eddie, at best there would still be Paraguay, and on a more constrained budget.

There in the safety of the cottage, I tried to imagine what it is like to be penniless, hunted by Syndicate and feds alike. A man of outsize appetites. I thought of Andrew Cunanan, the gigolo who shot the designer Gianni Versace. After nights in bathhouses and flophouses, Cunanan broke into a houseboat, luxury a greater consideration than security. Sukey believed Giampiccolo would opt for luxury. But he had not followed procedure, had not checked in for the codes he would need in Asunción. Instead, he had made a distinctive gesture. Touching you.

To be accosted by a man who looks like your father—creepy. Or poignant. Or inconsequential. A matter to be forgotten for a time and then recalled in passing, at the dinner table. This queer thing happened after school.

Why should Giampiccolo show himself? If he had negotiated with Big Eddie, that news could have come to Sukey from Eddie directly. The contact with you was a signal to me, a separate message. Delivered via a particular means of communication, accosting my son. And with particular timing. I assumed the deal must turn on my rumored *Today* show appearance.

But what was the deal? I sat at the kitchen table. A luna moth, milky green, flattened itself on the window screen above the sink. I remembered a night when you had tried to sleep over at Teddy and Janna's but needed driving home. I carried you from the car. A dinner-plate-size luna moth had plastered itself to the front door of the cottage. You said, as someone must have said eons before: green like the moon. You wanted to stay there in my arms, looking at it. And did, until you were fast asleep, dreaming of moths and colors and the night sky. Seeing the luna moth made me desperate to be with you.

I had let a bad man touch you. For your sake, I tried to sit beside Giampiccolo and look out at the world from his vantage, as in the installation phase of FtB I had sat empathetically with my Sesuit neighbors. I have listened to Giampiccolo's music, drunk his coffee, shaped his planks with his tools. I have felt the softness of his sheets and shirts and shoes. I should be well placed to discern the lineaments of his desire.

Anais's voice talked me through the problem at hand. The voice of Anais as she once was and might be again. Anais with her theory, about the spectacular moment we inhabit.

Theory and empathy, sound bases for action. What does a man want, who does not want millions in Paraguay?

Without knowing how I had gotten there, I found myself in bed. I drifted off and woke and dozed and woke again—many matters remained unsettled.

17

*

De Gustibus

My sleep was disturbed by images of Woodcock. Flash of light, tinkle of shattered glass, cold shock of bay at night. Then the beam of the chopper overhead.

I have not written about the Woodcock installation. Avoided the topic, out of shame. There is no ducking it any longer. Woodcock touches on the question of responding to Giampiccolo. Though when I fuss over Woodcock, Sukey says I am too self-critical, in the manner of a neurotic artist.

Get over it, she says. Woodcock is everyone's favorite.

Which does not allay the worry.

I undertook Woodcock for Sukey. She hated the building. An Eastern beachhead for West Coast wealth. The billiards tower above the roofline, the gym-cum-virtual-beach below the water table. Rarely occupied, built to be owned, not used. Guarded round the clock. The house was untouchable, proof that security could be purchased, which is why Sukey said we needed Woodcock.

Our successes mounted. Abrams, McIntyre, Giampiccolo. The

print media began to express grudging admiration, the occasional columnist conceding that it was something after all, to have enacted an anarchist program without harm to person. The press admired the technical accuracy.

One day I said, What if we can?

Sukey said, I knew you'd come round.

I had read my own clippings, that was the problem. Not that I failed to prepare obsessively. I still followed directions. For the mortars, I calibrated trajectories repeatedly. I ran drills, timed every step. I gave thought to the symbolic impact of the explosive I would use.

I decided on a return to thermite. It's an old concoction, three parts iron oxide flakes to two parts pulverized aluminum, topped with igniter powder. The recipe—powdered barium peroxide and powdered magnesium round out the formula—is known to all students of anarchist literature. Edward Abbey, the nature writer beloved of ecoterrorists, provided the details in a novel thirty years ago. The early thermite installations had been read by commentators as reference to the environmental disasters we have brought on ourselves. What with the mudslides in the West and the drought in the Southeast, I was content to allude to that theme once more.

If I remained attentive to detail, still my attitude had changed: At some level, I felt unstoppable. Which was the point, from Sukey's perspective. As a friend, she wanted me to flex my muscles, recognize my powers.

Woodcock was our only commando-style raid. The staging area was an empty property Sukey represented, on the north side of Woodcock. A panic sale—an uninsulated beach bungalow. The Vermitsky camp.

In her role as realtor, Sukey drove me there at dusk, in an old station wagon maintained by BaySky. She backed into the garage. I unloaded matériel and vacuumed the trunk. Sukey was dressed to the nines—en route to a dinner party. She would be out and about during the attack. I felt like a grunt bidding his hometown sweetheart farewell.

I waited until dark, then set about siting three small mortars in the beach grass behind the Vermitsky breakfast nook. Two were aimed at the Woodcock guesthouse. The third targeted a spot on Woodcock's environmentally incorrect seaside British lawn. I set staggered lengths of fuse. There was an additional long fuse for explosives, to blow the mortars themselves to pieces, and a fuse for fireworks, to indicate the authorship of the whole.

Over a swimsuit, I wore a jogging outfit borrowed from Giampiccolo. That and a backpack filled with the makings of thermite. I stashed the backpack on the beach below the Vermitsky camp. Up the steps to light fuses. Down again to don the backpack. Then cross the strand, scramble up the Woodcock beach stairs, throw myself on the grass.

The first two shells crashed through the guesthouse's glass doors, setting off alarms. The third had been modified to give off smoke, a flying smudge pot. It landed beside the main house, on the bay side. As the guesthouse roof caved in, I made out the figure of the guard, lumbering over to investigate, cell phone in hand. That had been our strategy—decoy the guard to the guesthouse, for his own safety. Under cover of smoke, I belly-crawled toward our principal objective.

For a moment, fireworks: the rockets' red glare. Frightened shouts, the thump of feet. I had ingredients enough to do two posts. I counted to myself, four one thousand, five one thousand. Eight seconds to unload the backpack and strip down. Another eight to fix wrapper to the posts, create pockets for the thermite powders, pour them in. I added the backpack and jogging clothes, sneakers included, so they would incinerate. I lit a short fuse. Wearing only a swimsuit, I slithered to the dune and rolled down, in the shadow of the stairs. Another explosion from the Vermitsky camp—the mortars blown apart. As eyes were drawn toward the source of the blast, I slipped into the bay. From the water, I imagined I heard the sizzling of the thermite, the groaning of boards, the tinkle of glass.

*   *   *

I was sweaty with excitement, and then chilled by the sea. A goodly distance, a mile and a half. I tried to keep my stroke efficient, silent. The longshore current was against me.

I felt as Sukey had hoped I would. Manly. I had grown up with visions of military glory. In kindergarten—kindergarten!—we sang a Burl Ives song about a Private Roger Young who sacrificed himself to save buddies from ambush in the Solomons. Later, while I knew that killing Vietnamese was immoral, I feared I had shirked a coming-of-age duty.

Swimming home, I thought of what Malcolm X said, that if you can be brave over there, meaning Korea, you can be brave over here. I considered the reverse, whether if I had been brave here tonight, it implied I would have been brave in Asia.

Something was wrong with my left arm, a pain in it, and numbness. A shoulder strain, I assumed. I pushed ahead, mock-heroic.

A helicopter beam swept the beach. I dove. I assessed my condition: alone, in pain, underwater, hunted by a Huey. At last I was the New Man, for one project assuming many roles: soldier, craftsman, athlete, teacher, father, husband, friend. Thoroughly unalienated labor. The man Anais signed on to marry. The search beam moved out to sea. The feds were guarding against a high-tech escape, speedboats, perhaps.

Back in the cottage, I vomited while the bath was running—a positive sign, by Manny's theory. Sensation returned to the arm. I thought grandly: the risks of combat. I was feeling the pride that (in my experience) portends a chastening.

It came the next morning. I snapped on the television. Before the Woodcock images appeared on screen, there was a news update from Miami. "Little John" Giampiccolo had been spotted. He had given police the slip, but only after having been seen enjoying a postmidnight snack with the boys at a popular crab house. An ex-employee, retired to warm climes, had recognized him despite the disguise, a blond wig and beard, and the inevitable dark glasses indoors. Questioned by a reporter, one of the alleged dinner companions answered, So what if it was?

What, indeed. By late summer, police and press had revived the single-bomber theory. The same figure had been sighted too often, a man resembling Giampiccolo. Repeatedly, the same hairs had been found at the bomb sites, the same clothing fibers. One bomber—and Giampiccolo was in Miami the night of Woodcock. I knew it would not be long before the FBI shifted gears. This was ten days before they leaked my name.

Giampiccolo was smart and we were foolish, jogging outfit and running shoes notwithstanding. It stood to reason that if we did real-time sabotage here, he would show himself elsewhere. I felt terrible. Indulging Sukey—indulging myself. And producing this result. Then the station ran its report on Woodcock.

It is night. The wall along the Beach Road side of the Woodcock estate is intact, so the camera crew are taping from a distance. They have set up a spotlight, like at the Oscars. The beam rakes the house. The upper story lists bayward.

Later a boiler blows, or a gas line. Smoke pours from the structure—smoldering wallboard, perhaps. Firefighters arrive, they breach the front gate. The cameras move in. Men are hacking their way through the front door.

Bonnie Luganis, the station's peripatetic local reporter, is interviewing the fire chief. He says it was a small blaze, easily extinguished. He is pulling his men out, in case there are other bombs. Large spools turn, the hoses snake toward the truck.

A cut back to Bonnie. Time has passed. She is interviewing Woodcock's security guard. A sleepy fellow, dazed, shaken. He says what we would want him to say, that in a sense he is grateful to the bombers, for having drawn him away from the main blast. He looks toward the house, thinking of the fate he has been spared.

And now unexpectedly, slowly the house begins to slump. The wires to the pumps have shorted, allowing seawater to fill the basement. Perhaps the firehoses added water weight. The foundation is defective, overwhelmed. Firefighters force the news crews and milling neighbors off the property, into the street. The house is collapsing layer into layer, like one of those telescoping drink cups you take on camping trips.

At dawn, the rising sun reveals the structure flattened—like a wedding cake sat on by a large guest, is how Bonnie Luganis puts it. Except that the phallic tower remains attached. Below the tip, a decided curve—objective correlative of Woodcock's impotence. The camera sweeps round to show the yards of stone wall, and the guard post at the gate. Then back to the detumescent billiard tower, sign of the Movement's triumph.

I recognized the problem immediately. Woodcock was boastful.

The early installations had been melancholic, ironic, darkly farcical—these elements in varying combination, qualities that stand against the dominant culture. Woodcock was mainstream, earnest, assertive. It had Sukey's energy but none of my pensiveness. Task and passion, but insufficient doubt.

Even the fall of Giampiccolo, our least ambiguous image, had a sense of inevitability, of deep humor that was lacking in Woodcock. Giampiccolo wanted to come down. Woodcock was forced into submission. Some of the difference arises from method. Woodcock turned openly on the machinery of warfare.

Watching the Woodcock images, I thought of the aesthetic James Joyce proposed, that pornography is kinetic and excitatory, while true art is static, achieving its emotional force through suggesting interrelations. Mining seawalls and homes, I had mostly aimed for quiet tableaux, in which connections are implicit but not insisted upon. Woodcock was pornographic.

True, we had not intended the devastation, had not counted on faulty wiring and substandard cement. But Sukey's wish to slap

down Woody Woodcock, and my own to prove myself in combat—
where had those impulses come from? It was as if in mysterious but
reliable fashion the prevailing culture had co-opted us, so that now
we displayed its signal traits: self-importance and a hunger for
glory. Far from embodying the New Man's virtues, I had acted as
Spectacular Man. I was certain I would pay a price for my transgression—aware that the descent into triumphalism is easy; the
climb back uncertain. I had been content for the Movement to be
humorous, unpredictable, inscrutable. I understood that now I
would need to take responsibility for the conventional excitation I
had aroused.

As I suffered these misgivings, Sukey phoned. Whom did I think
she'd seen at the party? Old Libby Howell. Looking remarkably
well—as though a burden had been lifted from her.

I said, I have the TV on. Too astonishing.

Sukey never wavered in her enthusiasm for Woodcock.

Nothing like a good shock to the system, she said.

It is true, Woodcock led to the flight of the wealthy from the
Cape. A multi-thousand-dollar alarm system, a full-time guard, the
assurance of specialists that a home is free of explosives—when
these together fail to ensure security, it must be acknowledged that
no structure can escape risk. The attack delivered a taste of the
inner city to vacationland. Bringing the war home. And the explosions kept in play the issue of distribution of resources, through
reminding viewers of the Woodcock squash court, the Woodcock
screening room, the Woodcock private beach.

Sukey loved Woodcock's punch. The best I can say for Woodcock is that indulgence and self-indulgence are elements of the
modern. In Charles Bukowski or Henry Miller, pornography is not
distinct from art.

I found the media response to Woodcock especially disheaften-
ing. When it was a matter of preplanted explosives, the talking
heads blathered on about sneaking cowards. With this lightning

strike, the Sesuibomber became an outlaw hero—like the guy who parachuted into the Rockies with the sack of cash, only here, not for profit. The Sesuibomber was Sam Adams and Robin Hood. I was like an indie director who had turned conventional—and become screamingly popular.

18

*

On the Road

Sunrise. The incoming tide, and for an instant, a true lilac sea. Surely it is sunset that pollution has corrupted, and not sunrise? I am free to take the lilac flash at dawn as a good omen—nature winking in my direction.

Sukey arrives. She is upbeat, despite the message, via Anais, from Giampiccolo. A bluff, Sukey says.

She still believes she owns Giampiccolo. She has her plan, however chancy, and we will stick with it. She is intent on catapulting me into stardom. Fame will bring you your son, she says. In America there is no resisting fame.

I am not sanguine about Sukey's machinations. The line is thin between irresistible and repugnant. The subject of the moment is always made nauseating by the excesses of the press, and this is true whether or not the person is a willing participant or even alive. Monica Lewinsky, Paula Jones, Princess Diana, the younger John Kennedy, Gianni Versace, the objects of our serial monomania. I have no wish to be nauseating to my wife and son, to the entire public.

Not nauseating, Sukey insists, when I express my worry. Stimulating.

There's irony: your father, Ritalin to the nation.

Sukey arrives, and then the handful of townsfolk who have voiced their belief in me. Friends from the neighborhood, the food co-op, the college. Harriet Bloxsom is kind enough to show. I believe she still feels guilt for the harm her comments did me in court. Grace and Dee and Tommy Madeiros join in. I thank them for their participation the other night and now. The plan is for a group swim, to show solidarity and afford me exercise.

I wear the powder blue trunks and cover-up. When we reach the water's edge, I remove the shirt and add the Day-Glo swim cap. For the cameras, the routine is reassuring. Visually it says, Chip Samuels is a man of habit, he can be relied on. Sukey believes the public favors repetition, as you did in childhood. Repetition and variation. Here is another story about the swimmer with the orange cap. What will befall him? *Curious George* for adults. Sukey insisted that to reach you I would need to compose that sort of tale.

Jolly and confident, Sukey beams at the cameras. For his part, Tommy looks fun-loving, as if he's out less for the swim than the beer with lunch that will follow. Dee is still the laughing colleen; her suit flatters her figure. Harriet has an implausible air of command. We would make good characters in a sitcom, if there were sitcoms about middle age. We could shuttle in and out of a bar or an apartment or an office, embodying our types, displaying our quirks, implying, Candide-like, that, however strange things seem, the world we live in is perfect in its way.

As we have done before, Sukey and I swim to our spot in the lee of Mooncusser Rock, only now, with friends in the water, there is more splashing and frolicking. We float, tread water, chat. Sukey has built tedium into the morning routine, to induce a loss of vigilance in the observers.

In time, a pair of rainbow-sailed windsurfers make their way into the cove. The sails obscure the cameras' view. Presently the swimmers' heads are visible again. There is splashing and conferring. The windsurfers sail off. Next, looking across the cove, a camera can catch sight of a board resting on the sand at the wrack line along Scargo Point. The rainbow sail has been hastily furled; it flaps in the breeze.

Later, Ollie Haas emerges from the bay onto our beach. Ollie used to baby-sit for you, though he is almost unrecognizable, with the trendy shaved head and goatee. Ollie gives the camera a naughty leer as he slips off his orange cap and runs his hand over his scalp, the gag being that there is no hair to protect from the salt water. At the top of the stairs, where reporters gather, Ollie speaks.

Bit of a lark, he says, bit of a good time, wa'n't it, help out an old mate. Studied under him over at the college, di'n't I, watched his son for him now and again when the missus was off gallivanting.

Ollie accents the *-van-*. He has a working-class British accent that Sukey has counted on to captivate the media.

This last bit, Ollie coming ashore, I saw only later, on the news summary. As for the more general pantomime, what happened is no mystery. Midway through the boring splashing, Sukey gave the signal for Ollie and a friend to sail in our direction. When he reached us, Ollie hopped into the water. In the cleft of the rock he slipped on an orange cap. At the cottage, I had entrusted Tommy Madeiros with a waterproof sack stuffed with a few essentials, this journal among them. Now I slid the sack into the front of the black stretch trunks I was wearing under the powder blue baggies. The bulge approximated Ollie's belly in silhouette. Sukey peeled the swim cap off my head. I handed her the blue trunks and pulled myself onto Ollie's board.

With the sail shielding me from the landside cameras and the second windsurfer blocking the view from the sea, I headed toward the point. There, I beached the board and made off in a nondescript rental car Sukey had left for me. When the group of merry bathers returned to shore, the cause and object of the festivities was nowhere to be seen.

Sukey says news stories must be simple. Obviously I had disappeared on the windsurfer. Obviously I was headed off-Cape. But the dramatic means of the exit—I mean the banal storytelling—left open the possibility of intrigue.

Once it became apparent that I was missing, the press made urgent contact with Wendy's office. Her partner, Bob Willis, held a briefing. I heard snippets on the radio, as I came off the Sagamore Bridge.

Bob has the folksy manner that says, All in good time. He maintains suspense, leaves open every possibility. That I am headed abroad, as is my right. That I am seeking privacy in the face of media intrusions. Or that I am off to make my fortune on television—yes, he has heard that rumor, too. The one detail Bob lets slip is that if my vehicle is identified, he may request a police escort for me, since there have been threats on my life. A light touch there, the presumption that since I am unindicted, the government will help me flee.

The neighbors' horseplay gives me twenty minutes, and by the time Ollie has entertained and Bob has filibustered, I am safely on the mainland side of the Canal. Wendy Moro is waiting at the car rental stand, Kippy's, in Buzzards Bay. She is there with Eric Souza, the Madeiroses' son-in-law, who will drive the limo. Sukey has thought through every detail, as exact in the handling of this charade as I am with explosives.

She has had a suit left for me in Kippy's trailer. Soft, summer-weight wool, charcoal. Tailored, I suspect, through compromise between the old jacket I wear to graduation luncheons and a Giampiccolo Armani. A snappy Italian suit and a black French T-shirt and silk boxers. More snow peas and salmon. The outfit is meant to position me precisely, as a rising star so confident that he makes no effort (sartorially) to take distance from his bad-boy reputation.

The risk is that I will be a laughingstock, all dressed up and no place to go. I am traveling to New York on the basis of a deal that has not been sealed. Wendy has been negotiating for me to appear on the *Today* show. Not as a suspect. Once accepted (so Sukey says) the suspect role cannot be shed. I must appear as an on-screen expert.

Sukey's attempted coup, Wendy calls it. Since the networks are hot for exclusive access, one of them will pay this price: I will join the news team. Wendy and the NBC negotiator, Harry Bolotow, have initialed a contract. Bolotow's higher-ups have the document and a deadline. It's take it or leave it. Sign by 2 P.M., or we open up the bidding to Fox and Turner.

I doubt that even Sukey and Wendy can pull off this farce. But I like the form of the demand. Without the argument's needing to be made, it says: Look, the networks make commentators of anyone. Convicted politicians, crooked financiers. Athletes who gamble, sportscasters who cross-dress. The guy who burglarized Watergate. War criminals, criminals who arm terrorists. Why not a man accused of mining houses? It's not as if I'd mined Haiphong harbor. Surely, in terms of moral depravity I can't hold a candle to Henry Kissinger or Oliver North.

I assume my uniform and join Wendy in the limo. It is white, a visual reference to O.J.'s white Bronco. Sukey says the public is used to watching white cars filmed from above. Most people believe O.J. was guilty, but for our purposes celebrity will count for more than innocence.

Eric has the divider shut—hear no evil. Wendy and I are alone together, staring out through tinted windows at the maples, oaks, and cedars that, along with the occasional cranberry bog, line Route 25 and then 195 West. She is demure, still, my melancholic defender, but she has about her a slight restlessness. There is color in her cheeks, as if she were mildly febrile.

It's up in the air, she tells me.

The gamble, the coup, the source of Wendy's stimulation.

I half hope we will fail. This morning, treading water, I asked Sukey, Whatever will I do on television?

Be yourself.

Which I took as a joke, since that is what no one in the media is. She said, Soft-spoken and indecisive.

The small-town teacher, out of his element in the limelight— that is the effect Sukey wants, the authentic self as image. The image of authenticity.

Or amusing, Sukey said. What was that word your wife used? *De-riveting.*

No, Sukey said. *Levity.* Black levity.

Sukey said: Who knows? You might paralyze them with levity. Or charm them with incompetence.

Sukey floated on her back. She said, That's what's wonderful about television. All a person has to do is appear.

I have no wish to appear, save for your sake—to bring resolution to the Giampiccolo matter. I don't need NBC, would settle for making a brief statement to the press. I want to say as much to Wendy, but she is proud of her role in the negotiations.

NBC is desperate, what with the exodus of audience to cable and the Web. The loss of NFL programming. The desertion of one news anchor after another. NBC is mainstream but slipping. Sukey says the key to success in America is to think like a Wall Street takeover artist. The opportunities are in name brands in decline.

Sukey dealt with Harry Bolotow, back in her PR days. He is an aging dealmaker returned from his exile in public television to revitalize the news lineup at NBC. Sukey likes that Bolotow has failures on his résumé, not least an ignominious trial as cohost for *Today.* She likes that he knows the stakes are real and losers suffer. She likes that he began as a radical—an engaged journalist, at Columbia College, back in 1968 when Mark Rudd and the "action faction" smoked cigars in the office of the university president, Grayson Kirk.

We are driving west on the interstate, and Wendy is describing the negotiations. She warms to her task. I worry that like your mother years ago, Wendy is not quite herself.

He needs the big kill, Wendy says, quoting Sukey, imitating the decisiveness and the titter. He needs a good get. To show he is not a *Masterpiece Theatre* type. To help NBC ape Fox—hyping the news with loud buzz. Of all the dealmakers at all the networks, Bolotow needs Chip Samuels most.

To have made the concept plausible to even one man who wields power, that seems something. We are just shy of giddy. Because of the risk we are taking. Staging the disappearance from the Cape when nothing is settled. Theater of the absurd.

We are being chauffeured in a limousine with a butter-soft leather bench, and Wendy is laughing out loud, openmouthed, hearty, though there is still sadness around the eyes. Wendy takes pride in the details of the package she has gotten Bolotow to initial. The penalty section is a key element, harsh consequences if the network fails to showcase me as an expert.

Unless I am indicted. Bolotow insisted on that one escape clause. The network can drop me if I am charged as a terror suspect. Which is likely. As soon as I appear on television, the feds or the Commonwealth will rush ahead. Even if they sign, the network executives will only be pretending to hire me as a regular. Whatever the initial uproar, in the long run they will look clever, reeling in the Sesuibomber and then throwing him back.

We are outside Fairhaven when a message from Bob Willis grinds out of the limo fax machine: Expect company.

Here's how Sukey envisioned it: Caddie Weymouth's office phones Willis demanding to know my whereabouts. I could be headed anywhere. Flight out of Logan, car ride to Canada. Embarrassing, for the AG. Weymouth and Willis strike a deal. I will not leave the country. Weymouth will make no sudden move to restrict my freedom. Willis fills Weymouth in on my itinerary.

Sure enough, in two minutes we are surrounded by state trooper cars. The cops wave to Eric. I take it they are pleased with the duty they have pulled. Secretly they identify with the outlaw who brings down trophy homes.

After the troopers come the rubberneckers. Traffic slows. We see drivers on their car phones, thrilled to have located the caravan, the alleged bomber on the move.

Inside the limo, Wendy describes the negotiation. She presented me as an expert, a man who had taught anarchism. Bolotow boomed: The literature of anarchism, at a junior college. And Wendy offered, Working person's college. As if to say, Where else would a radical teach? Implicitly referring to Bolotow's own show, *Dateline.* Reminding him that NBC viewers know me as a mentor to those versatile Madeiroses, a couple who fit every niche: worker, thinker, student, parent, grandparent. The elements in Sukey's plan meshed neatly.

Wendy does the voices. She manages to look ponderous when she plays Bolotow, a big man annoyed at having to dicker with a slight woman. She does herself as well, exaggerating the reticence: Wendy tactfully reminding Bolotow that I had done local journalism—which is how Sukey suggested Wendy label the Seasons of Sesuit essays. Giving Bolotow ammunition to defend what he had to do anyway. Sign the Sesuibomber.

Wendy's animation worries me.

Presently we hear the rhythmic thump of helicopters overhead, the media hyping the story of the moment. Wendy flicks on the limo television. We are the subject of the news briefs at station breaks.

By Fall River, crowds have formed. Curiosity seekers, yes, but also supporters holding placards through their sunroofs. *Free the Beaches! Samuels for President! Da Bomb! What a Blast!! Samuels = Legey!* The last, I gather, is the new slang for *legendary.* One sign makes me smile. It sports a single word: *Random!* Six months ago, *random* and *sketchy* did not mean up-to-the-minute. There's a new affection for the haphazard.

The interstate is highly random. From overpasses, well-wishers wave encouragement. Rest areas are filled with revelers, beer bottles held aloft, boom boxes blasting sixties music: "Eve of Destruction." "La Bamba." And Dylan's "Ballad of a Thin Man," for the chorus, Mr. Jones clueless. We get the new millennial sound as well, the Sino-Latina girl bands: "*Comidas chinas y criollas.*" "*¡No me tomes el pelo!*" Multicultural randomness. And eco-rap galore. The highway is a happening. Families are out to witness history. From convertibles, teenagers toss firecrackers, despite the cops nearby. Noisy homage to the Movement. On air, coverage becomes continuous.

I never imagined, I say.

I had been aware of the Sesuit Echoes, the sabotaging of Gulf-front homes in Mississippi and Texas, the outrages at Malibu, the disruptions to exclusive hunting clubs along the Great Lakes. They spoke to the Movement's attractiveness as a model for activists. But the echoes were few. Until today, I was ignorant of FtB's mass appeal and my personal acceptance by my fellow citizens. Until today I had ignored the truth Sukey insists on, that I am already famous.

A second fax comes through from Wendy's office, five lawyerly words: The thing speaks for itself. Which could be a motto for the Movement. Here Willis means that by generating this cavalcade, Sukey has made her point to the suits at NBC. It is safe to sign me on. More than safe, essential.

Wendy switches the TV to the local NBC affiliate and turns up the volume. The network is still hedging its bets. In the background is a helicopter shot of our limo's progress. The foreground is a news chatter show targeting upscale housewives.

What are they saying? the moderator wonders. The alleged terrorist and the lovely lawyer, what must they be talking about? The change in the nation's mood? I am stunned to see my thoughts invented, fictively, on television.

Aporia is the fancy term that has entered on-air speech, signifying not an impasse, but a marked change—a rupture between old era and new. Like O-ring or chad or serotonin, this word we had never heard before, *aporia,* is on every pundit's tongue as if it had been learned in childhood, from a Mother Goose rhyme. *Aporia* is serious, an accepted aspect of reality. On television, the two friendly debaters guess that Wendy and I must be speaking of the shift in the nation's sensibility.

What shit, I say. My response is less to the particular opinion than to the circus in whose center ring we have been dropped.

The century began, the moderator opines, not on January 1, 2000, nor even 2001. For America, the twenty-first century properly opens with the Giampiccolo installation. One woman speaks of a new generosity, another of a new level of unease.

Conspicuous consumption is out, the first woman says. She is a heavyset, dark-haired, deeply sincere type, enamored of her social observations. To her, one detail says it all: Where formerly the windshield of an oversize SUV would sport a self-interested No Radio sign, now it will display an explanation to the community: Five kids/House down dirt road. To justify the expenditure of fossil fuel. We want our neighbors to know we are of goodwill.

The second expert—blond, tough, cool—plays the cynic. Her worth consists in shallow practicality. Those are the stock characters in this commedia dell'arte, Pride in Pregnant Detail versus Aw, Get Over Yourself. The no-nonsense gal interprets the same omen. The cardboard signs relate to the mischief against SUVs, kids using epoxy resin to glue the gas caps shut. To her, symbolic crimes against property are the Movement's main effect.

The soft, deep one goes on about conspicuous generosity. The change goes far beyond beaches. On campus, not only anarchist wilding but also community service is glam. Corporations are suspect. Public interest law is in; the class action suits against the energy companies, modeled on the tobacco victories, are manned by volunteers. Few dispute the chain of harm: fuel consumption, greenhouse gases, climatic warming—and then five-hundred-year storms and insect plagues.

Yes, says the hard, shallow one, but generosity can arise from fear. She points to the open-door policy now in place at most gated developments. Since the outrages in Nomquit, in Padanaram, on Apponaganset Bay—the clubhouse and a dozen waterfront homes collapsed, tens of millions in damage—exclusive communities have instituted outreach programs, beach trips or pool visits for children in neighborhoods beyond the gates. But only because the members know they have to.

On the main point there is agreement: a society transformed.

The station cuts to a live reporter outside a McDonald's ahead, in Connecticut. Kids lean into the picture and wave. The reporter is saying that the highway on-ramps have been closed, for reasons of safety, for crowd control. Do not attempt to travel until the caval-cade has passed. Continue to watch as you are doing now, on tele-vision. We will be here live.

The two women are back on-screen. They are hip, superior, combative, intent on enhancing their own status—proof, if any were needed, that change is superficial. History seems to me disap-pointingly uniform, linked tales of greed and tribalism, competi-tion and exploitation, fanaticism and self-righteousness. The new tolerance? We saw it all in the sixties, Republicans speaking of community, bringing the nation together.

And yet it is hard to deny what is going on around us on the interstate. Young energy, a sense of release.

The fax machine squeezes out two more words: You're on.

Sure enough, the moderator interrupts the debaters with This Just In: Chip Samuels will join the *Today* show tomorrow. She does not say in what capacity, but neither does she any more identify me as the accused Sesuibomber. The network cuts abruptly to a straight news format, anchored in New York. All *aporia* all the time.

We are stalled at the Rhode Island state line, waiting for a new squadron. Wendy is sniffling and hiccuping. She is herself again, dejected in victory. I am glad to be represented by a woman who sees triumph's downside.

Crowd noise envelops us. Like at Nauset when you have thrown yourself into a large wave, a combination of silence and roar. If the public's sentiments were different, police alone could not protect us. We are creatures of the spectacle and at its mercy.

We have work to do. That is how we will settle ourselves. I slide in a videotape. Footage of Arlen-Pepper appears, and then Howell. I have an assignment, to prepare my segment, the one Wendy will insist on if the NBC producers ignore the terms of the contract and offer up a script that treats me as a suspect. For my time on-air, Sukey has in mind a variant of MTV, videomontage, only instead of music there will be my commentary.

Wendy is telling me about our mole at NBC—Arty Shahinian, the chief technician for *Today*, the man the corporation's reps embarrassed in the union negotiations last fall. The Arty Shahinian who worked alongside Mario Savio in the Free Speech Movement at Berkeley. Arty is another reason Sukey went with NBC, the chance of a kindred spirit on the set. The final piece in the jigsaw Sukey has assembled.

Rhode Island troopers join us in their brown uniforms. We set off again. Fans blow kisses. Men moon us. Women bare their chests.

I can see Wendy is unnerved by the size of our reception. We have won, but in a way that is a lot like losing. That is what we both feel, our absorption into the spectacle.

I am not blameless, I tell Wendy, I have been combative. I point to the images of Woodcock, explain why I will not show the tape tomorrow. I helped stir up this transmutation of politics into entertainment.

Wendy will not see matters as I do. She refers to the trouble I went through to spare the Woodcock guard. She seems to buy the label the networks impose on me, the man who changed history. Wendy is my Pygmalion, she has lost track of who I was yesterday, the hapless defendant.

I reframe Woodcock as failure. Because of the crowd noise, Wendy puts her lips to my ear when she speaks. Now she gives a light kiss, to say she sees past my humility. I have the fleeting thought: A man could get used to this.

A phrase your mother despised. We are already too accustomed to pleasure, she would say, too little prepared to forgo pleasure in favor of obligation. There is a midsixties Godard movie, *Two or Three Things I Know about Her,* that ends with a shot of consumer goods, mostly American cleansing agents, Ajax and Dash. Displayed on a lawn, the boxes stand on their bases or sides. The array anticipates the new downtowns of America's hypercapitalist cities— Atlanta, Houston—the rectangular office buildings plastered with logos. The camera lingers on a golden box of toothpaste whose brand name is Hollywood. In the voice-over, a man says that a radio show sponsored by Esso has lulled him into forgetfulness of the political horrors of midcentury. Torture, oppression, tanks rolling in. More than once, your mother referred to that scene when she heard the phrase, A man could get used to this.

Easy to imagine they are one's due, the admiring young woman and now the orchid in crystal. But Anais was right. Morality lies in discomfort. The great struggle is to resist the seductions of the spectacle.

19

*

On the Air

I know critics ridicule the new hosts of the *Today* show, Hugh Crale and Candy Aznavour. A high-water mark for perkiness is the verdict. Hugh and Candy do display a social facility so developed as to verge on the disturbing—in Manny's term, nauseating. But as a viewer I detect in them an undercurrent of world-weariness; their effervescence seems to mask and disclose private knowledge that life can disappoint. I would not have been ashamed to appear with them.

"Journalistic norms" is the reason they gave for avoiding me. As if we did not know that news anchors are entertainers. (And as if obeisance to norms were not itself part of the diversion. I remember the time Matt Lauer refused to interview O. J. Simpson, and Katie Couric stepped forward; each entertained—Lauer with the norms charade, Couric, with an episode of the O.J. panto.) Since the regulars refused to appear with a tainted correspondent, Harry Bolotow was dragooned into service. He had signed the contract, he would have to fulfill it.

On air, camaraderie prevailed, Bolotow joking about his past shortcomings as an anchor, Candy welcoming him back as a treasured alum. The news summary included a clip of my flashbulb-lit exit from the hotel lobby into the waiting limo. Watching the hosts on the set, I believed I saw unacknowledged pride in the show's association with the day's top story. We're number one! A stimulating feeling, however dicey the compromises required to produce it.

I hung out at the edge of the set. I had not been offered star's quarters, and Wendy would not let me enter the greenroom like a guest. She slipped her arm behind mine. Correspondent, she reminded me. Expert.

As we had expected, Bolotow asked me to commit to a script in which I played the part of the accused terrorist. Bolotow is a big barrel of a guy, the sort who inspires respect through physical presence. Wendy handled him with humility. He would understand that she would not be doing her job if she failed to hold the network to its commitments. Bolotow broke off communication. He was agitated because the regular producers would be walking out for his segment. Amateur hour, was what he muttered.

Wendy spoke with the tech crew, arranging for still shots of documents we might want to feature, reviewing the list of video and audio clips. Plan A, I had told her. The one where we save nothing for next time, spend it now.

You're in good hands, Wendy assured me.

She meant Arty Shahinian.

Wendy had only to mention hands for mine to resume their trembling. Too much was riding on this broadcast, since Anais's call. I thought of Sukey's assurance that any presentation of self would suffice. I vowed not to be falsely energized. To hold steady.

Bolotow began by badgering me about my role in the outrages, the composition of the Movement, my intentions. I was sufficiently paralyzed by the camera to appear to be resisting—as if moved to silence by principle. In truth, I was searching, to locate myself. Bolotow posed a question, and I wondered how I (in my everyday, noncelebrity state) would respond. Before I had decided, Bolotow moved on, creating television by grilling a nonresponsive witness.

Finally I mumbled: Harry, Mr. Bolotow, you seem to want to withdraw the invitation for me to appear as an expert. I am willing to agree that in the matter of the Sesuit installations, there is no expertise. They are expressive. To translate their message . . . I would diminish them.

I don't suppose my offer was comprehensible, to try to appreciate the bombings, rather than explicate them. Bolotow spoke with the staged annoyance common nowadays to interviewers and political candidates in debate: You are avoiding every question. Is the terror about beach access?

Wendy was nodding in my direction, lending me courage. And so I called for the videotape: Harry, Mr. Bolotow, you've asked about the gist or essence of the new anarchism. And I wonder . . . could we take the tape of the demolition of Johnny Giampiccolo's home and run it as a loop? Thank you, Arty. Would it help if we were silent for the first playthrough?

The behemoth shuddered and fell to its knees, sank into the dune.

I allowed myself to respond to the images as if on drift, seeing them afresh. Heidegger contrasts *Bestand,* imposing our will on nature, with *Gelassenheit,* letting be. The installation reminds us that we have strayed too far from the passive, observant role. I spoke my mind: How beautiful the beach is. Look—in that shot from behind the dune, when the monstrous house has disappeared. There is a sense of aptness, a return to the way the beach wants to be—if that is not too poetic a notion.

Arty continued to run the loop.

But what is the purpose of it? Bolotow insisted.

I was still engaged by the pictures, as I wished Bolotow, the sometime radical, might be. Letting my trance deepen, I said: The purpose of art is to open our eyes to the obvious.

Bolotow had done a special, for public television, on Monet's late paintings. It aired last spring. I found myself asking Bolotow about Monet: What is Monet's work about? Haystacks? Water lilies?

I take this posture in class sometimes. Thinking aloud, speculatively, in response to a student's overly concrete question. On air, did I sound incoherent? I meant that even public television does not carry specials about early-twentieth-century farming or botany. We are not interested in the immediate subject of a work of art.

I said: You are the expert, Harry, but, to avoid argument, could we agree that a critic might say Monet is about light and color? About the preciousness of individual vision. Perspective and decoration and our fleeting moment in this universe. And when we say these words we diminish Monet. They are less than what his painting is about. So when you ask whether the installations are about beach rights in New England . . .

All this while the loop was running.

Bolotow professed ignorance: You've lost me. What does Monet have to do with sabotaging vacation homes?

I knew I was floundering, but I was also gaining confidence, because on air I was myself, a man who flounders. I said, You are asking me about a movement that has captured the imagination of the country and at the same time asking me to disclaim any expertise . . . which I am willing to do, but then you bridle when I say what every viewer already knows . . .

What do we know, Chip Samuels? You have not told me what we know.

I was looking at the loop, trying to put my response into words. I said, As you insist, the explosion is absurd. But allowing ourselves to be moved by the image, we may come to see the house as absurd as well, and then to contrast the two absurdities. The house is absurd in a way that is insulting and demeaning to viewers, the explosion in a way that is playful and inviting.

Bolotow said: You are spouting nonsense.

Yes, exactly, I said, with enthusiasm Bolotow had not expected. Yes, these attempts at explication must fail.

I considered mentioning Walter Benjamin's essay, the one that says not all art is translatable, that translation is itself an art, and an exacting one. By now the crew was giggling, which I took as a signal that we were approaching levity. I sat and stared while Bolotow continued on his own tack.

He turned graver by the minute, speaking of the fatal explosions at the Army Math Research Center in Madison, Wisconsin, in 1970, and the Murrah Building in Oklahoma City in 1995. Bolotow did not seem misguided. The Sesuit explosions took place in the context of past violence. In contrast to it, is how I would put it. Sukey had taken such care, with diverted e-mail and sequenced cellular modems and cut-ins to alarm systems—Sukey's technical know-how applied to the single purpose of avoiding killing.

As Bolotow pontificated, it struck me he had captured part of the truth, that death is what the explosions comment on at this political moment. Deaths from poverty. Deaths from global warming. More deaths from natural disasters this past year than in any three years in the prior century. Hurricanes, typhoons, tsunamis— and the people crowded into floodplain slums. Or driven from them—over half the rivers in the world polluted today. Thirty million forced from their homes by water pollution this year alone. No more orangutans in the wild and no more pandas, whole ecosystems disappearing. First the animals and now the humans, and no ark to save us, nor a body of water safe to float one on. Some of these thoughts I expressed on air. I was hardly aware of when I was speaking aloud.

Bolotow got stuck on Timothy McVeigh, the Oklahoma City bomber. I remembered that McVeigh had fought in Desert Storm. Taught to kill, hired by our government into a unit that blew up Iraqis and plowed them into the sand. Powerless men, dissidents Saddam Hussein forced into the front lines, as cannon fodder. I recalled the term *blowback,* the notion that the Oklahoma bombing was the domestic price of imperialism abroad. I thought of the embargo we had imposed on Iraq. How every ten minutes an Iraqi child died. Hundreds of thousands of children dead, and we fret about beach houses.

I was wandering in my speech, I know, and looking off to Bolotow's side. My students make fun of the rapture I fall into when a new thought strikes. All the same, I was responding to Bolotow, making use of his suggestions. He stammered, appalled by what he had loosed on the network. Then he reverted to the deep voice that signals control. By no means could we see Sesuit as art. Tragedy, tragedy, tragedy, was his theme. Then cowardice, cowardice, cowardice—a confused discursion on the character of the perpetrators.

There was charm in Bolotow's decompensation. It recalled the performance of Admiral James Stockdale, the fellow who stumbled in the vice presidential debates some years back. Asking rhetorically, Who am I? Why am I here? The military hero stripped to his humanity. I had respected Stockdale enormously, for having endured with dignity as a prisoner of war. I admired him all the more for his discomfort on camera. How distinguished, in the midst of a staged entertainment, to ask the great and universal questions. Gauguin at the political dais. A bittersweet instance of *détournement,* a new use of the medium.

Bolotow is no hero, but he is large and conventionally manly. I believed that his confusion would have decided popular appeal, that if he wanted to return to anchoring, he was making a fair start.

Arty Shahinian was varying the images behind Bolotow, the Potter house and Howell and a flash of Arlen-Pepper. To have risked handling explosives to make these simple statements . . . even with Woodcock omitted, the pictures countered the charge of cowardice. I felt more comfortable now, seeing my work and Sukey's displayed to good effect. And so I motioned, scribbling with an invisible pen. Shahinian held up sheets of paper. I nodded—yes, the documents. Now the screen was filled with still images, with words in yellow, excerpts, superimposed. This was my moment, my toss of the dice.

The bomber can hardly be called cowardly, I said, if we assume he is Johnny Giampiccolo.

I did not speak eloquently. There were too many distractions. An impossibly tall and thin young woman—a producer—leaned into the set and waved her long arms. Bolotow interrupted. But the technical crew was on my side. Union men and maids led by Arty Shahinian, the worker-university alliance fulfilling its promise at last. My microphone took precedence.

I was telling a conventional fable, the sinner struck in midlife, like Saul at Kaukab, on the road to Damascus. The Saint Augustine story, the John Donne. The servant who at last invests his talents fruitfully: A man takes skills honed in a life of capitalist crime and applies them to art. Explosives, modems, organizational strategies, he puts them all to work in the service of a new ideal. In the case of Johnny Giampiccolo, if he is the Sesuibomber, destroying houses, including his own, which he knows to be unoccupied. In this one installation at least, he is less a terrorist than a creator of impressions. Is it a brave act, if Giampiccolo is the artist? To reverse course and declare in action the error of one's ways. To tear down what one has built.

The evidence appeared on-screen. FBI reports that Billy Dineen had felt obliged to pass on to Wendy. Charts and graphs documenting the forensic evidence: Giampiccolo's hair and footprints and clothes fibers found at the bombing sites. Explosives traced back to the mob. E-mail analyses linking FtB messages to the fragments of what were once Giampiccolo's computers. Credit card records listing the purchase of necessaries. Brokerage statements documenting the premature shorting of Northeast.

The producer gesticulated and Bolotow protested, but before we could be cut off, I saw the image I was waiting for, on a single screen in the panel of screens. Bonnie Luganis stood on her favorite rise of sand, smoke wafting in the background.

We have a breaking story, I said. News of a house blown up this very morning on Cape Cod Bay . . . in Sesuit . . . I wonder whether we can . . . do we have a remote report? Arty, can you patch in . . . ?

A technician made vigorous hand signals. I was to look right when addressing Bonnie, straight ahead for the audience.

Bonnie Luganis. You have news.

She began with the words that signaled my membership on the team.

Yes, Chip.

She was accepting me as the anchor in New York, the authority to whom she should report and defer: Yes, Chip, that's right. This is Bonnie Luganis, WHDH, NBC's Boston affiliate. I am reporting live from Sesuit.

It was our cottage, of course—gone.

No apology will suffice. And yet I hope you will come to understand and forgive.

Back when he'd chatted with me, Manny Abelman had remarked on my tendency to cling to the past. Living in my father's home, pining for my wife as she was in the sixties, cleaving to the principles she held then. Manny claimed to admire my loyalty and yet to look forward to a day when I would jettison my burdens.

Then the Antunes fertilizer bomb had landed on my doorstep. If I tried to discard the explosives, I would be caught and convicted. If I left them in place, the FBI would discover them, with the identical result. To attempt to reach you, I would need to forsake the six-on-six windows and the king boards and the sight of small ships at sea.

I took consolation in Thoreau: I see young men, my townsmen, whose misfortune it is to have inherited farms, houses, barns, cattle, and farming tools; for these are more easily acquired than got rid of. Better if they had been born in the open pasture and suckled by a wolf, that they might have seen with clearer eyes what field they were called to labor in.

I have disinherited myself, and you in the process, and my excuse is the one Thoreau alludes to, that possession can stand in the way of calling. On discovering the Antunes mess, I had first sought a different resolution; but within days, I came to understand that I would need to make a sacrifice commensurate with those I had imposed on others. When Giampiccolo touched you, the timing became clear.

I took my orts and shards with me. The matchbooks, the bit of brick, photos of you, this diary—those were in my belly pack. In the dark of night, I had thrown some larger items in the shed. Your teddy bears and your pillow. Mrs. Kuykendahl's set of Hardy novels, redeemed from a sidewalk sale at the Women's Free Library. My dad's bag, filled with rusty hand tools. Odd leavings I know your mother by: a silver-and-turquoise bead earring that turned up under our mattress, early crockery in the Grecian vein, her dog-eared radical tracts. The fertilizer bomb was closer to the cottage than the shed—near the utility room. Smoke damage aside, I assumed the keepsakes would survive, along with the potter's wheels. Still, I was prepared to lose everything.

At least I had believed I was prepared. The live shot of the collapsed cottage unnerved me. I blanched. I cocked my head. I mumbled. I looked for all the world like what I was, a community-college teacher and sometime handyman struggling to return to his senses. The effect was the one Sukey had hoped for, the image of authenticity. And perhaps the effect I had aimed for as well, a turning away from convention. The accused as victim as anchor as ordinary Joe—changing our notion of who might merit a seat at the table.

Bonnie said, It's your house, Chip. I'm sorry you have to learn in this way. The structure is a total loss, according to the fire chief. His men have soaked a nearby storage shed—it looks as though that should survive.

I thought of the harm to your bears and my books. I looked like a man who has learned his home is up in smoke but who is toughing it out in order to carry on with his job.

The beach grass is dry, Chip. As you can see here, the fire spread along this bank to the condominium complex known as Stone House.

That's (I was explaining to Bolotow) a substantial house, Federal, authentic. Turned into condominiums eighteen years back . . . Not stone, clapboard. Stone was an early owner. I lived there once, in childhood.

I fumbled, and at the same time it was clear that, as promised, I knew the details.

Chip, the firemen managed to quell the flames. Apparently they were alerted just as the bomb went off. You can see moderate damage in this shot of Stone House, in the section that was once the servants' wing, that charred wall. But the fire department tells me that if there are no further explosions, the bulk of the compound will not be affected.

No injuries? I asked. No matter the provocation, no matter the absence of alternative—the necessity—it was hard to bear the awareness that I had set off an incendiary bomb.

Harry Bolotow was shaking his head, disturbed at having implicated the network in this stunt. I suppose he was certain I had blown up my own house. Tell me, he said, are you going to apply for an insurance payment?

It was a hostile question, and it resulted in Bolotow's being silenced. Because the producers had turned a corner with me, decided I was a human-interest feature. An on-air journalist forced to take one of life's blows—the very blow that had occupied the nation's attention the summer long—while under the camera's eye. And who had done so with a stiff, or only faintly quivering, upper lip. If doubt remained as to my innocence, the remnant of suspicion only added interest. I was a commodity whose value was on the rise.

Was Bonnie Luganis trying to save Bolotow or sink him when she intervened? She said, Chip, I believe that like many Cape Codders, you are covered by Northeast Assurance, so the loss will be made good by the state.

I gave her a half-nod.

Interestingly, Chip, I understand the local police are privy to a recording—provided by your own defense team, if I am correct—a tape of what is alleged to be the voice of a federal agent, indicating that the insurer is itself under investigation.

I turned to Arty: We have a fragment of that conversation?

When the FBI dissident phoned, Wendy had managed to switch

on her answering machine to catch the tail end of the call. On air, we heard a mechanically distorted voice saying that a Northeast agent had been stockpiling explosives. What with the documents implicating Giampiccolo and now a recording that sounded like every person's impression of a G-man on the trail of bomb matériel, I was no longer the prime suspect. How much more likely that sabotage at FtB's level of complexity was attributable to the great players in the spectacle, millionaires and corporations.

Without my calling for it, a tape began to play behind me, a loop of our cottage burning to the ground. I understood that my task was to wrap up by doing more of what I had done already, speaking freely, as if from a trance. I talked about my father, the hardworking, patriotic immigrant, how he had built by hand. Sam would have reminded me that what is ours, we own thanks to those we live among. We should feel proud, not aggrieved, when for the common good the community reclaims a possession.

I had you and Anais in mind, that was the source of any sincerity you heard, the ease with which we sacrifice for those we love. Sukey had instructed me to end with sentiment if possible, and I was doing it in spades, sounding like a Gold Star Mother—but slightly off-key, in a way that let doubt persist.

Beyond the monitors, I could see Candy Aznavour, off-set, convulsed in silent laughter. Hugh Crale was trying to buck her up, slapping her on the back, urging her to pull herself together, which she did, barely. As the theme music swelled, they joined me, making it official, welcoming me to the team.

What was that you were doing? Hugh wanted to know—that spacing out in front of the video?

Our microphones were off.

I told him I had been thinking of *rap mou,* soft rap, the calm form of hip-hop that swept Europe last year. I had wondered if there was room for *reportage mou,* a less insistent form of journalism.

While the cameras ran, Candy Aznavour had held herself in control. Now she burst into spasmodic gasps and giggles. She said, I know it's awful, your childhood home. But you with a straight face—oh, stop me. In front of those video clips . . . And to think that the state will be paying for that shack . . .

I saw that I had crafted a work of fiction in the postmodern vein—multimedia, video- and audiotape, and performance art. I tried to make sense of its success.

The public evinces great sophistication these days, this truth is often noted. We can admire a president while believing him to be a philanderer and perjurer. We can understand the women in his life, his wife and his lover, to be simultaneously conniving and vulnerable, immoral and innocent. Anais would have said that these dichotomies are as gnats to swallow when we consider that a politician can, say, cast a blind eye on human rights atrocities and yet be styled a leader and even a moral beacon. For the spectacular performer, the challenge is to expand dichotomies—Ronald Reagan seeming kindly, say, or George H. W. Bush scrupulous, or W compassionate. The audience demands duality, punishes men who lack it. That was why Sukey ventured to send me on the air; she knew I would be attractive as a cultural critic precisely because I might be a terrorist.

Once the credits had run, I looked for Arty Shahinian. He had disappeared, not wanting to be thanked openly. My glance toward the crew gave a young tech apprentice courage to address me. She was bony and scraggly, like the Shelley Duvall character in *Annie Hall*. She grasped my hand and squealed, So sketchy!

The reward of creativity: to establish an aesthetic and then be judged by it. I asked the techie to convey my thanks to the crew. The workers, united, will never be defeated.

Hugh Crale slapped my back: Scoop of the year, the Giampiccolo bank accounts.

I swear I heard pity—rue in welcoming a recruit to the disappointments of celebrity. I liked him, thought he had every bit of the human depth I had imagined, behind the joviality.

Charming, Candy said. So much fucking charm in it.

The producer was at my elbow, reciting her wish list. The FBI was preparing a news release on the physical evidence implicating

Giampiccolo. The police in Sesuit would be updating their progress in the inquiry into the cottage bombing. A lawyer claiming to represent Giampiccolo was planning a press conference. The producer wanted me available to comment on breaking stories. This is the woman who had been waving her arms, trying to get me off the air.

I looked for Wendy. She gave me a shy smile. I realized I had seen her image on television a dozen times the night before. For days, she had been newsworthy, the accused Sesuibomber's lawyer. With the NBC deal, Wendy turned glamorous—the woman who transformed an outlaw into a network correspondent. Her face was "familiar," like that of any movie star once individual and now part of the definition of beauty. Enhanced in its worth, but stripped of its breathtaking particularity. Iconic.

Seeing Wendy, I understood that the mantle of stardom had descended on me as well, for good and all. Even my implicit denial of my role in the Movement—I mean my marshaling evidence against Giampiccolo—did not diminish my status. I had ridden south in the white limo, taken my place at the anchor desk, faced down Bolotow, given anarchism a voice. I had been seen seeing my cottage in flames. From here on out, I could be bumbling or sincere or quirky. Whatever posture I chose would be a posture of celebrity.

Wendy shepherded me toward the exit. She was speaking of feelers that had come through, by fax or phone—for me to host a talk show, produce news features, defect to a different network. I tried to gauge my feelings, to see whether I was experiencing a change in the direction and quality of my desire.

PART TWO

Celebrity

20

*

Triumph

Brief interval of inspiration: a week of fevered journal-writing, the week of Sukey's groceries. Then you returned. I felt no need to continue, now that I could speak with you or, better, refrain from speech and let you reveal yourself in action.

For nine-plus months I have not set pen to paper. Now, it is late June. You are asleep in the bedroom beside mine, in the servants' wing of Stone House. Two A.M. I have wakened to one of my colored nights, full of memory. I understand that I am meant to write. Your presence seems to urge me on, despite a father's inhibitions in face of his son. There's what caused the interruption, if I am honest: I dropped this journal before you returned—stopped writing when the affair with Wendy started. Even in imagination, I had no wish to describe that for you.

It began immediately. A limo took us from the studio. Crowds surrounded us. They roared. No one had produced a half hour of television the likes of the one we had given the public—the plot twists.

Wendy snuggled up against me. There was a new bond between

us. Not as between defense attorney and criminal client. As between darlings of the moment. As with Marcia Clark and Christopher Darden, the O. J. Simpson prosecutors, driven into an otherwise unlikely romance.

That is my excuse, if one is required. Like the ocean, celebrity hides enormous forces. Undertow, riptides, rogue waves.

That and Wendy's neediness. I had never met a woman so like me. Insecure, and yet relentless in the service of others. Susceptible to gratitude. Gratitude has its sensual side. Wendy thought she owed me something, for saving her from divorce law, perhaps, or from men who turn cruel in the face of a woman's melancholy. There was desperation to her kisses, as if she could not thank me enough.

That and Wendy's beauty. I would be lying if I did not mention beauty. A composition in perfect ovals: Modigliani, as I have said, or Matisse, or Edward Weston. Though here I may have moved from excuse to confession.

We were together—let me strive for frankness, in bed together—that afternoon when Sukey phoned. Hold all calls, we had said, but such insubstantial barriers are as nothing to Sukey.

No hello, no congratulations. Only: Switch on the damn TV.

A press briefing. New York Hilton. Giampiccolo at the rostrum.

Sukey, I mouthed to Wendy.

That son of a bitch, Sukey said. He's going to take credit.

Wendy sat propped against the pillows, hair up, fixed with a pencil. She spoke in a stage whisper: Tell her you're a hard sell.

Is Wendy with you?

That result was one Sukey wanted, one she thought was right for me. She would be free to go on her way, certain I was in good hands.

I'm a pushover, I said.

Sukey said, In every way. I can't believe you had me hand . . .

She had passed the Paraguay account to Big Eddie. Probably Eddie had funneled some cash back to Giampiccolo. A peace settlement.

Can they access the other? I asked, meaning the Swiss funds.

Damn his eyes, Sukey said.

On air, Giampiccolo looked the worse for wear. Anxious days underground, or a shortfall in hormone pills. Somewhere he had found a double-breasted continental suit for the occasion. When he spoke, he sounded slick, in control. He was available to meet with the authorities, that was his announcement. But he would invoke his right against self-incrimination.

My immediate thought was: My son will not be accosted again. I had the bends, from surfacing so fast. Wendy could not make out the source of my distress.

Shh, shh, she comforted.

Giampiccolo said he was happy to be back. His story was that he had reunited with radical friends from his youth, and they had turned him round. Convinced him to give up building, trash-hauling, horse-trading. Enlightened, he had chosen to disappear, make amends in secret.

He took the plotline I had offered, the Saint Augustine move.

At Giampiccolo's side stood XOXOX Patti. Warm, admiring. An answer to my question, where a man goes when he's on the run: to an early girlfriend. Patti Miller, now of Detroit, still a radical, organizing hospital workers, as your mother once did in Boston. Patti wore a loose-fitting dress with a Native American print. She was part of the show, the freckle-faced hippie companion, some meat on the bones now, aging earth mother.

Giampiccolo did not say outright that he was the Sesuibomber, but his speech was sprinkled with sixties left-wing jargon. Spectacle, drift, situation. Patti had prepped him. He must have achieved levity, because Sukey was laughing, cursing all the while.

Giampiccolo fielded questions like a politician, never confirming, never denying. The slipperiness gave him a look of competence. That's how the competent are, slippery. His presence made me seem by contrast ever less like a leader who had planned a long campaign, aroused a nation. Giampiccolo had access to tools, know-how, munitions. He was comfortable with risk. He had the character to wreak destruction—that was the real message. As in a presidential campaign, character is all.

At the same time, Giampiccolo denied involvement. He was assembling a dream team of defense attorneys. Top players were scrambling to get on board. Because his innocence was evident. Think of the attack on the Woodcock mansion, he said. The implication was that he would buy his way to safety, relying on technicalities, relying on whatever legerdemain had produced evidence of his presence in Florida while Woodcock was under way in Sesuit.

Where had he hidden? Why had he been underground so long?

Giampiccolo teased the press. He despised the cult of personality, he said. Better for the Movement to work its magic without its being identified with any one man. The joke here was in his obvious craving for notoriety. He had stolen history.

I had done well to rely on the theory Anais taught. Ours is not the society of the dollar but of the spectacle. The night of the day he accosted you, I had struggled to imagine Giampiccolo on the run. How must he have been greeted? As a low-end player on the outs with Mr. Big. Or as the rebel who had inspired a nation. Who would not prefer immortality? A man could get used to it. What does a powerful and elegant consumer want, when he does not opt for luxury? He wants to be legendary. As for your safety—in the modern world, celebrity trumps vengeance.

I don't believe Giampiccolo ever intended to harm you. His liberty depended on his remaining unconnected to me; it must be Giampiccolo *or* Samuels, each sustaining doubt as to the other's culpability. To touch you was the one way of contacting me that, if observed, could not be interpreted as collaboration. For a wise guy to threaten the son of a man who holds evidence against him is standard operating procedure, an accepted story line. A gesture that was the polar opposite iconically from what it was in fact, a means of coordinating our efforts.

Like Sukey, Giampiccolo is an artist whose natural medium is the spectacle. Accosting you was clever, but it was the press conference—his use of Woodcock—that best exemplified his dexterity. I had fretted over a trifle. Giampiccolo embraced contradiction. Like atomic particles that are never where you measure them, he could be at once here and yonder, with a probabilistic location only, baffling observers. Far from presenting an impediment, Woodcock made Giampiccolo's reemergence possible. For purposes of history, he was the Sesuibomber. At the same time, Woodcock provided the core of a legal defense.

Sukey cursed and sputtered, though I think she knew I had found the only way out.

You'll understand, Wendy said into the receiver, as she took it from me and hung up.

I was afraid you were out to get him, Wendy said. Giampiccolo's press conference had reassured her. I was not an aggressor intent on skewering a rival. I gave people what they wanted.

She began to kiss me all over, my soft chest, my doughy waist. Contrast was at the heart of our romance—her sleek, nervous body, my failing flesh. To be with an older man whose only violent acts were in the service of those he loved—this attachment comforted her. I worried over the age difference. May-December romance embodies the damage capitalism does to women's sense of worth.

Wendy mocked me for my scruples: The anarchist. The man without categories. Why not young with old?

She said: You have no notion of what goes on in America; we're barely August and October.

She asked: Is that all I am, the younger woman?

She had signed on when I was wanted for crimes against society and was still signed on, in full awareness of my guilt. She said, You are reliable, you are brave, you are funny. You saved my life. If you think love depends on reasons like that, if you think love rests on reason.

She said, Honestly, who can blame you?

Betraying Anais was not at issue. The Anais I knew was a forceful advocate and practitioner of free love. Even the Anais I'd heard on the phone two days before, even she would be uncomfortable with my abstinence. It was myself I betrayed. Abstinence can be a calling. Fidelity, too, however ridiculous. Faith and abstinence, traditional elements of vocation.

For all that I was inflated with celebrity, I knew Wendy had no business choosing me. I am worn. I am obsessed with antique dramas. What a young depressive needs is a vigorous, upbeat suitor who appreciates her depth.

To be famous and to take advantage of that status, to accept the permission the culture gives for a successful older man to find solace with a nubile lover—someone else's happiness. And yet it was mine as well. After years of celibacy, to be touched by sad and lovely Wendy—I hope that if someday you come upon these pages, you will understand and forgive.

21

*

Vindication

You will read them. I know as much, despite my claim of *to you and not for you.* Last fall, I needed that illusion, in order to write at all. No longer. I seem freed by your reappearance in Sesuit—freed or compelled, to bring this story up to date. The muse does fly low, setting the task, without explanation. If pressed, I would say I have resumed this journal in order to leave a collection of orts and shards for you to discover and interpret. When you are my age, perhaps. Well past the easy self-righteousness of adolescence, capable of sympathy with a father who loses his way.

For now, you are asleep, as you were last night, in your bed in the servants' wing. I am in the library, the least-changed room in Stone House. The panels proved too perfect for the condo owners to alter; the coarse Honduran mahogany available today bears no resemblance. In the light of the desk lamp, the old wood glows burgundy, as if soaked in wine. I feel embraced by my father's caring.

My appearance on the *Today* show brought you back to me. Not immediately. Your mother took time to warm to the idea of your visit. But there is no resisting the tug of celebrity. The media begged for a staged reunion. Presently, it came to seem odd that you did not contact your father—what was that about? Since on air I seemed an okay guy.

Wendy renegotiated my contract with the network. Bigger money. A pied-à-terre on Central Park West, with a view of the Sheep Meadow. When she was not at her practice in Sesuit, Wendy stayed with me.

I worked at a new craft, videomontage. Assessing the Echoes that broke the Sesuit Silence. Local photographers shot tape; I edited, added a sparse voice-over. In constructing my essays, I was courting you. I tried to imagine what a young man who is much like me, bookish and private, might tolerate. I took care never to press a point—to respect the viewer's skittishness. My favorite, of those early efforts, is the piece I called Toad.

We see a house on Boston's North Shore. It has a low profile with many gables, the canonical seven. The house is not without character. It is a small cottage, artfully expanded. An understated dwelling in a pretentious location—hunkered down over the private extension of Singing Beach. A weathered shingle home roofed in country-club green. A quiet signifier of New England aristocracy. L.L. Bean circa 1950.

Two rugged older men stand before the screened porch that runs the length of the east facade. One is the public health inspector, his name and title given by the chyron, the print at the bottom of the screen. The inspector explains something to the owner, who answers with a scowl. The video runs without sound.

Parathion, I tell the audience, the first case north of Georgia. The homeowner is a Southerner, Forrest Leigh, retiring CEO of Envirotrage, a company that pioneered the brokering of pollution rights. A man whose career consisted in helping business owners get the most pollution for their money.

Straight news stories have made the parathions familiar: the "cotton poisons" meant to be used in unpeopled agricultural fields where they break down in the sunlight. Despite restrictions on their use, these toxins have shown up in the food supply for years—parathions and now metathions, the industry's minimally altered variant of the banned substance. Every day, half a million kids under age five eat more than the safe amount. So that a few shareholders can get a competitive advantage. Poisoned fruit for children, fairy-tale evil with a Southern accent. For weeks, parathions and metathions have appeared in installations along the Gulf Coast.

Once absorbed into concrete, the poisons last for decades. Indoors, they cause stomach upset in the short run and cancer in the long, so the targeted structures are uninhabitable. No solution but to raze them. The installations are cleverer than FtB's—destruction of property, but (once the intervention is made public) with no risk to humans. And with an implicit environmental commentary: Why are we manufacturing carcinogens?

In Massachusetts, the choice of a Southern form of sabotage—and an environmental hazard—says the installation is personal, keyed to the owner's history. The invisibility of the damage conveys a message, that quaint exteriors can hide corruption, as in the Hawthorne novel, set nearby. Of the group that performed the installation, I speculate: Here is a different anarchist voice. One unconcerned with architectural aesthetics, one that addresses the deeds of the individual life.

On air, I try neither to celebrate nor to denigrate owner or home or installation. To display each as representative of an aspect of the time. I want the selection of images to have the effect of a teacher's ambiguous red slash in a paper's margin, a tick that might mean anything—affirmation or curiosity or a slip of the pen. One that causes the student to reconsider a sentence, to reassess what he believes.

Sometimes I imitate the authors of the books your mother left behind, the French obsessionals. There is a text by Francis Ponge, two hundred pages of attempts to describe a fig. Clichés: soft, gray. A poor gourd. Then more offbeat efforts: The fig is a poor church in the Spanish countryside. I have appropriated the right to be repetitive, and to indulge in flights of fancy. To locate verbally through successive approximations.

A grasshopper, I say, hoping to capture the effect of the gabled roofline, picked out in green. Or a toad—when we look from this angle, the head and shoulders of a squatting toad, the triangular up-and-down.

Reconsideration of the Leigh house suggests that the quality of the additions is not so fine. We cut tight to the house as it must once have been. A small, uninsulated "camp." When the house was expanded, a law prevented the camp's being torn down; the new house is technically an addition to the original. The camera zooms in and out, from former camp to present hunkered house. As we see the sequence repeatedly, we may come to believe that the saboteurs have expressed an aesthetic after all. Only certain load-bearing walls and the cement basement under the wings have been soaked. The camp had a clamshell-and-dirt floor, topped in recent years with plywood and carpeting. That floor was spared. Does it signify that the saboteurs are offering the owner an intact camp, a roof over his head?

The house will be torn down, the camp left standing—the town will require as much. There is no insurance anymore for this sort of thing; even the state's emergency provisions exclude claims related to toxins. Too easy to obtain cotton poisons, too easy for a man to spread them in his own basement. But Leigh is not strictly an owner—he had sold the house to his corporation. A privilege of the powerful, the executive leaseback. The cost of the pollution in his basement will be added to the cost of pollution in general, and the question for Envirotrage will be whether the cost can be passed on. Passing on costs—another potential theme. How corporations pass on costs, how the wealthy pass on costs, how America passes on costs. Polluted air and water. Droughts here, mudslides there. Thawing permafrost, rising tides that swamp all boats. Assets and liabilities.

All this in a four-minute package. That is the sort of segment I crafted, loosely linked words and pictures. Intending to attract the interest of a wary teen. Companionship, not expertise, was what I offered.

Did my work appeal to you? You never admitted as much—when I asked, you claimed not to have seen my Toad.

You did come. The legal system gave you a small shove. You had been abducted, that was the word used, from Massachusetts. Fathers' groups clamored for the enforcement of my rights, putting Caddie Weymouth under pressure to retrieve a child for a man who had until recently been the Commonwealth's prime terror suspect. Billy Dineen phoned you, on the AG's behalf, asking whether you might not return on your own. You were at risk of becoming an Elián González, a boy whose parental placement is a cause célèbre for a nation that otherwise does a fair job of ignoring children in need.

In the end, you came because you wanted to. But I understand how suspect matters of desire must remain, where spectacle corrupts private life.

You visited on your first school break, Columbus Day weekend. We avoided public drama. A chartered plane flew you to La Guardia. An escort walked you to my limo. The requisites of celebrity.

Suddenly, there you are. In the flesh. So much to absorb. Disorienting—like looking in a mirror that takes off the years. You are my height. Rangy, gangling, a work in progress. Myself as I was at your age, down to the slouch and the hooded eyes. I believe you are struck by the resemblance yourself, as if forced to preview what time will bring. You say, Hi, Dad.

There is no protocol for this sort of reunion. I do not know whether I can hug you, touch you at all. I grasp your shoulder, as if to help you to your seat. Electricity runs up my arm.

We sit side by side. I stare, slack-jawed. You are no better, unsure whether you can broach the Did You Do It question, all the more unsure, I suppose, now that fame has elevated me. Instead, you ask whether I will miss the cottage. I can only shake my head. What is missing a cottage to a man who has missed a child?

Here is how you look. Hidden. Camouflaged, in your baggy khakis and baggy Star Wars overshirt. Downy-faced, with cheeks touched lightly by the finger of Dame Acne. Vulnerable and unformed. Jumpy. Primed to take offense or flee. Large, real, present.

My son, already grown. An ordinary thought, one parents have when a child reappears after an interval—say, as he steps off the bus from summer camp. *Ecce homo,* zits and all. I think, My son is back with me, and we will talk and laugh and delight in the depth of our love for one another. Of course, it is nothing like, but the reality is also fine in its way. What reality lacks in neatness it makes up for in intensity.

You are in the limo, you feel trapped. You spot the well-stocked bar and reach for a Heineken. At eleven on a Saturday morning you take a beer in your hand and ask, Do you mind?

Once more your breathing is amplified. The sarcastic sigh as you await my response. I know I look puzzled. I am recalling what I learned from my students. Kids come right at you. They leave you no space to think.

I admire your challenge: *Do you mind?* It contains the truth that I no longer know you. Are you a young alcoholic in need of a pick-me-up? Or just a teenager challenging his dad? I lack even the standing to ask. I don't know if you are aware of the role alcohol played in my childhood. I see room to hope that your reaching for a beer is an act of connection, a taunt tailored to my private anxieties.

If not, if it is just a matter of you and liquor, I will face that truth. I have helped Sukey. I will try to help you. I am willing and eager to be a father to you, as you are.

All this in an instant. Do I mind? For me, fatherhood has always consisted of time overstuffed with meaning. I say, It's so early.

Meaning early in the day and early in our visit of reacquaintance. Taking reticence as consent, you twist off the cap. You gulp the first beer and take a second. Then you relax. I register the sequence. My son needs two beers to unwind. I feel thrust into the action of parenting.

Settling down now, you appear the quiet youngster I saw on television. I am witnessing the metamorphosis remarked on by all observers of adolescence, contentious adversary into compliant child. Reversible metamorphosis, that is the element missing in Kafka, the oscillation between bug and boy. Tracking your moods is like watching waves—coming and going.

Awkward, pensive, you do not so much converse as blurt out disconnected sentences, hardly expecting a response. Humming to yourself.

I've never seen New York.

I suppose we'll have time, to, you know, look around.

Mom feels bad for you about, you know, the cottage.

That Wendy Moro is, uh, your lawyer.

You seem exquisitely self-conscious. I try to put you at ease, ask neutral questions. About school and friends, the neighborhood you live in, music you favor. My emotion shows through. You clam up. And then, in our first hour together, you offer a gift. It is embedded in another of your challenges. You ask whether I like the new life. The chauffeur, the limo. You mean: If I was going to go for the money, why did I not stay with your mom, become the man she wanted on her return to the Cape, a go-getter?

I doubt I can explain that to join Anais in her happiness seemed soul murder. That as in a time-travel sci-fi flick, someone had to stay behind to guard the spot she would return to when she was herself. That celebrity is an element in the expedient cobbled together by Sukey—a solution to a crisis arising in the midst of our anonymous project of anarchy. Such transformations are common and difficult to avoid, situation into spectacle. Our contrivance at least had the virtue of calling you back.

I do not speak, let your objection stand. That is a hallmark of the relationship between adult and adolescent—misunderstanding difficult to broach with words. How right it feels to be the target of your scorn. I bask in it. Your mother used to complain about what her therapists called my inappropriate affect, as when I enjoyed her rage, but Manny reassured me that "not getting it"—not feeling what the other's challenge is meant to evoke—can be a talent. Manny says a man can have genius for inappropriate affect.

You break the silence with a welcome phrase. You say, It's like the monkey who eats the orange and throws away the rind.

That is the gift. A metaphor from John Galsworthy. Your quiet acknowledgment that you are a reader.

Late in the Forsyte sequence, four novels in, Galsworthy builds an episode around an oil painting. A portrait of a monkey with an impudent gaze, a white monkey seen side-on, its face turned to the viewer. You were referring to that passage, I was sure of it. The monkey has been caught in the act, eating an orangelike fruit. Empty peels lie tossed about. *Eat the fruits of life, scatter the rinds, and get copped doing it.* I loved that line, when I encountered it in childhood, and the discussion that follows: What should the painting be titled? *Modernity, caught out.* He is not embarrassed at getting copped, that monkey. Only annoyed that there is more he has not snatched.

Mon semblable, mon fils. The son who can read four volumes of Galsworthy and be moved by a trope. Best not to take your gift as an invitation to intrude. I can imagine how, given the private plane and limo, you might wonder whether I have turned smug or selfish; perhaps there have been selfish men in your mother's life.

I say, I hope I am not greedy.

As I speak, I understand the impression my affair with Wendy will give you, of my values.

Wendy had left for the Cape, to give us time alone, but that was the problem, too much togetherness, oppressive to you. Avoiding the media was a hassle. I intended to announce your visit after the fact. To say that we had met, and now everyone could back off. In the meanwhile, I did not want paparazzi dogging our steps. A curator gave us a private walk-through of the new guerrilla-art space at the MOMA. We slipped into an eco-rap concert via the stage entrance. Too precious, the special treatment. The second night, you said you preferred to hang out in the apartment.

That was the high point. Seeing you sprawled on the sofa, Paul Auster's *Leviathan* propped on your lap. You had been catching up on your anarchist fiction, in preparation for our reunion. You read, I washed dishes.

But shortly you said you had cabin fever. Could you take a walk?

Alone? I asked, and that was what you wanted.

Right after you left, your mother phoned.

While I have you . . . , she said. She wanted to remind me about your homework. You had a history report, you had procrastinated; the teacher was a bit of a hard-ass, if I knew what Anais meant. She chattered about your threat to get a new earring. I was not to let you out of my sight.

Welcoming the prodigal, a man does not worry overmuch about high-school transcripts or earlobe studs. And yet one must demand, inspire, cajole—else what does it mean, to father? That would be a goal for me, to care more about the everyday. I said I would look out for you. I was unconvincing.

Typical, Anais said. You want him to visit, but you don't want to take responsibility.

The dialogue pleased me, Anais's pigeonholing me as a run-of-the-mill guy in conflict with his wife. And so I tried to move matters further in the direction Anais indicated, joint parenting. I asked, Do you think Hank has a drinking problem?

It had just registered with Anais that I had let you out alone, at dusk, in Manhattan: He's wandering the streets?

I've never gotten the hang of authority. I said: He gets antsy.

I tried to reassure your mother, told her you would be safe in this neighborhood, that you knew to stay out of the park. My question for her was whether you would be trying to cadge a drink.

She said, no, you had never been disobedient with her in that way. But then she changed direction, began to confess. Liquor had been missing from the cabinet. She had overheard your friends joking. She had ignored the obvious. A single parent has so much to attend to. This past month had been rough on you. Your acceptance by kids who had ignored you. Your rethinking your young life. She would look into this matter of drink, would see what was available in the way of counseling. She had been negligent.

I valued her openness.

Anais asked if in the meanwhile I would speak with you.

Assigning me a fatherly task.

The relentless efficiency of capitalism admits of momentary lapses. One sees evidence of them here and there in Manhattan. Airspace not optimally improved with skyscrapers. A rent-stabilized apartment inhabited by a family of modest means. They are sources of hope, for the common man who imagines he can hang on a bit longer, for the entrepreneur who considers them springboards for the next leap upward.

McCorkle's is one such glitch. The old neighborhood bar. On a long-term lease, perhaps, conveyed in one of the intervals of irresolution that interrupt our commercial cocksureness. A refuge for the urban lonelyheart. No need to walk down the five steps to imagine what it looks like. Dark. Smoke-filled. With its stained oak bar and worn stools. Unvarnished floorboards, spaced and top-nailed, the crevices stuffed with cigarette butts. The rotating Budweiser banner. Mottled mirror, mercury worn thin. The array of dusty bottles, none exotic. A place to come for the usual.

Opening the door, I was suffused with a sense of the familiar. The moment of adjustment to the dim light. The barkeep's scowl. My apologetic nod, as I scanned the room. I stared into the depths. You were at the far end of the bar, where it makes a halfhearted attempt to turn a corner.

Once I started my walk, I knew you would be at McCorkle's. You would not be hiding. Defying, rather. And tending to your needs, as a drinker. Before I set foot from the apartment, in my mind's eye, I followed you here.

I visualized your movements. How to buy a drink: Pull your cap down. Walk quickly and confidently. Find the darkest spot in the house. Before the barman turns to you, flip a bill on the counter. Stand it on edge, tap it twice, then flatten it smooth in the film of water. A fifty—no, a twenty. In McCorkle's a twenty would suffice, a twenty and a false ID. What does McCorkle's know of Wisconsin? Besides, it's a holiday weekend. The few cops on duty have better things to do than sweep a B&G for minors.

A boy with the brim of his baseball cap obscuring his face. You slouched. I sat beside you, put my arm on the flat of your back.

There's none of that here, the barman said. No public display of affection, he meant, between men. All but admitting he knew you were underage. I glanced up.

Chip b'God Samuels, he said. The fellow from TV, goes on and on. Which was unfair. I say little. It's the looped images go on and on.

The barkeep was younger than I had imagined. Moon-faced, hair slicked back. Suddenly obsequious where he had been combative.

What'll it be? he said. And, to a fellow near the spigots: Andrei, look, down the bar, guy from the morning news.

Tipping his pale moon face in my direction.

Seen him in the neighborhood, Andrei said.

It seemed okay now for me to have my hand on the small of the young man's back. A perquisite of celebrity.

You ran a finger down the condensation on the beer glass. My father had that habit. Absentmindedly stroking the glass before grasping it. You asked, Whatcha gonna do?

You seemed self-possessed in your isolation. Unperturbed by my pursuit. I understood that, despite a certain social immaturity, on your own turf—alone with a book, say, or here now nursing a drink—you had substance, depth, self-possession. I could imagine how the setting appealed to you, the dusty, chaotic display of bottles. In contrast to the Midwest's happy order.

You emptied the glass in a gulp and asked me to fetch you another. I shook my head, no.

I imagined you were struggling with a question of meaning. What it meant to have an instant father, one you share with the world. A father whose face, in the billboard lineup of NBC News worthies, stares down in bemusement over Times Square.

Drinking slows life's pace, softens its challenges. Sam used liquor that way, to blur complications. Of which, in your case, I had contributed not a few. I began to acknowledge the justness of your anger, but you interrupted. What you had to tell me was simple: You were right, Dad.

You stared at your beer glass and picked at your eyebrows. Your intent was to communicate disgust.

You never had an attention deficit, nor a learning disability. You were a child on his own line of development, following his own interests. You had been placed in special classes in Madison, but when the child psychologists in Milwaukee tested you, they found nothing wrong. They took you off medication. Prescribed exercise and time for play and a mother's love. My own prescription.

You said, When I asked Grandma why my father was away, she said, Because he would not get you help.

It turned out you did not need help, except (this was the psychologists' assessment) socially. To diminish your awkwardness, your alienation. Traits your mother would once have seen as stigmata of blessedness—the disposition to remain an outsider in a corrupt society.

You looked up at me from the beer glass: Mom says I'm your clone.

You meant as a reader. You had plowed through Dickens, Hardy, half of Trollope. And the books that appeal to modern boys: Mailer, DeLillo, Tom McGuane, Richard Ford. Manly books. You blushed, not used to exposing this part of yourself.

I hope I let you know, through my posture, how proud I was of you for that confrontation in McCorkle's. A son is beautiful to his father. I wondered at the softness of the lines of your face. Like me, but with your mother's grace. Your effort to express yourself afforded me permission to peek at you while I struggled to take in your accusation, that I was right from the start.

Right about Anais, too. That she would not find fulfillment in financial success. You said you worried about her. She would lay a business coup at the feet of her mother but then rage at her for holding false values. When Anais was not desperate about men, she was dismissive. None had integrity, none understood what matters. Mom looks for you in them, Dad, is what you said.

You were controlled in that conversation. *Vindicated* is the word you used. Dad, you are utterly vindicated.

We believe and do not believe.

I had held out against your mother and the school system and the court-appointed experts. I had stood my ground against Anais's doctor and her women's groups and said, no, she is not herself, she will never find peace amidst the immense accumulation of commodities. I had lived by credos I trusted Anais would return to. Not enough! I did not believe with certitude, that was your charge. A man who knew, really knew, that his son was fine would find a way to keep him out of special programs. A man who understood his wife would manage to convince her of the source of her happiness. I had feared I was too extreme, standing fast. Sitting across from you, I realized my shortcoming was in the opposite direction, lack of fanaticism, insufficiency of faith.

A terrible thought seized me: that I had been a coward. That the reason I'd accepted being pushed aside was fear that the man I was, alienated from competition and consumption, could not raise a child in the world of This and More. I had misprized the aspect of self you most needed in me, my inability to get it. Like the Saggy Baggy Elephant, you had wanted to come home to a parent who shared your faults and qualities. Now I had reappeared, but as an insider—greedy monkey.

None of this did you say directly. You squeaked and mumbled.

You played with the coaster and glanced furtively at an overdressed woman who had wandered in for a quick hit to buck her up (so I imagined) before a foolish assignation. All the same, it was an indictment.

How can I make it up to you? I asked.

I want to be part of it, you said.

You meant the Movement. Your way of dealing with my transformation, incompetent into celebrity, was to follow in my footsteps. Unless it was only that you wanted to add your weight to mine, pulling your mother back over the line.

So confusing, fatherhood. To discover that I had been right in every regard—not overidentified. And in the same conversation to learn that your identification with me extends this far—to the point of action. How to dissuade you? The dream of a man who enacts terror, even of my modest sort, is that his son will not need to do the same.

Only after a moment did I consider the premise on which your request was based. Without asking the Did I Do It question, you knew.

22

＊

Thanksgiving

On the walk to the apartment, I made a decision. I would move back to Sesuit. As a dramatic gesture, to signal that your welfare was paramount. To provide a home where home had been for you. If a boy has to drink, safer to have him wander the lanes of a mid-Cape town than the alleys of Manhattan. I saw Sesuit as bucolic, reverting to hamlet status as trophy home owners fled.

Looking for housing, I turned to Sukey. The day Giampiccolo reappeared, she had asked Wendy's firm to draw up papers for a real-estate trust specializing in purchases of distressed properties. Sukey predicted that Massachusetts would repeal the remaining coverage for victims of terror, now that the Commonwealth owed me a small fortune for blowing up my own home. Worse—insurance companies were themselves suspect, and conviction of the Sesuibomber no longer seemed imminent. Sukey foresaw repeal and the panic that would follow. She said: In America, the direct path is through free enterprise.

Sukey had held on to some of the Swiss funds. She used them as seed money, to attract venture capital to buy beachfront cheap, in a corporation dedicated to community and profit both. The idea was that the beach would be free—privately held but effectively public, available for uses that town- or state-owned beaches could not entertain. Women-only days, where a gal could relax without being hit on by men. Gay days, nude days, inner-city-youth days. Native American days. Days of happenings, days of monastic silence. Even Twentieth-Century Days, where, by lottery, families could win exclusive right to a stretch of beach, in parody of the old way of doing things. Mostly the beach was to be open. Cape as People's Park. The best protection against anarchism is capitulation. The houses above were to be protected by the disorder below.

She would reestablish wild-berry patches on the open land.

Sukey's big project was a renovation of the Howell house and its neighbors on Saltworks Circle. She was creating a conference center. Grandeur offensive in a private home suited a communal setting. The outbuildings included bungalows reminiscent of the Cape in the fifties. A new Chautauqua—a site for revival. The zoning board was happy to entertain any project that might bring value to beleaguered properties.

Money flowed in, and Sukey spent it. Twelve, fourteen, twenty homes. Before she could rehab them, they were booked for rental, in anticipation of a summer of Happenings. The Cape drew radicals the way revolutionary France drew romantics.

I phoned Sukey and asked whether there was a cottage to be had in Sesuit. Two weeks later she showed up in New York. Le Bernardin for lunch.

She was back to designer dresses, Pucci revival, confetti curlicues, fuchsia and lime on black. She turned a cool cheek, to let me know the Giampiccolo resolution still rankled: Don't think you're forgiven.

She ordered us the tasting menu, and it kept coming. I was uncomfortable amidst the *luxe*. But I found I love urchin and urchin roe. The tang of the sea. I am not so effectively blindered by "not getting it" as I had imagined, not immune to temptation.

Before the coffee was served, Sukey slipped me a sheaf of official-looking paper. The deeds to Stone House, with both our names inscribed.

Not that you deserve anything, she said. But the condos came to market cheap.

Flames had lapped Stone House. Sukey and I knew those flames, a person does not forget clapboards ablaze.

Live at Stone House while you work on it, Sukey commanded. You need a hands-on project, I need a general contractor.

For when we retire, she said. Meaning she planned to forgive me in time. For now, she was busy enjoying dalliances with men of the sort who are drawn to older women when they achieve prominence in the spectacle.

On my next visit to Sesuit, I met with Bert Costas, to get the lay of the land. He had invited me for a formal interview. The inquiry into the fire in the cottage had bogged down—my guess was that evidence implicated the feds as passive conspirators. Bert had decided to take personal charge of the investigation, on the local level.

We met in the Sesuit station house, the shake-shingled Cape at Sesuit Four Corners, next to the prefab Wa Wa mini-mall. The town had already moved some police functions to a high-tech facility near Route 6—a brick cube meant to give the impression of security in insecure times. I preferred the old building with its beat-up filing cabinets and linoleum floors, a modest setting that signaled reasonable efforts to enhance order for a disorderly species.

Bert still had his curly hair, but with a monastic tonsure, as if he had won the laurels in some ancient race. I told him it was good to see him.

Tough luck, he said, about the cottage.

I have no information, I told Bert. No wish to testify.

He said, I thought that would be your attitude.

His tone conveyed respect.

I said, Bert, I'd love for you to solve this case, for all it would do for your career.

Bert said, Don't give a thought to my career.

I could see he had grown in confidence. But I wondered if I did not detect an edge, as if he still chafed under injustice—all those years he was passed over for promotion. He reminded me of my father. The quiet certainty. The hint of bitterness suppressed. A sweeter version: what my father might have been like had the disruptions in his life been less extreme.

Bert asked if I suspected Antunes, the insurance rep. I said Antunes hadn't the brains to pull it off. Bert said the physical evidence pointed to Antunes. Bags of fertilizer in the guy's basement, and a box of igniters. Looks bad, igniters in your basement, in Sesuit, if your job is selling insurance.

I asked, Off the record, what would happen if you used the fertilizer to grow blueberries . . . ?

Bert considered it. Bad for our reputation, he said.

If you lost the evidence, had to drop the case against Antunes, immunize him, go after the big boys? Assuming Northeast was out to get me. After all, you've had your successes.

I meant Parlequin. The Parlequins had sued the department and Bert personally for the false arrest of their son on drug charges. Late in the summer, I blew the front off the Parlequin house, exposing a drug lab behind a false wall in the basement. Parlequin was the only FtB installation that was not bayfront. One back, as the realtors say, with a view easement.

I told Bert about your drinking and my hope that a move here would settle you and me both. Bert knows about troubled kids. His son, Nando, your schoolboy friend, has been a handful.

Bert said he expected that with the emergence of an alternate suspect, the threats against me would wane. He suggested the old trio get together, he, Billy, me. I took Bert to mean that plans to indict me had been dropped, what with the physical evidence implicating Giampiccolo, and Americans' skepticism when it comes to complicated stories spun by the government.

The debriefing encouraged me to believe that you and I might be welcome home.

For your next visit, my plan was a Thanksgiving amidst the rubble: turkey and yams on a plywood plank on sawhorses in the Stone House dining room. You were disappointed. We had been invited to Candy Aznavour's in Manhattan. I told you my goal was to simplify. As much as possible to take up where you and I had left off, years ago. No, thanks, you said.

It is true, back when, your mother's Thanksgiving tales had upset you. Too many took place close to where we lived. Here on the Cape and nearby, one in six Wampanoags killed in King Philip's War alone, and the survivors sold into slavery. Anais did not spare us accounts of the massacre of women and children. I believe the worst for you was the image of Metacom's head on a stake—Metacom, the son of the sachem who had invited the Pilgrims to dine at that first feast. Bloody recompense: A native rescues settlers, and soon his son's severed head sits atop a pole. Still, it drew us together, to be bearers of truth about Thanksgiving and its aftermath.

Humor me, I said. But in the end you got your wish.

On West Seventy-seventh Street, beside the Museum of Natural History, urban wilders staged an attack on the giant balloons being inflated for the Macy's parade. I was recalled to New York to cobble together a commentary.

Local reporters had been on-site, recording Thanksgiving-eve festivities for the feel-good late-night news. Logos and icons, every balloon tainted by the market. Maurice Sendak figures advertised an insurance company; Snoopy, the same. Sugared cereals, sugared milk flavorings—a celebration of the purchase of childhood. Cameras captured the moment wilders emerged from the circling crowd. A glint of metal, then gashes in the prodigious effigies. The despoilers were dressed in store-bought Halloween costumes to mimic the creations they slashed. For a moment the tourists seemed to imagine it was all part of the show. Panic followed.

The pranksters dashed into Central Park, where a waiting van sped off. It was found moments later, empty but for the costumes, the perpetrators having scattered and merged with the fleeing crowd.

You accompanied me to the studio, watched my team edit images and prepare copy. The best clip, you agreed, was of the grotesque Pink Panther head with its disturbing rictus. Men in jumpsuits are inflating the balloon. A Native American princess dashes by and—flick!—a blade to the occiput. The panther's face speeds through half a dozen expressions, one more evil than the next. The final image is a flat forehead with a pair of wrinkled eyes. Atop them sits an enormous set of teeth, the nose and mouth not yet fully deflated. The montage looked like a video game, cartoon figure attacking cartoon figure, and much racing and chasing, with the police taking up the rear. I liked the red Indian image, wondered if the voice-over should make reference to the Boston Tea Party, that historic episode of wilding.

The staff and I discussed the ideological content of the essay, one of a series to be sprinkled amidst the coverage of the festivities the next day. We knew that Bolotow was ginning up a commentary. He would get the lion's share of airtime, expressing indignation at the way anarchists had ruined the Thanksgivings of millions of starry-eyed tots. My job was to suggest an alternative take on the same footage. To show how the wilders caused us to reconsider the object of Thanksgiving, our freedom.

The parade was held, in brave resistance to terror. Most sponsors chose to deck their floats with the ruptured balloons. The intent was to shame and defy the wilders, but I suspect the rebuke failed. The half-inflated figures had charm and originality. Birthday presents for a prodigious Eeyore. The National Guard presence notwithstanding, there was a small-town feel to the event. Americans marching, Americans spectating. As with the summer on the Cape, a sense among those who showed up of the best holiday in memory.

I introduced my own segment, in a live shot from the network's reviewing stand. My presence implied that the wilders were in sync with the Movement, using bloodless violence to target the self-evidently foolish excesses of capitalism. Refashioning absurd spectacle into absurd situation. Like the commentators who personified outrage, I showcased the curiosity-filled faces of children along the parade route. Following on those images, my montage posed unspoken questions: Of what had our sons and daughters been deprived? For what ought they to be grateful?

We joined Candy after all. Her extended family was unassuming—welcoming. You seemed especially comfortable with Candy's niece Pauline, perhaps because of her weight problem. I wondered whether you were like me in that way, better able to see yourself with a young woman if she had a slight cosmetic flaw.

Despite my increased tolerance for opulence, I found Candy's dining room disconcerting. Ocher walls with white trim. Gallery lighting. On the table, the heavy silver. Waterford crystal. Plates of Bernardaud Limoges. I don't think it was even the good china. Blinis with caviar led off the hors d'oeuvres. You liked the turkey stuffing, oysters, and exotic mushrooms. The grown-ups urged wine on you. Was I on edge? Hardly the holiday I had planned for us together.

Wendy had volunteered to come chaperoned by Hugh Crale, so that you would not be forced to assume, as the press did, that she and I were an item. They arrived late. Hugh had been held at the network covering the arrest of two suspects in the balloon slashings—working mothers outraged at the lack of funding for the City's public schools. I felt bad for the women, jury nullification their best hope. I suggested to Candy that I might do an additional videomontage on their behalf.

Can't keep you out of this town, was how Hugh greeted me.

Wendy had been negotiating for me to base my reporting in Sesuit. She had asked the network to set up a digital editing studio there.

Candy patted my forearm: Says he doesn't need the limelight. Yet there he is, mumbling away, day after day, with the camera on those hazel eyes.

This last was for Wendy, good-natured ribbing. What did Wendy see in me? Hugh and she made a handsome couple, his squareness of jaw, her ovals. A Grant Wood variant, *American Modern,* broadcaster and agent.

The company at large teased me about my incomprehensible essays.

You challenged Wendy: He's always with you. Has he explained the absurd?

You had read enough classical romance to know what a beard is.

I do wish, and doubt, that I could have explained myself. There is a passage, in *The Myth of Sisyphus,* where Camus writes of Adrienne Lecouvreur—an actress, in the eighteenth century, when the Church deemed theater sinful. On her deathbed, she accepted eternal damnation rather than renounce her calling. That constancy was her greatest role, Camus says—to choose a ridiculous fidelity over heaven. An absurd choice that is the essence of good faith.

I had tried to honor your mother and her ideals with my ridiculous fidelity. You judged me merely ridiculous. Absurd in the mundane sense. For having lived abstemiously in the cottage when there was all this to be had, frisée and mâche and designer olive oils. For priding myself on constancy when I seemed to enjoy what any celebrity might, the young and iconic lover.

Hugh Crale grasped Wendy's elbow. The table fell silent. You made a boardinghouse lunge for more stuffing.

After Thanksgiving, I told myself I would end the affair with Wendy. She seemed to have the same goal. She opened a New York office. Her work on my move north intensified.

The network saw it my way. I had never gotten the hang of on-set banter. Just as well to have the Cape Cod handyman appear by remote. I would return to the town where the Movement had begun. To bring my son home. That was how the PR people put it. As I took distance from the spectacle, my celebrity only increased. I was Cincinnatus, returning to the farm.

You'll be moving out? Wendy asked, more eagerly, I thought, than was seemly. This was after I had popped into the apartment late one night to find her ending a phone call: *Ciao, caro mio* and a hasty hang-up. I recalled Italian idioms larding Hugh's dinner conversation at Thanksgiving, as if those were something he and Wendy had together.

I asked, Whatever do you mean?

I was in New York with one suit and a plastic Baggie-ful of mementos when my cottage burned down. Since then, I had accumulated a change or two of clothes, but I was hardly a man for whom moving would be an issue.

Wendy said, Never mind, I love you.

I had hoped Wendy would find a lover close to her own age, someone stable, who was not a project. I had ignored the consequence, that she would want to bring him to this apartment, to our bed. That she would push me out.

Wendy was kissing me. Only you, she said.

Ordinarily our embraces were dark and tender, a melting into one another. That night, her lying aroused me. I focused on her with great intensity. The blue vein on her right temple, the tiny birthmark where the jaw meets the neck. Her young skin. As always, exquisite contrast: the age of the apartment—lead in the pipes, calcimine in the plaster—and the newness of the woman in my arms. She did seem to love me, keenly, in the bewitching and hopeless session known to all men: one last time.

23

＊

Restoration

I returned to Stone House, moved back for good at the New Year. I started the rehab by repointing the main hearth, mortaring in Sukey's chip beside a pair of old bricks that had each lost a corner. There it will remain until another mischievous child pries it loose or, as is more likely if less poetical, waves undermine the sandbank.

I was on indefinite leave from the college. I had tenure, but the dean said he would have to close the English Department altogether if I stood on my rights. I hoped we would resolve our differences. Meanwhile, my habit was to rise early and pitch in with the workmen, carpenters from the Azores, mostly.

I still took *Today* show assignments, editing, commenting. I did my own reporting for the piece on Martha's Vineyard, why the beaches haven't opened up there. A stubborn island, with a history of dialectical contradiction, tenacious beach ownership coexisting with radicalism that extends back to Congregationalist ministers who preached democracy before the Revolutionary War. The isolation makes it tough to import explosives.

Nationally, there was a lull in installations. I assumed innovative projects were in process, that they would emerge months hence.

Your mother had been talking with Sukey about design plans for the conference center; the starting point was a new line of dishes, AnaisWare, for that sixties look. Anais wanted a role on the Cape this summer, when you would be visiting me. For the rest of the winter, she would be in and out of Sesuit.

Once Sukey said Anais was in town, I daydreamed continually of welcoming her home to this eroding bank. She phoned in February: I'm here. We should meet. Now that we are both caring for Hank.

To her credit, she was walking up the flagstone path, cell phone to ear.

If only she had thrown herself into my arms. In the old days, when Anais came back, the hum of the wheel would summon me. That was our convention. She would head straight to the shed, acclimate. I would wait until I heard the wheel at full speed. Give space, even when she had returned. At last I would venture out. She would notice me, and when she had run a wire beneath the perfectly rounded base of a pot in progress and secured it on the shelf, she would hold her clay-wet hands high and fling herself for me to catch. Burying her face in my chest, in implicit thanks and apology for the time away.

That February day, she thrust forth a hand. I was the one to spread my arms wide. I had been plastering. Anais gawked.

My goodness.

Wondering, I am sure, at the return to bygone days. Me in painter's pants. Whole damn thing over again. When she had expected the man from *Today*.

Sorry for the mess. And the noise. Come in, come in.

But we stood on the threshold.

I was as shaken by her looks as she was by mine. She had the wavy hair and the cupid's-bow mouth. Those were good to see, but her manner was unexpected—gay, breezy—as if the goal were not reconciliation but seduction. She was fetching, with a gardenia scent, blond highlights, whitened teeth.

I should have known what Anais looked like. Back when men's groups were demanding your return, I had seen her in paparazzo shots, caught entering a restaurant on Buford's arm, en route to a working lunch. But evidence had vied with fantasy. I had followed her for years, in my mind's eye, had watched her age, using Sukey as a benchmark. Crow's-feet, creased cheeks, doubled chin. Coarsened hair. Bifocals, perhaps. Irascible Anais. She'd a shine to her nose and a bouquet of wrinkles. She smelled of new-mown lawn.

In my dreaming, I had not factored in the technology that intervenes on behalf of a chief operating officer. Standing at the door was a fine figure of a businesswoman. Young-looking. I know it is only my "not getting it" that made me focus on the hint of a death mask in the tightness of skin to skull. That and the slight asymmetry of smile. The odometer reset by scalpel and suture.

She noticed my perplexity. Not much to look at, she said, after that lawyer of yours.

Which was not the issue. I had been waiting for Anais.

Holding my hands away, I leaned and kissed her cheek. The rain-forest scent made me sneeze. *Quelle catastrophe,* she said; I understood her to mean not Stone House but our reunion. For the first time, I heard Anais's French as affectation. My distaste unnerved me. I was determined to think well of her.

I see you're remodeling, Anais said, and I had a giddy thought: *Love is not love that alters when it alteration finds.* I suppose I was responding to Anais's tone, of amused understatement.

She swept into the room. Plaster dust drifted down from the second floor. I lifted a drop cloth from the green wing chair and made a pass at swiping the velvet clean.

She was putting it together. That the Cincinnatus stuff was not for show. I was working with my hands again.

How had she imagined me? As described on air—by Deirdre, as

the Milquetoast who might conspire to found a library. The egghead, marginal to the main effort of the Movement, if involved at all. An observer and a doubter, as I had been in our college days. And then—as a man who turns mistaken identity to his advantage, rises to prominence on morning television. Who wants what the culture has to offer.

I sensed that I represented a dream, for her to quit the rat race of midlife dating. To come home to a man she was already married to and who had finally seen reason. An alternative worth pursuing. Only in my presence did it strike her full force—that I was the Sesuibomber.

She collapsed into the wing chair, heedless of the damage to the little black suit. Do you have water? she asked, putting her hand to her temple. Bottled, I understood. She took a pill, waited for it to work.

Seeing this refined woman collect herself, I feared Anais had been replaced, permanently, by Annie of AnnieWare. *All the truths of my position came flashing on me, and its disappointments, dangers, disgraces, consequences of all kinds rushed in in such a multitude that I was borne down by them and had to struggle for every breath I drew. I could not have spoken one word, though it had been to save my life.* I recalled Pip's words, the ones that accompany his realization that he has no special tie after all to the woman he loves.

I believe Anais felt the same disconnection.

She sat in the wing chair, hand to head. Teetering. Stay or run.

I'm not intruding? she asked.

You can never intrude.

We found ourselves in a comedy of manners, at the juncture when misunderstandings separate the protagonists and politesse abounds. Anais spoke my name: Chip Samuels. Won't you look at the two of us!

Once, Anais had known her feelings and acted on them instantly. Swimming the Chute, taking a lover, centering, leaving. Now she was weighing options, temporizing.

We were cautious and considerate. One word only seems worth mentioning, since it described the distance between us. I had referred to your dedication as a reader—intending to compliment your mother on how you had turned out. She heard me as judgmental, for the attention-deficit misdiagnosis. I made mistakes, she said. You'd overwhelmed me.

Overwhelmed, a word carefully chosen with therapists (I assumed) to stand in for oppressed, exploited, abused—concepts we once applied to the wretched of the earth. Did my loyalty overwhelm? I believed the true oppression occurred in Wisconsin, in Anais's dalliances with Gustav, Richard, Bo, PJ, and the others you had mentioned in conversation. Such men "get it"—they accept the hierarchy of worth assigned by the spectacle—and so sooner or later they will come to scorn a woman with a nonconformist past and an aging face. Anais had forgotten the lesson she had taught me, that spectacle creates inequalities of power and makes them feel like intimate truth, as if the weak one were disgusting and the strong desirable. The culture is cruel to single mothers and to women of a certain age. Anais used to say as much whenever a divorcée confessed to infanticide or a spinster shot her wayward lover.

Amnesia is the hallmark of spectacular oppression. Sixties radicals go underground. They masquerade as housewives and boutique managers. Soon they are subdued by what they work in. Given time on the job and mass-marketed comforts, Weathermen morph into housewives and boutique managers. Commitment, engagement, resistance—the ideals lose their imperative force. The housewife worries over her retirement account and brightens the kitchen with decorative mixing bowls made in China. She wonders, Was I ever that other way? When the police arrive, there is a moment of confusion: She thinks, They are arresting the wrong person. The process is accelerated, no doubt, if a woman turns to pills to medicate her sense of futility. Pills and possessions are notorious for inducing amnesia.

I was hurt at the harm done Anais. The intensity of her attempts at charm signaled the depth of her injury. She seemed hell-bent on joining me no matter my identity, like those nubile contestants and the ghastly multimillionaire on television. She made reference to her achievements, reflecting in her tone the valuations the oppressive men had assigned her, of diminished private and enhanced business worth. Forgetting who had left whom, she treated me like one more successful male who, whatever his past professions of loyalty, would choose the fresh-faced lover over the middle-aged wife who had raised his child.

I hoped she was wrong. I told myself I was holding back out of loyalty. I took my lesson from your accusation: *Not fanatical enough.* I had stood fast for Anais; I must stand fast longer, until she came to herself. The main thing was to get her help. She had been injured by the strain of ignoring what she knew about the state of the world—by queasiness outside awareness. I asked if she was all right. I recommended Manny.

I understood he was your therapist, she said.

I said: Sukey's therapist. I drove her there. He worked wonders.

What hell to see Anais walk back down the path, slump-shouldered. I have said that no artist or artisan worthy of the name understands his motivation. But in these intimate human choices surely a man should know something. Whether his reticence is a matter of principle—to help his wife recover—or of corruption of the self.

I had entered the spectacle, absorbed adulation. Once that line is crossed, bearings are hard to find. Anais's enhanced face spoke of amnesia and capitalist conformity, but it was also the stigma of her vulnerability. When had I stopped finding Anais's vulnerability compelling? If I could become an anarchist out of love for her, why not a network correspondent? Perhaps she was right: The problem was that I had touched Wendy. There was no last time with Wendy, or rather there were many.

I wanted my own session with Manny. Must I remain a man of the spectacle, for Anais's sake? If so, would a man of the spectacle choose Anais over Wendy? That was one way of framing my dilemma, and Anais's: The man she wanted would want Wendy.

24

*

Dovetailing

Did your mother say I had rebuffed her advances? You were cool to me on the phone. I guessed you wanted your parents back together, but when I asked, you said, I'll be in college in a year or two.

Anais and I continued to meet, when she came East. She seemed to imagine I wanted a woman who is ever more successful, more iconic. Buford held that what the corporation had lacked while Anais hid from me was a face. He planned to feature her in commercials for the AnaisWare line. She would sit for an interview for *Martha Stewart Living,* with talk show appearances to follow. Anais Speaks. Her depression, her struggles as executive and single mom, her advice on setting your table. Our separation would be papered over with platitudes.

She offered to take me on as a consultant to the AnaisWare subsidiary. I would be a boon to the product image: cups and saucers for the radically chic table.

She saw she was not reaching me: What's a girl got to do to catch a break around here?

I wanted to reach across the divide but found I could not, not on this basis. I declined the AnaisWare opening.

*   *   *

I had taken to eating breakfast with Bert and Billy, at Mello's Diner, another relic. Chrome-trimmed Formica tables. Eggs with chorizo. We ordered oatmeal, the only choice left to us, what with juice and coffee causing gastric reflux and everything else on the menu clogging the vessels.

Small-town American scene: cop, lawyer, and journalist sharing a booth. Chewing the fat, metaphorically if not otherwise. The usual: Billy's wife walked out. Worst thing that ever happened to him. A stage she was going through, she got angry and suspicious. He had trouble telling whether it was something he'd done. Turned out to be a thyroid problem, easily fixed in the end.

Silver lining to the wife's illness, he said. Puts work in perspective.

I told Billy, I'm sorry we haven't been closer.

He said, I feel we have been close, the last couple of years.

Bert spoke of job frustration. The town councilmen were tightwads. They might vote for bricks and mortar, a new police station with their names on a brass plaque at the entrance. The explosions had not convinced them to expand the force, not with property values plummeting. Now we've got free use of the FBI, was their attitude.

Bert had been injured, over decades, by the lack of respect for his efforts, and now by his being given the title of chief without the resources. His reluctance to pursue me, when he was first promoted, had brought him some glory, since the FBI's accusations soon seemed misdirected. But increasingly he was a fifth wheel, heading a department that issued parking tickets while the feds patrolled his town.

Bert was overwhelmed. Messy divorce, two teenage sons. Tough to raise kids poor amidst the highfliers. Too much This. Jags, Beemers, Hobie Cats. Coke and crack. Not so different from what we faced growing up, but the disparities seem greater and the effects worse. I imagined the explosions had appealed to Bert and Billy both, local boys who'd seen Sesuit ruined by wealth.

Bert said fishing was his dream. His uncle had helped him fix up his dad's boat. Bert hoped his boys would join him—keep them off the streets. He was looking for an excuse to leave the force. He said, A man returns to his roots.

A fine dream, Billy said. If there were still fish out there.

They talked of a fishery ruined by competition. Here was an area where their passions were similar to my own—socialism the logical solution.

Television seems to suit you, Bert said.

I told him I was pulling back: The glamour is bad for the family.

Billy said, I always had the impression you were drawn to carpentry.

I gathered implements. A few electric tools—jigsaw, lathe, drill. New hand tools, too—planes, chisels, files—where an application of Naval Jelly did not suffice to return my father's to service. I intended to repair furniture. Odd pieces Sukey had picked up in houses she'd bought from owners too scared or disgusted to set foot on the Cape. Nothing valuable. It would be years before I could be trusted with Goddard highboys, but I saw years before me.

Your mother came upon me when I was puttering.

You don't understand who you are, she said. You're a brandable name. You should make new furniture, your own line. Do it with Hank this summer.

She could find me a gallery placement if I made my pieces art.

We went back and forth about what that might mean. Performance art. Primed to self-destruct. A modem and an igniter in a desk's hidden drawer, say, wired to tiny amounts of low-sensitivity, high-brisance explosives at critical spots in the structure. Or tables—a tie-in to AnaisWare, if I could make kitchen and dining-room tables.

This was the conversation Anais engaged in nowadays, the sort that made her manufacturing company fly. We were "blue-skying it." Anais suggested a mock Duncan Phyfe that goes pop. Or a

George Nakashima or Maya Lin, if I preferred modern. Americana, multicultural. Anais would help with the design work.

There is a passage in the first chapter of *Capital* where Marx waxes poetic over the role of commodities. Form wood into a table. It remains wood, a sensuous thing, while adding a second aspect, utility. So far, nothing mysterious. Now place this dualistic object into the context of capitalism. Then, Marx says, the table evolves in its wooden brain ideas more wonderful than if it were to begin dancing on its wooden legs. Like Dotty Arnold's land, the table becomes *a strange thing, abounding in metaphysical subtleties and theological niceties.* The man who owns it may not only eat at it but also exchange it, for power over other objects and even people. The table embodies righteousness, dividing the blessed from the cursed.

I asked Anais if she'd had Marx in mind when she suggested I make tables. She gave me a look of incomprehension. Never mind. I liked the coincidence.

Anais envisaged furniture that would collapse without fire, without flying splinters—there was the engineering challenge. Loud noise, and a swift fall to earth. When an owner happens to make just the right series of phone calls, ones that correspond to the frequency sequences programmed into the modem. If the item has a modem. My contribution was to suggest that not all pieces be equipped. Randomness is a necessary element in absurdist art.

I would after all dip a toe into the pool of radical chic—a move toward your mother and toward you as well, I hoped. I had been reading textbooks, about adolescence and the romance of risk. Sublimation, that is the great recommendation. Not squelching the impulse to rebel, but redirecting it. Bike trips and rock climbing is what the authors have in mind, but I thought work with sharp tools might suffice, work linked to the Movement.

Come June, you joined me in the apprenticeship my father never offered. In the servants' wing of Stone House, together you and I learned to dovetail, not with the routers and many-fingered jigs you see on television, but by hand, estimating angles. Making sense of the wood. Hoping it would speak to us.

*   *   *

We match up two highly figured red oak planks. A large oval knot, deeply checked, mars each board halfway along its length near the edge. A puzzle for us. How to retain the knots, make use of them. Create a desktop that says, Tree. That says, Take nature as she presents herself.

We decide to cut around the knots, ovate curves. The desktop will be rectangular, but along the centerline the boards will meet yin and yang. I match grains, jigsaw the shapes in outline, lay the boards side by side. You will plane and rough-sand and trim and measure and re-sand.

You open up a bit, when you are intent on a task, among wood chips.

You sharpen your chisel by hand. You hum, you have your mother's hum. You think aloud. Will you finish school in Milwaukee? You do not say that you are happy here, but the thought is implied.

You have taken up with your old friends. Not so much Teddy and Janna; your pal is Nando, Peck's bad boy. Competent-looking kid, firm handshake, nothing to say to grown-ups. Old story, police chief's son getting picked up for petty mischief. Your mom says you had a friend in Madison, when you were there, who was naughty in a younger kid's way. A pattern, the shy with the misbehaving, like me with Billy Dineen. I worry that Nando can drink with the best of them, but I am glad for you to feel at home in Sesuit.

We work until we are bored with working, and then we swim. It occurs to me that we are recapitulating your summer of learning to read, but I do not follow the thought to its conclusion. What look like good times can end in crisis.

Pauline comes to the Cape. She is staying with friends in Brewster. Pauline, you, and I take a swim together, from Brewster into Sesuit, to the beach in front of the former Evrard estate.

The cold June waters cleanse us of our sins. I feel the bursitis in my right hip, and it is welcome to me. The tightness in my neck and shoulder, and the weakness in my left arm, these, too, are precious. Immediately after Woodcock, I consulted an internist, one assigned me by the insurer foisted on union men and women by the Commonwealth. He told me the symptom was nothing, inapparent on a cardiogram. He was wet behind the ears, but when the weakness recurs, I find his verdict reassuring.

Evrard is a recent donation to the charitable foundation, the Free Beach Institute, that Sukey established to complement her real-estate trust. The Evrards are old-line liberals ashamed to have controlled beachfront, pleased to find a way to give back to the community. Although, as the radio discussion about *aporia* implied, generosity can be hard to assess. The dune has receded to within yards of the Evrard deck.

We wander up to look about. The doors are ajar. Amid the worn furniture, two newish pieces stand out. Pauline throws herself on a sofa, Crate & Barrel British khaki. Bought, with matching love seat, at a yard sale from neighbors who fled the Cape early in the terrors, or received from them as a farewell gift—that is my read on the decor.

Pauline flops herself on the sofa in her wet suit, aware that the furniture will be discarded in the redecoration. She is plump and lively and comfortable. No-nonsense. You sit beside her, proud of yourself, in a first romance.

How would it be done? Pauline asks, glancing round the Evrard living room.

Though I do not need to guess what *it* is, I maintain a blank look. Not wanting to encourage your interest. Not wanting to endanger Sukey.

Mr. Samuels! Pauline urges, as if exasperated. She assumes a stagy Midwestern pose of good-humored frustration. She's a funny kid—fresh, unawed by adults. And not without a vixenish twinkle to the eye. I see a bit of Sukey in her. A happy choice for you, I think; Pauline looks like she can have fun.

Shall we head back? I ask.

The next day, when we are planing wood, you ask where the

explosives for the furniture will come from. It is a normal question, so I tell myself. On-Cape, there are no explosives to be had. Warehouses, businesses, even private homes, have been searched. Traffic over the bridges is subject to inspection, cars pulled off the road into lots built for the purpose. The Coast Guard feels free to board the smallest of boats. Tel Aviv has nothing on the security at Hyannis Airport.

A normal question, but on my swim to you it will return to me and I will wonder why I did not follow up, ask why you were asking. I thought only that you had been emboldened by Pauline, her joshing confrontation of me in the Evrard house. Understandable curiosity.

You and I do not need a source because we will not be mining the furniture, beyond one or two pieces, to demonstrate the principle. For those, I plan to install the explosives off-Cape.

I thought we had gone over this. My secret, my little joke, is that there are no explosive-filled desks or armoires. Beyond the demos, I am content to have every piece be a dud. So that you learn that excitement is not in the matériel. The concept, the symbolism, and the story line are what matter. Duds are expressive. Like Warelwast. The dud collector's item is a tale with a moral. What you see is what you get. There is no more to ownership than meets the eye. No enhancement of the owner. The dud is amusing and absurd. Parsimonious. Fraudulent. Eloquent. A fit symbol for our condition. I named our workshop Dancing Tables, as cryptic warning that what is most remarkable about the furniture is the value society accords it.

25

*

La Nausée

It is early on July 5, the wee hours. Windless, calm before the storm. You are asleep after an evening of fireworks. Sacked out on the library sofa, Zola's *Paris* spread facedown on the floor beside you. Perhaps you hoped to read before heading for bed, but the hour got to you, the hour and whatever else, beer or reefer. Still— my son asleep behind me in this room my father crafted, fondest dream. Your breathing sounds deep notes, the near-snore, basso profundo, suggestive of maturity.

I have been here with you since midnight, writing the entries about my move back to Sesuit and our work together, the dancing tables. I will continue until you waken, try to complete the journal in this sitting—since I assume my excess energy, my colored nights, will fade, now that your secret plot has played itself out. I under- stand better why I resumed writing. Like a man surrounded by preparations for a surprise party, I had a sense of plans afoot. An inkling that the events I was recording were drawing if not to a con- clusion, then to the point of momentary rest that we demand of sto- ries even in this decomposing world.

*   *   *

Consciously, all I knew was that I felt out of sorts, despite the pleasures of working beside you. The problem was my indecision with the women. It could not go on like this, not even in an anarchist interval.

Anais checked in regularly. She was encouraging, from the posture of a COO: My celebrity had survived the move north, the premarketing for the furniture was going well. She was less fanatically groomed, but I worried that the change was only a response to the new dictates of fashion—haute couture out, home-sewns in. Or that she was set on pleasing me. Complaisance is a decided aspect of her personality. I was beginning to understand that Anais-as-she-was would not return.

She is a strong swimmer still. In the water, it was like old times.

Sukey was in the picture. Flirting, touching, stopping by Stone House to hint that she could use a few more repairs, to astound the tourists. The showiest of our remaining installations, the Hoffmeyer compound, she had spent in April, on Patriot's Day.

Trust the proletariat, I said. The people will provide.

Sukey's flirtation increases when she is in a relationship with another man. The fellow of the moment is Schuyler "Tubby" Vanburgh. Tubby's a real-estate colleague with *Mayflower* roots and substantial land interests on Martha's Vineyard. He wears the yacht club uniform, faded cranberry pants and madras shirts. I worry that there is no more to Tubby than meets the eye. That this is the man Sukey will retire with, to the life she was born to, wealth and noblesse and fights around the liquor trolley. Sukey does know how to enjoy money. Although her cheeriness may have had a separate cause, the women's campaign against Giampiccolo, the one Wendy was coordinating.

*   *   *

Wendy was the force behind the civil suits. She had achieved one of her goals, to broker a fuller reconciliation between Sukey and me; Wendy was using her legal talents as a sort of couple therapy, an intervention in the tradition of Emmanuel Abelman.

She had encouraged four different women to enter filings against Giampiccolo, for harassment. She is the one who got the plaintiffs' lawyers to force the FBI to disclose the semen evidence. Aliquots of Giampiccolo's jism had been found on sheets and blankets in four of the blown houses. A guy who got off on planning explosions, it seemed. A pervert.

Paradoxically, the Movement's prestige was enhanced by the exposure of Giampiccolo's sexual aggression. The Clinton effect kicked in—those op-ed pieces that take the line, Who else is going to inspire a nation but a high-testosterone type? We expect these excesses in our leaders, the personal is not the political, etc., etc. The nation understood why the Sesuit cell had been able to do the impossible, ring up two dozen installations without so much as a singed feather on a pet canary—because the Movement had been orchestrated by an alpha male. Ironic, since I knew that the only high-testosterone type in on the disruptions was Sukey.

These successes should have left Wendy free to go. But nothing Wendy or I did seemed sufficient to end the affair. We had only to see each other to begin again, desperately.

I tried to feel out Bert and Billy over oatmeal, see if they thought I could pull off a reunion with Anais. The men were circumspect. Marriage had taught them that no one knows the answers.

Bert said, She was unhappy, out on the bay.

Billy asked, Does she know what she's getting into?

I phoned Manny and told him I was confused.

He said, Let's take a walk. First light.

I had never seen him outside his house. The Lady of Shalott.

* * *

As instructed, I came by at 5 A.M. Manny was standing at the end of his drive, staring longingly toward the Sears Woods. Hermit turned vagabond.

Nippy weather for this time of year, he said—the first time I had heard him exchange a pleasantry.

I drove him to what is still called the town beach, on Nantucket Sound. In April, a wildcat installation (that is, not one of ours) took out half of the town hall in Dennis, the side where beach permits are issued. Since then, the fate of town beaches has been up in the air. I like the idea of a town beach—one residents are proud to maintain and share with their neighbors and the world. But Dennis and Wellfleet are opting to donate their waterfront to the National Seashore. Sesuit may follow.

We stood still for a moment, watched the water brighten as the sun rose. The dry sand was rock hard. Manny strode across it. Despite the bottle glasses and Prince Charles ears, he looked almost dapper in his jogging suit. He'd a spring to his step.

Manny said, These explosions have done me a world of good. They make me want to get out and about. See what the Cape looks like, free and dangerous. I thank you, Chip Samuels. You cured me.

I?

You and Sukey Kuykendahl. Don't bullshit me.

Manny had a complicated explanation of what had liberated him. He had been under emotional house arrest. At home, the nausea was less intense. Then the explosions began. He found himself thrust out of doors. Moved to rise at two on a warm summer night, risk a skinny dip in Hoskin's Pond, snapping turtles be damned. Old man's stiff body in a freshwater lake, best feeling there is. The hell with the raw and the cooked. It's the rough and the smooth makes the world go round.

I agreed, tried to tell him about Wendy, my inability to let loose what I had grasped. But he was intent on the story of his own cure.

Absolutely right, you and Sukey. The Cape had become nauseating. High-tech mini-golf, behemoth supermarkets, cellular relay towers. On the beach, psychoanalysts on cell phones crowing over profits in biotech stocks. You changed the atmosphere. I began to taste it in the air.

I'm out of the business, I said.

With the raid on Woodcock and then the fire at the cottage, I had sensed the culture was pushing me to inconsiderate forms of installation, causing aberrations in FtB's narrative voice. So that further success would only serve the spectacle and its values: confrontation, self-assertion. That was where the ecoterrorists out West had gone wrong, I thought—too competitive, too purposive. I wanted to explain to Manny, but he waved me off, intent on his own line of thought.

He picked up a handful of pebbles and shied them over the shingle, to see stone carom off stone.

It's not the Dunkin' Donutses and outlet stores that cause the queasiness. That's what you taught me. It's the stasis. Change that is no change. Grand Opening of nothing. Same tedious plot. Jeopardy and resolution. High tide and low. Da . . . dum. Tired stories, that's the source of our nausea.

He needed to speak, so I listened.

It's obvious in the consulting room, to a psychologist. Tired stories. Early damage, later damage, self-damage, repetition.

I meet a woman in the market. She smiles at me, a smile of interest, but a trifle wan. A depressive. I am an understanding man, a stable man, a widower. She turns to me, offers a corrupt bargain. To overlook my homeliness, so that we can play a game of neurotic attachment, seeing which will emerge first, her contempt or mine. The second phase will come soon enough. Disappointment. Blame. Disgust. The standard endings.

Manny began to juggle stones. Unexpected talent. He stood juggling and talking, four round stones in the air, a way of speaking from trance: Have you noticed that we don't read novels? Skim them sometimes, but we haven't the attention anymore to get lost in them. Not even you—am I right? Attention deficit is a sign of the universal nausea. One more well-made story and we will vomit;

one more experimental story and we will vomit. We skim and complain of ennui.

Still juggling, rheumy eyes focused on stones in flight, he said: Ennui, anomie, attention deficit—it's all nausea. My new book includes a history of nausea, from late-eighteenth-century romanticism to our epidemic of bulimia.

He said: I have fallen in love with Sartre all over again. The importance of the viscous. *A handshake, a smile, a thought, a feeling, can be slimy.* You and Sukey have shown us that a house can be slimy. That an economic system can be slimy. *To touch the slimy is to risk being dissolved in sliminess.*

Still juggling, Manny said: What I long for is another planet. Aliens. The psychologist longs for aliens with different life courses, different family arrangements. Tell me something I don't know.

He was like a stand-up comic, the have-you-ever-noticed sort. High on anarchy. In monologue mode, as if making up for the years of listening: In the consulting room, I came to understand that my job is to give patients access to a greater range of denouements. Patients' nausea, repressed and denied, arises from the predictability of their stories.

Manny said: I have a new method. Handing patients tools. I am like you with your students, you with your son. Pointing to tools. Hammer. Saw. File. Awl.

You and Sukey gave me breathing room. Causing randomness to appear on television. I see the news without retching. When the histrionic divorcée in the Super Stop & Shop risks an encouraging smile, I smile back, to say, I, too, enjoy carting my groceries to a home that may be mined. I disagree with you about the parathion, by the way. Parathion degrades the Movement. The only joy is in explosion.

It was you, I said.

Listening to Manny, I came upon the answer to your question, where matériel comes from.

Pardon?

It never was Giampiccolo.

Manny gave me a stern look.

The secret donor.

We give and take, Manny said. That is what is meant by community.

I was able to give, Manny said, because a patient gave to me. I gave to you, and now you have given back.

Benny C., I said.

Manny admitted as much: One day Benny goes, Doc, you're an old radical, no? I'm going to surprise you when I'm gone, leave you something.

Benny challenged me: You know what your problem is, Doc? You're not active enough. You should do as you say. Take up a new skill.

Later I learned he had been released from prison, Manny said. Time off for good behavior. A model inmate, once he discovered electrical engineering. He went back to his business, applied his new knowledge. He became overambitious—that's the problem with psychotherapy, titrating the dose. Injured on the job, Benny was, in a warehouse fire. Died in prison, of old age. Left me the set of keys. UStowIt. I understood what the legacy must be. The tools of his trade.

Then Sukey told me about her dreams, and her plans for you. I thought about Benny's call to action, what it might mean in my profession. If words had come to nauseate me, I might attempt a different sort of interpretation. So I sent Sukey a care package.

A new psychotherapy, I said.

If it's not new, it's not therapy. When I began in this racket, naming sexual desire was psychotherapy. Now: old news—no effect, Manny said. Same as in your line, anarchism: To reach people at all, you have to surprise them.

We had arrived at the marsh, near Gull Pond. Time to turn back.

I understood that for Manny the bombings were not a matter of politics, or not directly. He was a doctor. He had hoped, in supplying the UStowIt key, to have me express and then experience what lay dormant within. The Movement had been a communal psychotherapy, Manny's handing a key to Sukey, our liberating him with it while we treated one another and the nation. I tried to ask Manny if that was what he had intended, but he was on to the next topic: He had finished his book, the long-awaited sequel to *So This Is Love*. Titled *So This Is Nausea*. A black jacket with white sans-serif print, at his request.

For a moment I imagined he was lobbying for a slot on *Today*. The thought was ungenerous. The launch would be tremendous—rumors that Manny had been my therapist had led the glossy magazines to snap up serial rights. But he had declined all invitations for on-air appearances, even from Oprah, who had offered to come out of retirement to chat with him about his prescriptions, when to strive to feel nausea, when to try to escape it. Manny forbade me to feature the book in my commentaries. The benefit he received from me was psychic. He said, I have enough and in excess.

Since he had mentioned comradeship, I reminded him that I had retired from the Movement. I am bourgeois, I said. I cherish time with my son. Access to the big house across from the cottage I grew up in. I'm drinking Pellegrino water.

The sun was behind me. Manny squinted in my direction. That's the rap on psychotherapy, he said. However radical its intent, it ends in creating conformists.

It was a joke, so I smiled. I took Manny's buffoonery as his way of declining guru status. But he understood what the times demand. A man needs to be in harm's way. I had confessed to bourgeois leanings. Those were bearable—Manny knew as much—only because I remain on the hook. A new scientific technique may point the finger at me, or a new witness, and I will be behind bars. An angry victim of the Movement may bomb Stone House. I am at risk, and the more balanced for being so.

I found myself saying aloud, The whole of Bangladesh is threatened by rising seas, and Madagascar, and much of Egypt.

Therapists are used to loose associations. Manny gave a psychoanalyst's hmmm of agreement. We were back at the car. Hoping for a scrap of advice, I said: I do have my own problem of excess.

Meaning the women.

As for that, Manny said, sometimes a man must wait for a sign.

26

*

Swim

One more explosion to describe. Yesterday's botched job. You know as much about it as I do. All I can contribute is a father's experience of terror, and my sense of wonder, finally, at the fullness of the day.

I had been up late the night of the third, on the phone, coordinating Fourth of July coverage with the network. Nationally, the big story was the weather. Quakes in California. Dust bowl in the Southwest, the path of precipitation pushed toward Canada. Flooding in Minnesota. In the Northeast, we were acutely aware of the situation in Florida and the Carolinas, August hurricanes massing a month early and the people praying for them, in the face of the months of Southern drought. For TV journalists, the crisis of climatic change would overshadow any events in Sesuit.

I had taken Independence Day off, to sit in the reviewing stand of our small-town parade, then enjoy the fireworks display at night. Hugh Crale had been sent to cover our festivities and to be on hand if houses blew. As for our own weather, the immediate forecast was for an old-fashioned summer day that would make any American remember the Fourths of his childhood.

Sukey was to join me at Stone House at nine for a cup of coffee before the parade. But nine passed without her, and when she arrived, it was a taxi that dropped her off. Her right arm was in a sling.

It's not as bad as it looks, she said.

It was, of course. I assumed the jumbo sunglasses hid a shiner. She had fallen off the wagon.

Bumps and bruises, she said. With her good arm, she pulled me to, for a peck on the cheek.

She said, I was driving the Lexus. A deer jumped in front, on Asa Phillips Way. Tubby was the hero. He used his cell phone to call rescue.

Which was as good a story as any. The deer, I mean.

Look here, she said.

On her good left hand was the diamond as big as the Ritz.

To celebrate. Champagne, only the one bottle.

She saw that *only one* was a mistake, both because it was a lie and because the phrase has no place in an ex-drinker's lexicon. She held me close, flirting for forgiveness. I thought of our work together in the service of her recovery. They had been good months. Friendship, like sobriety, is an endless task.

Come, she said, steering me to the staircase. Where's Hank? she asked, which made me understand she was serious.

Out, I said. AWOL.

The night before, you had borrowed the truck without asking. Now the truck was here but you were not. At Anais's, maybe.

Sukey was guiding me upstairs, and yet she took the time to ask whether you had settled in. You had been acting strange, asking her about explosives, assuming she knew how they were obtained.

I'll talk with Anais, I said. We'll keep a closer watch over him.

Spoken like an anarchist father, Sukey said.

In the condo era, the attic had been chopped into air-conditioned garrets. Sukey was having me take down walls, reclaim the space. The rehab job was half-finished. Sawdust coated the floor, wires poked out from the plasterboard. A boom-box radio, left on by workmen, played "Under the Boardwalk." At the far wall sat abandoned furniture, slated for Goodwill.

Not so elegant as the first time, Sukey said. Thirty-plus years. She snapped a drop cloth off a queen-size four-poster. We tumbled onto the mattress.

There is a line in Dickens, about Estella, no longer young, how after the freshness of her beauty is gone, an indescribable majesty and charm remain. I love the way Sukey's face has incorporated the years. And her body—for me, it refers to Titian and Delacroix. She takes joy in the sensual, with not a scintilla of modesty—immaculate lust. There is generosity, too, in her artistry, the lifelong attention to evoking pleasure. I knew she was saying good-bye—another "last time," if that label can be applied when there was only one former time. At the end, she asked, Can I do something more for you?

Which was a joke about memory, about the first time, when sex was new. I said, We should do all we can for one another.

The radio was playing a summer set, "Theme from a Summer Place," "Summertime Summertime," "The Summer Wind," "Summer in the City."

We nestled in each other's arms. Early as it was, I began to doze. It seemed half a dream, the Flash Newsbreak. Evidence stolen from the old Sesuit station house, fertilizer and igniters. Theft discovered early this morning. Cape put on high alert. Citizens warned to leave waterfront homes, police to go door-to-door. Regional high school open as an emergency shelter.

It was you. I was morally certain of it. You were on the lookout for explosives. You got wind of the opportunity—how?—through Nando? It fit together, the borrowed truck, your absence, fireworks planned for tonight.

Sukey had gone down a flight to answer the phone. She was heading back up, portable to ear: If I see him, I'll tell him. . . . No, no notion. Your boys can pick him up at the parade if you want, he's sure to be there. . . . You take care, too.

She roused me: That was Bert making like he's mad as hell—giving you a heads up. Did you hint you wanted to destroy the Antunes evidence?

We tumbled downstairs. Sukey was telling me what she had learned from Bert, that there was an all-points bulletin out for me and the pickup. A Wa Wa clerk had seen a red truck in the parking lot last night, though he was pretty certain it was a Toyota. The usual flawed testimony.

Not a bad scheme, I thought. You had parked the truck at the strip mall, no harm in that. Slipped across to the station house, entered by the bulkhead. While you knew I was home on the phone to New York, building an alibi.

In the kitchen, Sukey scooped up the keys to the pickup. Her plan was to beat the police to the dirt roads beyond Scargo Point, then lead them a merry chase. Show the truck on back lanes, let vacationers phone to say they had spotted it. Employing her realtor's knowledge of the byways of Sesuit.

The essential was for me to find you before the police did. You or the explosives. I told Sukey I would swim.

Evrard, I said, since that was my guess. I asked Sukey to phone Anais, have Anais clear you out of Evrard. I would look for the fertilizer when I arrived. If need be, let myself be captured in your stead.

Then it was out the back door and down the bank for one more mock-heroic swim.

High tide. Cool July water, blue-gray under the clear skies. I assumed your explosion was slated for nighttime, to accompany the fireworks. I could imagine it, an enormous blaze up the curve of coast, visible from miles away. To satisfy your wish for a role in the Movement.

I did not think you were at risk of death, and still I swam as if your life depended on it. Because of the old tale, idealistic youngsters blasting themselves to kingdom come. I swam to you and it seemed to me the thing I had done for the whole of your life, the exercise I do daily. Reach and pull. The constant task of father-hood, averting the improbable catastrophe. Praying that one's efforts are unnecessary, ready to revel in that most desired of out-comes, the nonevent. Reaching and pulling, to prevent your being misunderstood in school. To prevent your losing a friend or a mother, your being arrested or blown sky-high.

Families were clustered on the shore the length of our little cove. Scargo Point, Mooncusser Rock, places of pilgrimage for those who prize absurdity, resistance, situation. I was wearing the gym shorts you had left crumpled on the stairs. Tight in the waist. Shorts would have to do, no time to look for a swimsuit.

No one recognized me, nondescript balding head, standard-issue six-beat crawl. Mao says a guerrilla must be among the peo-ple like a fish in water. I headed for the jetty, cut cross the boat lane, into Quivet Cove.

I was in a state of panic, if panic can imply focus. I aimed to be efficient and unobtrusive. Reaching and kicking but barely break-ing the surface with my feet.

When you were an infant, I took you to Barnabash Pond. I held you afloat, my hand beneath your belly. In front of you I tossed a yellow building block I had made from a wedge-shaped wood scrap. You reached for the cheese. It moved away. You reached again, discovering that reaching keeps you afloat, pulls you for-ward.

Now I was reaching for you. The near-panic was accompanied by a sense of being in my element. The act of rescue is my element. I prayed you had not done something foolish, or that if you had, I might come between you and the harm. I swam to save you from your folly, which stemmed from my folly, the folly of loyalty to antiquated ideals.

Your mother is the expert swimmer. When we swam together, she could not help advising: Reach farther, pull earlier. I did not find it easy to alter the rhythm of my stroke. When the arm is at its limit, pull immediately.

From the start, my swim to you felt wearing, each joint crying out in its own anguish. And yet the mind does not stay focused, even on pain.

I loved the bay for bringing me to you. Anais was right not to move me from here. Childhood attachments: a mother, the sea—*la mère*, *la mer*. When one left, the other soothed. I understood my anarchism as a way of honoring early loves. My father, too. The explosions enacted feelings Sam never expressed, rage at inequities. As I say, this is how inspiration works. The causes emerge belatedly.

You must learn to breathe on both sides, Anais admonished. How could I live by the ocean and breathe on one side only? In a steady six-beat crawl, a stroke and a half between breaths. Breathe right, pull, pull, pull and breathe left. The swimmer who breathes on both sides will not stray off course. Swimming, I am what your mother made me. She is in my rhythm.

My shoulders ached. I took it as a good sign that the pain was not down the arms. I told myself that after the second mile, the muscle pain would fade. Reaching was my praxis, action intended to alter the future, to substitute my pain for yours.

Is it a terrible thing for a man to swim to his son and find that his mind wanders? Stray thoughts intruded. Hurricanes massing to the south. Remarkable what we know and do not feel. I monitored the water for a hint of turbulence. Or for the eerie stillness said to precede a storm. Nothing, just our familiar bay, rising and falling. This is our specialty, we humans, to know without feeling, and then to put out of mind. The planet warms, we run our air-conditioning. The storm is stalled off Hatteras. Here where the skies are blue we will have our celebration. Fireworks tonight, and you dead set on embellishment. If that is your plan, if you are the thief.

The waterlogged shorts chafed. I wanted to jettison them but could not, in the cove among the people. Past Barnabash Creek, I would drop them, or head to shore and run along the beach.

There was a sense of rightness in the swim. The loss of self. Simplicity. To will one thing. As I had not in the course of FtB. Mixed motives: to help Sukey, honor Anais, question capitalism, find you room to fly your kite. Less worthy drives emerged over time. There in the water, I willed your safety, as I had willed your mother health upon your birth.

But my focus blurred. As I swam past installation sites, I felt pulses of satisfaction. Giampiccolo, Howell, Warelwast. Everywhere, unprotected dunes, no seawalls left. We are the anti–Arlen-Peppers, ready to let the sands drift. Wherever they are laid down, the beach they form will serve the people. Then I caught myself—I saw that in counting successes, I was girding myself against the most terrible failure, the loss of a child.

As I neared the post-and-beam we had spared, a mild delirium set in and with it new cycles of self-accusation and defense. *Of course*, any sensible person would say, if a man engages in violence, his family will be endangered. But isn't this *of course* the complacency of the bourgeoisie? Passivity has its price. Oceans rise, mosquitoes flourish. The alternatives to action are not benign.

The *of course* crowd are right: Violence begets violence, and close to home. But not always. One time in a hundred, anarchist violence begets the fresh air we breathe today. I do not deny the role of luck. Most are not lucky. They fail, and their lives are absorbed into fiction, by Dostoyevsky, Conrad, James. An honorable fate, to be mocked by reactionaries of genius. What suits fiction is what *of course* happens, the ninety-nine defeats. The hundredth time: a journal. Credible only as history.

The radical must not feel shame for acting the fool. To cover long odds is the proper role of revolutionary activist and concerned father alike.

I was grief-stricken, sun-stricken. I was coming to terms with the truth that the spectacle always wins. To succeed is to make your son feel inferior, your wife, desperate. Ineluctable modality—the perceptual framework we cannot escape: the less-and-more of capitalism.

I would conform, I would blithely accumulate and consume, that was the deal I wanted to make. Existence is cruel for the child on the trash heap, the family in the floodplain. But I had done my bit. All I had ever striven for was what Perkins had commended years ago, the small life. I would retire willingly, insistently, as Anais had. Welcome amnesia. If I arrived to find my son safe.

My left arm felt heavy. The body is hard to monitor, the green-horn doctor's guess as good as any. The stance of late middle age: ignoring harbingers of death. Disaster improbable in the short run, certain in the long.

Before the mouth of Barnabash Creek, I heard a helicopter over-head. Surely Evrard had not blown—there would be smoke. Still, in my mind's eye, I saw you and Pauline slumped in the Crate & Bar-rel furniture, the two of you stoned on dope. Flames rise. You have mistimed a fuse. Fleeing, you trip on wires. Floorboards collapse. You are caught, consumed. You must forgive me—this ghastly vision was not a conscious comment on your abilities. Only a father's worry, made vivid by exhaustion and the chill of the water.

I made appeals to you, telepathically: Swim off, I urged. Let the bay wash away every trace of fertilizer. I will defuse the installation. I am content to be convicted of my crimes. All the while I was pray-ing that I had been faked out, jerked around—the good endings.

Your shorts had ripped. Passing the mouth of Barnabash Creek, I dropped them. What a difference! Only naked do we feel: menis-cus of brine on ass, privates swinging free. Unencumbered. How a man should be, en route to a destination that matters more than life itself.

Here was a surprise. The crowds did not thin. Long trek to the cove in front of Altschuler, but families had found a way, because of the holiday, because of the warning to stay out of doors. No hope of beaching and running. I was too well known, and too ridiculous in my nudity. Nothing for it but to reach and pull. The arm was heavy.

The nearer I got to Evrard, the greater my fear. I was delirious. What with exhaustion, water, sun, pain, the years. I had a vision, this one more detailed than the image of your incineration. I hope you will forgive me this second hallucination as well. Some partic-ulars proved jarringly exact, as if while thoughts strayed and arms reached, I had been putting together an ending to our story:

In this vision I see myself running through the surf, high-stepping like a running back. Across the strand, up into the house. I am naked. Pauline huddles with you on the couch. You look wrecks: eyes deeply ringed, faces puffy from insect bites. The room is sweet with the smell of marijuana. You drink beer from the bottle. I see the label up close: Leinenkugel's. The television is turned on loud. Parade coverage, Hugh Crale.

An armchair left by the Evrards is draped with an Indian-print cotton throw. I wrap myself in it. We are all apologizing: Sorry, sorry, sorry. I ask about the fertilizer.

Gone, Pauline says. She motions with her hand to indicate that it is elsewhere. You nod in agreement. You are crying large tears. I move to hug you both. An old man in a wet, makeshift sari throwing his arms around two beautiful children in distress.

I beg you to swim off, but you shake your heads. I collapse into the love seat. Your voice is weak. Your future stretches before you, reform school at best.

Shh, shh, Pauline comforts. She is your Wendy and your Sukey. You are Bonnie and Clyde, only you have screwed up in your first attempt at crime.

Your story comes out in dribs and drabs. You and Nando were talking, over drink and smoke, about conversations he had overheard. His dad griping. Understaffing at the old station house this week, hours being stockpiled to cover overtime for the Fourth. A lark—to boost the fertilizer.

You used Nando's keys and know-how to sneak in through the old bulkhead. Grabbed bags and igniters, hoisted them into the truck bed, headed off. Then everything went wrong. You and Nando fought. He wanted to blow Evrard immediately, you wanted to wait for the fireworks. Nando was driving. He turned the truck onto the dirt road into the Shiverick Woods. Unluckily—luckily—you had not latched the tailgate securely. When the truck hit a bump, the fertilizer slid out, the sacks split, you could not find the igniters. You spent what seemed like hours looking, everyone saying, Oh shit, oh shit, oh shit.

That image was at the center of my nightmare, three stoned fools being eaten by a hatch of mosquitoes from the bog.

There was an element of relief in this hallucination. No charred bodies. A father's dream: to find his son whole, no matter that the boy's hit bottom.

Then suddenly, the story takes a turn, as in those nightmares to which we append a happy ending as we wake.

Evrard's front door opens. Bert Costas strides toward us. He has the aura of the good sheriff. Bert asks if I mind, sits beside me in the love seat. He turns to me: The things we do for our kids.

He says, We found the remains of the Antunes evidence in the Shiverick Woods. Whoever lifted it made a campfire there this morning. Fertilizer scattered, the igniters burnt. Stuff was still smoldering when I arrived.

By building the campfire, Bert created a fixed point in time, a moment when the criminals were on the scene and you were elsewhere. I should think it would pain him, to have tampered with evidence. Here is an odd element to the dream: Bert sounds slick and conniving.

I understand he will do whatever is necessary to give cover for his son and mine.

A scene of misery and a tack-on happy ending. Amazing how much one can get right while missing the main point—the characters' motivation.

27

✳

Gifts

Crowds the whole way to Evrard. I lie flat and let the small waves wash me in. Only when my belly is on the sand do I rise, exposed. I dash onto the shingle and across the strand. A man yells, Look! From television! Chip Samuels!

Cell phones are in evidence. Reports will reach the networks. More immediately: Someone will notify the police.

I sprint up the path and into Evrard, back burned, bones chilled, eyesight bleached away, heart thumping, mind burdened by the vision of our meeting. I slip in past the sliding screen door. You are sprawled on the couch with Pauline. Despite the open windows, the room smells of cannabis. You are drinking Leinenkugel's. The television is on loud.

Even where it is accurate, imagination fails. Real life's extravagant. The welter of details: water marks left by the beer bottles on the captain's chest that serves as a coffee table. Pauline's alarm at my appearance.

I am the only wreck. You are your concerned, deliberate self.

Dad, you say, in a way that makes me understand how awful I look.

I say, The fertilizer—

And then I realize I have missed a step. I look for the throw.

Dad, you interrupt. I've done something, and I don't know why.

In my exhaustion, this seems the most wonderful thing you have ever said. You have experienced compulsion. You have acted freely, that is, with the freedom to follow compulsion. Now you feel confusion and regret, as any thoughtful man might, once he has taken a decisive step.

You swam the whole way? Pauline asks.

She is unused to our family, the extremes adults go to.

My shoulders are sore, but the arm feels more or less normal. I am telling you I will take the rap, only I need to know where the explosives are.

Dad, you say. I may have put Mom in danger.

Was that the compulsion, to help Anais? You are your father's son.

You say how sorry you are, for what I have been through, for the APB. You list precautions you took, double-lining the truck bed with black plastic.

Like any kid who's borrowed the car without permission and tried to make up for it by filling the tank or vacuuming the mats. I made it look easy, the two dozen installations. A son emulates his father. I am distraught, not angry. I say: There's something you couldn't know about. A conversation with Bert Costas—the feds must have bugged his office. My own indiscretion.

I say, You're here and in one piece.

You say, We weren't handling explosives. We were handling fertilizer.

The television blares. Hugh Crale is interviewing Wendy. She is speaking on my behalf, explaining my absence from the reviewing stand. The Fourth is the people's day. Best not to showcase any one man, we are patriots all. I give Wendy credit for deftness, wish we had never wavered from that line.

You point to the screen. We are waiting for news. You seem less tentative. As if you have gotten something out of your system. Proved you can do what your dad did—cross the line and return unharmed.

I hope there will not be too much of that.

*   *   *

As in my vision, Bert comes through the door.

He gives me the once-over, tells me I look awful, I should see a doctor.

I know I will. If I am not arrested, I will consult a top-flight New York heart man, accept a privilege not open to my union comrades. I want to live long, as your father. I am coming in from the cold.

Bert sits beside me, glances at you and Pauline.

Is Nando okay? I ask.

Bert nods: My men caught up with Sukey. She said you'd be here. She said you were home last night.

I was, I say. On the phone with the network.

That's good.

I try to apologize for what my son has done.

Never mind, Bert says. It was time.

Meaning he has been asked to resign, in the face of the theft of evidence. His standing as chief was always tenuous. This latest debacle is unacceptable, cops losing bomb makings on the eve of the Fourth.

Bert says, It's an ill wind that blows no good.

His cell phone rings. He says: Certainly, I know where it is. I'll have officers there. I'll be right there myself.

He glances at me. Samuels? I'm with him now, on the bay side.

I assume it is the feds.

Bert says: Bayside all morning. Many witnesses.

That part of my vision was right. Bert will not pursue this case. He will muddy the waters any way he can.

You are pointing at the television. An Action News Bulletin. The matter Bert is speaking about on his phone, the explosion for which you provided the ingredients. The new local reporter, Bonnie Luganis's replacement, is repeating what comes through her earpiece: As anticipated, Sesuit is witnessing violent disruption on Independence Day. The incident is across town, on Nantucket Sound. The target is the Farrel mansion, home to the former judge, the tobacco spokeswoman, Peggy Crow. There was no media alert, only the Movement's trademark fireworks visible above the trees.

A bystander has contacted the station to report a sighting, fifteen minutes before the event, of a swimmer swept out by the riptide, then emerging at the breakwater. We hear the eyewitness, by phone. She is an older woman with a Boston accent. She describes the sequence: lone swimmer, fireworks, single blast.

Nothing to write home about, the caller complains. Only smoke pouring out a basement window. It doesn't look like they managed to blow up anything.

She sounds disappointed.

A WHDH crew has arrived at the scene. We see the Farrel place. A plume of smoke rises on the landward side.

For what came before, I have no need of pictures. I can see her in the Chute. Narrow shoulders, lean arms. Hair wet against the skull. When the face emerges from the waves, there is rapture on it.

Better than anyone, I appreciate the effort. Your mother trespassing, installing, escaping. Flinging herself into the surf. What a girl's got to do, to claim a life with the man who is already her husband, once he's a celebrity.

A handcrafted gift. A feat of derring-do that is also an act of parenting, a gambit to reunite the family.

You are sobbing with relief, your mother safe.

Bert heads to the crime scene, and Pauline drives us to Stone House in her Jeep. We find Sukey in the driveway, using her good arm to drag a substantial rosa rugosa. The pickup bed is full of local nursery stock.

Lend a hand? Sukey asks.

You help her lower the roses to the walk, soak their root balls, hose out the truck bed. Always one step ahead, Sukey, creating a reason why traces of fertilizer might be found. Pauline goes off to phone the family she is staying with. I take a long shower, lie down to rest. Sleep does not come.

I find you in the kitchen, scarfing leftovers. Winsome sight, an unselfconscious teenager chowing down.

You walk me to the beach. We lean against the bank. I ask: How could Anais let you put yourself at risk?

You prefer to play your cards close to the vest, but you do not want me to think ill of your mother. You fill me in, enough to reassure.

Mom had been thinking about installations. A what-if game. Wandering Sesuit, considering sites, attending to gossip, who's home, who's gone.

Extraordinary, I think. Manny's hand in it. Anais asks what a girl's got to do. Manny invites her to seek her nausea. She goes on drift, as a way of finding her old self and courting her husband.

You understood what was on her mind. That was why you asked Sukey and me how to get matériel. Then an opportunity arose. You are too loyal to provide details, but I puzzled out this part in the swim to you. Bert griping, Nando picking up hints.

I say, You offered Mom . . . ?

You shake your head. You knew your mother would never agree to a scheme that put you in danger. You left her an anonymous note, telling her to expect a package in the trunk of her SUV. You used short, disconnected sentences, hoping Mom would think Sukey was the benefactor.

Danger aside, it is sweet, this feast of gifts, this potlatch necessary for the simplest of outcomes, reconciliation between man and wife.

Sukey brings us lemonade in Tom Collins glasses. There are pretzels, too, but the lemonade is the gesture. Implying she will go to work on the alcohol problem, as should you. I have no illusions about quick cures, but I believe you have been sobered by the anxieties of the day.

You make a request: Will I walk you through the history of the Movement?

I glance at Sukey. We are both thinking, Too soon, too many secrets.

I tell you there is a diary that will be yours, when we are all gone.

You accept that answer. You like history, you say. You like your history teacher. You have been thinking you will become a historian.

I am glad that you see a conventional future. College. Use of your bookishness.

Out of the blue, Sukey says: Momentary immortality.

She explains: What Giampiccolo is enjoying—if you're going to write history.

A uniquely modern status, momentary immortality. Giampiccolo will strut on the public stage, but he will not be remembered after all, unless as a con artist. In our time, the most eagerly accepted historical truths are those that arise from belated debunking, narrative meshing with physical evidence, as with Thomas Jefferson and Sally Hemings. The perfect use of this diary.

Sukey's phrase sets me to laughing. When you write, I hope you will give the women their due. They are the heroes. I include your mother. She provided the theory, she returned to the field today.

I am intent on expressing the lesson I learned on my swim. What happened in Sesuit does not happen. I say, There's no crossing the line without a price being paid. I should be dead. Your mom, too. And you and Nando in jail.

I am beginning to suspect the last is not true—that the danger to you and Nando was not so great. But I am reaching for a different thought. I say, It goes beyond explosives. Clear-sightedness kills. It's too dangerous, every time you glimpse a Nike T-shirt to see, woven into it, the starving kid on the garbage pile, scrounging for styrofoam.

Private references infest my speech, and yet I believe something gets through.

Speaking of my own intentions, I say, There won't be another day like today. My heart couldn't stand it.

You nod in agreement. But there is a glimmer in your eye. I see how much you look like your mother when she was young.

*   *   *

You leave to phone Pauline. I will head up soon, for a nap. First, I want a word with Sukey.

Are they still on? I ask. The fireworks?

She says, No one else is in charge in this town. We might as well be.

It is exhaustion that makes me laugh so freely.

Happy ending? Sukey asks.

I tell her I am worried about Bert.

You can do him some good, Sukey says. Play up the budget angle: Chief's Warnings Ignored—Town Council Hamstrings PD. Why not run it past Bonnie?

Bonnie Luganis has left NBC for ABC-Disney. She is their Chip Samuels, the montage essayist who knows the Cape. She might well do a piece on the Sesuit Fourth, slant it Bert's way.

It won't save his job, I say.

His reputation, Sukey says. I'm hoping Bert will be joining us. Billy, too.

Sukey has news for me about the real-estate holdings. She's going to slip them into the shell of a failing corporation that Buford controls, the former Buford Barrel Industries, listed on the Nasdaq. BBI will "buy" the real-estate trust with a majority of its own shares. Instant public corporation, Buford and Tubby giving the deal legitimacy. We will be rich.

Sukey is inviting Bert and Billy to head up a BBI fisheries division. They have plans to create an overarching co-op for Cape Cod fishermen, sharing skills, dampening competition, encouraging conservation. Getting the government to help out, what with Billy's connections and the new public sentiment against unfettered capitalism.

Hearing Sukey, I understand more fully why it was easy for you to steal the fertilizer. Bert's ill wind. Ordinarily, it would look bad for the Sesuit chief of police to jump ship and join the radicals. But when the chief is fired unfairly, why shouldn't he sign on with BBI?

If he takes a job that emphasizes cooperation among locals, one where he and his kids dirty their hands in his father's trade—that story might fly.

Regarding my hallucination as I swam toward shore at Evrard: It was flawed because I sold the spectacle short—underestimated its pervasiveness. Anais out to snag the celebrity husband. Bert set on monetizing his standing, moving from public sector to private. I don't suppose Sukey was in on the plot, but the Farrel explosion delivered what she required, "programming content" to suit the politically engaged tourist. All of us tainted, each providing entertainment and each profiting.

Was your theft sanctioned? Bert is as meticulous as I am; if he drew you in, there were provisions in place for your protection. I prefer to believe that his role was limited to leaving the evidence vulnerable. I wonder what you will think, when you learn of Bert's move to BBI. Just as well for you to discover that crime is rarely this easy. For you to see how hard it is to avoid co-optation.

I will approach Bonnie. To please my friends. To thank Burt and Billy for their scrupulousness this past year. But I dislike the assignment.

I see that we are winding down the anarchist situation, in favor of benign local socialism supported by conventional tools of the market. Chits called in, stories placed, shares pumped. A sad ending, I want to say to Sukey, the descent into spectacular politics. But given the terrors of the day, I cannot object to our backing off.

Sukey gathers lemonade glasses. About BBI—she wants me to head up a media division. Build a Web site to be the hub of the Movement, syndicate my reports from there as well as the network. Wendy will negotiate the details.

I'm retiring from journalism, I say.

Sukey says, What are you, a publicity hound?

It's true, the more I withdraw, the more I am in demand.

I want out, I say.

You'll think about it, Sukey says. You and Anais.

28

*

Fireworks

You were not yet home when your mother and I passed the library door. The house was silent. As we climbed the stairs, she said: You restored me, Chip. I had forgotten what it was like to swim the Chute.

It was good to be thanked. Still, I knew the Farrel installation was Anais's "last time," her farewell to radicalism. A woman does not mass-produce consumer goods, stake her claim as the next Martha Stewart, engineer a tricky reverse merger—she does not aspire to standing in the economy and in the spectacle—and then return to the role of ironic outsider. And yet, one never does know. That is what keeps our hearts beating, awareness that on occasion people we love will surprise us.

She took me to the master bedroom, once Mrs. K's. We went to look down on the bay by moonlight. I will travel with Anais again in any life she chooses, short of manufacturing in China. I am ready to sink with her into the immense accumulation of commodities as the oceans rise.

She fell asleep. I stood at the window. The moon laid a scalloped path on the bay. In the opening of *Dombey and Son,* Dickens shows us life through the capitalist's eyes. The earth formed for merchants to trade on. The contract of matrimony, designed for the perpetuation of family firms. The son intended for a destiny of commerce. Then, by way of contrast, Dickens writes of the sea. The sea from which life emerges and in which it disappears, the dark and unknown sea that rolls round all the world.

It had been years since I had thought of that passage, and it occurred to me, as it will have long since occurred to you, that for the whole time I was returning to my senses I had been acting in the service of Dickens's vision, twitting worshipers of property and honoring the sea. Or the vision is Hardy's or Galsworthy's, some antique ideal. For years I could not read my old friends, but in time I began to commune with them in action.

I looked out Mrs. K's window. Above was the attic where I had just closed a chapter with Sukey. Beside me was the canopied bed where Anais dozed peacefully. I wondered whether serving the loves of childhood is what defines a calling.

I knew I could not sleep. I wandered downstairs, to write these final entries. You were sprawled on the couch. I covered you with a quilt, knowing I would not often have the chance to tuck you in.

Soon I will waken you. Rouse a teenager if I can. Suggest you take a dip with the old man, on the ocean side, with the storm coming, and the big waves. Swim amidst the bluefish and the crosscurrents. Arm pain be damned. Your mother may join us. I envisaged that scene often, when you were young, the three of us in later life, out in the breakers.

I will waken you, but not yet. The moment is too precious. To have a son to worry over, whether he drinks to excess, whether we have injured him, whether he will follow too closely in his father's path. To have an estranged wife who wants to feel and offer love, who will make a project of it. To have comrades-in-arms. To have work for the hands. For the second time in a few hours, I find myself thinking of a line from Marlowe's *Faust,* one that was my mantra all those weeks I stood in other men's basements preparing installations: Run slow, O slow, you horses of the night.

*   *   *

Last night, Anais sat beside me at the fireworks. She has let her hair
go long and kinky. I could take the new look cynically, the hippie
cut required for AnaisWare, but after the risks she took at Farrel, I
do not. On the beach, she had the glow of a woman who has made
up her mind.

Sukey and I had entered into friendly debates over ways to stage
the fireworks. She wanted a traditional display, to stake our claim
to the patriot's role. I imagined offshore installations initiated by
telephone signals from the land, to evoke FtB's techniques. The
town fire marshal ruled that method out. Skilled pyrotechnicians
would ignite the charges. But my concept informed the final
arrangements.

It was your mother, the artist, who provided the choreography.
Fireworks reflective of the Movement, its respect for the arbitrary,
its notion that celebration should be ongoing and widespread. She
arranged for barges up and down Quivet Cove. She assigned ignition times according to a random-number chart. Silences and then
great bursts at unpredictable moments. Each installation must have
its peculiar beauty. Your mother was partial to devices with bird
and flower names: peonies, chrysanthemums, morning glories,
Blossoms after Thunder, Peacock Tails, Swallows and Eagles, Birds
Following Phoenix. (Seeing the catalogs, I thought of your old
friend Bilbo Baggins, the hobbit, seduced by fireworks in the shape
of lilies and laburnums.) Anais envisaged a postmodernist work.
Only the ending would be conventional—red, white, and blue, to
signal the Movement's American soul.

A fireworks plan that showed your mother understood.

Comme j'adore les feux d'artifice! she said. The fires of artifice.

Evidently, I answered, less in acknowledgment of the display
awaiting us than the one she had set off earlier that day.

We sat on a blanket Sukey's real-estate trust had provided for its luminaries. The air turned brisk, the sky darkened. We were at some distance from the nearest barge. At our age, we prefer quiet.

Wendy arrived, nestled against Hugh, letting him guide her. She seemed at ease. The attack on Giampiccolo has been good for her, frank aggression against a bad man. Wendy spread a blanket for Hugh and then walked behind your mother and me. She draped her arms over our shoulders and snuggled her face between ours. I love you both, she said. More than I can say.

She was wearing a puffy quilted outfit against the cool of the evening, but I could imagine her as she was in my arms, every oval. I took her half-embrace as a final good-bye and wondered whether she and Anais had talked. She, Anais, and Sukey together.

Your mother asked, Are you happy, dear?

Better and better, Wendy said. She had not let go her quiet gravity.

You were in the dunes with Pauline. Sharing a joint? A six-pack? I hoped not, hoped for good news on that front. Still, to have shaken some reason into your foolish parents—how could you not celebrate?

Sukey made her entrance as the first shell rocketed off a barge. She was swathed in multicolored scarves, as vivid as the flares above. Sukey is in her glory, rich and famous and outspoken. My co-conspirators, she said, meaning Wendy and your mother and me.

Tubby nodded obligingly. Pink-faced, hale fellow well met. He wore a knit shirt with a large logo embroidered over the left breast, a Rosie the Riveter gal hefting a sledgehammer, underscored with the label Ball Busters, Inc.

I could see it was the future, a corporation built around the three women, doing conventional good here on the Cape. Although you can never tell with Sukey. The radio carried reports of five explosions on the Vineyard this afternoon, echoes of our Sachem's Head installation—crater holes in the dirt roads leading from the private shoreline, stranding wealthy revelers at their Fourth of July picnics. Slow Coast Guard rescues, long day at the beach.

I could imagine the helicopter footage, miles of near-empty Atlantic coast on the national holiday. Handful of families on the broad stretches of sand. Contrast it with a public beach, blanket-to-blanket. Hard not to produce that photo essay: Where's the outrage, in the explosions, or in unpeopled beaches on the Fourth? What constitutes independence, freedom to exclude others, or freedom to wiggle your toes in the sand?

There was a hint of a Tubby-Sukey alliance in those explosions, which would explain her cat-who-ate-the-canary grin. I still worry that I haven't done as well for Sukey as she for me, that periodically she will need rescuing.

Will Manny be there to help? Sukey pointed him out. He was striding up the strand, a carefully coiffed blonde on his arm. His supermarket Juliet, no doubt. Manny said something witty; the woman laughed and went on tiptoe to kiss him on his bald forehead. She had a sort of leopard-skin shawl around her shoulders. (I remember your old joke: Because she wanted to be spotted.) Someone with a little life, Manny used to say. Men like us need women with life in them.

Nothing like seeing your therapist flirt, Sukey said. She beamed and waved.

Deirdre and Tomas wandered over, surrounded by a cloud of children—theirs, the neighbors', a multicultural group, swarthy and ruddy, Portuguese and Irish. I recognized your buddy Fernando Costas, shepherding a flock of grade-schoolers. He gave me a wink, to say all was well.

The children made it an American Fourth, boys with crew cuts, girls with tightly banded pigtails. They jerked their heads north, we all did, as a loud thud and a familiar crash, the sounds of a falling cottage, were heard from far up the shore. A wildcat explosion. Vox populi.

We turned back to the fireworks. The crowd laughed and gasped at your mother's unreadable art. You could tell that people were relieved to reach the conventional ending with its tricolor crescendo. Down the beach, the crowd counted four-five-six. Aah. Aah. Aah. Hurray. Someone had rigged an outdoor stereo to one of the liberated houses above, loud enough to send us a Sousa beat.

Slow, O slow, I thought. As if in answer, the great balls hung aloft, shimmering. I was in the right place. With my family and coconspirators nearby, and the great country before me, over the bay and on west for miles. I vowed not to regret a single wrong thing I had done, but to remember this moment of peace.

I gave your mother a kiss on the cheek and tasted her face powder. My madeleine. There was no hint of vegetable smell, but your mother knows that since childhood I have been partial to powder. I moved to kiss her again, and she turned to give me her cupid's-bow lips. She withheld, it seemed to me, very little. Her tongue had an odd taste, metallic or medicinal.

I was determined to rejoin her, but for that instant I panicked. She seemed to me to taste of capitalism, of the fifteen hundred advertisements a day, of neon and glitter. A rich flavor, delicious for those whose taste buds are attuned; I considered it a problem that mine were not yet. Manny had prepared me for the onset of nausea. Suitable affect, even in marriage, perhaps especially in marriage, in these conflicted times.

I knew I still reeked of gunpowder and the anarchist's unwashed hair. It was brave of your mother to offer herself to me. There is an upside to this matter of being permeated by what we work in. I am absorbing celebrity, will do so for your mother's sake and yours, to remake a family.

I sat beside Anais, with her lean swimmer's muscles and her relaxed hum. My panic subsided. I rested a hand on her shoulder. Above, the colors dissipated. The sky turned smoky. Parents issued commands, children protested and complied. Blankets were gathered, chairs folded, tote bags hoisted. Good-bye, good-bye. The audience, our fellow patriots, headed for the beach stairs.

Shall we walk home? Anais asked. I understood I was right, that my future had been decided, by the women. By you as well, catalyst of your parents' remarriage.

Anais made as if to rise. No, wait, I urged, and I held her arm.

Damp was setting in. She leaned against me for warmth. Our friends paraded by, saying farewells. Suddenly a volley of shells ascended from the barges. Boom! Boom! Boom! More Blossoms after Thunder.

Without letting Anais know, I had arranged to top off the display with a double ending. A tribute to the unexpected. The artisan's extra effort. Light & liberty. The crowd started and then cheered. Huzzah for the red, white, and blue. Your mother whispered, You do know how to surprise a girl.

We kissed. This time, I sensed the salt of the sea in Anais's hair, the sweetness of melancholy not quite banished, the wonderful papery texture of flesh as it ages. I held your mother tight and thought of you and felt the chill breeze off the bay. It occurred to me that I was *heureux* and *bienheureux* and *content,* lucky in love, blessed, and, yes, happy, as much as any man is in this mercantile moment.

Though its place names echo those of the Sesuit Neck neighborhood of East Dennis, the Sesuit of this book is a composite—a Cape Cod town of the imagination. On its bay side, the fictional Sesuit enjoys the rugged microclimate and topography of North Eastham; Sesuit's beachfront homes resemble ones to be found in Truro and on Nantucket and Martha's Vineyard.

Spectacular Happiness

Though it is built around the elements of a comic thriller—explosions, mobsters, federal agents, and a man on the run—*Spectacular Happiness* proves to be a romance and a thoughtful exploration of the nature of happiness: What sort of private contentment is possible in a culture focused on achievement, accumulation, and celebrity?

Discussion Points

1. How does the form in which this novel is written—a series of diary entries by the protagonist—enhance the story it tells? Does it succeed in focusing attention on the book's central themes of intimacy and disrupted family life? How would the novel and our response to the main character be different if its narrative were told more conventionally—in the third person, for example?

2. In his "interventions" on beachfront homes, Chip claims to take care to avoid harming people—to create absurdist theater. Is Free the Beaches a terrorist movement? To what range of activities can the tem *terrorism* apply? How do you think Chip's actions would be received in the current climate?

3. Chip tells us his therapist felt he was too timid and withdrawn. "When will you swing boldly into life? he asked. I have tried of late to answer that challenge" (pages 44–45). Chip discusses a number of philosophical motives behind the Free the Beaches movement, but might there be psychological explanations for his behavior, as the above quote suggests? Are there motives that Chip does not himself acknowledge?

4. One of the professed targets of the Free the Beaches movement is the "society of the spectacle," which American capitalism creates. When Chip strikes a deal to appear as a commentator on television, does he compromise his opposition to spectacle? Or, does he cleverly turn the weapons of capitalism inward? Is Chip's public success a victory or a defeat for his ideals?

5. "For as long as I can remember, I have found literature a reliable companion, surely the best guide to how we live when we are by ourselves" (page 23). How does Chip's devotion to literature inform his character? Does literature illuminate Chip's world or lead him astray?

6. "I find destruction to be an alternate form of collecting. A way to invite consideration of objects, their origin and function. Destruction preserves a culture at a moment, its artifacts, on videotape and in memory" (page 68). How is the Free the Beaches movement an act of preservation or documentation? Can destruction represent a valid form of political or creative expression?

7. "A man needs a calling and an awareness that it is a calling. As a specific against the nausea caused by tasks and goals the society imposes . . ." (page 77). Does Chip turn to destroying houses to express inner feeling—rage over his wife's leaving with his son, or ennui with an emotionally empty existence—or does it represent his vocation, the project toward which his life has been building?

8. "But then radicalism rests on the assumption that normative behavior can be deranged. Who, taking any distance from his life, would choose to be as inattentive to moral consequence as the average successful American?" (pages 83–84). Is it fair to say that the behavior of the average successful American is morally inattentive? Is the Free the Beaches movement justified in its attempt to waken citizens to the moral consequences of consumerism?

9. Chip's "summer of reading" shows him to be a dedicated parent. Is his later acquiescence to Anias—when he lets her take their son, Hank—a fulfillment or an abdication of the role of the devoted father?

10. When Hank's elementary school teacher wants him to start taking Ritalin, Chip stubbornly resists. Does Chip's refusal reflect, or contradict, the author's uneasy relationship with psychiatric medication as explored in *Listening to Prozac*?

11. "[F]rom early days I had subscribed to Miss Havisham's formulation, that real love is *blind devotion, unquestioning self-humiliation, utter submission*" (page 120). How do Chip's feelings for Anais influence his behavior after she leaves him? Is the romantic ideal viable in a culture with practical values and a fifty percent divorce rate?

12. "Arguments about justice trouble me. In an unjust society there is no privileged spot from which the right can be seen, as regards individuals" (page 178). Chip claims that his project is not intended to render justice against the homeowners. What, then, is his intent? Is he successful?

13. Why does Chip consider the famous destruction of the Woodcock house a failure and his first mistake? Is he right? What does this judgment say about his personality?

14. In the second section, "Celebrity," the novel becomes more openly satirical. Does the portrayal of Chip's ascension to fame—the televised limousine ride, the sympathetic demonstrators, the *Today*

show appearance—succeed in broadening the novel's scope? What do the comic scenes suggest about the role and nature of celebrity today?

15. In the last section of the novel, Chip must revert from lawless saboteur to responsible father. He contrasts the roles by claiming that the task of fatherhood is "averting the improbable catastrophe." But are there ways in which Chip's anarchism prepares him for fatherhood? Do we imagine him a better father in the end than he was during the "summer of reading"?

16. Does the book have a happy ending, or is it bittersweet? Is Chip's reunion with Anais a victory? Is Chip right when he says that imperfect or compromised contentment is the best one can hope for at this moment in history?

Discover more reading group guides and download them for free at
www.SimonSays.com.